STILL WATERS

A NOBLEBRIGHT
FANTASY ANTHOLOGY

FEATURING

JA ANDREWS
GUSTAVO BONDONI
CHRISTOPHER BUNN
M.C. DWYER
YVONNE ELIOT
FRANCESCA FORREST
CHLOE GARNER
CORRIE GARRETT
JOANNA HOYT
CATE ISERT
GLENN JAMES
JIM JOHNSON
VILLE MERILÄINEN
A. K. R. SCOTT
SHERWOOD SMITH
JOHN TALONI

AND EDITED BY

C . J . BRIGHTLEY
AND ROBERT MCCOWEN

CONTENTS

Acknowledgements

I owe a debt of gratitude to the talented authors who contributed to this anthology and to all authors who infuse their works with noblebright ideals.

Thanks also go to Robert McCowen, who assisted with every phase of editing this anthology from story selection to copyediting. His insight and attention to detail made *Still Waters* stronger and my job easier.

And of course, the greatest thanks go to you, dear reader, for believing in noblebright fantasy.

~ C. J. Brightley

FOREWORD

Noblebright fantasy is fantasy with a thread of hope even in the darkest hour.

A noblebright fantasy has at least one important character with noble, idealistic motives who does the right thing out of principle. The character is flawed, but his or her actions are generally defined by honesty, integrity, sacrifice, love, and kindness. The story upholds the goodness of the character; the character's good qualities are not held up as naiveté, cluelessness, or stupidity, but rather shown to be worthwhile. Good characters can make a difference. Noblebright characters can learn and grow. They can deliberately choose to be kind when tempted to be unkind, they can choose generosity when it hurts, and they can influence their world and other characters for the better. In a noblebright story, even villains are not without hope; their stories may have a redemptive ending, or they may have some kind of conversion experience (religious or not). It's not guaranteed, of course, but in a noblebright story, it's a possibility.

Noblebright fantasy is not utopian fiction. The world of a noblebright story is not perfect, and indeed can sometimes be quite dark. Actions have consequences, and even good characters can make terrible mistakes. But a noblebright story is generally hopeful in tone, even if there are plenty of bad, grim, dark things going on in the world.

For more information, please visit noblebright.org.

Thank you for reading.

~ C. J. Brightley

THE STARS' CHILL SONG

FRANCESCA FORREST

T rue cold has come, cold that causes frost to form along your windpipe and deep into your lungs as you breathe in, cold that fingers its way through any number of layers of clothing to find what's fluttering and warm and chill it, still it.

"They'll be singing tonight. Next couple of nights, most probably." The upland farmers are saying so, and the boatmen, and Mr. Parkhurst at Five Foxes Tavern.

A cold like this peels away the blankets of air between the earth and the heavens, and if you travel out at night, you can hear the stars singing. So beautiful, but so deadly, if you stop and unknot your scarf to hear those songs more clearly. The frozen faces of the unlucky ones are always tilted upward, lips parted, eyes wide, lost in rapturous attention. The animals too—one always finds a handful, frozen standing, out in the open, both predators and prey, wild creatures and domesticated ones whose owners forgot to shut them safe in house and barn.

Those songs etch permanent patterns in the windows of the houses of Orion Falls—flourishes and feathers of frost that never fade. That's what makes the glass produced by Orion Glassworks so valuable. When the cold comes, the foreman orders extra shifts, so all the glass made in the past months can be set out beneath the stars to catch the song and take its pattern. Sophie Brule is among the girls who have been assigned; like the rest of them, she would prefer to spend tonight at Five Foxes Tavern, because there will be dancing. Ezra Brown will be fiddling, but it's not to hear his playing that Sophie wishes she could go. Ezra Brown's fiddled in Orion Falls all Sophie's young life; he's as familiar as the hills and the hundred-foot cone over the Orion Glassworks furnace. Besides, he drinks. No, if she could go, it would be to spin on the arm of Elijah Spencer and to hear the trio of fiddlers that have come down from Lower Canada.

Anna Hapgood, on the other hand, longs to hear Ezra Brown play, but she will not be at the Five Foxes Tavern either. She will be with Sophie Brule's mother, who is about to have her next baby. The night being so deadly cold, Anna will no doubt spend it at the Brule shanty, up in the hills. Little Henry Brule has come down to find Anna this afternoon, and to bring a coat to his sister at the glassworks. He practically dances as he walks alongside Anna up to the brick buildings. Is he dancing to keep his feet out of the snow? When he runs ahead, Anna can see that the soles of his boots are thin at the heels and the toes. She imagines there may well be holes in his stockings, if he's even wearing stockings.

But his cheeks are rosy and his eyes are bright. Maybe it's excitement, and not the cold, that makes him dance this way.

"I'm going to be the leader of the rescuers," he announces to Anna, walking backwards in front of her, so the two of them are face to face. "Isaac Clark got to be leader last year during the first cold snap, and Matthew Bliss was leader after him, and now it's my turn. I'm going to take everyone out of the town and up into the hills."

Every time the stars' singing can be heard, the children of Orion Falls organize rescue parties for any loose dogs, cats, or even rabbits or squirrels that are unlucky enough to become smitten. Occasionally, stray lambs have been rescued. There are hot drinks waiting for the children wherever they should call on those nights.

A wind picks up, and Henry claps his mittened hands over his ears. He turns to face forward and runs ahead, to the doors of the glassworks, then dances in place until Anna catches up.

"I made a map of the route," he says, and pulls a square of paper from his pocket and unfolds it. Broken and unbroken lines curl this way and that; there are marks for houses and woods.

"That looks like your sister's pay envelope," says Anna, noticing Sophie's name on the other side.

"She let me use it. Look, here's the stream by my house, and here's the path down to town, and here's Main Street, and here's the glassworks. Here's where we'll meet up, by the school. And this is how I'll take them. Past the Abbotts' farm, and the Lamontagnes', and the Walcotts'. We're meeting as soon as it gets dark."

Which will be soon. In the west, the sky is the color of the glassworks' furnace, but in the east the fiery shades have already burned themselves out. The men who pull the glass on metal plates to make panes for windows are coming out in twos and threes; they hastily slip into coats and jam hats on their heads. And here come the girls, who wrap and store the glass, and who tonight will climb the ladder up the side of the furnace dome and circle round and round it on the catwalk, leaning the glass against the dome, forming a temporary layer of transparent scales.

"Why did they pick the dome as the place to set out the glass?" Henry asked his sister, the year she started working at the glassworks. "Are you ever afraid you might fall?"

"Oh no, it's wonderful to be up so high; you can see the whole town. I don't know why they put the glass there. Abby told me it's because it's harder for mischief makers to try breaking it, but Molly thinks it's to get the glass closer to the stars."

The other girls are going to get supper before returning, but Sophie stays just inside the door. She has a thick woolen shawl, but that's not enough against this kind of cold.

"Ma sends you this," says Henry, passing the coat to her. "She says with the baby coming, she's not going to be going outside, so you may as well use it." Sophie puts it on and looks sidelong at Anna.

"So you'll be helping with the birth? Not Mrs. Ellis?"

"Mrs. Ellis doesn't go out much now; her arthritis is bad and her sight is failing. It's mainly me. But I've got plenty of—"

"Oh, I'm sure you'll do fine. Ma could drop a baby with Henry assisting if she had to, anyway."

"Sophie!" says Henry, and it's embarrassment as much as the cold that's making his cheeks red now. But he can't spend too much time on outrage when he's got his own news to share.

"Sophie, I'm leading the rescuers tonight. I'm going to take them everywhere. We'll save more animals than anyone ever has before. This'll be a famous night for rescuing."

Sophie runs a hand through her little brother's dark curls.

"You're staying out all night with no hat? You want to end up with clipped ears, like that crazy fiddler?"

Anna feels a pang for Ezra Brown, but her face doesn't show it.

"I can do like this," says Henry, putting his hands over his ears the way he did on the walk over.

"How can you rescue animals with your hands on your head? Here, wear this." Sophie pulls her scarlet scarf off and holds it out to Henry. "I won't need it, not with the shawl and the coat." But Henry's not taking it. "Oh, go on," urges Sophie. "Don't make a face. Are you fussed about the color? Don't you know leaders have to wear something bright to distinguish themselves from their followers? This'll mark you as the leader."

That persuades him; he even looks pleased, now, with the bright scarf. Sophie reaches for something beneath her apron— coins—and gives them to Henry.

"A leader has to look after his followers," she says. "If you hurry, you can buy your friends some roasted chestnuts." Henry squeezes her in such a tight hug that she coughs, and then he dashes off down the street.

Sophie sighs, shivers as a tongue of wind licks by the entrance to the glassworks.

"Let's close the door," she says, and doesn't wait for Anna to answer; she pulls the heavy door shut.

The furnace fire has not been banked, but it will be. They say the fire is unpredictable on nights when the stars are singing. Maybe it's salamanders, as some say—or maybe it's the fire itself that rises to hear the song. Either way, the stars' singing arouses the flames far better than bellows ever do, and it's dangerous. So no nighttime glassmaking tonight.

But because the fire has not yet been banked, it's warm inside, even by the foreman's desk by the door.

"You're not having supper, Sophie?" the foreman asks.

"I'm not hungry tonight; too much excitement," she replies, lifting her chin. He gives her a quizzical look and goes back to his bookkeeping. Anna thinks on the coins Sophie gave to her brother and bites her lip.

"You remember the way to our house?" asks Sophie. She frowns slightly. "I should have made Henry walk back with you."

"Oh, no need for that—I remember the way," says Anna. "There's the path through the orchard, and then the path along the pasture above that, right?"

"That's right," says Sophie, and then, "Stay warm."

Anna nods and smiles. "You too."

And then Anna hurries off to Mrs. Ellis's house to pick up the things she'll need tonight, while Sophie lingers by the door of the glassworks, waiting for the other girls to return from supper.

Anna has put a small bottle of Mrs. Ellis's quince brandy in a cloth bag, along with packets of dried raspberry leaves and blue cohosh that she surely won't need for someone who gives birth as easily as Mrs. Brule. They're comforting to have, though; comforting for Anna, and comforting for Mrs. Brule— and the quince brandy even more so. She has wrapped her scarf around her head and ears and tied the ends at the back of her neck, and she has put on mittens. She won't need snowshoes; there's not that much on the ground.

It's dark out now, and there they are, overhead: the stars. So big, some of them, and so bright. Such colors, too, if you look—soft gold, cold white-blue, red, green. Anna can almost hear their singing, almost. What she does hear is the sound of fiddling coming from the tavern, seeping out like light from its shuttered windows, but only faintly and growing fainter. Anna is walking the opposite direction.

"Called out on a cold night, and no one to accompany you?"

Anna looks over her shoulder and sees it's Ezra Brown, his fiddle case slung over his back. The sight warms her to the tips of her fingers and toes.

"Henry Brule called me for his mother, but he's with his friends tonight, off to rescue animals. It's easy enough to get to the Brules' place without an escort," she answers, then adds, "You're not playing at the tavern tonight? They said you were."

Her heart speeds up as he begins to answer, because she knows what he'll say.

"A night like tonight, my first duty is to that song," he says, pointing upward. Anna smiles and releases the breath she hadn't been aware she was holding. It makes a cloud between the two of them; some of it freezes on the edges of her scarf.

Yes, that's what she thought he'd say.

When Anna was as young as Henry, and Ezra was perhaps a year or so shy of Anna's current three and twenty years, Ezra went out on a winter's night like tonight's, went out and didn't return. Mr. Porter found him halfway up the hill to Hunter Pond, almost frozen to death, and dragged him home. When Ezra revived, all he would talk about was the stars' singing. People could understand; it had happened to others before Ezra—Ezra was lucky to have been rescued. But when it happened a second time people muttered about folk who don't learn from experience. Between those two events, he lost three fingers from one hand and one from the other, as well as the tips of his ears and nose.

He hasn't needed rescuing since then, but still on nights like these he always goes out, fortified by spirits. People argue about whether it's the stars' singing that made him drink or drinking that makes him tempt death time and time again, but Anna knows drink is beside the point. It's love. All you have to do is listen to him play the tunes inspired by the singing, his stumps of fingers making the bow dance across those strings, to know it's love.

That love. It makes Anna heartsick, vicariously. It makes her blind to the young men in town. The only face she cares for is this one, with its deep creases, half-missing nose, nicked ears, and ghostly pale eyes, and it's not so much the face; it's what those eyes have seen and those ears have heard. It's how he makes the fiddle tell the tale.

"I'll walk with you as far as the Brules'," he says.

"You're going on to Hunter Pond."

"Yes. The sound is magnified there—I think the ice must reflect it back."

"I wish..." Anna begins, but trails off. She stops walking and leans back to catch a dizzying eyeful of stars. Concentrates. Maybe. Maybe she can hear something, now. She unwinds her scarf.

Yes. It comes as if on a breath of wind, though the night has grown very still, a sound she feels in her bones more as trembling than as resonating, trembling the way the stars tremble up there, though they can't be cold, can they? No, they must be trembling with the joy of their singing.

She has unwound her scarf but wishes she could peel off her ears to hear more clearly. She stands on tiptoe. Now she's four inches closer to that sound.

Something startles her and breaks her concentration. It's Ezra, wrapping her scarf back around her head. The whiff of song is gone, instead there's the sharp scent of alcohol and the damp warmth of his breath as he speaks.

"—waiting for you, isn't she? We should keep walking."

"You enjoy whole evenings beneath the stars when they sing, but I can't even steal a minute to listen?" The words tumble out before Anna can stop them.

"A minute becomes five and then twenty, and then… well, then there's a chance of losing yourself entirely. You don't want to risk that—you can't risk that. People depend on you. Me, now. No one depends on me; so I'm free to do as I like."

I depend on you, Anna would like to say, but those words are frozen in the back of her throat.

They walk on more swiftly now, in silence, through the orchard and alongside Henry's footprints across the pasture, and then, when they have nearly arrived at the Brules' ramshackle dwelling, Ezra suddenly grips Anna's arm tightly and points skyward. As piercingly as regret, a star flashes down from the top of the sky's dome and vanishes. Before Anna can say anything, another star, from another point high in the sky, follows the first.

"They're coming," he says. He picks up the pace even more, his hand still on Anna's arm so she must trot to keep up with him. They're at the door of the Brules' place now, and Ezra releases Anna. He's already walking rapidly away.

"They're coming to Hunter Pond?"

Ezra turns back.

"Yes. I hoped. I called. Each time they sang, I called… and now they're coming."

His voice is so warm that Anna can feel it on her cheeks, even at this distance. But he's turning away now, he's disappearing into the night, and Anna's cheeks grow cold again. The door in front of her is pulled open by a child with tangled hair and bare feet, and Anna hurries inside.

⟶ ⊙ ⟨⟨⟩⟩ ⊙ ⟵

Sophie, Martha, and Harriet don't speak much as they lift the plates of glass from their storage crates and lean them against the side of the glassworks' brick cone. They're working extra quickly because they're spelling Charlotte and Molly, who have gone off to the tavern. The foreman won't find out; he's not going to come out into the cold to see how many girls are up on the catwalk. In the end, all that matters is that all the glass is exposed to the stars' singing.

Charlotte and Molly have promised to return in time to let Martha and Harriet get some time listening to the Canadian fiddlers. As for Sophie, she no longer cares about hearing them. She will work the whole night through, and happily, too, because Elijah Spencer has been put in charge of banking the furnace fires, and when he's done, he'll come up and lend the girls a hand. And then—well, then Sophie intends to lead him along the catwalk until the furnace cone stands between them and the other girls, and in that privacy, she will rest her hands on Elijah's shoulders, lean in close, and see if a second kiss will be as good at that first one was. That kiss! But mustn't think about it while carrying glass on these narrow walkways.

Yes, it takes extra care. One can't handle the glass without gloves or mittens on; the air's too cold. One's hands will grow numb, and numb hands are clumsy hands. But hands in mittens and gloves are almost equally clumsy. It's carefully, carefully with each pane that must be leaned against the cone.

There are lanterns along the catwalk, so the girls can see what they're doing, and in their flickering light (wildly flickering—each little flame seems determined to escape its lantern's confines), the glass is shining. As Sophie makes her way back to the crate, she sees the plates she has already set out are already showing signs of patterning. She looks up at the sky—she can't help it—but doesn't unwrap her scarf. In sixteen years, she's never heard the stars—not to remember, anyway; never anything to make her want to stop and listen harder. And she doesn't intend to try and hear them now.

Just… when she sees the glass taking on those curls, those arabesques, that snowflake tracery, she does sometimes wish… what must it be like to be so touched? A tiny, tiny part of her asks, *Is it better than a kiss?*

But then she remembers the mad fiddler and his missing fingers. No, definitely not better.

A half an hour goes by, maybe an hour; it's hard to say. The stars are turning overhead, but Sophie's not looking. She and

Martha and Harriet have hauled up the next crate of glass and are unpacking it now; that leaves only two for Charlotte and Molly, when they come back. And what's keeping Elijah?

More time goes by—here are Charlotte and Molly (and there go Martha and Harriet; they barely turn back to wave goodbye), and here at last comes Elijah, looking anxious, with soot on his face.

"Fire won't settle down," he says. "Every time I think I've got it banked, it flames back up.

Something catches Sophie's eye, something up there. A flash, a falling star. And another. A vibration travels from her feet to her head. There's a sound like distant thunder coming from the heart of the cone.

"You have to try harder!" Sophie exclaims. "You have to settle it—you can't let it go wild." More vibrations; she fears she'll lose her balance, and he must feel the same—they find themselves clinging to each other and leaning against the cone, which is warm and growing warmer.

"Too late," he whispers, face pale as the snow.

Sophie hears Charlotte and Molly scream, then a tinkling of broken glass. Her stomach turns. How many panes have broken? How many weeks' wages have just shattered? The cone is becoming positively hot, but she doesn't dare pull away from it; the vibrations are too fierce, the catwalk too narrow, and the ground too far below. She coughs; suddenly the air is thick with smoke. If the stars are to blame for this, if the stars have put the fire in a frenzy, well, they're hidden from sight now.

"Look!" says Elijah. With their backs pressed against the cone, they can't see its top, but the flashing, twisting light illuminating the clouds of smoke tell them that the flames have found their way out the top of the cone.

Will her mother's coat catch fire from the heat of the cone? Sophie doesn't even care. It can burn, and her dress too, and the skin on her back can blacken, and it won't matter, because the fire is pouring its heart out to the stars, and Sophie knows this song. It's not about love; it's about longing. *I'm bright. I shine. Know me. Own me.*

"I hope the stars are listening," she shouts, so that Elijah can hear her over the rumbling and the roar of the fire. She's still clutching his left arm with both her hands, and he's still got his gloved right hand over her mittened one.

"I hope so too," he shouts back. "The fire's going to burn itself out soon; it's going to exhaust the coal."

No! For a second Sophie wishes she could throw herself into the fire, to help it burn a little higher, a little brighter, for a little longer.

But the catwalk has already stopped rattling and shaking, and there is no longer any dancing light reflected in the clouds. Voices float up from the crowd that has gathered at the base of the cone, and the sound of someone weeping.

"It sang itself to death," says Sophie, voice quavering.

"Star-mad, like Mr. Brown," murmurs Elijah.

"No, not like him!" Sophie pulls away from Elijah so abruptly that she stumbles, but quickly catches herself. "The fire's kin to the stars—isn't that so? The fire thought so. But no man was ever no star's kin. That fiddler, he's just a fool, but the fire..."

"The fire's left us with a bigger mess than the fiddler will, if he ever gives in completely to the stars' call." Sophie follows Elijah's gaze and sees that the glass leaning against the cone has grown dark, has taken on a smoky shadow. And now she hears the foreman's angry voice, calling her and Elijah.

Marguerite Brule is comfortable now, her newborn baby, a boy, asleep on her breast. Catherine Walcott condescended to be here for the birth, too; she has helped little Marie put Peter and Paul to bed while Anna was helping Marguerite with the delivery. The three women have been alternating sips of tea and quince brandy, but Marguerite is drifting toward sleep, and Anna and Catherine soon will lie down too, or so Anna is thinking, when Marguerite's eyes fly open.

"Henry's not returned yet," she says, sitting up.

"Won't he stay with one of the boys in town?" asks Anna.

"No, no. He boasts he's the man of the house when his father's away, now that Luke's working with the boatmen. Before he left, he put his hand on my shoulder, just like his father does, and said he'd see the other rescuers home, do a final circle of Hunter Pond, and return."

Hunter Pond. Anna thinks of Henry walking along its frozen margin, in the company of the stars, with Ezra fiddling in their midst... She stands up abruptly.

"I'll bring him home," she says.

20

The world of human warmth disappears like a candle flame blown out when Anna steps back outside and pulls the door shut behind her. Her eye is caught by another star streaking across the frozen sky. Is it heading to the pond? *You're late,* thinks Anna. *But I won't be late. Not too late.* She walks quickly and doesn't look at the sky again.

Hunter Pond is at the top of a wooded hill. Into the woods Anna goes, up and up; the climb is steep in places, and she finds herself breathing more heavily, feeling almost warm. Then the ground levels off, and white oaks give way to swamp maples, yellow birches, and highbush blueberries, for it's boggy by the pond. All these are nothing but skeletons right now, of course.

At last Anna is pushing through the blueberry thickets and onto the snow-covered ice of Hunter Pond. The wide, flat expanse of it breaks the tangle of woods, and overhead, bright and undeniable, are the stars. Not just overhead: in front of her too, wheeling and spinning just above the ice and perhaps right on the ice—it's hard to tell—the stars are turning in a huge, spiraling dance. Anna can't bear to look at the brightness full on but can't bear not to try, and through watering eyes it seems as if each dazzling sphere might resolve into something like a person, but maybe it's only desire that makes it appear so.

And the singing. It's not deafening because it's not heard with the ears; it's heard in the blood and along the nerves and the tree of the lungs, and down each chiming vertebra of the back. Anna's body is a bell that the stars' song strikes, and to resonate is to run toward those shimmering beings, to run and feel one is flying, to fall into a current that is more wild than a snowmelt flood stream, stronger than the tides, and older than the moon.

But her ears do catch something, one line of this polyphonic song, reduced to mere music, skittering toward her across the ice like a stone skipping on the water. What part of her was frozen just now, and melts on hearing it? She looks over. It's coming from Fisherman's Island, which is really no more than a collection of granite boulders possessively embraced by the roots of an old white pine. There's something silhouetted against the radiance of the stars at edge of the longest, flattest of the boulders; it's a thin smear of darkness. It's Ezra Brown, and he's fiddling. And that bundle beside him, is that Henry, leaning against Ezra's legs?

Anna lets the song current carry her across the ice and up to Fisherman's Island. Ezra's fiddling seems more full now that Anna's standing so near. She can hear the color of it—can the stars? Can they hear how he's added blueberries and pine needles to the melody?

She must collect her thoughts. Why has she come? To hear the song, of course, and to swim in its current, to dance. No, that's not why. Henry. She looks down at him, and he smiles sleepily up at her, then turns back to the scene on the pond. Anna sees him exhale, close his eyes, and adjust himself against Ezra's legs.

"Henry. Henry, don't go to sleep here. There's a bed for you at home for that. Come along with me now."

The words are little blots and interruptions in the song, and Anna hates herself for speaking and hates the task she's come to do, but she'll do it, all the same.

Henry doesn't open his eyes. "I want to hear the song. I'll come home when it's finished," he whispers.

Ezra doesn't speak at all, doesn't seem to notice Henry at his feet or Anna in front of him. The fiddle is racing now, speaking to the stars of autumn leaves.

Anna leans down and gathers Henry up in her arms. She staggers a bit at the weight of him and sucks her breath in at the coldness of his cheek against hers. There's hoarfrost in his eyelashes and he seems hardly to breathe.

"You should come too," Anna says, wondering if Ezra can even hear her. A small shake of the head tells her he can.

"You know how it will end, otherwise," she says.

"It ended thirteen years ago," he murmurs, eyes not leaving the pond, bow still dipping and rising on the fiddle. "Thirteen years, no promise that this night would ever come… you think I'll trade this night for an accumulation of more long and dusty years?"

"I'll come back when I've delivered Henry home," Anna says, to herself more than Ezra. Ezra doesn't answer.

"You! You're dismissed for dereliction of duty and for destruction of property. Do you have any idea—any idea? — how much this night's glass was worth? I've sent for Mr. Friedrich; he will see you imprisoned I'm sure. You had better just hope the furnace and cone are undamaged."

Sophie has never heard the foreman in such a rage. Martha and Harriet stand nearby with tearstained faces; they've been let go too for being away without leave, and Charlotte too for the plates of glass she knocked over when the cone began to shake. But most of the foreman's anger is reserved for Elijah. The force of his words has Sophie's heart drumming, though he has not turned on Sophie yet. Elijah just looks stunned.

"But sir," begins Molly, holding up one of the fragments of broken glass.

"Be quiet! I haven't asked you to speak."

Molly shrinks, but as she lowers her hand, the glass catches the light of the foreman's lantern. The smoky shadow that has laced itself into the feathers and spangles etched on its surface glints crimson and scarlet, ruby and cinnabar. As Molly sets it down, there are flashes of magenta and violet. Sophie gasps, and the foreman looks over. His eyebrows fly up and he reaches for the fragment. He turns it this way and that in the lantern light, and everyone can see the play of colors along the stars' patterns.

The foreman orders Molly and Sophie to bring down an unbroken plate, and by the time they return, Mr. Friedrich, the old Bohemian glass master who owns the Orion Glassworks, has arrived. He laughs and shakes his head when he sees the transformed glass.

"It seems," he says slowly to Elijah, in his accented English, "your mistake with the fire has a fortunate result. Our glass is already unique, and this batch is unique among our glass. You must speak with me further about what happened. We must investigate whether we can reproduce these conditions."

"Yes, sir," Elijah manages, and sends a quick, dazed look Sophie's way. She smiles back.

"This special batch of glass will more than compensate for the wasted coal and the broken plates," Mr. Friedrich continues, addressing the foreman now. "Let us forgive this night's missteps, provided everyone behaves as expected from now on."

The foreman nods curtly and directs the girls to start bringing down the rest of the glass. Something crunches under Sophie's boot; it's a fragment from one of the broken plates. Sophie picks it up, watches it sparkle wine red, royal purple, and tucks it away.

It takes longer than Anna expects to revive Henry, to warm his body and be sure his spirit is settled within, so that by the time he is tucked into bed with a sibling snuggled on each side and she once again stands beneath the dome of the sky, the world has inched closer to morning. The night is as deep and dark as ever, but Anna knows that in the east, the sun is creeping up toward the horizon from under the earth.

The stars' song has changed. There is a gentle melancholy to it now, like the recollection of an ancient sorrow. What sorrows do stars know? Anna can't imagine, but as she steps onto the lake's smooth surface, she feels that her bones know, and her blood knows. Her bones and her blood propel her closer to the stars' spiral dance, as close as she can come before tears from their brilliance make her stop, wipe a mitten across her eyes. Her tears on the mitten shine in the stars' light, salty diamonds.

Glorious and tragic as the song is, Anna feels a lack. It's a small thing, a lack of pine needles maybe, or a lack of blueberries. Her breath catches on its way to her lungs. She breaks from the dance and hurries toward Fisherman's Island, but sees no silhouette against the sky, hears no fiddle.

Ezra Brown is sitting with his back against the pine tree, facing the dance on the lake, his fiddle in his lap and the bow still in his right hand. Anna kneels down beside him. His body has become as hard and unyielding as the rock below; his face has been tattooed with the same feathers and whorls as the windows and glassware of Orion Falls.

Anna doesn't bother wiping her tears away now. *Now who will share the stars' songs with us, Mr. Brown? Not many of us dare to listen as you listened.*

She looks out at the pond, hears the stars echoing her own sorrow back to her in tones too alien to comprehend, and hates them for it. "Did you even know? Did you even notice how much he loved you?" she shouts, but her voice is a thin thing that lands at the edge of the rocks of Fisherman's Island, useless.

And yet, remarkably, as if in answer, now she hears clear summer sunlight, leathery leaves, dusty berries, midnight blue, each stamped with a star at the bottom—Ezra's fiddle tune, transformed. Anna rushes back out onto the lake, coming as close to the stars as she is able, and spins round, arms outstretched—she can't embrace the stars, but she can embrace the air around them—and repeats, "You did know, you did know, you did know," laughing and crying both.

Then autumn leaves flutter into the song, and Anna stops her spinning, surprised, and sees that she can look at the stars directly now, can approach closer, and so she does, and she sees they're wavering, like flames viewed through thick, thick glass. And yet surely dawn is still hours away? The sky is still black. The multitude of stars up there are as bright as ever. But the stars here on the pond have shrunk to firefly size.

"Are you–are you dying?" asks Anna, horrified. *The price of knowing blueberries and autumn leaves?* Anna looks back over her shoulder at Ezra, looks up at the dome of the heavens, looks down the path she's traveled to come here. Who can help her?

One, two, three... five, seven, nine... the dancers fade to nothing. Up above, so distant, the stars' melody is changing, but its sadness lingers.

The resonance in Anna's bones has become shaking in her shoulders, arms, and legs, and her teeth are chattering. It's time to retreat to the human world. She can mourn among the living, and maybe, some other winter night... but she won't even think about that now. She takes just one liberty—a quick kiss bestowed on Ezra's frozen cheek—and then it's back once again the way she came, the stars' chill song still hanging in the air.

About the Author

Francesca Forrest has lived in the United States, England, and Japan. When not working at her day job as a copy editor, she does volunteer writing tutoring and works on her own writing projects. She's had short *stories and poems published both online and in print, along with one novel,* Pen Pal. *She likes that Solzhenitsyn quote about the line between good and evil running through the human heart.*

According to Bill

Glenn James

Y ou could just see him, if you strained your eyes, and
Bill's eyes were very strained.
It didn't help that the young man was sitting in one
of the darkest corners of the club, and Bill found it hard
to look over there for too long without it being obvious.
Bradleys was a *musician's* bar, somewhere people came to play
and expose their soul, and the only lighting that mattered was
above the microphone. It was a place for shadows and avoiding
eye contact, although the gloom that filled the cavern of a bar,
with its high Victorian ceilings, actually owed more to penny-
pinching on behalf of the landlord than any deliberate attempt
to create atmosphere. Bill was used to serving the shadowy
customers who came to hear the blues without taking much
notice of their features, or their expressions, but this was
different.

Every so often the old barman found himself taking glances
at the youth in the corner, and it made him feel *uncomfortable.*
There was something about him...

Bill just knew him as Skaler, and he came and went with the independence of a cat. When he did appear, he would always come up to the bar and buy exactly the same thing, a glass of the most expensive Port, and he never, ever drank it.

After all these years pulling pints Bill could tell he definitely wasn't a drinker, you could see that for sure; you could tell the ones with alcohol or drug problems, and he didn't fit in with any of them. They would either knock it back by the bottle full and slowly vanish into their glasses, as that lost inner focus fogged over their eyes, or they would peck away at it all night, making their little pilgrimages to and from the bar, as their souls' struggled to the surface and quietly died.

This one was different; He really *was* there for the music, and somehow he seemed to almost inhabit the melodies and wrap them around him.

When someone with a little fire and life was performing he had noticed that Skaler would sit lost in the music, as relaxed as someone in a warm bath, but at the same time you could see that he watched the different singers and musicians with a keen eye; never less than engrossed in their melodies, but he followed their technique like a craftsman. He was a musician.

It was no surprise to Bill. Over the years he had worked in endless clubs, and by now he knew a musician when he saw one. Skaler had the air about him, and you could tell at once that he wasn't your run of the mill punter by his gothic New Romantic clothing, and that long black hair: The look suited him, it wasn't an affectation or an adopted pose. But there was something unusual about him that Bill couldn't quantify.

Bradleys was too dark for you to be able to clearly make out someone's eyes most of the time, and yet somehow, when Skaler smiled at you at the bar, you could really make out a gleam in his eyes and his grin. It was really unnerving; in one way it was the most heart-warming, human smile you could ever wish to see, but in another, it made Bill think he was very glad that there was a heavy wooden bar between them.

The customers came and went while the acts changed places on the tiny excuse for a stage, and Bill kept himself busy at the bar, tending the optics and cleaning glasses. He was never exactly ran off his feet, and he distracted himself with this and that, even occasionally listening to the different singers and bands... but every so often he couldn't help himself, and he felt his gaze drifting in the direction of the pale young guy in the corner in his old velvet coat.

If you had put Bill on the spot and asked him how long this particular customer had been coming in, he would have grinned hugely, and leant forward eagerly, with a gossips gleam in his eye to tell you all about it in a conspirational "just between you, me, and the doorpost" tone of voice ... but *then*, he would have had to stop before he uttered a word.

Bill would have sworn to you, as surely as bricks are hard that it had been ages. He was certain of this because that soused old so-and-so who always sits under the fire exit sign had fallen off his chair three times, from an over enthusiastic interest in Jack Daniels, and Bill had to put him into a cab again, so *that* meant that it must have been back in... But then he would blink, look really puzzled, and swear that it happened on another evening altogether.

Bill could never remember exactly when or how Skaler had first come into the club, and that troubled Bill.

That being said... there was one thing he could remember with a clarity as clear and cold as a February frost on a winter morning. That was the night when this Skaler had taken his turn on the club's stage.

Bill was unlikely to *forget* that, and it was the main reason why he kept looking across the bar at him with such curiosity.

Skaler didn't give much away in his appearance, despite his dress. No-one had taken much notice when the skinny youth in the long velvet coat had walked up to the microphone, brushing his long black hair out of his eyes and pulling back those battered lace shirt cuffs. Another one, Bill had thought to himself affectionately, recalling an endless line of rock mad kids in torn jeans and odd clothes, their eyes burning with earnest inspiration, as he watched Skaler lift a battered old guitar case off his shoulder and begin to tune his acoustic guitar.

Bill mixed someone a double, and glanced up to see Skaler touch the retro steel microphone, with a gesture that struck him curiously respectful. Skaler said something in an unassuming tone of voice, lost to the barman under a soused request for a bag of prawn-cocktail flavoured crisps, and he turned on autopilot for the till. It must have been about this time that Skaler's fingers caressed the strings, and with his eyes closed he sang into the microphone.

And at that point the world stood still. A melody and a voice filled the vaults and crevices of the room, unlike anything anyone there had ever experienced before. It was filled with sadness, and longing, and wisdom, and folly. A voice as lost in time as mariner on endless seas, as out of step with ancient times as it was with the modern world. It was unexpected, and familiar, strange, and all-known, and the way he played spoke eloquent of an eerie understanding of a stringed instrument, the kind of instinctive skill that made you think of the early blues greats, and suspicious bargains with dark strangers at remote crossroads in the thirties.

And as suddenly as he started, he was finished. One song, that's all he played. The dying cords hung in the air like the fading notes of a harp or a clear bell, and everyone present ached for it not to fade to silence.

Afterwards, Bill had never been able to figure out how long he had stood still listening, as if he had never heard music before.

He only knew he had suddenly become aware of himself again when the last note echoed into the silence across the room. The young man had opened his eyes, and with a smile far older than he should have been able to show for his years, he had quietly thanked the company for listening.

Then the barman had found himself standing next to an open till, one hand still raised and holding a ten pound note, whilst the other one lay dead in the copper tray like a deceased spider, fingers turned up and stiff. Three customers stood at the bar, and all of them were still watching Skaler in silence.

Bill found that his cheek was wet, and the shoulders of one man sitting near the stage were shaking with emotion.

Then something had seemed to snap, and suddenly men all around the room seemed to shake themselves and avoid each other's eyes, doubly glad of their solitude and the shadows.

And as Skaler returned to his usual seat, Bill had received the shock of his life. The Bar's owner was making his way across to the youth *very quickly*, actually pushing past customers both on their feet and seated.

Old Bradley never came into the bar, and never spoke to *anyone*. He was the most miserable human being Bill had ever had to the pleasure to meet, a sour faced, misanthropic man, who usually shunned anyone who frequented his club, ignored his bands and performers, and rarely even treated Bill to more than three word together, and Bill had known him for 38 years. His wiry, white-haired face was always stuck behind a Henry Winterman's Slim Panatela cigar, and a smile was never entertained either side of the tobacco.

29

Yet on this night when Skaler had performed, Bradley approached and *asked* if he could sit down!

Bill had watched in disbelief, as a man he believed had no vocabulary beyond a terse good night had spoken to Skaler animatedly for over an hour, quietly in the corner. Bill never heard a word of what passed between them, (despite his best efforts at eavesdropping) but when he got up to leave the table, Skaler had agreed with a smile never to play again on the stage at Bradleys.

Bill had lain awake at night more times than he cared to think trying to remember that song: something so longing and dark that it made him shiver to remember anything about it, but he tried time and again as hard as he could. A music that had ran through him like something he had known all his life but had lost forever, and he remembered with terrible sadness the longing he heard in that voice, orphaned by sunlight and adopted by the moon.

For weeks Bill couldn't stop thinking about it, and so, he came to a private decision. The next time that Skaler came in, and came over to buy his Port, Bill felt he would 'say something'. That was it, he would 'say something' about it. He didn't know what yet, but he felt he'd cross that bridge when he came to it.

And having reached that decision, that was when he really realised just how awkward and wrong footed he felt around this strange youth after having heard him play. Having heard Skaler's performance had given Bill the strongest feeling of acquaintanceship, as if he had known him for years and years, way back through his life. ALL his life. But the pot boy suddenly realised that they had hardly even exchanged words with one another, beyond those of bar tender and customer when he bought his drinks, and Bill didn't really know him at all except by name. But there was something witchy about someone who could play like that, and scared of him or not, Bill was going to speak to him.

So when Skaler did appear again, moving across between the tables, with the long tail of his coat spreading out like a galleon under sail, the sudden actual sight of him made Bill panic a bit.

Carefully concentrating on the optics, Bill avoided his eye, and quickly decided that it was best to remain within the safe bounds of bluff hospitality. As gruffly as he could muster, he said "Evening. Nice set, the other night."

Bill looked up briefly, thinking that was it, he had said hello... and his throat went dry when he could see that the young man with *the dangerous grin was staring right at him,* dead on eye-to-eye.

Skaler looked at him for a full twenty seconds in silence, unblinking, with his head tilted to one side, until the old man felt his hair at the nape of his neck bristle with the tension ... and then he flashed Bill that dangerous grin, winked, and said "Thanks," before picking up his drink and wandering off.

That was the first time Bill had noticed that smile, and somehow from that first glimpse it was uncomfortably knowing, as if Skaler had understood exactly how his music had made everyone feel... and what's more, it was deliberate.

It was a fact that Bill didn't know what to make of it at all, but he couldn't forget that music. Sometimes he lay awake next to his wife in the cold early dawn light, trying to recapture it. It had got to him in a way which he couldn't explain, and as much as he longed to hear the song again he couldn't bring himself to ask Skaler to play it. There was something downright dangerous about the guy when he smiled like that, something really frightening, and Bill was ashamed of the thought, being nervous of someone he was pretty sure he could snap in half with one hand if it came to it. So whenever Skaler reappeared, Bill caught himself looking across the bar, half desperately wanting to hear him play again, and spending the rest of the time avoiding his eye and avoiding speaking to him, chilled by that indefinable threatening aura.

Skaler carried on just as before, as if he had never taken the stage, and whether the whole thing had any significance for him it was impossible to say. He would sit in that quiet nook on his own, face half hidden by his long hair, half shrouded by the natural shadows, watching the other performers without a care in the world as if nothing had happened.

Sometimes Bill wouldn't see him for weeks and then he'd turn up out of the blue, buy his Port, flash Bill that startling grin, and then head for his corner as if he'd never been away. And so it went on, for well over a year after he had played at Bradleys.

But one evening, something happened which really did unnerve Bill, and he was trying hard to ignore it.

Everything was trundling along on autopilot, like a hundred other nights when you wander through chores, not thinking about anything in particular. Usually it was the case that Bill would stack glasses in the little dishwasher in the corner of the bar, and if Skaler was in, Bill had fallen into the habit of sneaking a furtive look across to his corner. Skaler never looked back if he was there, or made any sign to acknowledge his presence, other than when buying a drink. When Bill did this tonight, *he saw that the young man was looking right back at him.*

For a second it was such a shock that Bill actually jumped, and near dropped a glass, but the shadow of Skaler just calmly turned back to watch the stage. The hairs on the back of Bill's neck bristled with static, and that dangerous feeling knotted his stomach so tightly he thought he'd be sick. There was something in his eyes, something like a warning, and it had chilled him to the feet.

It unnerved him so much that for the first time since Skaler had played, Bill *avoided* looking across at him. In fact Bill made such a point of not looking in Skalers direction that several other customers found themselves looking over at his corner when Bill was serving them.

Bill was a very big man, well over two metres in height and heavy with it, and this bizarre feeling of being watched threw him such a curve that he didn't know how to deal with it. Over the years he had worked many a door in club land, and expanded on his natural muscles until he had a build which would scare off all but the suicidally drunk; But tonight, somehow, a sour sick taste never left his throat. An itch between his shoulder blades instinctively told him of eyes on his back from the darkness, and Bill found himself wondering urgently how he was going to get the guy outside at closing time.

The fact that he was so unnaturally aware and on edge undoubtedly caused a chilling sweat to break out all over his body, when a hand landed firmly on his shoulder at about 2 am.

The owner of the hand was on Bill's private side of the bar, and the thing which almost stopped his heart was the fact that he had not heard a sound to indicate they were behind him. Years of following the body language of customers had given Bill keen senses and personal radar attuned to threats, but he had not heard a sound. The hand was accompanied by something sharp, cold and pointed digging into his ribs, and that really took him aback.

Somehow it was disappointing, as although throughout this night of expectation and tension Bill had been waiting for violence of some kind, he never expected it to involve a knife. There was danger in his eyes, but that seemed too cheap and ordinary for the guy in the corner.

But the pressure on his ribs increased, and Bill turned to face the man behind him. The shock when they were face to face was almost too much.

A completely unfamiliar face stared back at him, unshaven and hard.

A man in his forties with feverish red eyes, wearing an old sheepskin coat which had seen better days. Bill was so surprised for a minute that he started to laugh, but then there was an urgent jab from the knife and he remembered what was happening. The stranger just indicated the till on the counter behind them with a sharp nod of the head, and simply said "open it."

No fuss, no bother, no lovable cockney rouges banter, just give me the money or die, it's your choice, thought Bill. It felt almost a pathetic let-down considering the aura of supernatural threat he had been anticipating in spades all night. Not being one to protect old Bradley's wallet at the expense of his life, Bill went to open the till.

But before he could, from somewhere over his shoulder Bill heard someone say "I don't suppose you've got change for a twenty?" He looked up urgently at the mirror behind the bar for assistance, but saw only himself and the robber. But then he saw the thief look sharply to his left, *felt his hand drop, and the pressure on the knife completely fell away.*

There was an odd intake of breath from behind him, and Bill turned cautiously around. Skaler was standing on the other side of the bar, and the stranger was staring intently into his eyes, which seemed to have become black with white pupils, in a way that oddly reminded Bill of the night sky. A halo around the moon shifted in the black surface of his eyes, and Bill felt himself swaying on his feet and had to steady himself on the bar.

Skaler and the intruder stood silently, locked together by their unblinking gaze. Nothing whatsoever was said between the two men, but then, the stranger's eyes widened in shock.

His name was Craig Atkinson, and he was experiencing a vision.

In his mind he saw a vivid flash of the future, a future where he had allowed his craving to get completely out of control.

Something which had started out as a recreational interest would cause him to wind up shivering under a canal bridge, gripped by a raging fever. He watched himself in his mind's eye slipping into hallucinations, and as the Blue Devils took hold. Craig Atkinson, aged 46, father of two from Wimbledon, saw this wasted, gaunt future-self forcing a rusty hypodermic into a vein at the back of his knee...

Then the bar snapped back into focus, and Atkinson went to scream, his whole body shaking, but Skaler silenced him by raising a finger and shaking his head.

Craig stared at him, and Skaler gave him that strange smile. "I really wouldn't take this money if I were you," he said, in his odd melodic voice, "It'll only bring you bad luck."

Atkinson shook his head in agreement, as if it was the best idea he had heard in his whole life, and Skaler grinned, "You know, I'd just nip off and get the next bus, if I were you. There's a really good old Billy Wilder film on TV later. Really funny, you know, one of his best..."

The stricken man gave him a look of almost insane gratitude, and nearly fell through the door trying to get out.

The old barman blinked hard, and rubbed his eyes. For a moment or two a perception had opened up to him, a vision of someone else's life. He - felt it, rather than saw it, but as reality dissolved back into the world of sticky circles of beer and a winking one armed bandit, he had the solid feeling that his life had been saved somehow.

The floor felt too hard under his feet, and his balance unsteady, and there was a violent discomfort across his shoulders. Bill's eyes were almost as wide as Atkinson's, and for a long minute he stood just staring at the door with his mouth open, unconsciously rubbing his side where the knife had dug into his skin.

Skaler was still standing there, a slight and perhaps not unsympathetic smile playing around his lips.

Bill was determined not to make it obvious that he had seen anything, or was impressed. He was still pretty scared, and as you do in circumstances like this, he bloody well carried on as usual. With a huge effort Bill picked up a glass, and automatically started wiping it out. He avoided Skaler's eyes, for a minute or so and then, as if noticing him for the first time, raised his eyebrows, shrugged his shoulders, and said "Yes?"

Skaler laughed.

Bill was not amused. He leant on the bar and gave him a fierce look, "You want me to ask you how you did that don't you? Well, I'm not going to."

Skaler might have been radiating innocence into the kilowatt range, "Sorry, I don't know what you're talking about. Can I have my change now, please?"

Bill noticed that there was a twenty pound note on the bar in front of him, and with a frown turned to the till. It was whilst he stood sorting through the change that he happened to look up… and saw only himself in the mirror. He turned sharply to look at Skaler, whose grin widened, but whose face *now* held the most unconvincing innocent look Bill had ever seen.

Turning back to the till he closed his eyes and took a very deep breath indeed. Then swallowing quite hard he turned back to Skaler and handed him his change. Skaler handed him back a five pound note as a tip, saying "have one on me," and Bill noticed how sharp his canine teeth were. Then with a solemn wink, the young man headed for the door.

For the second time that night Bill stood looking at the exit for well over a minute, until his thoughts were disturbed by a vaguely familiar, spirit-sodden voice somewhere to his left. When he turned around a shambolic figure was waving at him in a boozy sort of way, and rather grumpily asked "Are you deaf, I said I want a double scotch!"

Bill glared at him for a second and then shook himself, "You can have whatever you like mate, be my guest. The whole bars at your disposal. Champagne, Napoleon brandy, anything you want. Just don't ask me for a glass of Port."

And he rang the bell for last orders.

About the Author

Glenn James is a Dark Fantasy writer and artist who is carving a place for himself with his finely wrought shadowed tales. He has an ancient Celtic inheritance from both sides of his family, and has been described as having "A true talent for Darkness." An accomplished radio writer and performer, his dark prose has appeared in print *in the "Ripples" and "Horror Express" anthologies, "Second City Scares", "The Eerie Digest" and the Dark Hall Press "Ghost Anthology" in the United States. He is Co-Founder and originator of the genre open mic night "42" in Britain, alongside his wife Angela James, a performance platform designed for authors of Gothic, Horror, Fantasy, and Sci-Fi works. Creator of the vampire Skaler, Glenn is working on the first Skaler novel, and a collection of his short stories. Born originally in Birmingham, he lives in Staffordshire with Angela, and their two daughters Charlotte and Elizabeth.*

ICE AND FIRE

CHRISTOPHER BUNN

O nce upon a time, a baby girl was born. Her name was Matilda, and she was a princess. Matilda was the only child of the King and Queen of Lune. If you did well in geography class, you'll know Lune was a small kingdom situated several days' journey further west than the westernmost place you can find on your map. You'll also know the main source of income for the country was the rubies mined there. They were a lovely shade of red and brought excellent prices. The mine also produced emeralds and amethysts, but these were of little value in comparison to the rubies, and were used as doorstops, paperweights, or children's toys.

Matilda had many such toys, but she ignored them in favor of other pursuits. She was fond of gurgling and staring at stray bits of sunlight. She enjoyed flinging oatmeal from her high chair. She delighted in chewing on furniture or the Queen's best lace or the ears of the King's long-suffering hounds. But as babies tend to do, given enough time, Matilda grew up into a little girl.

She became good friends with the hounds, after they forgave her, and best friends with Peter, the only son of Jim Snow, the King's chief miner.

"I wish she'd play with other children," said the Queen. "More suitable children. Children who wash regularly behind their ears."

"You really are a snob, my dear," said the King.

"Perhaps if we made Jim Snow an earl?"

"If that'll make you happy," said the King.

The Queen conferred on Jim Snow the rank of earl. She gave him a purple silk sash that he was to wear to dinners at the castle. He trudged home for his lunch of boiled potatoes. He neglected to tell his wife about their recent social elevation, stuffed the silk sash into his sock drawer, and promptly forgot about it. His wife found the sash several weeks later and I'm afraid she used it to polish her china.

Matilda did not care about such things. She was more interested in catching frogs in the castle moat with Peter. The frogs were bright green, and none of them wanted to be caught. It was a splendid occupation for everyone involved. The castle hounds puttered along the moat's edge and occasionally jumped into the water. They gulped at the frogs with their slobbery mouths, but only succeeded in swallowing water. To the hounds, the frogs looked good to eat. What the frogs thought is appallingly unprintable.

Hunting frogs is hard work and it made the children hungry. They always ended up in the castle kitchen after an afternoon in the moat. The cook gave them bread and cheese, and a slice of sausage if she was in good temper. She was older than everyone else in the kingdom, and, therefore, was wiser than anyone else. The children, however, were more concerned with bread and cheese than wisdom.

As little girls sometimes do, Matilda grew up into a taller, older girl. By the time she neared her seventeenth birthday, she was almost a young lady. Almost, I say, because Matilda had a hot temper. Young ladies, of course, do not ever have hot tempers. They are pleasant, play the piano well, and do admirable needlework. Matilda inherited her hot temper from a great-grandfather who had been fond of invading neighboring countries.

It was to be expected, then, that Matilda got into many arguments with Peter. At least, she did the arguing. Peter was a miner's son, as you know, and miners always have a good amount of stone in them. This makes for sturdy, peaceable people. Of course, this also meant that Matilda found him infuriating when she was in the mood for a good knock-down, drag-out fight.

On a cold Thursday in December, the two of them were having one such argument. At least, Matilda was doing the arguing. Peter was merely being sensible.

"Well, if you won't take me down into the mine," said Matilda, "I'll go myself!"

"I don't think that'd be wise," said Peter.

"And why's that?"

They were standing in the front hall of the castle. Matilda picked up a boot from beside the coat rack and hefted it thoughtfully in her hand.

"Because," said Peter. "The mine's dark and dangerous and it's no place for a girl."

"Oh, it isn't, is it?"

"No."

"Dark and dangerous?"

"Particularly for girls."

"And I'm a girl?"

"Yes."

Matilda threw the boot at him. Peter ducked and the boot hit the chamberlain who was passing by.

"Speaking of which," continued Peter. "I've got to get there myself. We've opened up a new vein in the lower gallery and Dad needs a hand."

By the time Matilda grabbed another boot, Peter was safely out the door.

The miners had never gone so deep into the mountain before in all their years working there. It was stiflingly hot in the tunnels. The torchlight seemed subdued and diminished, weighed down, perhaps, by the awful mass of the mountain looming above them in the darkness. Pickaxes bit into stone with a bright, ringing sound. The air smelled of iron and fire.

"Look here, son," said Jim Snow. In the old miner's hand was a misshapen stone. The stone glowed a deep, fiery red. "Never seen a ruby like that before, eh? Almost like it's got a bit of fire trapped inside. Feels warm, too. Found it down in the new vein. Here, you better go show it to the King."

Peter hiked back down the mountain. The castle hounds came galloping out as he neared the drawbridge, hallooing and yipping. They slobbered on Peter and ignored the ruby in his pocket. To them it was inedible and therefore of no importance. They could smell the sausage and cabbage on him that he'd had for lunch, and they were keenly disappointed that he had not had the foresight to stuff some in his pockets.

Peter cautiously poked his head in the front door and found no one there. He did hear some commotion, however, around the back of the castle, so he made his way through the rose garden, the water garden, and the herb garden, until he finally came to the orchard. There, he found the King picking apples. That is, a dozen gardeners were picking apples and the King was supervising from below.

"Hi, you there!" called the King. "Get the one right above your – no, not that one! The other one! Well, then climb higher. Higher, I say! I don't care if the branch is breaking. Get me that apple! Ah, Peter. Cook's promised apple pie for dinner. My favorite."

"Sir, if you would care to take a look at this."

Peter dug the stone out of his pocket. The King looked. Then he blinked. Then he stared. He turned the ruby over and over in his hands.

"Are there any more of these?" said the King.

"Yes," said Peter.

The vein proved to be chock-full of the new rubies. The deeper the miners dug, the bigger the rubies became. Every day, Jim Snow sent a mule down the mountain to the castle, its packs stuffed full. The king was enthralled with the new rubies and converted the north tower of the castle into a treasury dedicated for the new gems. The castle carpenter built shelves and cabinets and display cases out of walnut wood.

"Aren't you going to sell these?" said the Queen, squinting at one of the rubies. It looked as if a flame glowed inside the stone. For some reason, that made her uneasy.

"Of course not!" snapped the King.

"They look like they have little flames locked inside them," said the Queen. "I hope you don't burn the castle down. Though, I wouldn't mind redecorating."

"You redecorated last spring, my dear."

"Really? That's a very long time ago. If you're going to burn the castle down, please schedule it for a sunny day. I'd prefer to have the maids take all the linens outside first. Besides, they could use a good airing. Also the tapestries. It's so very difficult to wash the smell of smoke out of fabric, you know."

"Nobody's burning the castle down!"

"They really do look like they're on fire," murmured the Queen.

That afternoon, down in the mine, down in the deepest tunnel, Jim Snow stared at the sight before him.

"See here, sir," said one of the miners. "We broke through the wall after lunch. Opened up into this here natural cave. Only, it ain't too natural, if you see what I mean."

Through the break in the tunnel wall, light gleamed. Jim could see into a vast space, an enormous cave bright with scarlet light. Hundreds upon thousands of rubies were embedded in the cave walls. They sparkled like candle flames. But only a fraction of the light came from them. The real source of the light came from deep inside the center of the cave. Jim's eyes widened. He stared for a while more, thinking, and then he turned to go.

The King was admiring his rubies in the north tower when Jim Snow climbed up the stairs.

"Gorgeous, aren't they?" said the King. "Lovely things. I almost wish I could eat them. Maybe squeeze 'em for my morning juice."

"Rubies aren't for eating," said Jim, who didn't have much of an imagination. "Hard on the stomach, I'd expect. I prefer cabbage and potatoes."

"Yes, yes," said the King. "Potatoes. Now, what do you want, Snow? A dukedom? Your son knighted? It's yours. Whatever you want. You haven't, er, brought me more rubies, have you?"

"No, sir. I couldn't bring the one I just seen. It's unusual. I suppose that's the right word. You'll need to come to the mine."

The King went. He had never been to the mine before. He had always intended to, but something had always come up. A ham sandwich. An unexpected and unwelcome visit from his Aunt Gertrude. Gophers pillaging the royal gardens.

"Good heavens, but it's hot in here," said the King.

"Wait until we get down to the lower levels," said Jim Snow. "This is nothing."

It took them two hours to reach the deepest tunnel of the mine. By that time, the King was sweating badly but still trudging gamely along.

"How – how much farther?" puffed the King.

Jim Snow didn't say anything. He just pointed in front of them. Light bloomed in the darkness. The air sizzled with heat.

A great globe of scarlet fire burned there in that endless night beneath the mountain. The King stumbled forward into the cave.

"Is that – is that?" He was unable to finish.

"Yes," said Jim Snow. "That's a ruby. Big one. Biggest one I ever did see."

The King gazed in shock and delight. He crept forward and touched the stone. He snatched his hand back. The ruby was as hot as a stovetop.

"I want it, Snow!" he exclaimed. "I must have it!"

"Ain't gonna be so easy," said Jim Snow gloomily. "You see how it's growing out of the stone pillar? Appears to me that ruby's holding up the ceiling, and it's right smack-dab in the middle of the cave. Might be holding up the whole mountain, far as I know. May be best to leave it be. Have to prop the whole cave with timbers and stone before I'd feel lucky enough to touch that thing. Take weeks at best."

"I don't care," said the King. "I want it."

"But it isn't yours."

The voice came from somewhere deep in the shadows. It was a whispery, crackling sort of voice. It sounded like the noise of flame devouring wood.

"Who's there?" said the King, stepping back. "Who are you? Show yourself!"

"We're here. We're there. We are the keepers of the mountain. We grow the rubies. They're ours. Ours!"

"Grow the rubies? Nonsense!" said the King sharply. "The rubies are mine. I own 'em. This mountain's mine."

The shadows rustled. "Foolish man. Yours is the outside. The thin skin of things. We let you take the cold rubies, for they are dead. They are worth nothing. But now your servants dig up the warm ones. The delicious, crunchy ones. Seventy-three, to be precise."

"He's right," muttered Jim Snow. "Seventy-three rubies, as of this morning."

"And now you dare steal the very heart of our mountain?" The voice rose in agitation. "It shall not be!"

"But I must have it!" cried the King. "I must. I'll give you anything!"

"Anything?" said the voice in wonder. The shadows rustled again as if conferring together. They whispered and mumbled and then giggled. Or perhaps it was only the sound of rocks grinding together. "Very well, king. You may take the heart of the mountain. In return, the next human to enter this cave shall be our servant for forever or a day. Whichever is longest."

"Fair enough," said the King. "Done! Er, Snow, would you mind calling in one of your miners? Not your son, of course, there's a good fellow."

"What?" said Jim Snow, aghast.

"Hello, Father!" called a voice from behind them. Both men turned. The King's face went white. Matilda stood at the entrance to the cave, a torch in her hand.

She grinned at them both. "Don't look so shocked. What a pair of geese you are. I've always wanted to see the mine. I followed you from the castle. Certainly runs deep! The air's so hot, I can barely breathe. I don't know how long it took me to make it down here."

"And down here you shall stay," hissed the voice in the shadows.

The darkness rose up. The flaming lights of the rubies in the cave dimmed. Shadow engulfed the Princess. The King and Jim Snow caught a glimpse of her frightened eyes, and then she was gone.

"Fair enough," whispered the voice in the shadows. "Fair enough, particularly for us. A heart for a heart. An excellent trade."

"Stop!" shouted the King. "You can't do this! You're monsters! She'll die down here!"

"Don't worry," said the voice. "We're monsters, true, but even monsters can be quite reasonable. We shall teach her to breathe fire."

And with that, the voice was gone, no matter how the King raged and pounded his fists against the cave walls until his hands bled. At his last blow, the enormous ruby dislodged and tumbled down at his feet. The King stared at it.

"I've been swindled," he groaned. "Hornswoggled. Ruined."

"Come," said Jim Snow. "We'll find her."

He bundled up the ruby in his coat, for it was still painfully hot to the touch. He put his arm around the King's shoulders and helped him from the cave.

But no one was able to find the Princess. Every miner in the kingdom hunted through the mine for the next seven days. They crept through galleries and tunnels. They climbed down into old, played-out ore holes twisting away through the darkness. They hammered on walls and turned over stones. But there was no Princess. There was only the darkness and the dreadful heat and the mocking echo of their footsteps.

Peter Snow hunted along with the rest of them. He did not leave the mine for any of those seven days, but carried along with him a sack of bread and water, as well as a blanket to wrap himself in for naps. If truth be told, he was more than fond of his old playmate, even though she was a Princess and he was only a miner's son.

The Queen did not take the news well. Her hair went white and she retired to her rooms. The King spent his days pacing up and down. Sometimes he would hike up the mountain to confer with Jim Snow. Other days, he would stand at the window in the north tower, staring out at the snowy peak of the mountain.

At the end of the seventh day, Jim Snow found his son searching an abandoned tunnel in the east galleries, torch in hand.

"She's gone, Dad," said Peter sadly. "I don't think she's anywhere."

"There're more places than anywhere," said his father. "But not today. Go tell the King I'm calling off the search for now. The men are dog-tired and need their rest."

Peter trudged down the mountain. The first snow of winter lay thick on the ground and heavy on the branches of the pine trees. He shivered in his woolen coat. After seven days in the heat of the mine, the frigid temperature outside was almost unbearable. Down in the valley, the castle stood shrouded in snow and the moat was iced over.

A fire smoked on the hearth in the castle hall. Peter tried to warm his hands while he waited for the King, but the flames were of little help.

"Ah, Peter." The King shuffled forward. He looked alarmingly old. "Have you...? That is to say – rather, is there any news? News of Matilda?"

"I'm afraid not, sir," said Peter. "My father is stopping the search for now. The men are very tired. Seven days, sir, as you know."

"Yes, yes, I know," said the King. He tried to smile, but could not. "Thank you," he said softly, and then he wandered off down the hall.

Peter made his way to the castle kitchen and poked his head through the door.

"Come in," said the cook. "Nobody's gotten a full stomach standing in doorways and staring at tables. Here, have some hot soup. Peppered cream of beet. That might warm you up."

It almost did. Peter ate two bowls, sitting at the kitchen table. He tried not to sneeze.

"Catching a princess is not like catching a frog," said the cook. "Especially this one."

"What do you mean?" said Peter.

The cook ladled him a third bowl. "Frogs are easy. You give them what they want. Delicious bugs. Now, what can you give those creatures under the mountain? What do they want?"

"They obviously wanted a princess," said Peter gloomily. "And they got her. I can't imagine wanting anything more than that."

"They're not you, though I daresay there's as much stone in their noggins as yours. Think!" She rapped him on the head with her ladle. "They live deep down under a mountain, a mountain forever reaching up into the sky. But does the sky belong to them? No."

"So that's what they want?" said Peter. "The sky?"

"Perhaps. Perhaps not. I really don't know."

"Then who would know?"

"The wind," said the cook. "You'll have to ask the wind."

And so Peter went to ask the wind. He buttoned up his coat, pulled his hat down around his ears, and wound his scarf tight around his neck. The cook gave him two steaming hot baked potatoes, one for each pocket, to keep his hands warm.

He trudged up the steps of the north tower. The King was wandering about his ruby room, sighing and glooming over the gems as they sparkled in the shadows. Peter tiptoed by and the King did not see him. A stairway led up from the room at the top of the tower. Peter climbed up, pushed open the trapdoor, and found himself on the roof. It was dreadfully cold up there. The world stretched out white around him. The wind whistled past, flinging snow into his face and whisking the roof bare.

"Hello?" he said, turning around as if he somehow might see the wind. "Excuse me. I was wondering if…"

The wind chuckled and hurried on by. Peter subsided into silence and tried to listen. He could hear the wind whistling past the battlements below. He could hear it shaking the icy branches of the apple trees down in the garden. He could hear it rattling the tower windows. There were no words in the wind's voice, only a rushing liquid murmur.

STILL WATERS

But Peter was patient, if anything. After all, he was a miner's son, and there was good stone in him. He stood and waited. The cold crept into him. He could not feel his nose or his feet or his ears. The potatoes in his pockets turned to ice. His hands froze. Icicles dripped from his nose. He was not sure if only an hour had passed or if he had been standing there for days. His eyes were frozen shut. The cold worked its way through him until he felt nothing at all except cold. His heart froze fast in the middle of a beat. He could feel the wind blowing right through him as if he had simply become part of the sky.

The wind laughed.

"Very well," said the wind. "Very well. You needn't be so stubborn." And the wind told him what he had to do.

Peter levered up the trap door and made his way back down the stairs. The castle was silent around him. Perhaps it was night? Perhaps his frozen ears did not work anymore? Ice formed on the floor where he stepped. The hounds drowsing by the hearth in the hall whined and cringed away at his approach. The fire died down to cold ashes as he passed by. He stepped outside. It was night, and the moon stared down at him with her single, silver eye.

Icicles hung down from inside the castle gate. They were enormous, as big around as a tree trunk. The wind whistled by and one of the icicles fell at Peter's feet. It shattered on the ground and an enormous, shining gem of ice lay among the shards. Peter picked it up and tucked it in his jacket.

He hiked up the mountain through the snow and the moonlight. The wind danced around him, swirling snowflakes into the air. The mouth of the mine gaped open on the side of the mountain. Peter stopped, but the wind urged him on.

The walls of the mine radiated heat around him. Flame flickered on the edges of his sight. Deeper and deeper into the mine he went. The air was almost unbreathable. But where Peter walked ice grew in his footsteps, and it clung to the walls when he reached out to steady himself. After a while, he reached the bottom of the mine and the enormous cave that lay there. Flames licked up the walls. Rubies shone in the shadows, full of fire and embedded in silence.

"I've brought you the sky," Peter said out loud. There was no answer, but the darkness around him seemed to become even more silent. Something was listening, he knew it.

"The sky," he repeated. The shadows rustled.

46

"The sky?" whispered a voice. The shadows crept closer. He was not certain, but he thought there were shapes in the shadows, many of them. Eyes staring at him.

"What is the sky to us?" There was hunger in the voice. "We are here, it is there, and everything we are not lies in between."

"True," said Peter, ice cracking in his throat, "but I've brought a piece to you. A gem of the sky, clearer than a diamond, as clear as the wind."

"Show us. We want to see! Show us now."

Peter removed the gem from his coat. It shone in the light of the flames with a flashing radiance that threw stars out twinkling into the darkness. Despite the heat of that place, the ice did not melt. Not a single drop of water fell, such was the dreadful cold of Peter's body.

"Ahh," breathed the voice. "We want it. We want it forever. Give it to us." Hands reached out of the shadows.

"Not just yet," said Peter. "Fair's fair. How can I give you such a jewel without something equal in return?"

The shadows trembled in agitation. "Rubies. Your weight in rubies."

"No. I'm tired of rubies."

"Perhaps the memory of fire? It will keep your dreams warm. Dragons will do your bidding. No? Would you prefer iron's strength? Your bones will never break, and your heart will never fail. You'll live forever. Who wouldn't want that?"

"No. Iron rusts in the rain."

"True, true. Perhaps true," said the voice. The shadows crept closer. "How about the secrets of a thousand years, plucked from the dust of dead men's bones, grain by grain? You could rule the world with such secrets, inch by inch, mile by mile, soul by soul. No? No, obviously not." The voice paused, faltered, and then strengthened. "We have a girl. A princess, no less. We filled her with fire and gave her a flame for a heart."

"I don't care so much about princesses," said Peter carelessly. "But a girl, now that might be something."

"Oh, she's the best of girls," said the voice eagerly. "Her touch can melt stone. Her eyes are full of flame. Her lips can –"

"No doubt," said Peter. He turned the ice gem over and over in his hands. Light danced through the darkness at its movement. The shadows trembled.

"We shall bring her," said the voice.

Stone grated on stone and Peter caught a glimpse of a vast, awful space looming away, deeper and deeper and down into nothingness. The very roots of the mountain, lost in darkness. A flame moved there, coming closer. A girl. Matilda. She stood among the shadows. Fire burned bright in her eyes and slid along the lines of her form. She opened her mouth to speak. He could see his name on her tongue.

"I suppose she'll do," he said, and she shut her mouth.

"Give the sky to us," said the voice. "Give us the jewel. Now!" The shadows snatched the enormous gem of ice out of Peter's grasp.

Peter took Matilda's hand. Flame licked up his arm. For a moment, he thought he felt warmth in his fingers, but then it was gone. The deathly coldness of his body was inviolate.

"Come," he said, his voice low and urgent. "Before it melts."

They fled from there, up and up through the darkness. Up through the long, lonely tunnels of stone. Their footsteps echoed in the galleries of rock and died away in the shafts that descended down into the roots of the mountain. Ice and fire snapped and guttered behind them. They came to the mouth of the mine. Snowflakes blew in with a sudden rush of wind. There was no morning sun, only a blinding white sky full of falling snow. Her fingers tightened on his. The snow hissed and steamed under her feet. The falling snow melted into rain around her.

Behind them, the mountain suddenly quaked with fury. Snow and stone crashed down from its steep slopes. The entrance to the mine collapsed in an avalanche of rock. On the wind, they heard moaning and wailing and the dim, distant fury of shadows. But then there was only silence.

Peter and Matilda came to the castle. The ice in the moat cracked and melted at Matilda's passing. But then it froze again as Peter walked by, for he followed close on her heels. The door scorched under her hand. Inside the hall, a page sat polishing boots before the hearth. He gaped at them. The fire leapt up in sudden heat as Matilda approached.

"Find my father, the King," said Matilda. The page scrambled to his feet and fled.

The King and Queen came in a fluster, beaming from ear to ear. The King swept Matilda up in his arms and then sprang back. Sparks smoldered in his beard.

"What's this?" he cried. "Water! Buckets! Quick! The castle's on fire!"

"Not at all," said Matilda. "I'm afraid whatever I touch becomes rather hot. I suppose I could become a cook and simply stick my hand in the soup to boil it. I do hope that ruby was worth it, Father."

"Nonsense," said the King.

"Oh, my dear," said the Queen, looking as if she was about to faint.

"I'm delighted you're back, Matilda," said the King. "I was about to call the army up, take the mine by force and, er, well, do something. Anyway, all's well that ends well."

But it didn't end well, at least, not in the castle. Matilda looked about for Peter, but he had slipped out the door and was gone. She went to bed, for she found she had little to say to her parents. Besides, when she did speak, flames occasionally fell out of her mouth. This seemed to make her parents nervous.

Matilda did not get much sleep. Neither did any of the servants. Her bed kept catching on fire, as well as the dresser and other furniture in the room. The servants stood outside her door with buckets of water. Whenever smoke seeped out into the hall, the chamberlain would knock and then usher in a bucket brigade. Of course, they all kept their faces politely averted, as it wouldn't do to see the Princess in her nightgown.

Most of the castle was in a bad mood by the time morning came. At breakfast, the King complained of smoke inhalation, the Queen fell asleep in her porridge, and Matilda set the table on fire. The pages yawned on their feet and the chamberlain was nowhere to be found.

"I think I'll have a chat with the cook," said Matilda, getting out of her smoldering chair.

"Don't set her on fire," grumbled the King.

The cook was baking bread in the kitchen.

"Here," she said, handing Matilda a pan full of bread dough. She watched in interest as the dough quickly baked in the girl's hands.

"Useful," said the cook, "but not exactly practical."

"No, it isn't," said Matilda. A tear slid down her cheek and boiled away into steam.

"I think what you need is a walk in the gardens." The cook sighed and nodded, and then tried to smile. "Make sure you don't burn down the apple trees. Here, take this."

She handed the Princess a leather knapsack. The leather started to smolder.

"Give me a kiss, girl," said the cook. "No, no, I don't mind a scorch or two. Heaven knows I'm always getting burned by the stove. Now, run along."

Matilda wandered out into the orchard behind the castle. Snow lay heavy on the ground. The apple trees stood frozen in skeletal outline. But there was something else standing among the apple trees. Peter. He looked up as she approached.

"Oh, hello. I think I must've fallen asleep." He smiled and the ice sheathing his face cracked. His skin was blue and he looked as if carved out of stone.

She took his hand in hers. The dreadful cold in his fingers receded a little. The flames licking over her hand retreated up her arm. For a moment, Peter thought his heart warmed enough to thud one slow beat. They stared at each other.

"Here," said Matilda, handing him the knapsack. "You'd better take this before it catches on fire. Cook packed it full of bread and cheese. And sausage, of course."

Peter slung the knapsack over his shoulder. Then, without a word, they set out. They went north, over the mountains, and past the great frozen sea. They were never seen again in the kingdom of Lune. It was said they finally came to a land of perpetual snow. There, Peter built Matilda a house of ice. She had no fear of burning such a place down. Her fire lent warmth to him. And, in the spring, his heart began to beat again. But whether due to the flame of her touch or simply her love, no one knows.

Author's Note

I traveled through Lune once, many years ago. It isn't so far from Switzerland where I was living at the time. If you catch the evening train from Lausanne, it's only an overnight ride, depending on how well you sleep. Of course, Peter and Matilda had already been gone for many years by the time I visited Lune. I heard their story while staying in a youth hostel not far from the castle.

About the Author

Christopher Bunn is the author of several novels, including the epic fantasies The Hawk and His Boy, The Shadow at the Gate, *and* The Wicked Day, *as well as the humorous fantasy* The Fury Clock. *A graduate of Wheaton College in Illinois with a Master's degree in TV/Film Production, he has spent many years working in television and children's programming such as VeggieTales, Bob the Builder, and Barney. He currently lives in California where he works on a farm. His website is www.christopherbunn.com.*

CAT GARDIAN

JOHN TALONI

T hunder cracked across the valley floor. The boom that followed was no ordinary rumble. A red, fiery glow that was not lightning accompanied the shockwave, which rattled foundations in the village. Another followed a moment later, causing small pieces to fall out of the ceiling.

The cat looked up, alarmed. The water bowl she was drinking from rippled, its still water disturbed by the rumbling ground. Her composure shattered as well. In short order she scooted across the room and hid under the bed.

A horn blew through the night sky. Soon shouts could be heard across the village. "We are under attack! To arms!"

The figure on the bed was already moving. By the time a knock came to his door, he had on his leggings and war boots. "Sigurd, it is the trolls! Come quickly! We shall meet the main body of the Aesir on the way! Odin himself will command us this day!"

"Soon enough," Sigurd called out. His sleep clothes lay crumpled on the bed. Returning to the bedroom, he put on his mail shirt and tunic.

"Ho, Kisa, this battle may go long," he said, his eyes catching those of the apprehensive feline. Sigurd went to his cold locker and pulled out a hunk of meat, placing it on a low table. "Be well until I return," he said. The cat jumped onto the bed, still fearful but somewhat calmer. Sigurd gave the cat a few quick strokes. She purred, a nervous, rapid sound, and nuzzled his hand.

Sigurd pulled on a window, leaving it ajar. Then with a few quick strides he gathered his axe, shield and helmet. Scant moments later he was out the door and into the night.

Soon the shelling stopped. Nevertheless, Kisa went back under the bed and stayed there until day shone full through the window.

The village remained especially quiet. None of the usual activity filled the streets. In the distance, an occasional boom broke the silence. The cat's ears twitched at each one. Echoes of great shouts whispered in the wind.

As morning stretched towards noon, Kisa emerged and had a few bites from the slab of meat. Then with a flick of her tail, she went to the window and jumped out. Cold food filled the stomach fine, but fresh mouse tasted far better.

When night fell the cat returned to the house. She took her usual spot at the foot of the bed. But the man did not return. He wasn't there the next day, nor the day after that. The water in her bowl shriveled and went dry. Kisa got by with water in small puddles around the house from morning dew.

On the fourth day an old man came to the house. "Here, kitty," he called out as he looked through the rooms. But Kisa didn't know this man, and she stayed hidden. He checked the slab of meat and noticed it was almost gone, then replaced it with another.

And so it went, for many days. The meat provided got smaller and smaller as time went on. But mice were plentiful, and the bed was soft.

Finally the distant sounds faded. On the following day, people came marching back into the village. The cat waited for her companion to return. Yet although many doors opened in the village, her door remained shut.

In the middle of the next day, Kisa was out hunting when a group came to the house. She returned to investigate. The old man was there along with another, much younger man.

"As you're his nearest kin, you're entitled to his belongings," said the old man. "Best to clear it out soon." He took a breath. "If you don't mind telling me what happened?"

"We were routed," said the other man. "The troll attack was a feint. They pulled us forward, past a strategic bridge. Then the Ice Giants appeared on our flank. We fought, but their combined forces took our full mettle and threw us back. Odin organized the troops for a strategic retreat while Thor harried the Ice Giants. We intended to cut the bridge behind us, but the Jotuns pressed closer and closer, and even Mjolnir was not enough to stop them. Thor pushed forward and was cut off from the main force, but he bought us time by harrying the Jotuns, leaving us to deal with the trolls. Sigurd rushed the men across, then held the bridge long enough for us to regroup. We charged back over, but it was too late for Sigurd."

"We shall drink to his name," said the old man.

"He dines with the Einherjar in Valhalla tonight," said the younger man. "Mayhap he will hear us."

"But that will be all," said the old man. "You know the ancient compact. Miss him you might, but the Einherjar are for Valhalla alone. They may not return."

The two set to packing. When they were done, the older man tried to catch Kisa. But she recognized neither of them, and would not be captured. With a hiss, she jumped out the window.

"Let her go," said the old man. "Never was a person other than Sigurd she would be around."

Kisa roamed through the outskirts of the village. When night came, she took refuge in a tree. She hadn't really understood much of the conversation, but Asgardian cats had a bit more intelligence than Earthly ones. Her companion was on a bridge somewhere? Then she would find him.

The next morning brought stiffness to her limbs. She had gotten used to sleeping in the warm indoors, on a soft bed. Still, a few moments hunting took the kinks out of her legs. Not too long later she had a juicy breakfast of fresh mouse.

Just outside of the village a small bridge crossed a river, barely bigger than a creek. Kisa went there and looked for her companion, who was not to be found. She crossed over and continued at the edge of the road, pacing through the grass and trees.

The next day she arrived at another town. It had a greater bridge over a wider river, this one running through the center of the village. She napped near the shallows, around a bend of the river, its slow-moving waters comforting her. But Sigurd was not there, either.

She went to many towns over the next few weeks. And while the mousing was good, still she missed Sigurd's companionship.

After searching for over a month, one night she saw lights in the sky: a vast river of deep and colorful waters. She headed towards them, even though the night's dark kept her from making swift progress. The lights were so far away that she didn't reach them that night. She hunted in the morning, then rested through the day. That night she set off again.

Early the next morning she arrived at the source of the light. It was the biggest bridge she had ever seen, its rainbow colors stretching further than she could look. Standing at the entrance to the bridge stood a familiar looking profile.

She walked up the figure and rubbed against his legs. "Brrdddtt?" The figure looked down. It was close – very close – to the figure of her companion. But it was not him.

"Ho, little one, what are you doing here on the Rainbow Bridge?" He reached down a hand. Though he wasn't the man she was looking for, his approach was similar. And she was very hungry. She allowed him to pet her head and scratch behind her ears. She extended her tongue and licked around her mouth.

"Ah! Hungry, are we?" said the figure. "I doubt you would like my mead, or a slice of golden apple," he continued. He opened a bag that seemed to contain provisions of various kinds, "Let me see – ah!" He unwrapped a bundle, then used a small knife to carve off a piece. "Here you go," he said, holding out the meat.

The cat sniffed it, then grabbed it greedily. Fish! She hadn't had any since Sigurd left. She took it and hurried away, out of reach of the figure's arms. With an indulgent smile he cut off a larger piece and placed it on the strange surface. Though the bridge was solid, it was not like any ground that Kisa had ever been on. Nor was it like regular stone. The colored bands felt like a carefully polished floor, not rippling like water, but almost slick.

"Now, are you a messenger from Freya?" the man mused. Suddenly Kisa felt his eyes boring into her. His gaze left no portion of her unscrutinized. "Nay, a simple house cat," he murmured. And though his eyesight was the best in Asgard, he did not detect the faint whiff of Sigurd's scent that remained on Kisa's fur.

Then the gaze dropped, and Kisa rubbed around his legs again. For though he was not Sigurd, still he had his manner.

When darkness finally came to the Rainbow Bridge, the figure turned away from scanning the heavens. With a wave he invited Kisa to join him. "Come, it is time to rest in Himinbjörg." Kisa came along, her tail high with a slight twitch at the end.

Once inside the dwelling, the figure prepared a small plate of meat for the cat. And though Kisa would not know the name Heimdall, it could be no other watching the Rainbow Bridge.

Kisa ate lightly of the meat provided. She had consumed her fill of fish earlier, and this house had many mouse scents in it. She purred near him for a moment, then went off hunting.

Thus it went for many days. Kisa accompanied Heimdall to the Bifrost, although in her feline way she did not always stay nearby. She hunted in the fields behind him, and as for the house, the scent of mouse diminished considerably. She became at ease wherever Heimdall went.

One day, Kisa felt a creeping sense of alarm at the Rainbow Bridge. A sense of something strange filled her. She pranced up and down the bridge, tail twitching, unable to detect a reason for her mood. Except...there! Her nose detected a faint whiff of something unexpected. She hissed, and meowed urgently.

"What is it, little one?" said Heimdall. He focused his eyes and ran a sweep of the area, but detected nothing. His eyes were the best in the nine realms, but Kisa's sense of smell was better than hisunmatched by man.

She hissed again, but though Heimdall searched, he saw nothing. Eventually he stopped looking. During this time Kisa went behind his legs and walked as if leaving the Bifrost.

Moments later she came back, seemingly unconcerned, and wandered around in front of Heimdall. Then with a mighty leap, she sprang into the air. To Heimdall it appeared as if she jumped at nothing. But she seemed to land in midair and hang there. With her front claws and her teeth, Kisa dug into the flank of some hidden animal. She raked the body as deeply as her claws would go.

"AROOOOOOO!" came an animal cry. The spell of invisibility protecting it shattered at the cry, betraying the presence of a large wolf.

"Fenris!" cried Heimdall. He snatched up the Gjallarhorn and blew several loud notes. Behind Fenris an entire wolf pack revealed itself.

"Our cover is blown, Houndlings!" howled Fenris, saliva dripping from his mouth. "Attack!" But Kisa was not done. She scampered up the wolf body, towards its neck. There, she hung on with claw and tooth, harrying Fenris as much as her little body was able. After digging with her front paws she clung with them, alternating scrapes with one back paw at a time while holding on with the other three and her teeth.

Heimdall drew his sword and charged Fenris. "Let go of her, Wolf!" he cried out. But the bloodlust had risen in Kisa and indeed, it was she that would not let go of him.

Behind the wolf pack stood a figure clothed in a grey cloak that only revealed her face. The grim visage appeared half colored in blue and half in flesh. The horns of her helmet reached high. No living figured stood near, but wraiths wisped beside her. The death goddess Hela stood ready to attack once the wolves broke through.

But Heimdall's warning had been in time, and the advance troops of the Aesir were not far behind. When they arrived they saw Heimdall fighting for his life, surrounded by a pack of wolves. They also saw one very angry cat, holding on to Fenris' neck. "GET IT OFF!" howled Fenris, but his brethren were busy themselves.

With the sneak attack exposed, the Aesir soon began pushing back the main body of wolves. Heimdall turned to face Fenris, but he was many fathoms away. With a cruel snap of his jaws, Fenris finally got his teeth onto Kisa's body. He yanked, and threw her into the air. She hit the ground and crumpled. Fenris bayed and the wolves began to retreat.

Grim-faced Hela turned as well. Her forces less retreated than evaporated, dissolving as if they had never been there.

The battle won, the Aesir started to pull back. Even the Valkyries turned and started the flight back to Asgard astride their winged horses.

And then, as Heimdall rushed towards Kisa, she breathed her last.

The hindmost of the Valkyries wheeled her horse in midair and headed back. Had not a brave warrior just fallen in battle? And yet, she hesitated. For some dogs had gone to Valhalla, battle hounds bred to the warrior's life. But never had a cat been chosen.

A one-eyed figure at the edge of the battlefield nodded. The Valkyrie approached the cat's limp form.

Kisa woke, confused. She had felt the jaws snap, then the crunch. And yet she seemed to have no injuries. Kisa licked her pelt and saw that it was clean. There was no dirt, nor even any saliva from the wolf.

She found herself in a room that she had not seen before, yet seemed oddly familiar. There was a plate of food that smelled good, although after a few bites Kisa realized she was not particularly hungry.

She trod around her new surroundings. The house contained a few small rooms. She found the bed comfortable enough, and dozed there in the afternoon.

As night fell, the door swung open. A familiar figure came through. Sigurd! Kisa jumped off the bed and ran to him, purring.

"Ho little one, let me get my battle gear off first!" Sigurd placed his ax and shield in wall mounts, then removed his gloves and mail shirt. "You are looking better," he said, scratching behind her ears. "They told me what happened. What were you thinking, taking on the Fenris Wolf?" But Kisa responded only with purrs.

The next morning Sigurd left early. Kisa went mouse hunting and found one next to the house. Delicious! She gave it little thought, and spent the evening curled up around Sigurd's feet.

As she went hunting the next day, she found a mouse in the same position. After devouring him she went on her way, puzzled. As the days went on she found that a mouse was always in about the same area.

Sigurd saw her there one morning, her tail twitching. He gave a smile. "All are resurrected nightly in Valhalla," he noted. "Even the mice."

Over the weeks that followed, Kisa was always glad to see Sigurd. She spent her days prowling the vast green meadows of Valhalla. Its many lakes provided a place to nap after a meal. At night she would return to the house. If he did not return by the door, he would appear mysteriously in the middle of the night on the bed. For sometimes Sigurd won in the daily battles of Valhalla, and sometimes he did not.

But over time, she missed the company of others of her kind, for there were none in Valhalla. And though she still liked Sigurd, Heimdall had been a good companion as well. She thought it might be nice to go where the mice at least had the decency to stay dead.

One morning Sigurd saw her pacing restlessly, her tail switching back and forth, and guessed the reason. "You miss your other friend, don't you?" He opened the door, a symbol of parting. "Go, then. The fort hasn't been built that could hold the likes of you, and you are not bound by our compact. But the way is long. Follow the colors in the sky to the Rainbow Bridge."

Kisa stood at the door, her tail twitching. She wanted to go, but also wanted to stay. Sigurd remained there, holding the door as she looked out. "Well, little one?" he said.

As he spoke, a Valkyrie fluttered through the nearby sky on a flying chariot with two winged horses. They landed on the street in front of his house.

"She has friends," said the Valkyrie. "She need not travel alone."

"Freya," said Sigurd. "I would recognize your veiled power even were it midday."

"Must it be Freya?" asked the Valkyrie. "For if she were to visit the realm of Odin's chosen among the slain, then the visit must be noticed. And perhaps that would open the door for Odin to trespass in her own realm. No, this is simply a visit by an ordinary Valkyrie, a common sight for the Einherjar."

"I wondered why you did not take Kisa yourself," said Sigurd.

"It was Odin's turn," she replied. "And anyway, the cat chose you. Just as she now chooses to be elsewhere, for a time."

Kisa walked up to Freya and nuzzled her legs, then went back to Sigurd.

"Go then, kitty," said Sigurd. Kisa stretched up and put her paws on his legs. Sigurd reached down and lifted her up. "She'll take good care of you. Visit when you can." Kisa nuzzled his hand, but when he handed her to Freya, Kisa cuddled easily into the crook of her arm.

Without further discussion the woman took off, her chariot following behind the stomp of the horse's hooves, pawing through midair as they ascended. As they neared the edge of Sigurd's eyesight the horses flickered, then turned into two large cats pulling the chariot through the sky.

They soared through the vast expanse. For a person, perhaps, the view would have been exhilarating. For Kisa, it was simply nerve-wracking. Yet such was the great speed of the chariot that they were soon at the Bifrost.

"Kitty!" said Heimdall. Freya put her down, and she sauntered towards him, purring lightly.

"You may call her 'Kisa,' as Sigurd does," said Freya.

"I am like to call her Wolf-Smeller!" exclaimed Heimdall.

"Well, if you must," replied Freya, her nose wrinkling faintly. "As a title. Infrequently."

The two gods chatted then, and Kisa prowled the area. Something was odd. It was as if a new sense had been awakened in her resurrected body, one that she was only now starting to appreciate. She paced at the edge of the Rainbow Bridge and yowled.

Freya came by and stood next to her. "What do you see, little one?" And then she made a small gasp.

Heimdall came up beside them, squinting. "I see it as well. Like a mist, but with the suggestion of shapes."

"Mau!" exclaimed Kisa.

"Hela's presence stirred the afterlife," said Freya. "They gathered here. They sensed her likeness to them. And...there is something more."

"The warning," said Heimdall. "Collectively, they cried out. Their souls are so small, I did not hear. But she did. Just enough."

"Mau MAU!" insisted Kisa, stamping her paw.

"I think I know what she wants," said Freya. "And they deserve a boon."

Freya made a complex motion with both hands. The gesture unloosed a small amount of ghostly substance. She gestured again, tapping into the vast well of the Bifrost, the frozen spectrum of energy separated into its component layers, and released a small, steady stream of energy made form. The stillest of still waters stirred and sent a ripple through the membrane separating the living from the afterlife. The ghostly matter coalesced into a cloud.

The cloud began to separate into shapes. Cat shapes. Though not near as substantial as Kisa's soul form, they had some modest presence.

"I see them," said Heimdall. "But how? Why them?"

"They are the spirits of cats loved by people," explained Freya. "As you have been kind to her, so they are attracted here."

"There is plenty of space for them," said Heimdall. He waved expansively behind himself, towards a wide field. The cats each walked up and greeted Kisa with a body touch or nuzzle as they passed, heading towards their own section of Paradise.

On a faraway bridge stands a figure, eternally keeping watch. He is frequently alone, but never lonely. He can often be seen with his cat, or any number of other pets wandering in from the fields behind them. The animals replenish their spiritual forms as needed from a deep pool of otherworldly liquid, still fed from the small stream Freya left open.

Over the years the souls of the humans came in search of their pets, and found them on the Rainbow Bridge, as they walked out from their fields and past Heimdall to meet them. Some passed into fair Asgard, as the gods there created an afterlife with a middle ground between Hel and the life of the brave slain—although exactly what they are not telling. Others greet their pets and both move on, to other afterlives of their conception. Many pets warned their human companions of dangers on the road to their various heavens. So whether the people saved their pets, or the pets saved their people, none could say for sure.

About the Author

John Taloni has been reading SF/F since he was eight and stumbled across a copy of Alexei Panshin's "Rite of Passage." His major influences include Anne McCaffrey and Larry Niven. Taloni is a long-time attendee at SF conventions, and he met his wife while dressed as a Pernese dragon rider. Their daughter asked at the age of four if they could watch more of the show with "the robots that say 'exterminate,' and the entire family has happily watched Doctor Who together ever since.

EMBRACE OF THE DEEP

GUSTAVO BONDONI

W e're not supposed to go in there," Kista said, pulling away.

"Relax, there won't be anyone around. It's just us. They keep the pool locked after hours," Jav replied. He pulled the card he'd taken from the security room out of his pocket and placed it against the reader. "Fortunately, I know where they keep the keys."

"If they catch us, they'll fire us both."

He turned to look at her. "You can go if you want. I spend every single day cleaning up after the rich bastards who pay a hundred years' worth of my salary to stay here a week, just so they can go into that pool. I want to know why. I want to see what drives someone who has everything to pay a fortune to come here. Do you know the waiting list is twenty years long?"

She didn't say anything, but she followed him through the door, which made him happy. Even if the magical pool wasn't anything special, watching her strip down to swim would be worth the price of admission.

But he knew it would be special. The door had opened into a glass elevator that descended slowly into the glowing waters.

The Pool. That was all they called it. Anywhere in the galaxy, people knew what it meant when someone talked about it. Other pools, pools with a lowercase 'p,' were called this pool or that pool. When someone simply said 'the Pool,' they were referring to this one.

The name didn't do it justice. The huge expanse of water, hundreds of meters in diameter and deep in proportion, was actually the lower half of a huge spherical complex. The upper section was where the rooms were located: rich tourists occupied the skin, each enormous suite boasting endless windows and terraces, while the lower levels, eternally lit with fluorescent light, were for the staff. Jav's glorified broom closet didn't even have its own bathroom—he had to share with the rest of his janitorial team.

The entire resort floated on the trackless ocean that made up the surface of the planet. It was the only man-made structure in the system, and that was how management liked it. A huge fleet of security ships kept trespassers out.

"So, what now?" Kista asked. There was a twinkle in her eye that said it wasn't the first time someone had brought her somewhere weird in order to get her alone, and that she had a pretty good idea of what came next. Jav wasn't surprised. She was the prettiest woman he'd ever spoken to: olive skin and brown hair, almond-shaped eyes and a slim though well-muscled body. If she hadn't been a penniless refugee of the Tau Ceti Civil War cleaning toilets for a few credits against her indentured servitude—just like he was—she would never have spoken to him. He knew he looked good enough, but in normal times, she'd have been hobnobbing with the college set, not with the menials.

Still, she'd agreed to come. That had to count for something, didn't it?

"You may not believe this," Jav told her, pulling off his shirt. "But I actually do mean to take a swim."

"Naked?" she asked with the hint of a smile.

"I didn't bring trunks."

"And I notice you didn't warn me about where we were going."

"Hey. I may be obsessed with this pool, but I'm not stupid. If you're coming in, you're going to have to remove at least some of your clothes. But it's your choice."

She watched him take everything off. As he stood next to the edge of the platform, she said: "Aren't you the least bit concerned that the sea is fluorescent, and that there are bright pink patches in it?"

"If the rich guys can take it, so can I." The entire ocean was like that, all over the planet. In fact, the water beneath them was just water from outside, which filtered into the bubble via grates on the sides.

"The Pool is full of lifeguards. When it's open, at least."

It was true. The resort employed hundreds of swimmers. He saw them trooping to and from the elevator in their black suits. One of them had once told him that the suits were hermetically sealed, and that they were forced to shower—with their suits on—before returning to their chambers. None of them had ever felt the water. "True. But again, if they're letting the fat cats in here, it has to be safe. I'll bet the lifeguards are just there to keep them from drowning and having their family sue the place."

He jumped into the water, aiming for a light blue tongue that intersected with the platform. He treaded water for a moment, trying not to think of the empty fathoms beneath him, or of how long it had been since the last time he swam.

"So, how is it?" Kista asked, tossing him a flotation cylinder on a line connected to the platform.

"It's fine. The water is warm, and it kind of keeps you afloat. It's pretty salty. But other than that, it feels like water."

"Any weird side effects?" Kista asked. She pulled her shirt off.

"What?"

"Stop drooling. I asked if you feel all right."

"I feel the same way I always did. Maybe the effects come later? Maybe the water gives you immortality or something."

"I'm coming in," she told him. She picked up a twin to his flotation device and sat down on the edge before lowering herself gingerly in, leaving all her clothes in a pile on the platform.

She swam right over to him, planted a kiss on his mouth and brushed against him. Then she laughed and swam away.

He began to paddle after her, but an unexpected chime stopped him short. It was a sound unlike any he'd ever heard before: a deep, rumbling bass that had to be well beneath the threshold of human hearing. It felt as though the tones were inside his head.

"Well, aren't you coming? I'm beginning to think you don't want me here."

The sound of Kista's voice, sweet and seductive to him mere moments before, was suddenly jarring. He turned away.

"Hey, what's wrong with... oh." Her voice trailed off, but he had already stopped listening. She was just background noise.

An image flickered at the edge of his vision, but disappeared when he tried to focus on it. Then it came again, flashing across his field of view. He closed his eyes and shook his head, but the sight, white and ghostly, was still present.

It coalesced into a face.

"No, it can't be," he said.

"Yes, it can," was the response, felt, sensed more than heard.

It was Dianne. She was here in front of him, looking the same as she had back when she was still present, back when the world made sense and they had a small daughter. Before the second planet of the Tau System declared itself an independent kingdom, leading to the war which had torn his little family to shreds and turned the whole sector into a wasteland. He didn't know whether Dianne and Melinne were still alive when the refugee service had shipped him out. They'd promised him to look into it, but when he woke after a four hundred year trip spent in a stasis pod, all they could tell him was that he was now an indentured menial at a luxury resort, working off his passage out of the Tau meltdown, and was lucky to have a job. Many refugees did without, and faced a future as slaves, not menials.

Then he was at a party. The party was the celebration of Melinne's first tooth, a true milestone that didn't depend on the orbit of some long forgotten homeworld to have meaning. Happy Toothday.

Jav remembered being angry that Dianne had spent a fortune on decorations and food, and had invited everyone they knew. The kid will never remember this, he reasoned. But, on this one occasion, Dianne hadn't sought consensus; she'd bought everything on her list and a couple of items on impulse while shopping for the rest. Money would be tight for the rest of the month.

Now, though, the anger was a memory. He ran his fingers over his infant daughter's face, savoring the softness of the skin and the flaxen suppleness of her hair. Melinne pulled away, not wanting to waste time on cuddles when there were so many new things to reach out and grab. Things she probably shouldn't be touching. A balloon caught the baby's eye and she gave her patented toothless—well, nearly toothless, now—smile. His heart sang to the beat of the subsonic roar.

Water got into his mouth and he opened his eyes. When he realized where he was, at best light-years away from his beloved daughter, at worst having outlived her by four hundred years, he nearly broke down and cried. Since he'd arrived at the Pool resort, Jav had tried to convince himself that his past was dead. He'd attempted to live the best life he could. Drank when he could, and got a girl in his room when he could. He wanted to move on, not to be tied to memories he could never recover.

The tears falling into the pink sea were proof that he'd failed.

More movement in the corner of his eye suddenly became a kaleidoscope of colors that took over his entire world.

He was in a throne room. Gold and pink and orange coral covered every surface, while water swirled all around him in the impossible colors of the planet's sea. He realized that he didn't even know the planet's name. He didn't care. A beautiful mermaid swam towards him, green locks flowing behind.

Then he realized that it wasn't a mermaid, but a fully human woman. Her legs shapely and creamy-white, a color that only the richest of humans could obtain by editing their genes. Of course, blue was a much more popular choice for the truly daring.

On cue, the woman's skin turned blue. She moved to face him, and her orange eyes made a startling contrast with her pale cyan skin.

The world was suddenly more vivid than anything he'd ever seen, heard or felt before. The water brushed his skin and activated nerve endings that had been dormant all his life into an electric frenzy. The sound of rhythmic rumbling soothed him and energized him at the same time. And the colors... he didn't have words for those soft swirls that went beyond the visible spectrum, seen not with the eyes but with the spirit.

He realized that it wasn't just a blue girl before him, but the whole sea, personified within a body he could understand. It was the mother of everything on the planet and it would nurture him and protect him. He knew, without knowing where the thought came from that his life from that moment on would make everything he'd ever lived before seem washed-out and grey.

It was as another dimension had been added to his entire existence. Not just colors and shapes and sensations, but emotions. There was a feeling of safety and oneness: he was floating in the ocean while the ocean was floating through space. All was as it should be.

She took his hand. It was a simple, careless gesture, but suddenly he felt every ecstasy that a human could experience. All at once. The most obvious was the rush of physical pleasure, tingling all over his body, as if synapses that had been used for other things his entire life suddenly learned to love. But that was only the most strident, the child yelling for attention at a party for grownups.

Masked, but at the same time heightened, by that pleasure were the subtle, deeper sensations. The sensation of a first salty bite after a week without food combined with the sense of a glass of hot water on a warm day; the feeling of muscles relaxing during a massage session; the satisfaction of a job well done; the smell of fresh-baked bread and just-mown grass; the nothingness of nirvana.

It was all happening at once, and Jav felt himself letting go.

Why worry about being indentured and working away a passage when he could drift off into the arms of this perfect blue princess of the waves and exist in eternal bliss forever?

At the thought, the impossible pleasure intensified further, as if the ocean was rewarding him for his loyalty—as if he were a dog being given a bone. But even though he was conscious of it, all he could do was to wag his tail: he gasped with a mouth that belonged to a different plane of existence, an existence of crass and unfulfilled numbness.

He was filled to the brim with the knowledge that he could be there forever, enjoying the perfection of life in the womb of the sea. All he had to do was to let go.

And as his fingers, of their own accord were releasing their grip on the flotation cylinder, a pale memory appeared before him. It was inconsequential, a mere ghost compared to what he was experiencing, a washed-out nothing.

But the image had a strange power and he watched it. It smiled, showing him a single tooth peeking out of an otherwise bare lower gum.

Afterwards, Jav was never able to explain to himself how he managed to get out of the water. He had vague memories of sobbing on the platform, devastated from the loss of the perfect world beyond the human capacity to perceive. His only thought was that he had to get out of there before the resort's security people found him.

Even the discovery that Kista's cylinder floated alone with no sign of the girl felt like nothing when compared to that overwhelming shock and pain. He remembered thinking that the cleaning crews would probably discover her body the next time they dredged the bottom for sediment.

He envied her for a moment and almost dove back in. Perhaps she was still in the arms of the sea. Perhaps she truly was dead. He would never know.

The next morning, he woke, tossed the incriminating keycard into the atomizer and asked his supervisor to assign him to the most dangerous, highest-paying job on the facility: a job that would allow him to burn off his debt and make enough for a passage back to Tau in less than a year.

The man gave him the fish-eye. "You've never been much of one for doing your own job, and now you're asking for real work. What's gotten into you?"

"I want to see if my daughter is still alive."

He glanced down at his records. "You left Tau four hundred years ago. It'll take you another four hundred to get back."

"I know. But she could still be there. She might have been in stasis, or traveling. She might be old enough to be my grandmother. But I don't care. I have to know."

He sighed. "All I have is deep-sea duty and radioactive waste classification. Both of those are risky as hell, but you'll be out of here in no time."

Jav shuddered. "I'll take the waste cleanup."

"Really? Why?"

"Because I'm not going anywhere near that creepy pink sea."

"Whatever. Suit yourself."

As the man filled out the form, Jav realized that the urge to return to the arms of the sea had subsided. Well, somewhat, anyway.

I'm coming, Melinne. Hold tight.

About the Author

Gustavo Bondoni is an Argentine novelist and short story writer who writes primarily in English. His debut novel, Siege, *was published in 2016, and his second,* Outside, *in 2017. He has nearly two hundred short stories published in fourteen countries. They have been translated into seven languages. His writing has appeared in* Pearson's Texas STAAR English Test cycle, The New York Review of Science Fiction, Perihelion SF, The Best of Every Day Fiction *and many others. His website is www.gustavobondoni.com.*

THE GLASS SLIPPER

SHERWOOD SMITH

We'd just stepped off the school bus and were starting up the long hill toward home. We passed a couple of old storefronts and had reached the vacant lot when all four of us saw a flash of gold in the gutter right below our feet.

"Hey!" Lissa exclaimed.

"What's that?" Nikki yelled.

I crouched down on the edge of the curb, poking at the trash that the rain had piled up in the gutter. In the midst of the withered leaves and soggy papers and mud gleamed a roundish thing kind of like an extra-large gold coin. As the other three watched, I picked it up and shook it off.

"What is it, Margo, a badge or something?" Pat asked.

"I don't know, but I like it," I said. Sunlight glanced down between a couple of clouds and made the thing glitter and shine so it looked like liquid flame in my hand. It would be great in my collection of Weird Things, I decided—if no one else wanted it.

"It's pretty," Lissa said, touching it daintily. "I wonder who lost it?"

"Is that carving on it?" Nikki pushed her curly black hair out of her eyes as she peered down at my hand. "It looks like something is written on it."

"No, it's leaves," Lissa said, setting her backpack on the sidewalk and bending over my hand.

I tipped my palm so everyone could see the thing. The glitter was so bright it almost hurt my eyes.

Lissa gasped. "There are words on it! Look... It's kind of old-fashioned, but I can read it. Here's an 'I', and there's 'molder' —"

"Holder," Nikki said. She grabbed my fingers in her strong brown hand, staring down at the talisman, then up at us, a funny look on her round face. "It says, 'I grant the holder one wish.'"

"Whoa." I felt kind of like little electrical shocks were zinging through my entire body. Had I, Margo O'Toole, found real magic at last? "Lemme see—" Nikki let go of my hand and I nearly smacked myself in the face. "You're right," I said, examining the fancy letters, which looked like something from a fairy tale book.

"D'you think it's real?" Nikki asked, rubbing her hands.

"No way." Pat crossed her arms. "Toss it. It's all gross with mud and gunk, so it's probably crawling with germs."

"If you do, it's mine," Nikki said. "In fact, didn't I see it first?"

"We all saw it at the same time," Lissa said quickly, flinging her blond braids over her shoulders. "You know we did. Margo just picked it up first."

Nikki grinned at me. "But if you don't want it—"

"Who said I didn't want it?" I retorted quickly. "That was Pat."

Everyone looked at Pat. All four of us girls are the same age, and we live on the same block in a not-so-safe part of the city. We've been going back and forth from school together for several years, because we aren't allowed to go alone. Pat's the tallest, and sometimes it feels like she's the oldest. Her lips were pressed together in a familiar line, and her dark eyes were, well, *austere.*

"You guys, it's not going to work. Let's get home before we get into trouble," Pat said. She sent a worried look up the street.

"Just a sec." I turned it over in my hand. "Well, it's not like there's a name or address on it. I say finders keepers."

"We can make a wish first and then toss it." Lissa looked my way, wrinkling her nose. "And after that, you can wash your hands."

"Let's go." Pat's voice was sharp. "I can't believe you're messing with that thing at all."

Nikki and Lissa gaped at her. They were obviously thinking, was this really good old Pat, who was always so quiet, and fair, and so kind she couldn't even step on bugs?

I knew she hated any mention of magic these days, but I couldn't tell them that.

"So, if we only get one wish," Nikki said, "we better think a little."

"If it's even real," I said, sneaking a look at Pat.

It didn't help. "I can't believe you dummies," she muttered, and whirled around so all we saw was her skinny back. Next to us was a weed-choked vacant lot, left over from a fire. Stalking in the direction of a charred old tree stump right in the middle, she yelled over her shoulder, "I'll get started on my homework while you waste your time on that thing."

We all watched her march through the wet weeds, drop down onto the tree stump, and yank her notebook out of her backpack. Lissa and Nikki turned back to me and shrugged, looking down at the talisman. Nikki's brow puckered, and Lissa threw her braids back. "What do you think? Should we wish for a thousand wishes?" she suggested.

"I've never read a story where that worked," I said. "The magic might just split up a thousand ways and you'll get a little of each wish—like, just the front porch if you wish for a mansion, or if you want a really cool pair of shoes, you'll wind up with half a shoelace."

Nikki gave a loud snort. "That's one thing I really hate—those stupid stories where the person is granted a wish, and goes for something that seems perfectly okay, but then it turns out to be a total disaster."

Lissa bit her lip, and did a little jazz step, backing away. "You think that thing is going to zap us? It was in the gutter, after all. Maybe it zapped someone else."

I thought over all the magic stories I'd ever read—and I've read a lot. "Someone might have tossed it," I said, "but then maybe, after it grants its wish, it might just kind of jump into space, and land anywhere."

"That's one big jump, Margo." Nikki grinned sourly as she looked around at the familiar rundown apartment buildings and crummy old stores of our neighborhood. "I haven't heard of any sudden millionaires around *here*."

"Is that what we should wish?" Lissa asked. "For a million bucks?"

"Or a billion?" Nikki added, closing her eyes.

For about ten seconds, it felt great. I thought about my mom and me getting away from our dinky apartment and buying a house with my share of the money. A mansion! With an entire theme park in the yard. And a limousine—for each of us.

Then I thought about what would happen if we couldn't prove how we'd gotten the money. "I wonder if the IRS would believe us," I said. "The FBI sure won't."

"Who says the IRS would have to know?" Lissa demanded. "We'll keep it a secret, of course."

"Margo's right." Nikki threw her backpack down next to Lissa's and rubbed her chin thoughtfully. "Anybody who suddenly spends big amounts of money gets investigated by nosy tax agents. I've seen it in a million detective shows. They'll think we're with some kind of creepy gang."

"We won't spend big amounts." Lissa fluttered her hands, turning a pirouette. Then she stopped and sighed. "But then, even if we spend tiny amounts, we'll get investigated by nosy families. At least, I sure will."

"Me, too," Nikki grumped. "Heck—I buy a single candy bar with my babysitting money, and my mom wants to know why the money didn't go into my college fund."

I closed my fingers over the talisman. "I'm just wondering if each of us might get a wish," I said. "I mean, if I wish, then hand it off to you, Nikki—you'd be the new holder. Then to Lissa." I was thinking, *And if it really works, we could give it to Pat.*

"But it might disappear," Nikki said, toeing the trash in the gutter, as if another talisman might be uncovered. A car hissed by through the wet street and Nikki jumped back from the dirty splash.

"Let's agree on the first wish," Lissa said. "If it stays, then we agree on the other wishes."

"Fair's fair." Nikki kicked mud off her shoe.

"Okay," I said. "So what'll it be?"

"A mansion, maybe?" Nikki threw her arms wide. "Everyone has her own room. No, two rooms. Five! A bathtub like a swimming pool for each!"

Lissa closed her eyes and sighed. I grinned, thinking again of royal palaces with rooms and rooms of fun stuff to do.

But then Nikki snorted again. "Wait a minute. It's only one wish, you hogs."

"What?" Lissa exclaimed.

"We have one wish," Nikki repeated, looking from one of us to the other, her brown eyes wary. "If we wish for a palace, we might get one, but I bet it doesn't come with furniture. And even if it did—" She made a terrible face. "—who's going to clean up a million rooms? Not me! It's bad enough being stuck with cleaning our little place when my mom's too tired."

"And who's going to let a kid keep a palace in the middle of the city?" Lissa shrugged her shoulders hands out.

I groaned. "I can't think of anything that won't backfire. Like, if we wish for an unending supply of ice cream—"

"—We end up barfing at the sight of it," Lissa said. "I just thought of that as well."

We stared at each other.

"Maybe we could fix things in our lives," Nikki said slowly. "All four of us have had divorces happen in our families. Maybe it would work for all of us—even Pat—if we wished our parents were back together again, and all happy."

We looked at each other. Lissa turned another slow pirouette, then faced Nikki. "I hate to say it, but do you really want your dad back?"

Nikki's head dropped and her hair swung forward and covered her face. I couldn't see her eyes, but I didn't have to. The few times her dad had visited, it always ended up with him getting drunk and though Nikki never complained in front of me, I think her dad was pretty mean to Nikki and her brothers and sisters.

She looked up. "I don't, but my mom might. At least, she'd like another paycheck, or the child support he owes us, or something."

Lissa said, "I like my step-parents now. If the magic brought my parents together again, what would happen to my half-brother Sean, since his father is my stepdad, and how about the new baby my stepmom is expecting?"

I'd been thinking while they talked. "In the stories, forcing a change onto someone else's life always turns out rotten. Even if you did it for the best reasons."

"It would be a good thing in Pat's family," Nikki pointed out seriously. "I mean, except for my dad, who's just a flake, at least all our parents want us. Hers don't even want her any more—and that aunt of hers is mean. She just uses her for a maid and a babysitter."

"Which makes it extra rotten," Lissa added, "because there's no one in the world who works harder, at school or home, than Pat."

"Or is more fair to other people."

"I just don't see why she's so mad," Lissa added, whirling in another pirouette, and then stopping to glance at Pat on her tree stump.

I opened my hand again and stared down at the talisman, thinking hard. Pat and I lived next door to each other so we'd spent a lot of time together. When we were little we'd acted out the adventure stories we read and loved. I'd started collecting Weird Things in first grade, and Pat used to help me—we always hoped one of them would turn out to be left by aliens, or would transport us to another world. Then the problems started at Pat's home, and trying to test the magic from books to see if it was real turned from a game into a kind of quest.

Lissa and Nikki knew about my Weird Things collection, but not about the quest for real magic. I thought about how in fourth grade Pat and I used to run into thick fog banks, hoping they'd turn out to be a magic gateway to Middle-earth, and how we tried to open the backs of our closets to see if we could get to Narnia.

Once we tried a love potion on her parents. That was before both of them left, and her grandmother moved in. Pat's grandmother really loved her, but after only a year she died, and Pat's aunt moved in—with her kids. Pat's life was now exactly like Cinderella's—except there was no fairy godmother, and Pat no longer believed in magic.

There she was, sitting on the stump crouched over her math book. I couldn't see her face, but her bony shoulders looked fierce. *That's why she's angry*, I thought. *It'll hurt too much if this thing doesn't work.*

But I couldn't say anything—I knew she'd hate it if I talked about all our tries to get to Narnia and Oz. I turned back to Nikki and Lissa.

"We can't bring her grandma back to life," I said.

Nikki made a face. "Yeah, Margo's right. She might come back a zombie."

"Eeeeeugh," Lissa and I groaned together, exchanging gross-out looks.

"But if her parents were together again, and loved her?" Lissa asked.

My mind was racing now. "Would it really work, though?"

"What do you mean?" Lissa and Nikki exclaimed at the same time, grinned at each other, and then turned to me expectantly. Another car whooshed through the rainy street, but this time neither of them noticed the splash.

"Well," I said, "is it right to make people go back to the way they were, without asking? I mean, how would you like it if a magic spell forced you to be like you were in first grade?"

Lissa said slowly, "We're talking about getting them to love Pat again."

"But they don't," Nikki said, frowning. "I think I see it—it'd be fake, wouldn't it?"

"Right," I said. "At least, fake or not, it would be fake for Pat. She'd always know they were back together because of the spell, not for her. Or even for each other."

Lissa hopped again. "I see. They might not even act real—but like programmed dolls, or something, if we force them to change." She stuck out her tongue. "Heck, there's always a chance this won't even work in the first place." She glared at the talisman on my palm. "Will it really matter to us if it doesn't?"

Again we looked at each other. "Not to me," Nikki said, smacking her hands together. "I got my life planned out. College, law school, then goin' after corporate pirates."

Lissa whispered, "If it just were mine, I might have wished that I'd get a scholarship to a good dance school—except then I'd have to worry that I was good enough once I got there."

"You want to wish you would be the best dancer in the world?" I asked.

Lissa's whole body tensed as she closed her eyes, then she said, "No. It's like what you said about Pat—I'd always know the applause was for the talisman, and not for me. I'd hate that."

"So what do we do, throw it away?" I asked.

"There's a chance it's real," Nikki said.

76

"I know," Lissa said. "I'm just wondering if we could ask Pat if there's something she would want."

"And get our noses bitten off?" Nikki rolled her eyes, grinning. "She already let us know pretty clearly she thought this whole thing was stupid."

They turned to me. "She wouldn't touch that talisman," I said. "Though she's the one who needs it most."

"So what do we do?" Lissa asked. "We can't change her life for her—and she won't take the thing and do it herself."

I said, "Maybe we can't send her to the ball, but we could give her a glass slipper."

"What?" Nikki asked, making one of her faces.

Lissa's eyes went wide, and she laughed. "*I* know what you mean!" She whirled into a little dance step on the sidewalk, her beaded hair swinging out gracefully. "When Cinderella had that slipper, it was her proof that magic had happened—and it could happen again. We could give Pat hope. I mean, if magic is real just once, then it could happen again."

"Anything could happen," I said, thinking of all the stories I'd read—and all the ones I hoped to act out some day, on the stage.

"She might even start looking for it," Nikki said, nodding slowly.

"So we're all in favor?" I asked.

Lissa smiled, making a graceful dancer's bow, and Nikki smacked her hands together. "Do it, Margo."

I raised the talisman, the other two reached up to touch it as well, and I said, "We wish Pat would see magic."

Then we turned to face Pat, not knowing what—if anything—to expect.

For a moment, nothing happened.

Then Pat's head came up, and she looked at us. It was a long look, an odd look, as if she saw something else besides us. I felt a weird tingling in my bones, and around the edges of my vision light flickered, like tiny stars, but I didn't dare move. Turn my head, even.

For a long time we all just stood there, and then Pat got up. And she smiled.

It wasn't a big grin, like Nikki's best, or a giggly smile, like Lissa when she's feeling silly. It was a little one, but it glowed in her eyes and her cheeks and her forehead—it made her all bright.

She picked up her books and came down the hill, still smiling.

I looked down at my empty hands—the talisman had disappeared. But it didn't matter, I realized as I stooped to pick up my backpack. It didn't matter because we'd each gotten a gift after all. We'd given Pat her glass slipper, and the look in her face gave it right back again.

"C'mon," I said, laughing as I looked at the others. "Let's go, or we'll be late for the ball."

About the Author

Sherwood Smith studied in Austria, finally earning a master's in history—she's been a governess, a bartender, and wore various hats in the film industry before turning to teaching for 20 years. She began her publishing career in 1986. To date she's published over forty books, nominated for several awards, including the Nebula, the Mythopoeic Fantasy Award, and an Anne Lindbergh Honor Book. Her website is www.sherwoodsmith.net.

Eyes Full of the Sea

Yvonne Eliot

They had been at sea for three days before he realized that the sickness which had overcome him was different from that which afflicted his fellow passengers.

Eyes swollen closed, he heard someone rush past him and heave their guts over the rail. The sudden acrid stench was blessedly swept away by the breeze, the sharp tang of seawater cleansing the air. Rory McTavish thanked the stars that, whatever else might be ailing him, at least he had a strong stomach. In fact, he found the ragged swaying of the ship among the waves almost comforting in its motion.

So what was wrong with him? Instead of nauseated, he felt massive, weighty with a slow, inexorable momentum. At the same time, he felt constrained and awkward, as if his body was too small to hold how big he was. He felt cold beyond comprehension despite the warmth of the sun against his skin. His blood seemed to ebb and flow with currents that had nothing to do with the human form, and he seemed to go on forever.

Disoriented, he slitted his eyes open, getting his bearings. He vaguely remembered hauling himself out of the already fetid hold and trying to wedge himself out of the path of the busy seamen. He was lying in a nearly fetal position, the rough grain of the deck's planks pressing against his cheek.

As he blinked the salt and grit from his eyes, seemingly random shapes and angles started to arrange themselves into beams, ropes, and shadows of slowly undulating sails. It must be near noon, perhaps a bit past. With great effort, he levered himself into a sitting position, wincing as a splinter jabbed into his palm. He squinted at it, then carefully pulled out the wood and sucked the wound. Looking up, he found that the man sagging against the railing–his pallor resembling the belly of a day-old haddock–was the portly Sir Alasdair Murdoch, his recent employer.

Rory checked his hand. It didn't seem too grievous a wound. The last thing he needed on this wretched voyage was a festering sore. Had it only been a less than a week since he'd been sitting in a corner of Tad Flaherty's tavern, finishing the chair he'd carved for Tad's little Bridget? So much had changed since then.

The tavern had been dark as usual at that late hour of the evening, the flickering from the fireplace and lamps casting a warm, indistinct glow around the room. It didn't bother Rory; he really didn't need to see to work. The wood hummed quietly in his hands as he traced the courses of the latent moisture in its veins. His blade moved surely, smoothing curves and fitting pieces such that the greener wood would tighten closely around the others as it dried. He smiled at the thought of the beating it would get from the three-year-old. Bridget might be an adorable little girl, but she was also a hellion and a half.

Two gentlemen kept glancing in his direction, watching the way he caressed the edges of the little chair. After conferring, the stout, balding one looked around until he found Tad at his usual place behind the bar. He waved to catch Tad's attention, gesturing for him to join them.

The hairs on the back of Rory's neck started to prickle as it became obvious that they were discussing *him*. Tad smiled and answered their questions, beaming at Rory from across the room. Although the taller of the two strangers seemed doubtful, the rotund one looked satisfied, and Tad returned to his work. More murmuring between the gentlemen, then the taller man had shrugged dismissively and turned back to his ale. Rory wasn't sure whether to be relieved or disappointed, so he busied himself with polishing one of the legs of the chair.

To his surprise, a darker shadow fell across his work. The stout gentleman stood by Rory's side, hand on his hips, surveying the young man.

"I am Sir Alasdair Murdoch," he announced abruptly. "We have received a commission from King James himself to colonize the glorious paradise of Nova Scotia. Unhappily," he frowned and clasped his hands behind his back, "one of our party is no longer able to join us. Since the commission requires that we provide a full half-dozen able-bodied men to work the land, we find ourselves at a loss. Specifically, we find ourselves in need of a good carpenter. Tad Flaherty has a fair reputation in these parts, and he says you're a worthy lad. Would you be interested in joining us?"

Rory felt his whole body grow hot, then cold. Leave Scotland? Leave the land? Leave... but no, Mairead had already left him. His blood started to rush a little more quickly in his veins. Why not? He thought briefly of his uncle, but the ripple of habitual guilt was quickly swept away by a tide of fierce exhilaration.

Opening his mouth to reply, he found it too dry to speak. He swallowed and tried again. "I would indeed be interested. When would we be leaving?"

"We have already made arrangements with a boatmaster to convey us upon the morning's tide two days hence." Sir Alasdair looked at him almost apologetically from under heavy brows. "I hope this is not too inconvenient for you."

Rory shook his head and rose, still holding the little chair. "I have little enough to pack. Just tell me where and when." *Too fast*, a voice hissed at him, *it was moving too fast*... but he wanted this.

Sir Alasdair eyed him curiously, "Have you no family, no provisions you must make before embarking on such an endeavor?"

Rory shrugged. "I'm an orphan." That much was true, anyway. Sir Alasdair seemed to take the declaration at face value, for he nodded and gave instructions for meeting at the dock. Another nod, and he rejoined his companion, leaving Rory dizzy.

And so it had happened. Tad's wife was tearful in her goodbyes, and even Tad himself got a bit misty, but they reassured him that they wished him every happiness. Rory managed to avoid seeing his uncle entirely, leaving a note with the Flahertys to pass along to him after Rory had left.

Now he was here, crouched on the deck of *The Golden Thistle*, bound for heathen lands. He shook his head to clear it of both the lingering memories and the general, befuddling fog. The odd weightiness had subsided a bit, settling into the background of his awareness. Laughter startled him, and for a moment he thought it was part of his imaginings, since it seemed so out of place. Following the sound, he saw two women emerge onto the deck. The older one was plump, her dark brown hair threaded with heavy streaks of grey, while the younger woman....

Rory became aware that his mouth was open and closed it abruptly. It wasn't so much that she was physically beautiful, although her cloak parted to show a pleasingly curved form and her light brown hair glinted strands of red and gold in the sun. The freckles that sprinkled her nose couldn't detract from the delicate structure of the bones. Instead, they gave her an impish look that even the pair of round spectacles couldn't hide. But what caught him most was that she was so *alive*. Her laughter was matched by dancing eyes and light feet, expressive hands gesturing as she described something to the older woman.

Looking up, she saw Rory and paused. His world narrowed down to the sun on his back, the swell of the sea, and the way the lenses of her spectacles intensified the hazel of her eyes. Part of him was aware of a sailor walking past him and of her companion's sudden, piercing gaze, but that was distant and unimportant. She tilted her head slightly, her gaze curious, then said something to the watchful woman beside her. The elder responded sharply, and the girl—she looked to be about Rory's age—laughed again, turning from him as the two continued their walk.

It was enough to bring him clumsily to his feet. He had to meet her, to speak with her, to know her. He ran stiff fingers through his unruly red hair and futilely attempted to straighten his clothes. Watching them as they perambulated around the deck, it seemed to Rory that the girl's gaze seemed to drift his way rather more than strictly necessary, but that could have just been his heart teasing his mind. In time, their route brought them again in his direction. The older woman obviously tried to talk her companion into withdrawing below deck again, but the girl paid her no heed and continued to approach where Rory was utterly failing to look calm and nonchalant. She came next to him and leaned on the railing, looking out at the sea.

"You must be the new boy," she said. "Roderick, is it?"

He flushed. "Rory, ma'am."

She giggled and looked askance at him. "Oh, don't 'ma'am' me." She leaned on one elbow to face him directly. "I'm Catriona Sullivan. My da's Sir Gregory Sullivan, one of the aspiring baronets."

That made sense. Rory had discovered that there were three parties aboard, each headed by a man hoping to take advantage of King James' promise of the title of Baronet as a reward for colonizing Nova Scotia. Sir Alasdair's tall associate at the tavern had been another, a Sir Lachlan Fraser. Rory was glad that Catriona was unrelated to Sir Lachlan, as the two men had taken an instant dislike to one another.

"If that's what you want, ma'am—Miss Sullivan," he stammered.

"Catriona," she chided. The matron who had come up to join them frowned deeply. Catriona sighed. "Oh, ma—we're going to be stuck on this ship for months, practically sitting in each other's soup. After that, in the New World, we'll be working too hard to pretend that frivolous formalities matter one jot." Her mother's nostrils flared disapprovingly, but she seemed to reluctantly acknowledge the truth of the argument or, at least, the futility in continuing it. She imperiously held out her hand to Rory.

"I am Lady Sullivan," she proclaimed. He gingerly took the proffered hand, unsure whether to shake it or kiss it, so he settled for an awkward bow.

"Rory McTavish, carpenter for Sir Alasdair Murdoch, milady," he responded, releasing her hand.

Her keen eyes studied him, and, unexpectedly, she nodded. "You'll do." Lady Sullivan then addressed her daughter. "Come, Catriona. I do believe we have taken sufficient exercise for the time being. Let us return to our cabin." She inclined her head toward Rory. "Mr. McTavish."

As she followed her mother back toward the stairs leading below, Catriona murmured, "Rory," and smiled at him.

Rory watched them disappear, stunned by the whirlwind of emotions rushing through him. But then the alien weightiness returned more strongly, the motion of tides and currents filling his veins. He closed his eyes and allowed himself to be one with the sea.

Days soon fell into a pattern. After spending the night in the hold, Rory would wake in the morning to the grunts and stenches of his fellow laborers and, in another compartment, the livestock. He'd tumble out of his hammock and stow it for the day, then make his way to the galley to eat whatever hard and salted but otherwise tasteless grub was being served. Of course, the newly-minted baronets and their families lived on an upper level complete with cabins and something approaching real food, but those were luxuries not granted the common man.

He spent as much time above decks as possible, carving spare bits of wood into small toys the shapes of birds or fish, helping mend damaged spars, or simply staring at the vastness of the ocean, feeling its depths and currents. He had stopped trying to understand why he could feel the sea as he did, his pulse matching the tides, accepting it as part of this whole, strange journey he was on.

Of course, his activities were designed merely to occupy time while waiting for a chance encounter with Catriona. Rory chuckled at himself for the thought; he was pretty sure that Catriona left very little to the fickle whims of chance.

Sometimes, usually when the weather was worse than usual, he'd catch only a glimpse of her cloaked form. Once or twice, when storms had raged throughout a day, he hadn't seen her at all, and he moped, allowing his connection with the ocean to pull his blood and body into a languorous stupor beyond the reach of surface turmoil.

But more days than not, they talked. They shared stories about the time her parents had taken her to Edinburgh, and when he'd found the badger's burrow; speculated about what they might find in their new home; and argued amicably about whether the bird which had been following them was an albatross or merely a common gull. She confessed that she used to hate having to wear spectacles, but now she was far more grateful that they helped her to see.

As the days became weeks, the stories became deeper, more personal. He told her about Mairead, her dark eyes and wild, black hair; the way her songs could hush the stubbornest woodpecker and shame a lark. She was older than he, but he'd loved her and thought she'd loved him in return until she proved otherwise by abandoning him. The beauty of her voice had carried her off to a laird's household, and he'd never heard from her again.

He found himself talking about his childhood, something he usually avoided. As a toddler, he'd fallen into a cistern and nearly drowned. His mother had rescued him, but caught a chill in her lungs that proved fatal, leaving him to be raised by her brother. He'd never known his father, who had died soon after Rory's birth.

Catriona's eyes were so gentle, so sympathetic behind their lenses that, as he told his tale, he could almost forget the acid of his uncle's tongue, the abuse heaped upon the little boy who was always too slow or too stupid. He wanted to let her caring wash away his uncle's accusations that he was cursed, that he would always bring destruction to anything—or anyone—that crossed his path.

It almost worked.

Something else which had become part of his daily routine was being the butt of Sir Lachlan's taunts. Sometimes it was something as simple as the tip of Sir Lachlan's foot protruding just enough into Rory's path to cause him to stumble. Sometimes the baronet took great pleasure in mocking Rory's lack of education or the bits of carving he made.

"Why, Rory," he'd exclaim, "once we reach the New World, I'm sure Sir Murdoch will be eternally thankful to have brought along such an accomplished crafter of doll-things. Do you make little dresses as well?" His witticisms were met with titters and guffaws from nearby passengers, adding to the humiliation.

Rory knew it was foolish to allow the man to get under his skin, but he could feel his face flush every time. And every time he swallowed a retort, the bile grew until he was seething with the sickness of it. They still had almost a month before the crew expected to sight land, and Rory doubted he could stomach much more.

Rory stirred fitfully in his sleep. He felt cold and immense, immersed in darkness. He'd become accustomed to his bond with the ocean's massive swells, but this was different. He sensed fish scattering before him. Above him, the curve of the ship's hull swayed with the ponderous rhythm of the sea. Anger and a lust for revenge filled his alien heart and found a focus in the unsuspecting vessel.

Rory hauled himself up the ladder between decks, moving from the hold to the cabin level. As he approached the stairs to the upper deck, he heard the familiar, mocking voice behind him.

"If it isn't My Lord Carpenter." Sir Lachlan sauntered up to him, his arrogance unaltered by the roll of the ship. As improbably impeccable as usual, he languidly surveyed Rory's disheveled appearance, then waved him aside so that Sir Lachlan could mount the stairs first. Rory's jaw clenched but he obligingly moved back a step to allow the man to pass. He imagined Sir Lachlan missing a step and tumbling in awkward disarray — and, in fact, as he thought it, the ship *did* lurch, forcing Sir Lachlan to frantically grab Rory's shoulder to catch himself. Their eyes met: Rory's angry and smug, Sir Lachlan's a mix of disgust, hate, and maybe just a touch of fear. He righted himself, let go of Rory's shoulder, and climbed onto the deck, unconsciously wiping his hand on his trousers.

Rory waited. He had no wish to be seen to be following Lachlan like a lapdog, so he concentrated on breathing slowly and deeply until he felt he could continue, then went on deck. He needed air. He needed to think.

Rory recognized Catriona's footsteps coming up beside him, but he didn't turn, keeping his gaze outward toward the sea. She hesitated, then leaned against the rail, unconsciously mirroring his stance.

After a moment, she asked, "What do you see?"

He didn't answer. They stood there, swaying with the rocking of the ship, surrounded by the creak of the boards and rigging, the soft splashing of the waves against the side as the vessel moved through the water. The icy, salted wind scoured the clammy stench of the hold from his skin but did little to assuage his anger.

After a time, he spoke. "I see power." He watched the undulating surface of the waves, feeling its connection to all that lay beneath. "I see fear." He finally turned to meet her curious scrutiny. "And I see... hunger."

Her eyes widened, startled. For a moment, he thought he could see himself reflected in her lenses, but his eyes looked filled with the sea: a deep, shifting bluish green that rippled with the motion of the ship. Then he blinked, and the reflection showed him eyes of his normal clear blue. He shrugged, disturbed, trying to convince himself it had been a trick of the light. "What does anyone see?"

She tentatively raised a hand to his face, as if unsure whether she should be frightened, then let her arm fall before she touched his skin. "I see... you," she said, wonderingly.

Rory stared at her, torn between wanting her to understand how scared he was and wanting her to reassure him that he was imagining things. But he knew what he'd been experiencing was more than mere fantasy. How could she not *feel* what had been tracking them from the depths that they had so carelessly traversed? Except that he knew that wasn't it. Catriona was so sensitive to nuance and things at the edge of perception that he half-believed she had some form of the Sight; she *had* to have sensed that power — hunger, he had named it — yet she seemed unafraid. He wanted to shake her, to *make* her see.

It was Death.

But he couldn't do it. He couldn't breach the distance between the darkness of his knowledge and the innocence of her trust. So he simply turned away again and resumed his sightless vigil, erecting silent walls to close her out. Eventually, she left him.

He ignored the ache in his chest. It was better that he be alone.

The inevitable happened two days later.

He'd been avoiding Catriona since their encounter at the railing. She'd come on deck and he'd turned from her, pretending to be busy with his carving. She hesitated, wanting to join him but respecting his isolation. Out of the corner of his eye, he saw her stand there a moment, then go back down the steps.

"Seems a shame." The hated voice, so close at hand, startled Rory. Sir Lachlan leered in the direction Catriona had taken. "Such a beautiful girl, so lithesome, just waiting to be taken by a fine gentleman. Too bad about those spectacles, though. Why, I'm sure that I would be doing her a favor if I took her below and..."

Whatever he had planned to do was cut off by a blow that slammed his jaw shut, followed by a thud as he hit the deck. Rory was standing over him, breathing heavily and cradling his stinging fist. Sir Lachlan lay there stunned for a moment, then tried to regain his dominance over the situation.

"My goodness, McTavish, are you really resorting to fisticuffs? Really, that is so *common* of you. Although I'm sure I shouldn't expect anything other than...." He trailed off, the smirk fading along with the color in his face as he saw Rory's expression.

No. Too many times, he'd taken it. Too many times, he'd backed down. The rage that had been building to a simmer beneath his skin would no longer be denied.

Enough was enough.

The sea surrounding the ship began to roil. Passengers and crew alike started murmuring, staring wide-eyed at the seething surface, chattering nervously, trying to hide their fear. Waves built in size and force, crashing together and apart off the bow of the vessel as *something* started to rise.

Rory didn't have to wonder. He knew what was coming to demand its due.

From the center of the turmoil rose a column of dark, sinuous glass. The dragon was formed from the sea itself, fish and waterweeds caught up in its snake-like body. The head was as large as one of the cows moaning frantically in the hold, the torso at least thrice the thickness of the mainmast. Sprays of water lifted from its back to form monstrous wings that *whooshed* a gale of droplets and a stench of salted decay upon the terrified knot of huddled humanity.

Its eyes were a deep, shifting bluish green that rippled with the motion of the sea.

Rory felt it pulling at something deep inside him, and he let it touch his consciousness. Two visions filled his mind: the man saw the dragon, while the dragon looked down upon the cowering, shrieking people. Rory recognized many of those who had laughed at him and was filled with bitter hatred. His human sight faded as he felt himself expand and merge with the dragon, seeing only through its eyes. It—he—screamed vengeance to the sky, showing teeth like needles as long as a man's arm, then swooped down to sink those teeth into the mainmast, snapping it in twain. It shook the timber with its mass of rope and canvas like a terrier with a rat, then let it fall to the deck. Rory, watching from the dragon's eyes, felt a grim satisfaction as the insignificant beings below scattered to escape.

Storm clouds, drawn by the violent energies surrounding the ship, coalesced overhead, darkening the sky and hurling gusts of icy wind into the fray. A lightning bolt shot down and impaled the dragon, shattering into countless streaks of electricity ricocheting within the rearing frame.

Rory exulted at the lightning quivering through his ophidian self, but it wasn't enough. He could sense a darkness at the core of the creature, a darkness which was the core and fuel of its power, and he wanted it for himself.

He strained towards it, but it eluded him, slipping away from his grasping psyche. Again and again, until he gathered all his desire and *lunged* at the darkness. It seemed to struggle, then relented, and he was inside.

Immediately, he was assaulted by emotions and image. With a shock, he recognized them.

His uncle's bitter, scornful face, telling him yet again that he was a worthless slop of mud.

Sir Lachlan's contemptuous disdain, barely even acknowledging his existence as more than an inconvenient annoyance.

Mairead's joy and relief at finally being rid of him.

His uncle's face, again, this time turning from his sister's grave with hate-filled eyes condemning Rory: *You did this.*

And he suddenly understood. The fuel wasn't rage. It wasn't power. It was fear: fear that they were right. Fear that he was cursed. Fear that the world would have been a better place if he had been stillborn, never inflicting his crippled soul on those around him.

Anger swept through him, anger and defiance. He'd show them. He'd *destroy* them.

Unbidden, Catriona's amused voice floated above his anger. *Oh, really?* it asked. *And this proves them wrong, how?*

The voice was joined by a sense of her presence, and Rory's rage stuttered and began to lose force, dissipating in her warmth, leaving him full of shame and anguish. *Oh, Catriona. What have I done? What can I do?*

He could feel her smile. *Have faith.* The smile deepened. *Create faith.*

Create faith? How could he force other people to have faith in him when he had no faith in himself? How could he change the disgust, the contempt, the hatred they threw at him?

Look again, she said.

Reluctantly, he looked.

His uncle's bitter, scornful face rose before him, then began to crack, shedding pieces that fell and whirled away. Beneath the façade, a younger version of the man looked out, face crumpled in grief over the death of his beloved sister. He looked at the little boy before him and panicked, realizing he had no idea how to care for a child, let alone try to comfort him while lost in his own mourning.

Sir Lachlan's contemptuous disdain suffered the same transformation, the mask breaking apart to leave a huddled, awkward little boy who was never very good at anything and was always teased by the neighborhood children.

And Mairead.... She *was* filled with joy, but it was because of the opportunity to share her gift with the world. What he hadn't noticed before was that the joy was tinged with sadness and regret that she couldn't join her in the adventure.

He reached out and touched each of these faces wonderingly. How could he hate people for being in pain or for wanting joy?

Catriona's approval spread through him like a warm, tropical current. The darkness enshrouding his fear lost its sense of menace, becoming translucent wisps that shredded and wafted away to dissolve into light. The electricity still coursing through the dragon's body slowed and widened, becoming a soft glow that illuminated the sky, burning off the storm clouds above.

Rory was again inhabiting two bodies, feeling the dragon, yet now aware of his own body as well. He was unsurprised to find Catriona at his side, clasping one of his hands in both of hers, the dragon's glow reflecting off her lenses. Seen from outside, the water that comprised the dragon's body had clarified, shimmering like striated glass, wings now shifting, iridescent rainbows. Its eyes were a bright, clear blue.

It still hovered over the ship, yet its purpose was no longer malignant. It opened its mouth to pour forth delicate streams of water that wound around the fallen mast like liquid ropes, raising it to its former position and carefully setting it into the stump of its base. Rory felt the moisture soaking the timber and knew how to change that moisture, drying some of the splinters more rapidly and thoroughly than others to hold it together, healing the rift. The streams retracted, leaving only a hint of magic securing the pieces. The yardarms were next, receiving similar repairs. Then the rigging was restrung and the torn sails remounted. To mend the sails, the dragon spread its very wings wider and wider, becoming more and more transparent, until the ghost of the dragon drifted *through* the ship and melded its wings to the sails.

Rory turned toward Catriona.

"Thank you," he murmured.

She smiled. "I told you I saw you." And she kissed him.

About the Author

Yvonne Eliot loves painting with words, using language to explore all the myriad nuances and expressions of human experience. She believes that the most important stories are the ones we tell about ourselves. Other than the occasional piece of flash fiction, this is her first publication.

RUNS LIKE WATER

CHLOE GARNER

D enise's daddy gave her two main things in life: a horse, and a restless sense of adventure.

Pretty much everything else in her life, she got from her momma, Grandad Evans, or Granmomma Pritchett.

Standing next to the stream a couple of miles from their house - across the barley field, the cart path, and the sheep pasture, through the big trees and down the rock bank - Denise felt the pull of the water, the same way her momma said her daddy always had.

"He needed to be moving," Tabitha said. "Always moving."

Granmomma had tcht'ed from her knitting, and Denise had looked over at her paternal grandmother, wondering how a traveler, an adventurer, had come from that woman of stone. But there were mysteries in the world that took too much inspection, and she'd stolen bread from the table and gone running outside, instead.

Granmomma would be there when the sun went down, when Denise had to go home again, and maybe tonight Denise could get her to tell a story about Johannes, the boy whose feet never found home soil.

Grandad Evans was the one who came looking for her, this day, calling her name from upstream, out of sight, and Denise answered.

"I'm here."

Grandad came into view, shuffling over rocks like a man built of rubber bands, and sat on a rock nearby.

"You catch anything?" he asked.

"Where does it go?" Denise asked. Again.

Grandad grinned, showing tea-stained teeth that gapped where his old gums were pulling back further and further.

"It goes a long way," he said. "Down this way and that, growing trees, watering cattle, finding its friends."

"Who are its friends?" Denise asked. Grandad nodded at the water.

"You know. This creek and that stream, buddies from way on back. Thick as thieves, can't tell one water from another, when they get together."

Denise nodded.

"And where does it go from there?"

Grandad scratched the back of his head, dramatic tension.

"From there, it'll hit a river. Lotsa people like to name their rivers, but I figure the river doesn't know any better and calls itself whatever it wants. Rivers go deep and they go slow, except where they go fast. You can find lots of good fish in a river."

Denise giggled.

"I don't want to catch a fish," she said. "I want to go with them."

"Not yet, young one. Not just yet."

And he stood, tussling her hair and taking her hand to walk back up the rocks toward the soft, sweet, mossy dirt below the trees.

"You barefoot again?" he asked. "We buy you shoes, Dennie."

"But it feels better," she answered, and he bounced her hand against his hip.

"Don't let Granmomma see you like that," he said. "Quick, run down to the creek and wash your feet off. I'll carry you home."

He let her hand go and she climbed back down to the water, rinsing off the dirt from her feet and ankles and picking her way back up the rocks. Grandad swept her up in his wiry arms with a grunt.

"Not much longer now," he said, "you'll be carrying me instead of me carrying you."

"Never," she answered with a smile, and he kissed her forehead.

"From your lips to God's ears," he answered, carrying her back to the house.

Johannes wasn't dead. Denise knew that. Well, she believed it, and so did Tabitha. Granmomma often suggested that he was, while Grandad speculated on what adventure Johannes might have been on, at that moment.

Johannes had left for the first time when Denise was still unborn, and he hadn't returned until after she could walk. Denise couldn't remember that first time, though she remembered the second. She'd been eight, and he'd brought home with him the single most important creature in her life outside of the adults she lived with: a slender roan filly named Petra.

She was only just a yearling, newly separated from her dam and nervous about the world, but even then she'd had attitude. As a grown mare, she was still lighter than the local crop of weanlings, but she was twice as smart as any other horse Denise had ever met.

She hadn't yet met a gate or door that could stop her, so she slept where she chose and grazed where she chose, so long as it wasn't in the barley field. Grandad had hobbled her for two days, the last time she'd sneaked in to graze the young barley, and while she'd gotten out of it easily enough at night, he'd spent both days with a pitcher of water and a mug, watching her endure her punishment.

Denise had wanted to intervene on the mare's behalf, but that was their food for next winter, both her and the mare, and eating it while it was new would keep it from making harvest.

After that, Petra had kept clear of the barley, but she'd let herself into the house and gone through Grandad's room, unmaking his bed and dropping his books on the floor, open but undamaged.

94

Denise loved that mare like a best friend. She took every opportunity to ride into town on errands, and she spent evenings whispering to Petra about the wide world. It made her sad that the mare had seen more of that wide world than Denise had, and Petra was *much* younger.

"Momma, can I go out riding tonight?" she asked most nights after dinner.

"Not tonight, baby," Tabitha answered. "I don't trust those clouds."

"Not tonight, baby. The boys from town have been ranging out further at night, and you know Petra's afraid of them."

"Not tonight, baby. There are potatoes to peel for tomorrow's dinner."

In point of fact, Petra wasn't afraid of the boys. They just made her dance, and Denise didn't have enough experience in the saddle to stay on when the mare skittered sideways and reared up, kicking at the dust. It might have looked like fear, and the boys might have come out of their way to get just that reaction, but Denise knew Petra better than that. The mare wasn't afraid. She was clever, and she always wanted to be on her toes when something unexpected was happening.

Like boys throwing sticks at her.

So it was, as on most evenings, that Denise was in the run-in out on the cow pasture, rubbing Petra down with burlap to make her coat shine and feeding her vegetable scraps from dinner, when she saw a horse's ears come up over the hill that led toward town.

She slipped up onto Petra's back to see better—her mother hated her riding without a saddle, but Denise had grown almost a foot since last summer, and she was tall enough to scramble onto Petra without a stirrup, so she did.

She could see the horse's silhouette down to the eyes, and the top of a man's head, hatted with an outlandish shape.

It could be a merchant. Sometimes they wore funny hats to identify themselves, but Denise knew. She just knew.

"Daddy," she called. Petra bolted, and Denise clamped her legs around the mare's slender ribs, tangling her fingers in her red mane and just managed not to fall off.

She thought Petra would try to dump her over the fence by running most of the way to it then turning sharply—she'd done that before—but instead the mare went straight at the fence, gathering just a stride short to jump, and giving Denise no more warning than that.

She popped over the fence like it was barely knee high, and Denise slammed nose-first into the mare's neck, rubbing her face hard as Petra got her feet back under her and kept on.

The man on the road hadn't sped up, nor had he stopped. He just kept coming, the sun setting behind him and his strange hat.

"Denise," Granmomma scolded, and Denise turned her head to look just as Petra jigged left. Denise lost her seat— without stirrups, she was toast—and landed lightly on her feet.

"You aren't to ride her without someone watching you," Granmomma said. "You know that."

"I wasn't *riding* her," Denise said. "I was just sitting on her so I could see better. And she took off."

Granmomma's loose, wrinkled face settled into a deeper disapproval, and Denise shrugged, pointing.

"It's Daddy."

The woman's eyes lit up for a moment as she scanned the road, then she glowered at Denise again.

"It's been years since he was last here," she said. "That's just a merchant."

Denise shook her head.

"It's him."

Granmomma waved her off, and Denise ran past a prancing Petra. The mare followed on quick feet. Denise hung on the fence, waiting as the man got closer. Beside him, there was a shorter person, a boy. Denise's heart fell.

Johannes traveled alone.

She waited anyway, holding herself up on her palms and letting her toes bounce against the wooden gate while Petra pretended to eat her hair.

"Knew a princess once who lost four feet of hair to a horse, letting him do that," the man called. Denise vaulted the gate.

"Daddy!"

She ran to her father and hugged him, looking up at the tall black horse he was leading and then at the scraggly boy at his side.

"I like your hat," she said, and Johannes laughed, taking it off.

"It's yours."

She took his hand, separating it from the reins to lead his horse herself, and she walked the rest of the way to the house, peeking around him at the boy from time to time.

"This is Sean," Johannes said. That was all. He didn't offer any more explanation than that, and Denise didn't ask.

"Where have you been?" she asked. "Tell me everything you saw."

He laughed, picking her up and throwing her onto the tall horse's back.

"Tell me everything you see," he said, looking up at her.

She opened her eyes wide, scanning.

"The barley field, and beyond that, the sheep. The woods where the stream goes through. The cows and their lean-to. The road. The fence. Petra."

"Every place is just like this one," Johannes said. "But different."

She grinned, and he led the tall horse through the gate while the boy waited, silent and watching.

The horse's back was laden with parcels. Two sleeping mats, saddle bags full to bursting, and canvas bags tied at the top and pierced with leather thongs so they wouldn't fall. She wanted to go through everything, to touch all of it, to smell her father's scent again and make him tell her all his stories.

She looked down at the boy again as he came through the gate and closed it, giving Petra a quiet greeting as she sniffed him. He looked up at Denise through shaggy bangs and he might have smiled. She smiled back.

Tabitha came out of the house, wiping her hands on her apron, and she ran to Johannes, wrapping her arms around his neck.

"It is you," she said.

"You promised me a son," Johannes murmured.

"We'll just have to try again," Tabitha answered. Denise stuck her tongue out.

"That isn't my boy out there," Granmomma Pritchett called. "Couldn't be. *My* boy would have come home before now. *My* boy is long dead."

Johannes tipped his head against Tabitha's.

"She still sore at me?" he asked playfully.

"Is she ever anything else?" Tabitha asked. With a grin, Johannes spun, clapping Denise's leg then offering her his arms to jump down. She slid off the horse on her own, landing on her feet.

"You shouldn't be riding barefoot," Tabitha said.

"I wasn't *riding*," Denise started to argue, but Johannes' laugh intercepted any need to.

"You really expect to keep her off a horse?" he asked.

"First the horse, then the road," Tabitha said. "That's how it happened with you."

"The road will always be there," Johannes answered, then he kissed her nose and Denise stuck her tongue out again. Sean laughed behind his fist.

"Hello, who's this?" Tabitha asked. "Have you taken up a squire?"

"This is Sean," Johannes said. He looked at Tabitha, his mouth drawn to the side, and Tabitha shook her head.

"Oh, no, Johannes Pritchett. I'm not taking in wanderers."

Denise stiffened as Johannes pointed at the gate.

"We can keep wandering then..."

Tabitha grabbed him by the ear and dragged him out of sight around the corner of the house. Denise looked back at Sean. He ducked his head, then looked at the black horse.

"We should get Rusty put away," he said. Denise frowned.

"Rusty?"

"Your dad rescued him," Sean said. "He had a nail through his hoof and his owner was going to leave him to die."

"Rusty," Denise said, looking at the tall horse once more. "All right. Let's go see if I can find you some mash."

Sean put his hand out to brush his fingers across the glossy black coat, smiling.

"Have you eaten?" Denise asked abruptly. He shook his head, still admiring the horse.

"Let's see if we can find some mash for you, too," she said.

Denise finished rubbing Rusty down while Petra watched with a critical eye, dropping the burlap into the corner of the lean-to and going to look at the horse's feet.

A horse's feet were everything to it. Denise knew that. She took great pains to care for Petra's feet, cleaning them religiously and keeping them trimmed. To bring a horse back from something so dire as a nail through his hoof was amazing, and Denise wanted to see the scar, to see how bad it had actually been.

She couldn't find any sign of the injury, no matter how hard she looked. She lifted each of Rusty's feet, one by one, looking at every surface of them, but they all seemed completely healthy.

She looked up to find Johannes watching her.

"Why aren't there any marks?" Denise asked. "Was it not as bad as his owner thought?"

Johannes shook his head.

"No, he would have died if I hadn't helped him," Johannes said. Denise patted Rusty's face, shoving Petra out of the way and going to stand across the fence from Johannes. Tabitha came out of the house, and he looked over his shoulder at her.

"No," Tabitha called. When Johannes had first gotten home, and then over the reheated remains of dinner, they'd teased each other, picked little fights that made each of them smile. This was different.

Denise only rarely heard her mother angry, but that single word, that might have been the angriest she'd ever heard her.

"It's time," Johannes said. "She deserves to know."

"Know what?" Denise asked.

"Is this why you came back?" Tabitha asked. "To dump an orphan boy on me and tear my daughter away?"

"What is she talking about?" Denise asked her father. Johannes looked back at Tabitha once more, then closed both hands in fists, resting his chin on his crossed wrists.

"The world is bigger than you know," he said. Denise climbed the fence and sat on a post with one foot on either side, waiting for what he would say next. Tabitha looked up at her, eyes afraid.

"I'm not going to fall, Momma," Denise said, and Tabitha shook her head, wiping her hands on her apron.

"There's magic out there, just like there's magic here," Johannes said, watching the field in front of him. Denise sighed, looking off to the side, looking for whatever magic he could see *here*.

"I love my home," she said. "But I want to see that world."

"That's not what he's telling you, baby," Tabitha said. Johannes stood, coming to stand next to her and running his thumb over the scab on her knee from a fall over by the creek.

"He doesn't have a scar because his feet are whole, like they were always supposed to be," Johannes said, applying a slight, warm pressure to Denise's knee. The scab disappeared, and he let his hand drop. Denise frowned, grabbing her shin to pull her knee up where she could look at it, and tipping off to the side. Johannes grabbed her elbow, pulling her back up onto the fence post. She looked an apology at Tabitha, who gave her a resigned laugh, shaking her head. Denise looked at her knee again.

"Where did it go?" she asked.

"Gone," Johannes said. "Like it was never there. There's *magic* in the world."

"How'd you do that?" Denise asked, hopping down.

"The same way you can," he answered. "Your Grandad can teach you, the same way he taught me. He's a scholar, and he knows more about magic than anyone I've ever met."

Denise looked at Tabitha, and Tabitha nodded.

"I always knew your daddy," she said, "but I fell in love with him because of all the time he spent with my daddy, studying."

"Does Grandad do magic, too?" Denise asked. Johannes shook his head.

"No. It runs in our family a long way back, but you need someone to teach you."

"Then let me come with you and *you* teach me," Denise said. He put his thumb to her jaw, cupping his fingers around the back of her neck.

"Do you know how much of a waste it is, to have two healers in the same place?"

"But I'm not a healer," Denise said. "And if I have to learn anyway, why not do it with you, instead of here?"

He kissed her forehead.

"I can't do that," he said. "I can go where I'm needed, and I can do what I'm gifted to do, but I can't take you away from your mother and deprive the town of a healer, apprentice or not."

"Then you stay, and I'll go," she said defiantly, and he laughed.

"I'm sorry, Tabby," he said. "I didn't know."

"That she's *exactly* like you?" Tabitha asked. "Yes. She is."

Denise looked sullenly from one to the other of them.

"Sean got to go with you," she said. Johannes sombered.

"You wouldn't ask for what he's had, if you knew how he got here," he said.

"Tell us," Tabitha murmured.

"It was a fire. It took most of his village, and I didn't hear about it until days after it had happened. They were tending the survivors as best as they could, but burns that bad... It was just a matter of time for most of them. His entire family died, and I only got there in time to save him. His village had too many losses for anyone to take him in..." Johannes looked at Tabitha. "The road is no place for a boy his age."

"You weren't much older," Tabitha said. "The first time you went out."

"It makes a difference," Johannes said, and she nodded.

"Okay. Okay. We'll make it work."

Johannes nodded, putting an arm around Tabitha's waist and the other across Denise's shoulders.

"Let's go sit inside. I have stories to tell, and a roof over my head is a luxury I'm not going to miss out on."

"You told her?" Grandad Evans asked in the dim of the late evening, after they thought Denise was asleep.

"Yes," Johannes answered. "Will you train her?"

"Of course," Grandad said. "When are you leaving again?"

"Tomorrow," Johannes said. "I've heard of a town a few days' walk from here with a pox."

Denise looked at the boy sleeping on the floor in her room, huddled under a spare blanket and pillowed by a wad of clothing.

"I wish I were going with him," Sean whispered.

"I wish I were, too," Denise answered.

Sean was a far better rider than Denise. Now that there were two of them, most of Tabitha's excuses to keep Denise in failed, so they took to riding along the road for hours, some nights, coming in late after dark under Granmomma Pritchett's glowering gaze. They talked about the people and the animals and the lands that Sean had seen in his limited time with Johannes.

"Why do you think he wouldn't let you stay with him?" Denise asked one evening as she reached up to touch leaves overhead. The barley harvest would be a good one, this year, and soon the men from the village would come to help take it in. Tabitha acted as the town midwife, and part of the exchange was that the men helped when there was work that overwhelmed Grandad's ability to get it done. Denise thought they would have done it, anyway, but she did worry what would happen to them when Grandad Evans wasn't able to plant and tend any more.

"Because I don't carry my weight," Sean answered. Denise was surprised that he was as unconcerned with it as he was. Sean shrugged. "Not yet. But I will. My brothers were all big. I'm going to get big, too, and then I can help with... things. You know? Earn my keep." He tussled Rusty's mane. Johannes had never explained why he was leaving the horse, but horse and boy seemed devoted to each other.

"What then?" Denise asked.

He grinned, his teeth flashing in the dim light.

"Maybe he'll come back, and then I can go with him again."

"You watched him heal people," Denise said. Sean nodded.

"I did."

"I'll be able to do that," Denise said. "And then..." She sighed. "I *want* to go."

Sean was watching her.

Even in the few months he'd been there, he seemed to be filling out. Denise had a guess that there hadn't been enough food for both him and Johannes most of the time they'd been traveling, but she'd never asked.

"Hey," he said, slipping to the ground. "Come on."

She dropped to the dirt path as well and followed him through the woods. The stream, here, was further from the road, far enough that Denise couldn't hear it, though she knew it was there.

They left the horses at the top of the bank and slipped down toward the water, working by feel more than by sight, because the trees overhead took up what little light was left to the evening.

They found water, and Sean sat, pulling off his shoes to let his feet rest in the water. Denise rested on her elbows, her fingers trailing in the stream. The bugs were out, and soon it would become unpleasant, but for now it was nice to just enjoy the running water.

"It goes somewhere, you know?" Sean asked.

"Of course," Denise said, insulted. "It joins up with other creeks and then it meets a river and it goes down to a big lake a long way off."

Sean laughed, and Denise bristled silently.

"Your dad said that the world felt like a hill to him, and he was water. He just couldn't stop."

Denise sat up.

"He said that to you?"

"He did."

She frowned, looking at the glints of reflection on the stream's turbulent surface.

She felt like that.

"That's how it is for you, isn't it?" Sean pressed.

"I don't want to leave Momma," she said. "Who's going to take care of her when Grandad gets old?"

"You think your dad didn't feel that way?"

Denise looked at his dim silhouette, and Sean stood.

"We should go back to the house."

"No," Denise demanded. "What do you mean?"

Sean started up the hill, and Denise dragged him back down by the back of his shirt.

"What does that mean?" she asked again.

He shook her loose.

"He wants to be home with his family," Sean said. "He talked about you all the time."

"He never met me," Denise said, not sure why she was taking Granmomma Pritchett's side in this conversation.

"He knew you existed," Sean said. "And he talked about you, out riding in the woods, or going to town to buy fruit, or meeting a boy and spending the whole day walking in the sun, talking."

Denise shook her head.

"I don't do any of those things, except buy fruit."

"But he liked imagining it," Sean said, edging away again and starting up the bank. She followed. He found Rusty, and Denise started back toward the road on foot, listening for Petra. The mare would hide until the last minute, and then pretend she hadn't been hiding when Denise finally found her. Back on the road, she mounted up and waited for Sean. Rusty took longer to pick his way back through the woods.

"He wanted to be here," Sean said. "And I think he would have been, if it weren't for the healing."

Denise was getting better at it, the healing. The first progress had come in leaps and bounds, and she was slowing, but she was still getting better. Grandad was a good teacher, just as her daddy had promised, and once she knew she could do it, it wasn't hard. Tabitha was talking about starting to bring her to deliveries, to help if things went wrong. Denise didn't want to be there when babies were born. Not after the description Tabitha had given her over the years of what that was like.

"You have to understand," Sean said. "You're just like him."

Denise looked over at him. The light was almost completely gone, now, though a nearly full moon was set to rise soon.

"Who's going to take care of them?" she asked.

"I know," he answered.

Summer went. Winter came, with its short days and inside chores, and then spring with its planting and tending lambs and calves.

It was a good year for the lambs and the calves. Denise helped with the deliveries—much preferable to being there when a woman was giving birth, she thought—and when things went wrong, Grandad talked her through how to help. They didn't lose any of them, and Denise went with Grandad to nearby farms when they got word that things had gone wrong with the larger animals. That spring, Denise got to lay on the ground with a brand new foal in her arms, holding it as its spirit wavered, pulling it back, holding it together as she went looking for the pieces that had broken and mending them. Grandad squatted in the ground in front of her, giving her just a word here and there, and then standing long before it was done. His confidence in her was everything she needed.

It was a good spring.

She would go out to the creek some days after she'd seen to Petra, standing above it and watching the run of the water, feeling the pull of it, like gravity.

Sean would come and find her and just stand next to her.

They said nothing.

Tabitha delivered Denise's little brother late in the spring. There was no more avoiding it; Denise caught her brother, held him as Grandad cut the cord, then let Granmomma take the new baby to clean him as Denise healed her mother and lay her on her bed to rest.

Sean spent the entire afternoon outside looking pale.

"Are they okay?" he asked when Denise came out, late in the afternoon, almost dinnertime. He looked horrified, looking at her, but she shrugged.

"Momma's fine. The baby's asleep."

"You don't love him?" Sean asked. Denise smiled, leaning back against the wall and looking up at the sky.

"He's a baby," she said. "He doesn't even have a name yet. How would I love him?"

"I loved my little sister," Sean said. "From the very beginning."

Denise looked over at him, wondering if he was odd, or if there was something broken about her.

"Go get washed up," Granmomma said from the doorway. "You're going to help me with dinners until your momma is back on her feet."

"How long do you think that will be?" Denise asked.

"Up to her," Granmomma Pritchett said. "Until then, you're taking on anything she normally does."

Denise blanched.

"Roberta is due any time," she said, and Granmomma nodded, crossing her arms.

"It's a lot your momma takes on. You're going to get to see it, up close."

Denise looked at Sean, who ducked his head. She sighed and went back into the house to change her clothes.

She made it all the way to the next summer before she ran away the first time.

One day, she was just out in the field with Petra, and then she was on the mare's back, cantering down the road, the wind lifting her hair off her shoulders and her laugh carrying behind her on the breeze.

She had no idea where she was going.

She just couldn't stand it anymore. Knowing that the world was bigger than the boundaries of the town, and never having seen any of it.

She rode at speed for a long time, hours, before she saw anything other than little farms and wild land, but then—oh, then—she finally saw the first town that wasn't the one she'd grown up in.

Granted, it looked exactly *like* her town, save she didn't know any of the shops or buildings, and all of the people were strangers, but it was *something*. She was *here*, and it wasn't where she'd ever been before.

She left Petra to roam and be bothersome outside of the general store, and she went in, peering at shelves and mooning at produce that she could have just as easily gotten back home, but this was different.

This was *somewhere else*.

She talked to the shopkeeper, a graying man of portly girth named Trevor, and she watched the other customers.

There was a scuffle outside, and Denise went to the door, watching as Petra picked a fight with a pair of tied geldings. Just like back home, the other horses were all inches taller than her and hundreds of pounds heavier, but it hadn't ever stopped her. She nipped at them and bobbed her head quickly, darting out of reach as they tried to nip back. As Denise opened the door, one of the geldings had turned to try to square up a kick and Petra danced away. A man came running.

"Why is that mare untied?" he demanded, looking around. "Whose is she?"

"If you know a knot that would hold her, I'd love to learn it," Denise answered, stepping forward and snatching at Petra's reins.

"You need to control that mare," the man said, "or I will."

Denise drew her head back.

"I'd like to see you try that," she said. His hand flew to the side, intending to strike her backhanded across the face, but a woman screamed, drawing his attention as well as Denise's.

Down the simple street, a woman was holding a young boy, lying in the dirt.

"What happened?" Denise asked, dropping Petra's reins and running toward the woman. No one she passed could tell her. Denise shoved a man out of the way as he squatted to look at the boy.

"What happened?" she asked.

"Help him," the woman said, looking past Denise at the man.

"Tell me what happened," Denise said, taking the boy's hand between her own and feeling for what was broken. Hands gripped underneath her armpits and someone tried to drag her away, but she let her arms flop up over her head and fell back to the ground, scrambling forward to take the boy's hand again.

"Tell me what happened," she demanded. The woman took her in, shocked, then shook her head.

"He was playing, and then he just... fell."

Denise nodded, letting her arm go limp as it jerked behind her, someone else trying to pull her away.

There was disquiet inside the boy, but everything felt like it was where it was supposed to be. The strength of him was there—his bones were probably fine. There wasn't any loud pain that she could find.

She thrashed as two men grabbed her at the elbows.

"Leave her," the woman yelled. "Let her look at him."

Everyone paused, and Denise looked up at the two men, seeing them for the first time. One of them was clean-shaven and neat. The other had a beard that hadn't been shaved in perhaps a week, and he wore leather clothes designed for hard wear and little maintenance.

Doctor. Farmer. Rancher, maybe.

Denise jerked again, putting her hand over the boy's forehead.

There it was.

Heat. Disruption. Things that were out of order.

She started sorting again, putting things in their right order, small to big, stacking them so that heavy, big things went on the bottom and light, small things went on the top, the simple shape of the world that it always preferred to take. Grandad had taught her that, and once she started seeing the patterns of how the world wanted to be, she could start putting them that way intentionally, just like reaching out and plucking a blade of grass to weave into a hat.

The heat dissipated slowly as she worked, and she heard conversation behind her as the doctor said angry things about not wasting time.

She stood up.

The woman looked up at her, and Denise saw her tears for the first time.

"He's fine," she said. "He's asleep now. You can wake him up."

The woman looked down at the boy, giving him a tentative shake, and his eyes fluttered and opened. Denise grinned.

Simple.

She didn't look back as she went to recover Petra from where she was breaking into a tailor's shop, picking a direction and setting off anew.

She scavenged her meals, having no coins and nothing of value for trade, but the summer was ripe with mushrooms and fruits and herbs. She had good meals, if they did cost her in work, and Petra was happy to graze anywhere they went on patches of sweet clover, but Denise wondered how her father made it through the winters.

How did he buy food? Did he just store up enough? She couldn't imagine Petra carrying enough food to feed them both through a hard snow, not to mention an entire winter.

But that was a problem for another day.

She saw things.

After the boy, none of them were quite as exciting, but she saw them anyway, crossing a stream once that she was certain was her very own stream, meeting up with its friends on its way down to the river, whatever the locals might be calling it.

She turned to follow it, taking this path and that and doing her best to keep it always just over there, but eventually she lost it as the roads didn't go the right way, and she let it be. Water always showed up again, if you watched close.

She had no idea where she was, and while she might have expected that to frighten her, she found it intoxicating.

Petra was having fun, too. She bothered wildlife and farmyard animals alike, racing penned horses just to keep going long after they hit their fence corners, chasing and nipping after chickens and rabbits and goats.

Oh, how Petra hated goats.

Eventually, Denise thought of her family, of Grandad milking the cows and tending the sheep, watching over the barley and the lambs. Of Tabitha and Marlet, sitting in the kitchen splitting peas from the garden, Marlet eating them with his four tiny teeth.

Of Sean, standing by the creek, wondering how far downstream she was.

And she turned back.

She arrived home three weeks after she left, give or take, her clothes torn and dirty, her hair tangled and matted, and hungry as she'd ever been for bread and meat, but happier than she could remember. The sight of the little farm made her heart sink, and she hated herself for that, because everyone she loved was there.

She was exactly like her father.

In all, Sean had taken it the hardest.

Denise could see it in her mother's eyes, that Tabitha knew it was only a matter of time before Denise left and never came back. Granmomma Pritchett didn't speak to Denise for days after she got back, but it was out of an old, dry anger. Grandad had just asked if she'd done anything interesting, and she'd told him about the boy in the first town.

Sean was livid, in his quiet way.

They went to sit on the rocks by the stream, watching the water run deep and cloudy from a heavy rain a few days back.

Denise had slept under a tree, sopping wet, in that rain.

She wished she was out there, now.

"Why didn't you tell me?" Sean asked after a long time.

"What would I have said?" she asked. "I didn't know I was going to do it until after I did."

He looked at her, bursting with something he couldn't express, then he exploded, turning back to face the stream with a yell as he threw his arms in the air. Denise tipped her head.

"I didn't," she said again.

"I know," he said, his voice still loud. "I know, but... how could you just leave me?"

"I left everyone."

"I would have come with."

That stunned her for a while, and she turned, tossing pebbles into the water.

The pull of it was tangible, on her shoulders, on her knees, deep in her chest. She wanted to chase that water.

"I saved a boy's life," she said.

"I heard you when you told Grandad," Sean answered. He didn't sound impressed. He threw a larger rock that splashed up on the far bank.

Denise wondered if she could jump that far.

"I'm going to do it better, next time," she said. Turned to look at Sean. "What does Daddy do for money?"

He looked at her, sullen, then sighed.

"Sells things he gathers. People pay him for healing their livestock and stuff, sometimes. If they can't afford it, he doesn't let them, but if they can, sometimes he does." He looked over at her, less sullen but more angry. "It's *hard*. Neither one of us ever had *enough* to eat, the way we do here. Yeah, we never know if the garden is going to fail or if there won't be enough barley for the winter, but there's *enough*. I was *always* hungry, with Johannes."

"That's because you were a boy, and you didn't carry your own weight," Denise said. "You'd do better now."

Sean laughed bitterly.

"That's exactly what he'd say. You know, I don't think he ever noticed that we were starving. He was always so eager to get going again, sometimes we didn't even stay when someone offered us a place to sleep at night. We'd walk a few miles out of town and sleep on the side of the road, instead."

Denise knew it was supposed to sound bad, but it was exciting to her. She'd never considered that she could do that.

"How does he do it?" she asked. "Sleeping outside, like that? What does he bring with him?"

Sean looked at her and shook his head.

"I won't tell you unless you promise you won't leave without me again."

"If I wait and come to find you, they might try to stop me," Denise said, and Sean frowned, thinking.

"I don't care," he finally said. "I want you to promise, anyway."

"Okay," she said. "I promise. Tell me."

She lied.

She hadn't intended to lie.

She hadn't even intended to go out again, but as summer drew to a close and the leaves started to change, she started going out on long rides after lunch, while Marlet was napping and Tabitha was working. Denise had chores at home, and she knew that if she didn't do them, someone else would have to, and no one else had the time or energy to spare most days. So she did them gladly enough, for what they were.

But those rides were the one thing she lived for.

Some days, Sean would come with her, and they would talk. Or not. Time with him was pleasant; Sean was the only friend she'd ever had, of her own age.

"Why would you go out with me, again, when they need you so much at home, and if you hated being out, wandering, so much?" she'd asked him once, but he wouldn't answer.

He'd grown taller than her, that summer, and his shoulders showed the work of the farm. He'd started shaving, though he often cut himself, and he finally looked like he belonged on a horse Rusty's size.

He liked life on the farm, and Denise's family loved him as one of their own. Sometimes Denise assured herself that if she did one day leave for good, he would take good care of them, but she knew he'd meant it when he told her that he wanted to come with her.

Later, she promised herself that that hadn't been why she didn't tell him she was going. That she hadn't known she was going to do it, in advance, just like last time, but it was a lie and she knew it. She'd packed a bedroll and some bags for hunting edibles in the forests, and she had gone to get them that morning and left them out by Petra's lean-to when she went to feed the animals.

She'd known, and she hadn't told him, because she was afraid of what would happen to Grandad, to Granmomma, to Tabitha, to Marlet, if she left with Sean and didn't come back.

She wanted to know that he would be there to take care of them, even though it made her feel even more guilty than before—even more aware of how guilty she felt, leaving all of them.

She loved them.

Marlet was walking more and more, and she could make him laugh until he cried. And her mother deserved to have someone in her life who didn't just disappear. Grandad at least seemed to understand, but in some ways that made it even worse: that he expected her to desert them.

And yet, she went.

She loaded Petra with the minimal supplies and she rode her hard at the south fence, jumping it to avoid going out the gate and past the house, not slowing until Petra was blowing hard and needed to ease, not until Denise could imagine that no one would follow her.

She picked a new road, wandering until the light was nearly gone, then she hopped down and wandered through a field, leaving Petra to graze as she unrolled her bedroll and went searching for her supper.

The second time wasn't as much fun as the first. Knowing how upset Sean was going to be when she got home just spoiled it, and she spent much of the time worrying that something would happen to Marlet and she wouldn't be there to put him right again. He was walking everywhere, but he was clumsy, and Tabitha could only watch him so much.

She found a new stream and followed this one up towards its source, passing through small towns and hamlets, staying now and again with a family here or there who were willing to feed her after she'd done them some small healing service unasked. She kept her bags full of forest goods that she could trade, and she did much better for food this time, though she began to miss fires at night for warmth and light. Cloudy nights were frightening, when she could hear animals roaming around her. Surprisingly, this seemed to bother Petra little, though Denise figured the mare was just expecting that whatever it was out there, it was much more likely to catch Denise first.

Denise stayed out for four weeks or a little more, as the season turned colder. Then she found herself at the front gate of the house again, tempted to just keep riding because she didn't want to face her family. But she got down and led Petra through to the pasture, taking her tack off and storing it, then going to look at the barley field.

It was bare.

She'd been gone for the entire harvest.

She'd known that; she'd ridden past dozens of grain harvests over the last few weeks, but to know that she hadn't been here for the most work-intensive event in the farm's calendar, that Sean had been here and she had not, she didn't know how to feel.

A pair of elbows came across the fence next to her and she turned her head to look at Grandad.

"Granmomma didn't think you'd come home," he said. "Johannes stayed out after his second time away this long. Came back when you were a few years old."

Denise nodded, watching the horizon.

"I don't *want* to go," she said. He laughed.

"Yes you do. You don't *want* to abandon us."

She looked over at him, in pain, and he gave her a sympathetic smile.

"You'd never know it, the way Granmomma talks about him, but your daddy loves your momma more than you've ever loved anything in your whole life."

"Then why isn't he here?" Denise asked.

"Sometimes you have to choose," Grandad said simply. "And he chose to go do important things, out there. To listen to the person he was built to be."

"I love it," she said. "And I hate myself for loving it."

Grandad nodded.

"I can't tell you what to do."

"Does Sean hate me?" she asked. Grandad laughed.

"He might have been hurt most of all, when you turned up missing again, but he knows Johannes as well as any man alive. I think he understands."

She turned, finding Sean leaning against the gate at the far end of the pasture, watching them. Denise looked at Grandad, tucking her mouth deep to the side, and he patted her on the back.

"Enough avoiding," he said. "Go do what you have to do."

She nodded and started walking.

Sean opened the gate for her wordlessly, leaving it open for Grandad to close on his way out, and they walked to the front gate, going through and crossing the lane, the sheep pen, the woods, going to sit next to the stream in a suspended silence.

"You said you'd tell me," Sean said finally.

"Grandad needed you," Denise answered.

"One of the rams died," Sean said. "A wolf came in and he was defending the flock. Grandad and I got there and chased him off, but not before he hurt the ram too bad. You could have saved him."

Denise rubbed her face.

"I'm sorry."

He nodded.

"I thought I might never see you again," he said.

"I'll always come home," Denise said. "This is my family."

"But I'm not," he said. "What if I start a family somewhere else, before you come back next time? Your dad doesn't wander around the village, seeing old friends again."

"You'd leave Grandad and Momma and go somewhere else?" Denise asked.

He looked at her for a long time, then back at the water. Denise hadn't considered this.

"He says it's like water running," Sean said after a long time. "You can hold it back for a while, but it's eventually going to get out, and it's going to run again."

"I'll stay," she said. He looked at her with a deep frown.

"That's not what I'm asking."

"They need you, and if you're going to leave, then they're going to need me. So I'll stay."

He threw another rock.

"You can't promise that."

She looked at her hands.

"Maybe I can't, but I'm going to, anyway."

She kept her promise for two years. Denise was sixteen summers old, a woman, now, and she stood in the field with Petra watching Sean and Marlet and Grandad work at planting barley.

There would be accidents this season, around town. The plows and the randy young bulls meant that someone always needed her to patch them up, which also meant that, come harvest, another young man would turn up to help Grandad with the barley.

And Sean was staying.

Day by day, she knew even more clearly that he was staying for *her*.

The world was a difficult place for a man without a family. He had no land and very little money to his name, but he could have gone out with Rusty—a sturdy charger of an adventuring horse, if Denise had ever seen one—and he could have found his fortune. Sean was a head taller than Denise, now, and he did almost all of the heavy work of the planting while Grandad supervised with an expert's eye.

He was a handsome man to Denise's eye, Sean was. Perhaps a bit homely to some, with a face that might never lose all of its roundness, but he had clever eyes that always picked her out when she was around, never took her for granted. He had workman's hands, strong but articulate, and sometimes while they went walking he would take her hand in his, and they wouldn't speak for a long time. She thought she might have loved him, but she wasn't sure.

She still felt very young and very out of herself.

She'd stayed, but she'd traded a part of herself to do it.

Yes, she'd gotten to stay with her family, and she'd been here when Marlet had fallen out of a tree and snapped his ankle, put him back together so he walked normally, where he might not have been so lucky, otherwise. And she was grateful for that.

But just like Sean always noticed that she was *still* here, so did she.

She was *still* here.

The fantasy that she could just run away was gone.

She couldn't do that to Sean again, not with his loyalty and the pain it would have caused him for her to do it, but she also couldn't take him with her. As children, it had been simple to say, but as adults, it meant something else, and she was very aware of that, now.

There was an expectation that she would marry, and there were quiet words that men and women would exchange with Grandad when they had the opportunity, pointing with quick, subtle motions at Denise, and then at some young man or another whose face Denise knew, but whose name invariably escaped her.

She was expected to court, and she was expected to marry, and running away with Sean was an entirely different thing than it might have once been.

Petra stood often at the corner of the pasture, smelling the air, as if that—at least—could bring her stories from the vast *over there*, but Denise didn't even have that.

She wasn't miserable. She was often happy, in fact. But she was always *still here*.

She thought of Sean's words, about chasing the creek until it hit the river, and then following that to see where it led next, but she stayed.

Sean looked up, finding her standing there next to Petra, and he waved, jogging across the rutted field to come lean against the pasture fence. She picked her way across the pasture to come talk to him.

"Go," he said.

"What?"

He nodded.

"Go. We're okay, here. And I know that spring is always the worst."

Was it?

It was.

He nodded, reaching for her hand to take it between his dirty fingers, bringing it to his mouth and kissing her knuckles.

"But come back to me. To us."

He nodded, and she looked around.

Grandad was watching her.

The bag was in the lean-to. It had been for a week, covered in old straw.

Tabitha was leaning against the house, arms folded, also watching.

Sean let go of her hand, and gave her one last firm nod.

"Go. Come back soon."

She turned, and she tried to walk back to the lean-to, but when she looked down, her feet were running.

That was the best summer.

Her skill as a healer had grown in her time at home, and she could sense where there was pain or sickness around her, like a force drawing her this way or that. She gained a reputation among some of the traveling merchants, and they would tell her about communities that needed her, as she crossed paths with them now and again.

It was a good summer, but as the grain crops around her grew topsy, she turned once more for home, at the same time like trudging uphill and like going back where she most wanted to be.

She'd missed Sean.

She'd missed Grandad and Merlet and her momma and Granmomma, certainly, but the warmth of Sean's hand in her own, the way he saw her like no one else did... She missed it like she was incomplete without it.

He met her in the lane, coming home, and she let Petra go, running to meet him and letting him sweep her into a great hug.

"I didn't know," he murmured.

"Always," she answered.

Another year. Sean told her she could go out again, if she wanted to, but Grandad was ailing, and Denise couldn't bear to leave him to disease, should it strike. She couldn't fix old age, but she could keep him from falling prey to something else.

And she didn't want to leave Sean. She simply wanted to be with him more than she wanted to be elsewhere.

So she helped him with the spring planting, going with Tabitha to deliver four babies one after another in the course of two weeks and saving the life of one of the mothers and one of the babies for having been there.

She couldn't go.

They needed her here.

And she watched the summer wear on, tending the sheep, the cows, Petra.

It was a good summer, but she didn't know how much longer she could do this. The need to be here and somewhere else at the same time, it was something no one else seemed to be able to understand, though Sean sympathized.

They went out walking one evening late into the summer, picking their way along the rocks at the side of the creek, a long way downstream. He hadn't talked much, and Denise thought that he thought that wandering this far would help her. It didn't, but she loved him for thinking it.

"Should be a good harvest this year," Sean said.

"Looks like," Denise agreed easily enough, hopping across a larger gap in the stones. The water was high and it was running loud, tonight.

Sean said something, and she turned to face him, trying to pick out his words above the sound of the water.

"Why are you all the way back there?" she asked, going back to where he'd stopped.

"Because I'm afraid of you," he answered.

"Are not," she teased, but he didn't seem amused. She frowned. "What's going on?"

"It's never going to stop," he said. She looked around, for the moment not certain what he was talking about. The crops? The water? "You wanting to leave."

She shrugged.

"I'll learn to live with it," she said. "When Grandad..." Her throat closed and didn't let her say the next word, but Sean nodded that he understood. "Someone has to feed Momma and Granmomma and Merlet. And I'm not leaving without you again."

He nodded.

"I know you think that, but I don't believe you."

She shrugged.

"I can prove it. Just give me enough time."

He took her hand and put it to his forehead, shaking his head.

"That's why I'm afraid of you."

"What are you talking about?"

"I want you to be my wife, but asking that… it would mean that you really would be agreeing to stay with me for the rest of your life. And I can't ask that."

"You want me to marry you?" Denise asked.

He sighed, rolling his head to the side.

"What else could I possibly want? You're beautiful and my best friend, and I've been in love with you since the moment I met you."

"You have?"

He nodded.

She looked at the water for a long time. Then she turned and took Sean's hand, walking up the bank and through the woods back to the road.

"What?" he asked.

"We should go home," she said. "It's time."

He squeezed her hand and they walked. Denise was troubled, but not by Sean. She could do this.

She could.

They got in view of the house, though, and they both stopped.

There was a big gray draught horse standing by the house that neither of them knew, and a man standing next to it who was holding Tabitha in his arms.

They ran.

Johannes turned as Denise hit him at speed, hugging him as hard as she could. He pulled her away, looking her up and down.

"For as terrible a father as I've been to you, you've turned out amazingly well," he said.

"Are you kidding?" Tabitha asked. "You brought her her two favorite things in the whole world."

Denise frowned.

"Are you crying, Momma?"

"Just wait," Tabitha said. Johannes shook hands with Sean.

"I brought you to them for your sake, but it sounds like

they've needed you more than you've needed them," he said, and Sean nodded.

"Thank you, sir."

Johannes looked at Denise again.

"Where's your bag?"

"What?" she asked.

"You heard me," he said. "Where is it?"

She glanced at Sean.

"Out in the lean-to with Petra," she said. Johannes nodded.

"Go get it."

She looked from him to Tabitha without understand, but did as she was bidden. When she'd put it at his feet, he went through it, nodding.

"There are a lot of pieces missing, but it's a good start. You can have what you need out of my stuff." He paused. "I'm not going to need it."

"What?" Denise asked.

Johannes put his arm around Tabitha.

"Just a couple of weeks ago," he said, his voice bemused, "all I wanted to do was come home. I'm done, Denise. I followed my path and now I've found my still water. I can stay here, and I can rest."

"There's not much rest around this place," Tabitha warned, and he kissed her forehead. Tabitha wiped her eyes again.

"But what about...?" Denise asked, looking at Sean.

Johannes looked from Denise to Sean and back with a conspiratorial smile.

"I would have thought that the two of you would have come to an agreement by now, the way Tabby was talking," he said. Denise blushed.

"You can see the minister in the morning," Tabitha said. Denise looked at Sean, who took her hand.

"I've always wanted to know where that creek ended up," he said. Johannes hugged Tabitha then let go of her, putting one hand on Denise's shoulder and the other on Sean's.

"Go," he said. "See the world. Make it better." He grinned. "Then come home and tell me all about it."

About the Author

Chloe Garner acts as the conduit between her dreaming self and the paper (or keyboard, since we live in the future). She writes paranormal, sci-fi, fantasy, and whatever else goes bump in the night. When she's not writing she steeplechases miniature horses and participates in ice cream eating contests. Not really, but she does tend to make things up for a living. Find her on Twitter as BlenderFiction, on Goodreads and Facebook, or at www.blenderfiction.wordpress.com.

LIFEBLOOD

A. K. R. SCOTT

I n the middle of the desert there stands a forest where all
the trees have faces.

Or so they say.

Teiran's eyes narrowed as she glanced past the dusty
market, beyond the edge of the village, to the dense green that
thumbed its nose at the sea of sand from which it grew. She
had never seen the faces. But by this time tomorrow, she'd
know for certain if the stories were true.

"Anything else, dear?"

The old woman squinted up at her, offering a gummy smile
as she patted the bowl of dried purpletop flower buds. Teiran
shook her head. Too expensive. Besides, if everything went as
she hoped, she wouldn't need them, anyway. She paid for the
roots and herbs in her hand and placed them in her basket.

"Give your mother my best, won't you?" asked the old
woman.

Teiran bowed her head. "I will. Thank you."

She hefted her water jug back onto her strong shoulders and headed home. The sand shifted under her sandals, and the wind blew low to the ground, spraying grit against her ankles. She tugged her hat lower and scarf higher as she approached the small mud house she shared with her mother. Sweat traced clammy fingers down the back of her neck.

The tiny porch provided a welcome reprieve as Teiran ducked beneath its pocked ceiling and settled the full water jug against the side of the house. The coals left over from breakfast were still glowing in the fire pit, so she added more fuel and stoked them to life. Then, stepping lightly, she slipped through the front door and into the relative cool of her home.

Her hat and scarf took their place on the hook by the door, and she moved carefully, giving her eyes time to adjust to the dim light. Shallow panting coming from the mat in the far corner of the room reassured her, and she ghosted through the space, gathering various spices and tossing them into a bowl with the roots and herbs she had purchased in the market. A quick turn with the pestle and she was back outside, filling the bowl with water before placing it over the small fire.

Teiran tucked herself under the shade of the porch. She sank onto the rug and pressed her back against the hard mud. With a deep sigh, she let her muscles relax, borrowing support from the wall, but keeping a watchful eye on the bowl.

Such was her routine twice a day, every day, for the past three months. But tomorrow would be different. One of the neighbors would be here to keep watch.

Two more times, that's all. Then, she'd have the cure.

In the space of a blink, the clear water in the bowl became bright orange. Teiran leapt to her feet and grabbed the tongs, yanking the bowl from the fire. Using the hem of her tunic as a buffer, she carried it back into the house.

Slow wheezes had replaced the panting in the far corner, so she didn't bother sneaking this time.

"I have your tea, Mama," she said, straining the liquid into a mug.

The straw mat rustled in response.

Teiran carried the tea to where her mother lay and settled down on the floor beside her. Setting the mug aside, she hooked her arms under her mother's shoulders and helped her sit up. Her heart clenched at the feel of the frail body, little more than a sack of bones, and weighing no more than a handful of sand. Nothing like the woman she had known and loved her whole life. But Teiran shoved down the ache as quickly as it rose. One more day. Then she'd have her mother back.

She blew across the top of the mug before lifting it to her mother's lips.

"Careful, it's still hot."

The minutes stretched out in silence, broken only by faint slurping noises, as tiny sip followed tiny sip until the mug was empty. By that time, the tea had begun to work, and the wheezing was almost inaudible.

"Thank you," rasped her mother as she rested her head back against the thin pillow.

"I'm about to make supper," said Teiran. "Can I get you anything else right now?"

Her mother managed a weak smile. "Tell me... about your day."

Teiran chuckled and set the mug aside, pulling her knees to her chest. "A wealthy spice merchant arrived today. He rode into the village on the back of a pure white stallion, as grand as you can imagine, with an enormous herd of camels, draped in cloths of purple and gold, and carrying more jars and boxes than I could count. He was interested in buying the salt mine. The whole mine! I happened to be nearby when he approached, so I showed him around. And I must admit, it was hard to stay focused on my task. Up close, he was so handsome, with dark eyes and a kind smile."

Her mother's own smile broadened.

"I must have done too good of a job, though, because by the time we'd finished the tour, he said he wanted the mine, but only if I came with it."

A strained huffing noise which passed for her mother's laugh, overlaid Teiran's story. It carried with it the stench of illness and decay, and she struggled to keep her tone light even as her throat tightened.

"Well, naturally," she continued, "I declined his offer. I told him I wasn't interested in marriage right now, though he was still welcome to the mine. I'm sorry to say, he was devastated. And he decided not to buy the mine. He said it would remind him too much of the woman who had broken his heart." She finished the story with a dramatic sigh.

It was a game they played. With her mother confined to their tiny house, Teiran was happy to feed her imagination. It was nicer than the truth—another sweltering day toiling in the salt mine.

She wondered what story she would have for her mother the next time she asked. Would she be able to give an account of the trees with faces? Whatever she'd have to tell, it would be interesting.

Which reminded her.

"Mama, I've heard of a... a healer who may be able to help you. She's not too far away, about a half day's journey. I'll be setting out early in the morning tomorrow to visit her, but Mrs. Ashtani will be here to check in on you and help with anything you need."

Her mother's face pinched in on itself as if she'd just eaten an unripe bongoaberry, and she struggled to sit up.

Teiran placed her hands on her mother's bony shoulders and gave a gentle squeeze. "It's only for one day. And I'll be home before you know it. I promise."

It was a promise she wasn't sure she'd be able to keep, but she needed to reassure her mother. Worry would only speed her decline, and that must be avoided at all costs. This was the reason Teiran hadn't told her mother where she was really going. It wasn't a lie, exactly, just a partial truth. If her mother knew she would be entering the forest tomorrow... Teiran shuddered.

But it was their only hope. If Teiran succeeded, her mother would be well again. If not, then tomorrow they would both see their last sunrise.

The crowd was already thick when Teiran arrived at the forest's edge. Torches danced against the backdrop of the night sky, lighting a path from the onlookers to the enormous silver gate that stood like a sentry at the line where the sand turned green.

No bars, no fence, just a gate. Nothing else was needed. Everyone knew those who went into the forest uninvited never returned. Only when the gate stood open were people allowed to enter, and then for only a short while.

In the center of the forest was a pool that few had seen but of which everyone had heard. In that pool lived an ancient naiad, though how she or the pool came to be there was a mystery lost to time. She ruled the waters there and the forest that surrounded them.

Once a year, at sunrise on the summer solstice, the naiad would open the gate, welcoming in anyone who wished to enter the forest and drink from her pool, if they could find it. Her water was magical, granting anyone who drank it one hundred years of youth and beauty. Teiran had seen a few men and women who proved the veracity of this claim, and it was for this reward that most of the hopefuls gathered. But Teiran had a different goal. The water's transformative magic also cured the drinker of all physical ailments as it restored their age and appearance.

She rubbed her hand over her pocket, feeling the outline of a small bottle. If she could find the pool and bring back the water, she could cure her mother.

But it wouldn't be easy.

She scanned the array of contestants. They ranged in age from maid to crone, though most of the hopefuls were younger, like her. But who was to say age and constitution determined success? One would assume so. But no one knew what dangers they would face in the forest. Most people who entered never returned, and those who did had no memory of the trials they had endured while on the other side of the gate. Often, many years would pass with no one finding the pool.

The buzzing crowd faded to silence as the village chief stepped onto the small dais.

"Welcome, contestants," he boomed. "In a few moments, the gate will open. But first, a few reminders. You will have one full day and night to find your way to the pool and return to the village. The naiad's hospitality is not infinite. You must be out before tomorrow's sunrise. I repeat: you *must* be out by tomorrow's sunrise." He looked out across the crowd, his face a mask of solemnity.

"The naiad's generosity is also not infinite. Only the first one to make it to the pool will be granted her water. As a courtesy to your fellow contestants, we ask that if you are fortunate enough to be that first person, signal your success so that everyone else can begin to make their way back to the gate." He gestured to a large urn to the right of the dais. "Each contestant please take two of these surge stones. If you are the victor, simply raise the stones above your head and strike them together."

Teiran fell into line with the other contestants as they peeled away from the crowd and took their turns at the urn. The number of hopefuls was smaller than one might imagine. While some people found the possibility of the naiad's gift irresistible, most people shied away from it. One hundred years might seem nothing to a naiad, but to a human it meant outliving your loved ones. That was a price most people weren't willing to pay. She hoped her mother wasn't one of those people.

Lost in her thoughts, Teiran didn't notice the line move. She hurried to catch up, snagging the toe of her sandal on a ripple in the sand. As she double-stepped to right herself, her shoulder collided with a passerby.

"So sorry," she mumbled. Then, she looked up and gasped. Her spice merchant, the one from her story, was staring down at her. His dark, almond-shaped eyes sparkled with reflected torchlight. He reached up, brushing a midnight-black curl back from his forehead and drawing her attention to the scar that slashed across his left eyebrow. If anything, it made him even more dashing.

What was she thinking? Her spice merchant was fiction, something from her imagination. This man was very real.

"No harm done," he said. His full lips curved into a sultry smile, and Teiran's heart shuddered. Try as she might, she couldn't pull her eyes away from his handsome face. He stepped towards her, and she froze as he leaned down, bringing his cheek close to hers. "At least with grace like that," he said in a low voice, "I know you're one less contestant I have to worry about."

His words iced her rising temperature in an instant, and she gaped at him as he stepped back. Then, he winked—actually *winked*—at her before strolling back towards the gate, his stride matching his attitude.

Teiran rolled her eyes and shook her head, admonishing herself for the momentary distraction. Of course, vanity motivated most of the contestants, but it was ugly to see it play out in front of her.

The urn was before her now. The small, azure surge stones were flecked with gold and glittered like precious gems. She took one in each hand and placed one in her left pocket, and one in her right. There was no reason to chance that they might spark on their own.

She resumed her place before the gate as the rest of the contestants collected their stones. The stars had faded, and a thin red-orange line painted the horizon. Not long now.

"One final point of interest," bellowed the chief, as the last contestant collected her surge stones. "This year is unique from any other in our recorded history. This will be the first time a victor will enter the forest for the second time."

The crowd rumbled at the chief's surprise revelation, and a beautiful figure stepped from their midst. Teiran gritted her teeth as she watched Kesara glide past the rest of the contestants towards the dais, basking in the attention. Her hips swayed provocatively as she sashayed to the urn, her strong dancer's body the picture of an ideal. She bent lower than necessary over the stones, no doubt very aware of how to best display her assets. Then, in one fluid movement, she whirled to face the crowd and clapped her hands together over her head.

Blue light shot from her fingertips like a bolt straight up into the darkness before it split into a dozen smaller beams, curling and spiraling across the sky and raining golden sparks down around the crowd.

Kesara laughed as she tucked the surge stones into her loose-fitting pants, catching the chief's disapproving glare.

"Just checking," she shrugged.

Teiran's fingernails dug into her palms, and she shook her head, trying to loosen the tension from her shoulders. It wasn't fair. Kesara had claimed her reward only last year. One hundred years were hers, so why would she try again? Perhaps when she was close to the end of her time, after she had enjoyed decades of vitality, it would make sense. But not now when the possibility of success was so small. Why risk losing the time she'd fought so hard to get?

The crowd was as confused as she.

"...think she's going to sell it. How much would you pay..."

"...heard her father begged for some of his own..."

"...hasn't taken a husband yet. Maybe she's planning ahead..."

Teiran turned her eyes back to the gate, blocking out the whispers. Whatever Kesara's reasons, it had nothing to do with her—just another distraction. Sure, Kesara had been victorious last year, but the naiad had wiped her memory of the trials. She had the same chance as anyone else.

At that moment, the horizon flamed, and a blade of orange sliced across the desert, reflecting off the silver gate. The crowd stilled as the gate split down the middle, its two sides gliding open like a pair of ethereal wings.

Teiran secured her pack across her back and whispered a hasty prayer as she waited for the gate to finish. She could begin in three…two….

"Good luck!" shouted the chief.

Teiran broke into a sprint. Her heart raced as she saw others enter the forest ahead of her, everyone disappearing in a brilliant flash of silver light as their feet crossed the threshold.

This was it. This was her chance.

She would reach the naiad first.

She *would* save her mother.

Teiran leapt through the gate, and vanished.

She landed with a soft thud, her feet springing slightly on the spongy, foreign ground beneath her. She sucked in a breath and coughed. The air was sticky and dense, and a strange blend of sweetness and must filled her nostrils. It was darker than it had been only a moment ago, and she turned back, expecting to see the sunrise beaming through the forest's gate.

She saw neither.

Instead, the forest stretched out behind her, beside her, in all directions. Enormous trees reached high overhead, their branches dripping with lush foliage. No wonder the light had disappeared. The forest was so thick she could hardly see twenty paces ahead of her, much less all the way to the horizon.

Teiran wasn't sure what she'd expected to happen when she crossed into the forest, but this wasn't it. There was no gate and no path. Just trees. She shivered despite the muggy air. The naiad's magic was powerful, but that wasn't surprising. It was actually experiencing it that put her on edge.

She set her jaw and tightened her pack. There had to be a way in and a way out, otherwise no one would ever come back. But which way? Her neck strained as she looked up at the trees, eyes searching through the gloom.

That one.

She hooked her arms over a sturdy branch and scrambled up. After half a life spent going up and down ladders in the salt mine, climbing the tree was second nature. As she broke through the canopy, her eyes widened. The forest spread out infinitely in every direction. But that was impossible. The forest was big, yes, but she could make out its borders from the village - at least some of them. It must be another trick of the naiad's magic.

No matter. She found what she sought. The sun, like a ripe apricot, hovered just above the eastern tree line. She climbed down and put it to her back. The naiad's pool was in the center of the forest, due west of the gate. Never mind that the gate had disappeared. She had just come through it, so that had to count for something. And it was better than picking a direction at random.

The forest brightened as the sun rose, its beams piercing the canopy and striping the trees with bands of pale yellow. Teiran had never seen so much green in her life, and her eyes devoured her surroundings, even as her feet sped through it.

But where were the faces?

Now that morning lit the trees, everything shone clearly. And there were no faces. Instead, large, oval-shaped disturbances marred the bark of every tree, as if someone had stirred the grain with a spoon and let it settle where it liked. If she squinted and tilted her head just-so, perhaps she could imagine they were faces. But it would take a lot of imagining.

Another thing that struck her were the ovals' positions. Most of them were above her head though a few sat as low as her shoulders. And all of them were on the trees' western sides - facing the same direction she walked.

As interesting as the ovals were, she had no time to waste investigating them. She pressed on, removing her hat and scarf. The forest was duplicitous, protecting her from the sun's rays, all the while trapping its heat and baking her like a holiday roast. Teiran couldn't tell whether the moisture which coated her skin was her own sweat or rather came from the air around her. She paused long enough to take a swig from her flask, in case it was the former, then marched onward.

After a few hours, her steps had slowed noticeably. Her knees ached from walking on the soft ground, and the humidity taxed her body in a way the dry desert heat never had. She'd seen nothing but trees since entering the forest, and she had begun questioning her decision to travel west when she spotted something dark ahead.

Teiran frowned as she approached. It was a door set in a wooden wall, which towered over her and snaked through the forest to her right and left. Before the door stood a pedestal, atop which rested a vase with a long, narrow neck.

Her first trial.

A wave of relief washed over her, followed at once by a pressure in her gut as she focused on her task. It was clear that she had to go through the door. But how to do it?

She pressed her hands against the wooden panel and shoved. The door didn't budge. Not that she'd expected it to, but it was worth a try. She spotted a small keyhole in its center and bent down to peek through. The forest continued on the other side.

She turned away from the keyhole and focused on the vase. Crafted from a creamy, translucent stone, it seemed to glow with an internal energy, and was about as tall as the distance between her wrist and elbow. A shadow within caught her eye, and she peered into the hole at the top for a better look.

Lying on the bottom, illuminated by the bright stone, was a slender, wooden key. One key, one keyhole. Simple enough.

The stone was smooth, and surprisingly cool, under her fingertips as she grasped the vase. But when she tried to lift it, it wouldn't budge. Nor would the pedestal. A crease formed between her eyebrows. She stuck a finger down through the top, again not because she thought it would do any good, but because she didn't know what else to do. Her knuckle snagged as she pulled her finger out, and she was glad the opening wasn't smaller, or else she might be stuck, literally, at this door.

Teiran paced away from the pedestal and surveyed the fallen branches that littered the forest floor. She selected a promising one and snapped off two thin twigs. But they were of no use. The neck of the vase was too long and narrow to use the them like a pair of tongs. And she could forget using one to slide the key up the sides. The curvature of the vase made that impossible.

She tossed the twigs aside and circled the pedestal. She didn't have time for this. The sun was nearing its apex, and she wasn't even through the first trial. There had to be an answer, and she felt like she was staring at it without actually seeing it. She couldn't pull the key out. She couldn't dump it out. She hadn't tried breaking the vase, but something told her that would be a pointless waste of energy.

Teiran growled as her frustration mounted. The blasted heat didn't help either. She pulled out her flask and took another drink. The moment the tepid water hit her tongue, an idea flashed.

She lowered the flask from her lips and swirled it around, estimating the amount of water inside. The vase was tall, yes, but not wide. She should have plenty left over.

The water sparkled in the sunlight as Teiran tipped her flask over the vase's opening. When she had poured in enough, she looked down to see the key floating just below the neck. A smile threatened the corners of her mouth, and she leaned back and poured in a little more. She checked again. The key still floated on the water's surface but wasn't any closer to the neck. She poured again, more this time. The key moved slightly but still wasn't within reach. The hint of a smile vanished as she sacrificed more of her water to the vase. Her estimate must have been off, but she didn't think it could have been that bad.

When it became clear that it would take all her water to get the key, Teiran barely flinched. She would get to the pool, or she would die trying. And if lack of water was the cause, so be it.

As the last drop entered the vase, the key handle bobbed through the opening. Teiran snatched it out and hurried to the door, slipping it into the keyhole. She turned the key, listening for a click, but none sounded. Instead, a soft gurgling noise came from the vase. She approached the pedestal and looked inside the bright stone in time to see the last of her water disappear. Then, she heard the click she had been waiting for.

The door moved with the lightest touch this time, opening with ease. She slipped her empty flask back into her pack and stepped through the wall.

How long had she been walking? The summer solstice was the longest day of the year, but it was more like the longest day of Teiran's life. She felt the loss of her water more keenly as the hours passed, and the wall became a distant memory. The fresh fruits tucked among her rations were the first to be eaten, their sweet juices dulling her thirst for a short time. But they were gone, and she had seen no sign of water since entering the forest.

Nothing but trees.

If she ever got out of here, she didn't care if she never saw another tree in her life. And now, with the afternoon sun scorching the air, they did even less to shade her. This part of the forest was less dense than it had been. The trees were not quite as tall and the leaves not quite as thick. Younger, was that the word?

At least the strange ovals provided a welcome diversion. The swirls appeared not as random as they had been. Bits of bark clumped tightly in some spots, and less so in others, almost in a pattern. Teiran could see now why some might have thought they resembled faces.

The tinge of smoke laced the air, tickling her nose. She surged forward, spurred on by the promise of something new, whatever form that would take.

The moment she laid eyes on the vast, flaming canyon, she thought again. Waves of heat rolled out of it, marbling the landscape beyond. The fire roared below, tossing sparks into the air like confetti and filling her with dread. Her heart sank when she spied the crossing. A single rope traversed the gap, anchored to the ground on either side. She approached with caution and tested its stability. Tight as a tick on a camel.

Her throat burned as she inhaled, the heat scorching the path from her nostrils to her lungs. The fire seemed to have dispelled all the moisture from the air. Teiran had been wishing away the oppressive humidity all day, but this was far worse. She backed away and fished her scarf out of her pack, wrapping it around her head and securing it tightly over her nose and mouth. For the first time in her life she was glad for her long days in the mine, harvesting and toting salt bricks, practicing the habits that formed her well-muscled arms and legs. She'd need every bit of strength to make it across. She crouched beside the lip of the canyon and reached for the rope.

A blood-chilling scream ripped through the air, and Teiran jumped back. The sound echoed through the trees, slow to fade, and coming from somewhere not too far away. She wasn't alone after all. The realization of what must have happened to one of the other contestants pushed Teiran's lunch back up her throat, and she just managed to pull down her scarf before expelling it onto the dirt.

She wiped a shaky hand across her lips and swallowed hard. What a horrible way to die. Suddenly, the mortal dangers of the challenge she had so eagerly embraced were as real to her as the ground upon which she now rested. What was she thinking coming into the forest? She knew the odds of making it out. It was a fool's dream.

She rolled over onto her side, and something pressed against her leg. Righting herself, she slipped her fingers into her pants pocket and clutched the little bottle. It was warm in her palm, and she gave it a gentle squeeze, her determination renewing even as the impossible task lay before her. She withdrew her hand, pulled the scarf back up over her face, crawled over to the rope, and latched on.

With her belly against the rope, Teiran stretched out over the pit. Her vision filled with nothing but the flames beneath her until all she could see was a wall of orange and yellow. She wrapped her legs around the rope and pushed away from the ledge. A squeal escaped her lips as her body swung around and hung beneath it. Despite the fire now at her back, her eyes were still under assault - this time by the blazing afternoon sun which beamed down through the break in the forest's canopy. She squeezed them shut and moved across the rope, hand over hand and ankle over ankle.

Heat choked her, heedless of the scarf, and her skin tingled and tightened the longer she hung over the flame. A rabbit on a spit, that's what she was. Sweat slicked her hands and soaked her clothing in unbelievable quantities. Droplets ran down the sides of face and into her ears, tickling them. She gritted her teeth against the urge to reach back and scratch.

Hand over hand, ankle over ankle.

Her muscles burned. Her insides burned. The whole world was burning around her, and she dangled above it like an offering. And a pitiful one at that.

Another scream echoed off the canyon's walls overlapped by yet another. Teiran jerked, and she struggled to hold onto the rope as her wet hands slipped and slid across it. Sweat dripped from her body now, a stinging, salty rain. She squeezed her eyes tighter, blocking out the sound of death and regaining her grip.

Hand over hand, ankle over ankle.

Her head bumped into something hard. Mustering her resolve, she pried her eyes open and tilted her head back. The canyon wall. She'd reached the other side.

Teiran hooked her elbow up and over the rope, pulling strength from reserves she didn't even know she had, and hauled herself out of the canyon. Her aching muscles, baked skin, dehydrated body, all begged her to rest against the forest floor, even if for only a moment. But she struggled to her feet, determination drowning the weakness, and staggered back into the forest.

Without question, they were faces.

Teiran's skin crawled as she slogged her way through the forest, keeping her eyes trained forward. At least this way she didn't have to look at them. But she felt their eyes upon her back. Those beautiful, horrible, wooden faces, twisted in surprise or terror - some with features pinched and taut, others slack with mouths agape, all shadowed in the evening light.

The forest continued to thin and grow younger as she walked. And the faces on the trees to the right and left of her had begun to shift. She hadn't noticed it at first, but the further she went the more they moved, angling towards her. Watching her.

Ahead, she spied a gap between the trees. It winked in and out of view as she walked, growing larger as she approached. And in the space of a single step, she was out of the forest.

Hope sparked within her chest.

The pond, dappled in shades of peach and honey, was the most beautiful thing Teiran had ever seen. Her cracked lips and parched throat rejoiced in the relief it promised. Survival took over, and she scrambled away from the trees, over rugged stones, to the sandy shoreline. She knelt at the water's edge and plunged her hands into the shallows. A sound caught in the back of her throat, somewhere between a cry and a laugh, as she cupped her hands and brought the water to her mouth.

Just as the cool liquid touched her lips, Teiran jerked, flinging her arms wide and spilling the water on the sand. She shook her head to clear the physical need which had clouded her judgement and surveyed her surroundings.

The forest encompassed the perfect circle of tranquil water, and every tree, every face, looked inward. Watching. Waiting.

The naiad's pool. This must be it.

She squinted in the evening light. Her eyes darted around the shore, looking for other contestants, but she was alone. And she had seen no blue and gold light the sky.

She was first!

But where was the naiad?

Teiran leaned forward and crawled back to the edge of the water. Despite the setting sun, she could see her reflection clearly. Her hair was a tangled, matted mess. Her face was streaked with dirt and soot with dark shadows masking her eyes.

But as she stared, the image blurred. It wasn't her face she saw, but her mother's.

On a worn, straw mat lay a shell of a woman. Bony hands rested across her sunken abdomen. The skin of her face was taut, accenting every outline of every bone, and the more Teiran looked, the more skeletal her mother became.

No.

What trick was this?

She wanted to look away, but it was as if a pair of heavy hands rested on her shoulders, pushing her ever closer to the water. Her breath quickened as she pressed back against it, but she couldn't tear her eyes away.

No! This wasn't how it would end.

A rustling in the trees behind her provided a moment of distraction, but it was enough.

Teiran shut her eyes. Her growl reverberated across the pond as she tossed her head back, lurching away from the water.

She whipped around in time to see Kesara emerge from the forest. Her shoulders were hunched, and black streaked her perfect face. But there was a fire in her eyes and a smirk on her lips.

"Well, well," she said, her voice hoarse. "Who would have thought?"

Teiran eyed her warily, rising to her feet. "Sorry, Kesara. I was here first."

"You?" Kesara spat, taking slow, measured steps closer to the pond. "What business do you have here? The naiad's water can only do so much." She gestured to Teiran as if that explained everything.

Teiran took her meaning. "It's not for me. My mother is dying."

Kesara's expression verged on boredom as she cleaned the dirt from under her fingernails, still inching ever closer.

"I said *dying*," Teiran barked. "The naiad's water is her last hope." Indignation flared within her. "And what about you? You've won your prize. What more could you want?"

"Isn't it obvious?" Kesara gave her a patronizing smile. "What is a hundred years, when you can live forever?" She slithered her way over the rocks. "Another drink, another one hundred years. For someone like you that must sound like a prison sentence. But for someone like me," she swept an arm down the length of her body, "well, you can imagine."

"You're too late," said Teiran. "I was here first."

A stick cracked, and their heads snapped to the right where another figure stepped out from the trees. Across the lake, the twilight shades shifted revealing yet another one.

Kesara's humorless giggle grated against Teiran's eardrums. "Stupid. If this is the end where is the naiad?" She hopped down from the rocks and landed in the sand. "I may not remember the trials, but I do know one thing. The only way to go is forward."

Kesara sprang on her toes and dashed for the water, but Teiran was quick. She stepped forward and lowered her left shoulder, catching Kesara in her midsection and knocking the breath out of her. Kesara landed on her back with a groan. Teiran turned to the water. Before she had taken two steps, a hand wrapped around her ankle, fingernails digging into her skin. Teiran was stronger, but Kesara was tenacious as she clawed her way up Teiran's legs.

Movement caught her eye, and she saw more people exiting the forest and heading to the water. Panic gripped her chest. The water, her mother's hope, was within reach. And nothing would stop her from getting it.

Teiran twisted around, grabbing one of Kesara's arms. Spinning in a circle, she swung her light-weight opponent like a doll, back towards the forest. She released her grip, sending Kesara sailing towards the rocks, before diving into the water.

Her eyes again blurred with the vision of her mother as the phantom hands pushed her deeper and deeper.

Then, she was standing in her little mud house. The silence was overwhelming, and the air smelled of rancid meat with a trace of something sweet. In the shadows of the back corner, her mother's outline was still as stone. Teiran raced to her, reaching for her hand.

"Mama..."

The fingers beneath hers were cold and stiff.

"Mama!"

Hair strung across her mother's face, and Teiran reached up to brush it aside. Her mother's eyes were closed and her mouth slightly agape. The skin across her forehead was rough to the touch.

Teiran's insides twisted, and a strangled sob burst from somewhere deep within her.

"Hold on, Mama. I'm almost there. I got to the water first! I'll get what you need, and then everything will be fine."

She sobbed and gently rubbed her mother's cheek.

"You'll see, everything will be fine."

Tears streamed down her cheeks as grief overtook her. Teiran buried her face against her mother's lifeless form, wailing. Her keening echoed off the mud walls, and it was a sound that would haunt her the rest of her days. Hiccups punctuated her cries, and before long, they choked her. She sat back gasping for air, but her lungs would not be filled.

Her vision darkened, and everything disappeared.

Teiran fought for breath as her head broke the surface of the water. It was dark, and she sputtered, gulping huge mouthfuls of air as her feet found purchase.

"Your gifts are acceptable. You may claim your reward." The voice was like a liquid tremor.

Teiran wiped the water from her face and gasped.

This wasn't the pond, and that wasn't her mother.

A pair of glistening green eyes studied her with interest. The naiad stood before her, waist deep in a small silver pool, her black hair clinging to her shoulders and chest and accented with wisps of algae. Two pointed ears peeked from beneath the hair, and her skin shimmered with an iridescent quality.

The pool rested beneath an arched pavilion made of the same translucent stone as the vase which had held the key. A warm glow radiated out from the stone, challenging the moonlight. The trees pressed against its perimeter. Watching. Waiting.

The naiad cocked her head to the side as if she, too, were waiting.

At such a time as this, thoughtful conversation seemed the best course. Instead Teiran stated the obvious. "You're the naiad."

"As you see." The naiad's voice tickled Teiran's ears, fading in and out as if it was coming from all directions at once.

Teiran forced her breathing to return to normal, and she swallowed. "What gifts? I have brought nothing to give you." Immediately, she regretted her words. Why would she think the naiad would give her water freely? Of course, there must be payment. But to what was she referring?

"But certainly you have. Your very lifeblood has refreshed me, and I give you my thanks along with your reward."

"I have given you no blood."

"Not blood." The naiad's giggle tinkled across the water and rang through the stone arches. "Lifeblood. That which you gifted me at every trial."

Teiran gazed at the naiad. Water droplets glistened over the surface of her body and dripped from the ends of her hair. And when she cocked her head to the side Teiran spied the small slits that formed her gills just underneath her ear.

Of course. Not her lifeblood, the naiad's.

The three trials.

Water. Sweat. Tears.

She had indeed paid the price.

"You're welcome," said Teiran, awkwardly. "And thank you for the reward."

She reached a hand under the surface, into her waterlogged pocket, and removed the bottle. She uncorked the top and dipped it into the pool, filling it to the brim before returning it to her pocket.

"Yet another one?" murmured the naiad. "Interesting."

Teiran opened her mouth to ask what the naiad meant, but a popping noise sounded behind her. She turned in time to see a green shoot burst from the ground. It groaned and creaked as it twisted up and branched out. Tiny leaves exploded from the tips of the branches as it finished, and Teiran stared, wide eyed, at the result.

A fully-grown tree stood before her wearing a face as perfect and detailed as if it had been painted on, though it was made of the very wood of the tree. It was a face she knew.

Her spice merchant.

She might not have recognized him, so pinched were his features, save for the scar across his left eyebrow.

"He took far too long at the first trial," said the naiad, to no one in particular, "and never really had a chance after that. Met his end at the bottom of the canyon."

Teiran tore her eyes from the handsome face and looked around the pavilion. She recognized most of the faces. Some, she knew from her village, others she had only seen just that morning. But almost all of them were familiar.

"Why?" she breathed.

The naiad blew out a soft sigh. "So many years spent, so lonely. Not much water in the desert, you know. But I'm not lonely any longer. Their spirits keep me company."

Teiran chanced to look back at the naiad and saw her peering at the new faces, her expression serene.

Teiran's heartbeat quickened.

It was all a trap.

The naiad played upon their vanity with the chance to remain young and beautiful, but it wasn't from any sense of generosity. It was so she could surround herself with them. Collect their spirits to keep her company.

"What of me?" Teiran's voice quavered as she spoke.

The naiad turned her glittering eyes back to Teiran. "What of you? Do you plan to stay in my forest forever?"

Teiran shook her head.

"Then this is the last time we shall meet."

Teiran exhaled slowly.

"And do feel free to help yourself to the pond water. It's not magical, but you'll need some if you want to make it out by sunrise."

Before Teiran could respond, the bottom of the pool vanished, and she plunged into the depths below.

When Teiran's head surfaced, she shoved her face back into the water, drinking deeply until the need for air forced her chin up. She'd been without water for most of the day, and the heat had taken its toll. But, she didn't want to overdo it and make herself sick.

She pulled her flask from her pack and filled it as she dragged her body out of the pond. The water was silent and empty, except for her. She wondered if the others had turned back, or if some of them now lay on the bottom of the pond, their spirits forfeit to the naiad.

Once on the shore, she fished the surge stones out of her pockets, held them over her head, and struck them together sending bright, blue light streaking into the night sky. When the last of the golden sparkles vanished, she tucked the stones away and headed for the trees. She'd have to move quickly. The stars overhead brought a welcome break from the heat, but also warned that sunrise would be here sooner than she would like. It was the shortest night of the year, after all.

With no other direction, retracing her steps seemed the only course of action. Now that she had made it to the naiad, the gate had to be there. Otherwise, how would anyone get out?

She'd been walking for about a half-hour when she heard a disturbance ahead of her.

Grunt, drag. Grunt, drag.

She approached cautiously, squinting into the darkness.

"Kesara?"

The gorgeous dancer whirled on her. "Get away from me, you filthy animal!"

Teiran stumbled back, then spotted the cause of the commotion. Kesara's right ankle was twisted at an odd angle and trailed behind her as she limped through the forest.

"Isn't it enough you stole the water from me!?" Kesara shrieked. "You've come to gloat over your handiwork as well?"

Guilt washed over Teiran as she replayed her fight with Kesara - how she'd practically thrown her away before diving into the water.

"The rocks," she whispered.

"Yes, the rocks," spat Kesara. "You've crippled me, you heartless beast. Now go, and leave me alone. I can't stand the sight of you."

Grunt, drag. Grunt, drag.

Teiran stared at Kesara's back. Yes, she thought she would have done anything for a chance to save her mother. But she never meant to hurt anyone.

"I'm sorry," she called, lamely.

"Just stop talking!" Kesara gritted out. "Go. Sunrise will be here soon. Take your water to your precious mother. Go!"

For all of Kesara's winning personality, Teiran couldn't leave her behind. Kesara's injuries were her fault.

Teiran stepped beside Kesara and grabbed her arm, slipping it around her own shoulders.

"What are you doing?" said Kesara, trying to pull her arm away.

Teiran's grip held fast. "There's no way you'll make it back to the gate before sunrise without help."

"Ha. Like you care."

"Yes, I care," Teiran shot back. "I didn't mean to hurt you, but you will excuse me if I don't want to watch my own mother die while there is something I can do about it."

Kesara grumbled something inaudible, but allowed Teiran to lead her.

140

They made a slow but steady pace.

When they arrived at the canyon, the fire was gone, and a thin, sliver footbridge spanned the opening. Teiran took advantage of the break in the canopy to inspect Kesara's ankle. Even in the moonlight, she could see it was getting worse. The surrounding skin was discolored and tight, puffing up through her sandal straps.

"Stop poking me with your dirty fingers," grumbled Kesara, as Teiran probed the injury.

Teiran lifted her eyes to the stars, judging the time. Then without asking, because she already knew the answer, she swung Kesara up over her shoulder. Kesara yelped angrily and hurled a few choice insults at her.

"We're too far in, and you're too slow," scolded Teiran. "If you'd stop squirming, I can get us to the gate by sunrise."

"I won't have you deliver me back to the village like a sack of horse feed," said Kesara.

"Then you can stay here," replied Teiran. She made no move to set Kesara down, but her comment had the intended result, and Kesara fell silent.

Despite Teiran's best efforts, and Kesara's relatively light weight, exhaustion and dehydration dealt their winning hand. The wooden door already stood wide open when Teiran approached the wall and unceremoniously dumped Kesara against it before dropping to the ground herself. She lay on her back, panting, searching the sky for a sign. But the stars were fading.

"We're not going to make it," she breathed, tears pricking at the corners of her eyes.

Kesara, who had been uncharacteristically silent for the last hour, struggled to stand.

"No, we're not," she said quietly. "But you can."

Teiran sat up. "I can't leave you here." The guilt which she'd pushed to the back of her mind returned in full force.

"Yes, you can," said Kesara. Her voice was strangely calm as she spoke. "I'd give anything to have my mother back."

The confession hung in the air between them. Then, Kesara continued. "If you have a chance to save her, you have to take it. She's the whole reason you came into this forest. You go ahead. I'll be right behind you."

Hope warred with guilt as Teiran weighed Kesara's words. Kesara was releasing her. Not pushing her away, but giving her permission to leave. Teiran stood, searching Kesara's face in the moonlight.

"This is what you want?" she asked.

"Yes," said Kesara. "Now go."

"I'll see you back in the village?"

Kesara smirked. "Do you really think I'm going to get stuck here? The gate is opening again next year, and I plan to be there when it does."

Teiran nodded, then turned and walked through the doorway.

Every step she took was heavier than the one before. Who were they kidding? Kesara wouldn't make it back to the village. It was just like the game she played with her mother. A story was much better than the truth.

Teiran's throat clenched, and she fought back the tears that once again threatened to escape. She couldn't leave Kesara here. Not when there was a way to save her.

She spun on her heel and went back through the door. Kesara slumped against the other side of the wall weeping silently into her hands.

"I can't leave you here with no water," said Teiran, slipping her hand into her pocket and removing the small bottle. Kesara looked up, her pale face streaked with tears.

"Drink this. I'll refill it." Teiran handed her the bottle.

"Thank you," whispered Kesara, removing the stopper and pressing the bottle to her lips.

Teiran watched Kesara's throat bob as she swallowed.

Kesara gasped, and her eyes flew to Teiran's. "What have you done?"

In the space of an instant, her color returned. The dark circles under her eyes vanished, and her skin plumped like a newborn babe's. Her ankle, once mangled and useless, righted itself, and she leapt to her feet.

"My mother," stammered Teiran, "she still has a little time. I'll try to figure out something else. But you...what happens to those who don't make it out of the forest...it's worse than death."

Then Teiran remembered the naiad's vision - her mother's gaunt, cold shell. She pressed the heels of her hands against her eyes as if she could force the memory back into hiding, hoping it really was only a vision.

Kesara's voice brought her back. "How could you—"

142

"Shut up, Kesara," snapped Teiran, dropping her hands, "and run."

Teiran took off through the door with Kesara right behind her. Her body protested every step, but her will was in charge, urging her ever forward until her limbs were numb and her chest burned with each breath. Kesara soon pulled ahead, the effects of the water washing away her exhaustion, but she remained in sight, glancing back over her shoulder every so often as if to make sure Teiran was still there.

Branches whipped Teiran's face and arms, but she didn't care. She watched through the treetops as the sky turned grey. Then gray-green.

Then it was there.

The gate stood in a clearing, open wide. It welcomed them. Until it didn't.

Fear gripped Teiran as those two silver wings began to close. Kesara vanished between them in a burst of light, and Teiran dug her toes into the springy ground, barreling forward and shrieking like a madwoman.

In a flash, she was gone.

"I have your tea, Mama."

A frail hand rested on Teiran's leg as she brought the mug to her mother's lips. The wheezing was worse than ever, and it took longer for her mother to drink.

By the time she finished the tea her mother breathed a little easier, and Teiran settled her back onto the mat.

"Tell me... about your trip," whispered her mother.

"The roads were dusty, naturally," began Teiran, as she set the mug on the counter.

"No," interrupted her mother. "Tell me... about the forest."

Teiran froze, then snuck a sidelong glance at the back corner.

Her mother's thin lips managed a weak smile. "Mrs. Ashtani... let it slip."

Teiran's first instinct was to apologize - for half-truths, for putting herself in danger. But she wasn't sorry. If she had another chance to save her mother, she'd do it all over again.

"It was beautiful. And horrible." The memories were fuzzy, like a dream that hovers at the edge of your mind. There had been trials, but what exactly they were, she couldn't remember.

She recalled trees and faces, a pair of glistening green eyes, and a small bottle filled with magical water.

She was debating whether to mention that water when there came a light rap at the door.

Teiran rose and opened it. When she saw who stood on the other side, she stepped out onto the porch and closed the door behind her.

Kesara radiated in the sunlight. She had always been beautiful, but Teiran thought she looked even more so now than she had before the race, if that was possible. She practically glowed.

Teiran clenched her teeth. This was how her mother should look now. Not that she regretted giving Kesara the water. She regretted her own actions which made that choice necessary.

"Kesara," she said flatly.

Kesara shifted on her feet. It was the first time Teiran could remember seeing the dancer unsure of herself.

"I never got a chance to thank you for what you did for me in the forest," said Kesara.

Teiran huffed. "You mean for bashing you against the rocks?"

"No, you know what I mean."

Teiran took a deep breath and let it out slowly. "Yes, I know what you mean. I'm sorry it was necessary, but I couldn't leave—"

"Just stop talking and let me get through this."

Teiran pinched her lips together.

"I know what it's like to lose your mother. My mother was my best friend, and when she died...." Kesara's eyes grew distant and her voice trailed off. She stood frozen for a moment, like a lovely stone statue. Then she sucked in a quick breath, her eyes snapping back to Teiran. "It wasn't her time. And then when you said you wanted the water to save your mother... I mean, why did you get that chance, and I didn't?"

Kesara's eyes shone with unshed tears, and Teiran shook her head. She couldn't answer that. No one could.

"Anyway," Kesara sniffed, grasping Teiran's hand and pressing something cool and smooth into her palm. "I want you to have this."

Teiran looked down at the small, pink bottle, then back at Kesara. Hope she dared not acknowledge flared in her chest. "Is this..."

"What else would it be?"

"But where did you get it?"

Kesara tilted her head to the side. "I got it last year, don't you remember? The victor returns, and all that." She waved a hand dismissively.

Teiran shot her a questioning look. "But why do you still have it?"

"Youth and beauty," said Kesara, matter-of-factly. When Teiran still didn't seem to understand, Kesara gave an exasperated sigh. "I'm already young and beautiful. I was saving it for a time when I actually needed it—buying a few more years into immortality."

Teiran searched Kesara's face, but there was no haughtiness there. Just open honesty as if she was merely stating fact.

Her fingers closed around the bottle and she wrapped Kesara in a tight hug.

"Thank you."

Kesara stepped back awkwardly. "Anyway. Give my best wishes to your mother."

Teiran nodded, then hurried inside. When she presented the pink bottle, her mother's eyes filled with tears.

"Oh, my… darling," whispered her mother.

Teiran helped her sit up and tipped the contents of the bottle into her mouth, slowly, until there wasn't a single drop left.

Her mother gasped. Her fragile body, a skeleton wrapped in paper-thin skin, transformed before Teiran's eyes. Angles became curves, hardness grew soft, and golden tones replaced pallor. Her mother's hair, thin and patchy from months of illness, bloomed in a riot of chestnut, auburn, and bronze. Wrinkles and blemishes vanished, and the woman who remained exceeded Teiran's wildest imaginings.

She rushed to her mother, pulling her to her chest and feeling her heartbeat, her softness, her *life*.

Yes, they had a new set of problems to face. They looked more like sisters than mother and daughter, now. And it was a near certainty that her mother would outlive her. Teiran could only imagine the shadow that would cast over them as the years passed.

But for now, they were well. They were together.

And the gate would open again next year.

———————————⇒∘⊂⬯⊃∘⊂———————————

About the Author

A. K. R. Scott is a musician, actor, and lover of the written word. This native South Carolinian spent her childhood devouring books, whether tucked away in her bedroom, up a tree, or hidden under the dinner table. Now, she lives in Texas with her husband, two daughters, one rascally dog, and an ever-expanding library. Her website is www.akrscott.com.

IRON AND FROST

CATE ISERT

W inter in the mountains of Omsk was long, cold, and dark. By the middle of January, it was so cold that nearly all the moisture had sublimated out of the air, thinning it to a crystalline sharpness. There was no water left for future snowfalls, and the last of the humidity had dusted the ground with a thin, powdery layer that melted away to nothing when you kicked off your boots in the warmth of your kitchen. The small farms and villages lay under a pristine layer of white, because the ground was too frozen and the air too dry for the previous months' snow to churn up into muddy slush that ruined the storybook snowdrifts of warmer climates.

It was, therefore, with great astonishment that Ksenya opened her kitchen door one morning to discover a thick pond of ice had spread across the yard of packed dirt behind her little log house.

With her head stuck out into the cold and her skirt still firmly in the kitchen, a quick investigation revealed that the pond spread around the right corner of the house. To her left, she could almost touch the edge, if she stretched out her foot as far as it could go. As a peasant, Ksenya did not know much about water formations or mathematics, but she had enough logic in her brain to figure out that the pond's center was somewhere close to her goat shed. Luckily, that was exactly where she was headed.

Two steps onto the ice Ksenya's feet shot out from under her, landing her flat on her back. The ice was not smooth, for all its glassy stillness. Its surface fanned out across the ground in flat layers, creating small hills and ridges as if gentle waves had been frozen in the very act of forming. After catching her breath, and with thanks to whatever beings looked after the production of multiple petticoats and thick woolen coats, Ksenya picked herself up and shuffled carefully toward her goats, watching her feet to keep her balance. She did not see the other addition to her yard until she had bent her nose on it.

Or, she would have, if she hadn't had been wearing three scarves. Ksenya's first thought, staring up at the tall, thick pillar of crystal-clear ice, was annoyance, much as she would have felt if a tree or a large boulder had suddenly appeared in her path. Her second reaction, which logically should have been her first, was incredulity.

The pillar's circumference would have challenged at least three Ksenyas holding hands to span it completely. Suspended in the middle of the column, her pointed little shoes at least two feet above the ground, dangled a tiny old woman. She wore all black, from the blouse and shawl tucked around her skinny shoulders to the long skirt and stockings hugging her bony ankles. Her gray hair wisped out from under the black headscarf knotted tightly under her pointed chin. One hand was fisted tightly, the other pointing at something behind Ksenya. The old woman's pinched mouth and narrowed eyes tinged Ksenya's astonishment with gratitude: at least *she* wasn't the one from whom this old woman would be eventually seeking retribution.

Then again, thought Ksenya, coming a little closer, the vengeful look might have just been the old woman's regular expression. It was a little difficult to tell around the long nose and all the wrinkles. But ten years of living with her back fence running up against the forest had taught Ksenya to be polite to everyone, so she curtsied (a little awkwardly, as one does when one is bundled into six layers of clothing) and pulled the scarves away from her mouth to speak.

"Greetings, Grandmother," Ksenya said, and then immediately felt a little foolish, since talking to a column of ice – human inhabitant or not – provoked very much the same reaction as talking to a tree.

Her answer, instead, came from behind her.

"Greetings, child," boomed a loud, bass voice. Ksenya jumped and turned, just in time to see a tall, white-bearded figure appear inside her fence. At least, she *thought* she saw him appear. There was a chance that he might have climbed over the fence, though his apparent age made it seem unlikely. Actually, his whole presence made it seem unlikely. He was dressed in the long, fur-trimmed coat and hat of a boyar, and the staff he carried was made of silver – certainly not the dress of someone who climbed over fences. As Ksenya bobbed a curtsey to him as well, an explosion of shrill noise burst from the direction of the frozen column.

Actually, Ksenya noted, clapping her mittens over her ears, more like the suggestion of noise. Covering her ears had done exactly nothing.

The man in the long coat burst out laughing. "Caught you at last, you old hag," he said, walking up to the pillar and slapping the side of it. Without moving so much as an eyelash, the old woman managed to convey the thought that her eyes were about to bulge out of her head. Her shrill chatter congealed into distinct words, and Ksenya watched in fascination as the long-nailed fingers flexed ever so slightly within their casing of ice.

– *get what's coming to you, Moroz, you thrice-blasted, worm-eating chicken gizzard* –

Moroz laughed again, his voice cracking through the cold air, while the old woman's escalating complaints squealed like metal across ice. Ksenya's fingers curled more tightly over her ears, and finally she decided that politeness had its place, but enough was enough.

"Excuse me," she said, cutting across the noise. "I'm sorry, but have we met?"

Moroz turned toward Ksenya, and she had to tell her feet very firmly *not to move* as his silvery blue gaze flicked over her.

"We have not, mortal," he said, amiably enough. "You should count yourself lucky."

The old woman cackled. *She doesn't know who you are, you old demon*, she said. *And you thought you were so famous.*

"I'd be more respectful, if I were you, Jaga," Moroz thundered back, his white beard brushing against his coat as his head turned. "Unless you want to stay there for the next twenty years."

Twenty? mused Jaga. *I wouldn't be too sure of that.*

The air shimmered, a light mist rising from the column around Jaga. The old woman's fingers flexed further, and her nose twitched slightly as her thin lips pulled into a grin. Moroz frowned and took a step back. Grasping his long staff horizontally in both hands, he planted his feet and thrust the staff toward Jaga's pillar of ice. Mist billowed, meeting the invisible wall that Moroz pushed toward Jaga, and tiny droplets plinked to the ground as the temperature dropped even further. Ksenya, thinking wildly of her poor goats trapped in their own block of ice, gritted her teeth against the cold and put her foot down.

She put so much enthusiasm behind the action that her heel skidded on the ice and she sat down hard for the second time that day, but the stomp was valid and the mist disappeared.

The corners of Moroz's mouth curled up. He took a step forward. At least, he tried to. His tall felt boots stuck to the ground, and if he had not caught himself with his staff, his knees would have bruised themselves as he fell. Frowning, Moroz started at his feet and tapped his staff on the tips of his boots. Neither boot moved. Jaga snickered. The snicker turned into a shriek as she discovered that she was frozen. Again.

Ksenya picked up her bucket and walked back to the house. It appeared that if she wanted to either feed or water her goats, she would need the small hatchet to break them free, and she hadn't used the hatchet since the ground had frozen several months ago. By the time she had found the hatchet and had made her way back to her visitors' tableau, Moroz had apparently discovered that he could not remove his feet from his boots, and his staff did not seem to be working either. As she passed him on the way back to the goats, he stopped trying to wedge the end of his staff under his right boot and reached out to collar her by the back of her coat. She dodged the grab and continued on to the shed.

"Come back here, you impudent child!" Moroz boomed. "Release me at once!" He tugged again at his feet. Ksenya turned, but didn't stop.

"Many apologies, Grandfather," she said, feeling rather more in control. "My goats are hungry. I will come back right away to discuss –" she waved her mittened hand at the icy coating around the yard "– all of this."

The lack of choice in staying or going did not stop Moroz – nor Jaga, for that matter –from expressing their vast displeasure at the situation. While Ksenya chipped away at the goat shed door, Moroz alternated between threats and bribes, while Jaga sniped equally at the two of them. Ksenya ignored them both, which seemed more and more to amuse Jaga and further infuriate Moroz. Though she put up a very good front of disinterest, Ksenya still breathed a sigh of relief when she was able to shut the door of the shed behind her and concentrate solely on her goats.

She stayed in the shed perhaps a smidge longer than she needed to, waiting until her captives on the other side of the door had argued themselves into silence. Then, squaring her shoulders, she pushed back into the cold.

She was met by a glower from Moroz and the impression of a raised eyebrow from Jaga.

"What," insisted Moroz, in tones of threatening bass, "have you done?"

"I've taken away your magic, Grandfather," Ksenya said, as politely as she could. "Well, it's more that I've blocked you from using it. You're stuck in place until I let you go."

"Not possible," rumbled Moroz, as though he had not spent the last hour trying to tug himself free. "You are mortal. You have no power."

Ksenya stayed silent, holding his gaze in what she hoped appeared to be calm disagreement. In actual fact, the sticking-people-to-the-ground trick was the only one she had, and it wasn't even really hers, but she felt that to disclose that to someone as powerful and irate as Moroz would not be very wise.

Moroz leaned forward, supporting himself on his stick. "Let. Me. Go."

"You were endangering my land," Ksenya pointed out. "And the minute I let you have your magic back, you'll put *me* into an ice column. Or worse. I'm not going to let you go until you promise to leave us alone."

Good luck, dearie, Jaga said scornfully. *Moroz thinks he's a law unto himself.*

"*You* are an interfering old witch," Moroz countered with careless accuracy.

"What did she do?" asked Ksenya, after a pause.

Nothing, retorted Jaga.

"You ruined my work!" Moroz fumed. "Everything was perfect, and you smashed it to pieces."

Hardly, Jaga sniffed. *And Vasilisa wouldn't have worked out for you anyway, poor girl.*

Ksenya stared at Jaga. "What did he do to *you*?" she asked, fascinated.

As always, Jaga's expression didn't change, but Ksenya could sense the mental equivalent of an eye roll.

"Yes, yes," she hastily amended. "I meant besides trying to freeze you for the next twenty years."

He tried to kill my granddaughter, Jaga said. *Well, great-great-granddaughter*, she amended, after seeing Moroz's sarcastic eyebrow.

Moroz sniffed back. "I wasn't trying to kill her," he insisted. "I was trying to adopt her."

By inflicting her with a pack of bloodthirsty relatives.

"I planned to rescue her!"

"Stop," Ksenya insisted, seeing where the discussion was going – again. "I wish you the happiest of times with each other trying to pay and pay again, but I really must insist that you take your argument off my land."

Moroz straightened, folding his arms across his chest. "I do not take orders from mortals."

"Very well," Ksenya said. "I will bring you a stool so you do not become too tired."

She turned on her heel to go back to the house, then hesitated.

"Forgive me, Grandmother," she said, turning back to Jaga. "I do not think I could let one of you go and not the other without asking for trouble."

Jaga said nothing, but her small snort seemed to confirm Ksenya's suspicions. Ksenya fetched the stool for Moroz, positioned it so that it was less likely to teeter on the ice, and then left her two visitors to themselves.

Four days went by. On her thrice-daily trips to the goat shed, Ksenya was careful to greet her guests and offer them food or more blankets, but Jaga was the only one who would talk with her, and there really wasn't much Ksenya could do without unfreezing the pillar. Moroz preserved a sullen silence, his chin sunk down on his chest and his eyes watching Ksenya from under white-beetled brows. By the evening of the fourth day, his thunderous silence had almost gained enough solidity to follow her into the goat shed, and she seriously considered spending her nights amongst the hay.

Instead, she put up her chin, snugged her scarf around her neck, and marched outside.

"You seem unhappy," she said when she had drawn abreast of him. She folded her arms across her stomach.

"Observant child," he replied, mimicking her stance.

For handful of seconds, they stared at each other, then he exhaled noisily.

"Agreed," Moroz grit out. "Free us, and we will take our differences elsewhere."

"You will do nothing on my land?" Ksenya insisted.

"Nothing."

Ksenya turned to Jaga for affirmation.

Nothing, Jaga confirmed.

Ksenya stamped her foot again.

The ice under her boot splintered, shooting a spider web of cracks across the yard and up the length of Jaga's pillar. Jaga shook herself, flinging off pieces of ice. Moroz growled when one of them hit his leg. Jaga cackled. The sound of Jaga's voice against the cold air after so long of it being only in Ksenya's head had the girl rubbing her hand against her ear, and Jaga cackled again. Ksenya's breath caught in her throat at the sight of Jaga's grey, pointed teeth.

"Many thanks, dearie," Jaga said, and she skipped over to the fence with a spryness that belied her years. One hop over and she was gone.

Moroz also walked toward the fence, though his long coat necessitated a statelier stride. Remembering his appearance, Ksenya watched closely to see if he would also jump over the fence, or if he would disappear before he reached the barrier.

He did neither. One second, he was inside the fence, and the next second he was outside of it. He turned back just outside of the forest. Safely outside the reach of Ksenya's land, he pointed his staff at her. A single snowflake blossomed out of the end and drifted back across the fence.

"Be wary, granddaughter," Moroz said as she watched the snowflake float closer. It was large and almost blue, with silver glinting along the edges. "I can do nothing to you on your land, but if you walk the woods in the winter, we may very well meet again."

"Until then, Grandfather," Ksenya said amiably, and then, in a sudden spray of snow, he was gone.

The snowflake remained, drifting down over Ksenya's upturned face. She closed her eyes right before it landed and felt the cold of it as it melted against her forehead. Silver flashed briefly at the corners of her vision and then was gone. *I wonder*, she thought as she swung her feed pail on the way back to the house, *if that marked me for good or for bad.*

Ksenya went into the house, hung up the pail, and shut the door. In the yard, the shards of ice glittered in the last light of day.

About the Author

By day, Cate Isert is a mild mannered office denizen, and by night she is usually asleep. It's really in the mornings and evenings that she is able to indulge her artistic side and find time to write (and sing, and sew, and cook, and dance, and read, and...). Inspiration for this story came from her high school years when she lived in Russia. This is her first fiction publication.

THE BLACK HORN

JA ANDREWS

T he bag with the Black Horn bounced against Eliese's back like the prodding of a little sprite, cheering her on to adventure and victory. She raced after her twin brother Rellien, his red curls jouncing wildly as he ran down the goat trail winding high along the cliff. Behind her she could hear Marcus's quick breaths and footsteps. A pebble knocked loose by her foot shot off the side of the path and bounced down the steep slope disappearing into the gorge. The rust-red cliffs stood out in sharp relief against the empty blue sky. Eliese's black hair soaked in the heat from the summer sun, making the top of her head feel like it was too close to a fire.

The bag was lighter than she'd expected. The fabled Black Horn had always looked so grave presiding over the great hall from the mantle. It was a thing of legend, of magic, and though she'd stared at it for hours on end, she'd never before dared to touch it. Until Rellien had set his mind to blowing it and they'd hatched their plan. But now that she'd held it, it felt like... well, it felt like a common ram's horn. A bit big, perhaps, but that was the only difference between it and the horns the watchmen blew.

Still, she couldn't quell the thrill of what they were about to do. Carrying the horn made her feel like some sort of battle maiden fighting valiantly in an ancient tale.

"I think I should blow it first," Marcus called from behind her.

"Why?" Rellien demanded.

"Because I'm older. I'm already twelve."

"Eliese and I will be twelve next month," Rellien objected. "Being barely older doesn't count. I'm blowing the horn because my father is the captain of the keep, and some day I will be too." He turned to give Marcus a serious look. "I may have to blow it for real some day."

Marcus opened his mouth to object, but Eliese broke in. "Just let him or he'll argue with you all afternoon."

Marcus scowled from under drooping, sweaty brown locks and kicked a spray of tiny rocks off the thin path, letting them skitter down the slope. But he didn't say anything.

"Lookout Rock!" Rellien declared over his shoulder as they rounded a curve in the cliff face. He clambered off the trail and out onto a huge boulder hanging out over the gorge. "From here we shall see the whole of our fertile land stretched out before us!"

"Fertile?" Eliese asked, looking at the barren cliffs.

"Fine," Rellien said. "Our land rich in ore. And precious metals."

"I'm pretty sure it's just rocky," Marcus said, and Eliese giggled.

"And from this, our lofty watchtower," Rellien continued, ignoring them both, "we can spy our enemies from afar!"

Eliese climbed up next to him, the dry and dusty breeze blowing past her. Far below, the narrow gorge twisted off to the west. At the bottom a thin road plodded along next to a small, parched stream. To the east, the gorge wound up toward the pass at Stone Gap. And at the top of the pass, lodged between the road and the sharp southern cliffs, sat the keep.

"And our great palace." Marcus said with an unenthused sigh. "Also made from ore and precious metals."

"I like it," Eliese came to its defense. "It looks solid. As strong as the cliffs themselves."

"That's because it's made out of the rocks of the cliffs themselves," Marcus pointed out.

"It will keep us safe," Eliese insisted, "and that is what it is meant to do."

"Not if a horde of Wildmen come," Rellien said darkly, crouching down and peering west through the canyon. "If wave upon wave of the vicious men come, they'll crash past the keep and spill through onto the plains, ravaging and killing everyone in Queensland."

"That would take a lot of men," Eliese pointed out.

Rellien shrugged. "They're Wildmen. They grow from the grass and rocks. There are countless Wildmen."

"I'm pretty sure Wildmen come from wild women," Eliese said, "not grass and rocks."

Marcus laughed.

"Could you two be more helpful?" Rellien asked, irritated. "You're destroying the moment."

"Right, sorry," Marcus said. He stepped up to the edge of the rock and shaded his eyes and he looked west down the empty gorge. "Captain!" he cried. "The countless hordes approach! And with them come... um..." He looked around for a moment. "...giants! Giants to destroy the walls of the keep."

"The Black Horn, fair lady of Stone Gap!" Rellien cried, holding out his hand to Eliese. "The army of Wildmen approaches, we need the horn! We need its power! We need it to raise again the legendary army from the very rocks. Indestructible and loyal only to us."

She reached into the sack and wrapped her hand around the horn. Under her fingers the inner curve was smooth as glass. But the outside was rough with ridges like a miniature range of mountains, lined up one after another.

The sunlight sank into the horn, warming the blackness. It called to her for a moment, called to something deep within her, pulling at her gut.

"Fair lady!" Rellien said, wiggling his fingers impatiently at her. "The army approaches!"

Eliese hesitated another moment, but the Black Horn had settled into just a horn, hollow and lifeless.

"El," Rellien sighed, "You can blow it next. You can be the Queen Lady of the Keep. Have an army of trolls coming. Whatever you want. But you already agreed to let me blow it first."

Eliese stretched the horn out toward her brother.

"Thanks!" he said, grabbing it. "And if you could swoon or something at our impending doom, that would be great."

157

"I don't swoon." Eliese said, indignant. "I'm perfectly capable of helping solve whatever problems come up. After all, I'm the one who climbed up the mantle to get the horn, and I'm the one who discovered we could get out the watch tower window to reach this goat trail." She scowled at her brother. "Swoon," she muttered.

"Shh!" Rellien whispered, peering down into the empty canyon. "The enemy is right at our feet! It is time!"

Rellien held the horn for a moment, then glanced at Eliese and Marcus. The three of them stood perfectly still.

Eliese's heart quickened. Her brother lifted the horn up and it looked too dark against the sky, too black. Marcus stepped close to Eliese, his shoulder up against hers.

"What if it works?" he whispered, his voice barely audible. "What if we raise an army?"

Eliese opened her mouth to tell him it wasn't possible, but her mouth felt too dry to talk. She leaned against him, suddenly frightened of the horn. Rellien brought the horn to his lips and drew in a breath. Eliese grabbed Marcus's hand and squeezed, drawing back. Rellien blew out a great burst of air.

And out of the horn came a weak honk.

Like a goose. Coughing.

There was a breath of silence before Eliese's fear rushed out of her in a laugh and the boys joined in.

"Blow it again!" Marcus called.

Rellien did, and this time the honk ended in a squeak.

Their laughter echoed off the canyon walls.

"My turn!" Eliese said, reaching out for it.

She took the horn from her brother. It felt warm, but... vacant. She set her lips against the unyielding opening and taking a deep breath, blew as hard as she could.

The horn let out a sickly warble. The boys fell into gales of laughter, but Eliese didn't join them. Against her hand, the horn hummed. And something in her gut stirred, as though the surface of a deep pool had been disturbed.

The laughter of her brother and Marcus turned to great war cries and their voices rang out, the noise doubling and tripling back on them until the entire canyon was full of it.

Eliese closed her eyes. The horn felt alive and restless in her hands, and the something inside her reached for it, longing for... what, she wasn't sure.

The boys' yells echoed loud and wild, filling the air and crashing against the cliffs until the ground beneath her feet trembled and her eyes snapped open. Marcus and Rellien were jumping and hollering near the edge, but the rock was shaking with more than that. She turned to look up the slope above them. The rocks were moving, rushing toward them like a river of stone.

She cried out to the boys and grabbed for them, pulling them down and huddling together as the stream of rocks rushed down the mountain, crashing down only an arm's reach past the rock they were on. Eliese clutched the horn to her chest, feeling its warmth and that strange calling again.

They clung together for a half dozen breaths while the sound of the rockslide faded down the cliff. Peering over the edge they saw the thin, light path of the avalanche leading straight down to a pile of rock on the gorge floor.

Silence reigned over the canyon.

"Maybe it's time to head back," Rellien whispered, the words shaky.

"Agreed," Marcus said quickly.

The two turned back toward the goat trail, their eyes wild and wary. Eliese placed the Black Horn back into her bag.

"So much for the legend of the Black Horn," Rellien whispered with an unsteady grin as he passed her.

Eliese forced a smile at him, disappointment and uncertainty swirling through her. She let her fingers linger on the horn for an extra breath, but the horn sat silent and empty.

"So much for the legend," she answered slowly.

But the boys were already dashing ahead on the path toward home.

TEA WITH A KEEPER
Seven Years Later

Eliese hung the kettle over the fire and turned toward the table in the great hall where Keeper Oriana leaned back in her chair. The curly red head of her twin bother Rellien and Marcus's brown mop leaned over a dice game at the far end.

"Is the king as bad off as we hear?" Eliese asked, hoping the question wasn't impertinent, and hoping her voice didn't sound as nervous as she felt. Eliese's father had been a child the last time a Keeper had come to Stone Gap. There were only ever a few of them in Queensland. As preservers of knowledge and history, and wielders of magic, the Keepers stayed at court to advise rulers or witnessed and recorded the most crucial events in the land.

The fact that one was here at Stone Gap made Eliese's gut turn to stone. No one this important ever made it all the way here, to the edges of the civilized land, unless there was something truly perilous happening.

Oriana nodded. "His mind wanders and his body weakens." Her hair was long and almost completely grey, but there was an alertness about her face that kept her from looking old.

"But the king is so young," Eliese said, setting out teacups and a teapot. The king was barely older than herself.

"Too young. It began as a hunting injury, but has turned into a dreadful illness. And with no heir, the last thing this disaster of a succession needs is a warlord like Noreth invading."

Eliese's heart clenched at the name, the fear that had sat in her gut for weeks rising up again. The Wildmen had lived on the edge of Queensland for as long as anyone could remember, bringing skirmishes, and occasionally attacking in force. A generation ago, in an attempt to establish peace, the last king's cousin married the Wildmen's war chief. And for a time it worked—until their son, Noreth, grew into power. Now his connection to Queensland didn't lead him toward peace, it gave him hopes of attaining the throne. As the present king lay dying, families with royal blood all across the country were angling for the throne, creating alliances. And in two days, Noreth would be here with an army of ten thousand to stake his claim. "Will the reinforcements from the king reach us before he does?"

The dice game stilled as both Rellien and Marcus listened for her answer.

Oriana paused. "I'm not sure."

"They have to come," Eliese said, clutching a cup in her hand so tightly that the ridge along the bottom dug into her palm. "We're a small garrison. We've enough men to keep the bandits in the hills under control, but we're not equipped to stop an army!"

"We'll stop anything that comes through the gap," Rellien said. "The keep is well positioned, and no matter how large the army is, they still have to come through the pass a few at a time."

"But they will just keep coming," Eliese said. "They'll exhaust us and kill us and then nothing will stop them from reaching the plains."

"We just need to hold them off until the king's army gets here, El," Rellien said.

"How can you be so calm?" Eliese demanded, thrusting aside a lock of black hair that had fallen in her face. "We don't even know when Noreth will get here. We've had another whole day of this blasted fog, which is never going to lift, none of our scouts have returned—" Eliese shut her mouth, trying to quell the fear that ate at her. It didn't matter how close the reinforcements were. The sixty men stationed at Stone Gap couldn't hold the road against Noreth's force of Wildmen, even for half a day. They'd be slaughtered.

"We might not be enough," Marcus said quietly. "But we have to try."

She turned away from them and looked out the window, wishing she could see through the thick fog that had sat in the gorge for days. But the evening outside was a dreary haze.

Bread and cold meat were brought in and Rellien, Marcus, and Oriana served themselves. Eliese forced herself to put some food on her plate.

"I don't suppose the king's army is bringing with it a dragon," she asked Oriana, "Or some great magical talisman that can defeat an approaching horde?"

Oriana gave a small smile. "When I first became a Keeper, I thought magic could fix anything. In theory, there could be magic strong enough to stop an army, but practically speaking, it's impossible. It would cost too much." She shook her head. "Magic always has a price."

Eliese fidgeted with a piece of bread. "Always?"

She waited for the Keeper to offer a quick nod, brushing off the question. But the woman looked at Eliese for a long, thoughtful moment.

"All the magic I've ever heard of does. What you call magic, the Keepers call energy. And it can be manipulated. For instance I can draw heat from the fire, and put it in the kettle." She paused a moment and the kettle over the fire began to hiss as the water inside of it boiled.

Eliese glanced at Marcus and Rellien and saw their eyes wide, staring at the boiling kettle.

Oriana winced and rubbed her hands together. "But moving the energy... hurts."

"I've heard that." Eliese pulled the boiling kettle off the fire and poured the water into the teapot, watching it steam in wonder. It should have taken at least three or four more minutes to boil the water. "And if you tried to do too much magic..."

"It would kill me." Oriana looked into the fire. "Heating the kettle causes a little discomfort. But doing something strong enough to stop an army? There's certainly no one alive who could wield that sort of power and survive."

"What we need," Rellien said, grinning, "is the Black Horn."

Eliese started at the mention of the horn. She'd thought of almost nothing else for days. She looked up at it, sitting still in its place on the mantle. Her dreams had been haunted by it and her waking hours spent wishing the legends about it were real. Twice, when she'd been alone in the great hall, she'd almost picked it up, remembering the way it had pulled at her so many years ago, the way it had hummed against her hand.

"Is that it?" Oriana said, peering up at the horn. "I've heard the legend of the horn."

"So have we," Marcus laughed. "But it turns out it's just a horn."

Eliese measured tea leaves into the first two cups.

"And not even a good horn," Rellien added. "If you want to find anything magic around here, you'd be better off looking in Eliese's tea."

Eliese's hand froze and she shot him a scowl. How dare he bring this up in front of a Keeper? Joking about it among the family was one thing, but this...

She braced for a laugh from Oriana, but the Keeper turned to her, interested.

"Is your tea magical?"

"No," Eliese said.

"Maybe," Rellien said at the same time. Next to him Marcus nodded.

"It's just tea!" Eliese said.

And it was just tea. Usually. Although sometimes she was almost positive it wasn't. But whatever went on during those times wasn't anything she could explain. Or even anything she was sure actually happened. It certainly wasn't something she wanted to claim in front of a Keeper who actually could do magic.

162

"Why do they think it's magical?" Oriana asked.

Eliese shot her brother and Marcus a black look. "Sometimes if my father is having trouble sleeping, my tea helps him. But it's just the tea."

Rellien shook his head. "It might be more than that. If there's something Eliese wants from you, or for you. If she brews you some tea and you drink it, well, the thing... sort of... happens."

"It's just coincidence," Eliese said. "Marcus, tell her."

Marcus grinned at her. "It might be coincidence. But if you were mad, there's no way I'd drink tea you poured for me."

Eliese glared at him and pointedly poured water into one of the cups. The tea leaves swirled, staining the water a thin green. She leaned across the table and placed it in front of him. "Like this?"

Marcus eyebrows raised and he leaned back away from the cup. "Did I mention how lovely you look today?"

There was a scuffle under the table and a thunk. Marcus grunted in pain and grabbed his leg, giving Rellien a black look.

"That's my sister," Rellien said, "and she does not look lovely."

Eliese raised one eyebrow. She poured water into the second cup, leaned over the table, and set it firmly in front of Rellien. Her brother looked at her for a moment, then slid the cup away with one finger. "I mean, you are a vision. And I'm not thirsty."

"It's just tea." Eliese laughed, turning back to Oriana. "Would you like some?"

The Keeper studied Eliese for a long moment. She glanced back at the men, neither of whom had taken a drink. "Your mother was from a foreign land, was she not? I have heard that you take after her."

Eliese nodded and pushed her thick black hair over her shoulder, self-consciously. "My father met her on a island in the Southern Sea and she came back as his wife. She died when Rellien and I were born, but the people of Stone Gap say that they'd never seen a man so smitten as my father, that my mother bewitched him. But everyone agrees they were happy." Eliese paused. "She became a sort of... talisman to the keep. They would come to her to be blessed. She always did what she could to help him in their troubles and the people said her touch was charmed. But she never claimed it was magic."

Oriana looked at the teapot for a long moment, then met Eliese's gaze. "Do you think you brew magic tea?"

There was no mockery in the question, and its sincerity caught Eliese off guard. The honesty of the question made her feel... anchored. Made whatever it was within herself feel more real.

"I don't know. I know when I want something..." She looked at the Keeper, trying to put it into words. How could she explain the... whatever it was that she could find sometimes, deep within herself. The hidden well that she could dip into and splash out just the tiniest bit, somehow infuse it into the tea. "'Want' isn't a strong enough word. When I'm *desperate* for something while I brew tea...sometimes it happens." She paused, thinking about how mundane the results always were. "Although it's never anything that can't be explained another way.

"I love my father, and... sometimes I think he just feels that. And it calms him."

Oriana smiled. "It's astonishing how often love and magic are mistaken for each other." She considered Eliese for a moment. "Does it tire you? Or hurt you to brew it?"

Eliese shook her head. "It doesn't hurt."

"But she sleeps like the dead that night," Rellien said. "If she sleeps past dawn we know she's been up brewin'."

Eliese pressed her lips together, but said nothing. It was true. When it worked, when she could find that deep place inside of her, those nights she could barely get up to bed before falling asleep. She searched the Keeper's face for something, some sign of what she was thinking. It sounded stupid saying it out loud. "But it's not actually magic. It's just tea."

Oriana considered her for another long moment. "Brew me some."

Eliese laughed. "It won't work. I don't want anything from you."

"Nothing at all?"

Of course there was something. The worry that had gnawed at her for a fortnight shoved its way to the surface. This was a Keeper. Here. In Stone Gap.

Eliese set the teapot down and took Oriana's cup. She picked out some tea leaves and set them gently in the bottom of the cup. Then she let her worry rise, let the fear that she'd been carrying lift up to the surface, opening something up. And there it was, the deep pool filled with yearning and want. She tipped the teapot over the cup and poured out the hot water, adding to it her longing, dripping it out in drops of fierce desire.

"I want the men of the keep to be safe," she whispered, handing Oriana the cup.

Oriana took the cup and held it before her face, looking into it for a long moment before taking a drink. She closed her eyes, sitting very still. Eliese watched her, barely breathing.

"Do you not wish for your own safety?" Oriana asked, finally looking up.

Eliese let out a short laugh. "I am always safe behind these walls." She shot another glare at her brother and Marcus. "We could all stay safe behind these walls. It is those who would leave to fight that need to worry."

"The tea is delicious." Oriana took another drink. "And I have no idea if it is magical. I feel... something. But it may all be because I'm looking to."

Eliese nodded. "That is what I tell my father." *And myself.* "It's just tea."

"Hmmm," Oriana said noncommittally. "Perhaps." She glanced up at the mantle. "Would you mind if I looked at the horn?"

The foggy day left the room gloomy, and on the mantle the black ram's horn sat like a curl of blackness, darker than the shadows. Eliese reached up, her hand hesitating only a moment before picking it up. It felt like nothing other than a hollow horn. When she handed it to Oriana, the woman's hands looked thin and pale against it.

"Tell me the legend as you know it," Oriana said quietly, turning the horn over in her hands.

"When the masons were building this keep," Eliese gestured to the walls around her, "before they had completed the outer wall, the Wildmen of the west came with their vicious war bands. With no protection from the approaching death, the people fled. The last to leave were a mason named Kellen and his younger brother Tann, whose legs were weak.

"Before the two could leave, Kellen was bitten by a rock snake. Kellen wouldn't survive the journey home and Tann didn't have the strength to flee on his own. The brothers knew they were doomed. But an old healer woman appeared as if by magic. She closed herself in a room with Kellen. When she emerged, Kellen had died and she held this Black Horn.

"'Your brother's final gift,' she said, handing the horn to Tann. 'His strength for you when you need it.' Then the woman disappeared.

"Tann got himself to the front of the keep. Below the bands of the Wildmen were winding closer along the bottom of the gorge like a stream of poison water.

"He lifted the horn to his lips, and blew with all his grief and fear and fury." Eliese paused. "And an army arose from the very rocks of the gorge. An army of warriors with Kellen's face, indestructible as stone. They swept down on the Wildmen and crushed them."

Oriana raised an eyebrow. "That would be handy about now." She ran her hands over the black ridges, then closed her eyes and bowed her head over it. Eliese watched for something. Anything. The Black Horn lay still and lifeless in the woman's hands.

Oriana looked up, her brow knit. "It holds no power," she said finally.

Eliese felt something within her sink.

"It holds no ability to make a horn call either," Marcus said. "It's the worst horn I've ever heard."

Oriana smiled. "I didn't mean it didn't have the ability to hold power, just that it's empty of power right now. Or it was, until I put some into it." She looked at the horn for a long moment. "It is holding that. It has an echo. A memory of... purpose." She shook her head. "But it's empty. And the emptiness feels very, very old.

"If it did once raise an army from the rocks, it doesn't have that power to any longer."

"Can you fill it?" Eliese asks quietly.

Oriana shook her head. "The amount of power this can hold is vast. Far more than I could supply." She looked at Eliese sympathetically. "If I were to try to fill it, it would kill me. And even then, I don't think it would raise an army. It's empty of more than just energy. It would need a spell to use that energy and turn stones into an army. Honestly, I don't even know if that's possible. If it were filled, it would just be a horn, holding a lot of power. And doing nothing else."

She stood and handed the horn back to Eliese. "But don't lose hope. There may not be armies of stone coming to your aid, but there is an army of men. More than enough to hold the Gap against any size army that Noreth can bring."

Marcus and Rellien rose too and walked with the Keeper toward the door while Eliese put the Black Horn back on the mantle. It was so light she could have lifted it with a finger.

"I will send a raven to the army, urging them to hurry." Oriana paused at the door. "And I can't fail."

Eliese turned to find the Keeper smiling warmly at her.

"You made me tea and wished for me to keep your family safe. How can I do otherwise?"

Eliese forced a small smile. The others left and she sank back down into her chair. The Black Horn sat on the mantle looking smaller and less black than it ever had. The worry that had taken up residence in her gut flared to life like a fire, burning her stomach.

She set some leaves into her own cup, picked up the teapot, and paused for a moment.

"I want my family safe," she whispered. The longing rushed through her, filling her chest like a surge of water rising from that deep, primal place. "I want my home safe. I want no enemy to come near."

She tilted the pot and the water poured into her cup, a smooth river catching the silver, foggy light from the window. Dipping into the well of emotion within her, she added her longing to the water. She set the pot down and picked up the cup. Her hand shook, sending ripples across the surface. She closed her eyes and took a drink.

The teapot had gone cold and a rush of tepid water flooded her mouth. It was so weak it tasted like tainted water instead of tea. Thin but sharp, and it cut through her mouth and sank down into her, slicing through any small hope that had grown.

Anger at the approaching army and the slow reinforcements and the useless tea surged up like a burning flood.

Eliese took the cup and hurled it into the fire.

The Offer

The evening dragged on interminably. The tea and the food had been cleared away, but Eliese couldn't bring herself to go up to her room. It felt too distant and lonely. She wanted to be here, in the heart of the keep, with the quiet bustle of activity always within earshot. Sitting in one of the tall chairs near the hearth, she stared into the fire, willing herself to think of anything besides the approaching army.

Marcus appeared after a while, dropping down into a chair next to her and stretching his feet out toward the fire. She waited for him to speak, to say something that would make her smile, but he stayed silent.

For a long stretch the only sound in the room was the cracking of the fire. Eliese's thoughts tumbled around each other. Fear of the fighting that was drawing ever closer to her home, thoughts of Marcus, her brother, her father lying dead on the rocky floor of the gorge, Noreth's army flowing past Stone Gap unhindered. Flashes of memory of Rellien and Marcus as children, grinning, laughing, running off to do something reckless.

She closed her eyes and took deep breath, trying to control the dread that was rising in her.

There was a rustle and Marcus's hand closed over hers. Her eyes snapped open and she found him staring up onto the mantle, his hand gripping hers tightly.

"It's a shame the horn doesn't work," he said.

His hand felt warm around hers and she hoped he couldn't feel her terror. Eliese followed his gaze up to the mantle. The Black Horn sat crooked on its stand where she'd put it earlier. It looked off-balance, precarious.

"Yes it is."

Silence fell between them again

"When the fighting comes," he began.

Eliese squeezed his hand. "Please don't," she whispered. "I can't bear to think about it."

"Next year," he began again, glancing at her for just a heartbeat before looking back at the fire, "when the position of watch captain opens, I had planned on asking your father for it."

Eliese turned toward him, the coming battle momentarily forgotten. "That's a brilliant idea! You should be watch captain. The men already follow you. There's no better choice in the keep."

He gave her a tight smile. "I've been trying. I've been joining Rellien in his strategy lessons and when Rellien is captain of the keep, I think I could help him…"

Eliese shifted in her chair, resolutely shoving aside the voice that told her that it was foolish to discuss any future past the next few days. She felt a surge of happiness at the idea of Marcus getting a position of such regard. "My brother will need you," she said. "He's so focused on what could be that he loses sight of what actually is. You've always brought him back down to earth."

Marcus shifted in his chair, keeping his focus on their clasped hands. "Yes, I want to help your brother. And help the keep. But..." He glanced up at her. "...it's also the only position in the keep that your father might approve of as a possible match for his daughter."

Something breathtaking and vaguely painful clamped down in Eliese's chest and she opened her mouth to say something, but Marcus hurried on.

"I know this isn't the right time to say this, and I don't need you to tell me what you think of the idea, I just—Noreth will be here in two days and I don't know if I'll—" He clenched his mouth shut for a moment. "I just wanted to make sure you knew."

The tangle of emotions in Eliese was too much to decipher, but underneath it all ran a deep rightness. Marcus's face had never looked so frightened. She reached over until she held his hand in both of hers.

"Please still be here in a year," she whispered. "Promise me you'll tell me this again in a year."

He opened his mouth to say something when footsteps rang out from the hallway.

"Marcus!" Rellien's voice called out.

With a last squeeze of Eliese's hand, Marcus stood and walked toward the door. Rellien burst into the great hall.

"My father's called a council. One of our scouts has returned. Noreth will be here by dawn."

THE COUNCIL

"He'll be here at dawn?" Eliese rose out of her chair as her panic flared. "How could he possibly be here this quickly?"

"He must have pushed his troops as fast as they could go while the fog held. It's probable he knows that our reinforcements aren't here yet."

Eliese took a step toward him. "What are we going to do?"

169

"Father's considering what terms to offer Noreth."

"Terms?" Her voice sounded shrill. She looked at Marcus, but found his face unreadable. "Noreth will never agree to terms. He wants himself set up as king. Nothing else we offer him will be enough. He doesn't want terms, he wants us dead."

"No one expects him to agree to them, El," Rellien said tiredly, rubbing his hands across his face. "But maybe it will give us a little time before we need to actually face him."

Eliese's mind crashed up against the idea like a wave on an immovable cliff. "You can't face him before we have reinforcements. The garrison couldn't hold the pass against an army of Wildmen, even for an hour. You'd be slaughtered."

"Thanks for the vote of confidence," Rellien said dryly. "You know we can't sit here and do nothing. If Noreth gets past the keep he'll be on the plains and a battle there will be a massacre for both sides." He gave a heavy sigh. "Everyone but you has already accepted that this was coming."

"Please don't do this," she grabbed at his arm. "There must be something else."

He leaned forward and kissed her on the forehead. "There's no time for other options." He disengaged her hand from his sleeve. "Marcus, the council is starting." Without another glance at her, he strode out of the room.

Eliese followed after them, straight into the council room.

Her father Captain Joran, Keeper Oriana, and several others were bent over a map, discussing things quietly. When Joran caught sight of her, his brow creased. She wasn't officially part of the council, but she crossed her arms and raised her chin. With a disapproving frown, Joran turned back to the map. But he didn't tell her to leave. She grabbed a chair between Marcus and Rellien.

"We have multiple confirmations now," Captain Joran said to the room. "Noreth will reach the gorge during the night. He must have pushed his troops hard to get here so quickly, so they will be tired. But if he did that, we must assume he knows that our reinforcements aren't here yet.

"We'll parley to offer terms." Joran looked around the room. "But unless someone can come up with terms that Noreth would actually accept, I don't think we can hope to put off the battle for more than a few hours.

"The reinforcements won't be here before late tomorrow night. And even that might be optimistic." Joran ran his hands through his hair. "So if anyone has ideas of anything we can offer Noreth that he'd at least be willing to consider, or any ideas how a battalion of sixty men can hold the pass against an army of ten thousand, I would love to hear it."

The council offered half-hearted ideas, but there was nothing that a small keep in a rocky gorge had to offer a man who wanted nothing more than conquest.

Eliese looked around the room, her heat sinking. There was nothing they could do. All these men were going to be killed in a doomed effort to hold the pass.

Beside her, Marcus's hand sat on his leg, his knee bouncing nervously. She thought of how it had felt, holding her own. How the idea of marrying him, of the future they could have had felt so full and good and right.

She felt a surge of warmth at the thought that he'd planned so much to marry her. It was an odd feeling, this realization that she had something, that she *was* something that someone would value that much.

And Noreth wanted to take it all, not because he hated her, just because she and her world stood in his way.

If only she had something Noreth would value that much.

The answer sprang into her mind and clamped around her heart. For a moment she couldn't breath. She put her hands in her lap and clasped them together so no one could see them trembling.

It was the only way. But Noreth was a horrible, vicious man. The stories of the things he'd done to people...

She looked at her hands, clenched together. What she wanted was Marcus's hand back around hers. She wanted something to keep everything she loved safe. But what if that something was her?

This was the way to stop Noreth, and no one could offer it but her. She took a deep breath and prayed that her voice wouldn't shake. At the next lull in the conversation, she leaned forward.

"Offer me."

The room went silent and every face turned toward her.

"Noreth is looking for a wife," she continued. "He thinks it will give him a legitimate shot at the throne. Offer me. We're a noble family, the King is a cousin--"

"No," both Rellien and Markus said flatly.

Her father's face darkened. "Absolutely not."

"It's an offer he would at least consider," Eliese pointed out, her heart pounding both from fear of the idea, and from anger at being dismissed. "The best offer that anyone in this room has suggested."

"It is," Joran answered.

"It might actually buy us some time—" Eliese stopped short at her father's unexpected agreement.

"And if we'd tried sooner it might have even worked." He looked at Eliese and smiled sadly. "Not that I ever would have let that man near you. But it doesn't matter any longer. We've also received word that Noreth has agreed to a marriage with Lady Sielan."

The room sat silent for a breath, in shock before it erupted in talk. Lady Sielan was devious, constantly vying for power. She was also one of the closer cousins to the king.

"Peace," Captain Joran said, and the room quieted reluctantly.

"But if he's allied with her," Eliese said, a spark of hope flaring, "won't he call off his attack? He can't invade a country he's trying to ally with."

Her father glanced over at Keeper Oriana.

She shook her head. "I don't believe he'll call off the attack. He has no reason to. The country is in such disarray at the moment that it might splinter into duchies at the slightest pressure. Noreth isn't a man to shy away from such an opportunity. If his invasion succeeds, he'll gain a great deal of power. If not, he'll cash in on his alliance with Lady Sielan. If his troops strengthen her own, there isn't much in Queensland that could stop them. Both he and Lady Sielan are clever and ambitious enough to see an opportunity like this and seize it." She looked around the room. "I don't see any way to stop the attack now."

Eliese shrank back in her chair. Marcus sat stiffly beside her and Rellien dropped his head down into his hands. The room was silent until Captain Joran cleared his throat.

"Well, then, if there is a fight coming, let us plan our part."

Someone spread a map of the gorge out across the table and the men stood to look at it. Eliese hesitated for a moment, but she couldn't sit there and listen to them plan their deaths. She slipped out of her chair and fled from the room.

AN ARMY OF STONE

Eliese had meant to go to her room, but she found herself instead in the great hall, sinking back into her chair by the fire. The world outside had fallen into darkness and the corners of the hall were full of shadows.

A wave of exhaustion swept over her and she leaned back in the chair, her body feeling too heavy to move. A small laugh escaped her when she realized she'd brewed tea twice today—once for Oriana and once for herself. The fire burned lower and the shadows slipped closer. Feeling cold and small, Eliese closed her eyes.

When she opened them again, the fire had burned down into dark coals breathing out only occasional deep red light. She sat up straight, looking out the window, her heart terrified that she'd see the light of dawn creeping across the sky. But the world still lay in blackness.

She sank back, covering her face with shaking hands. She had to stop it. If the men of the keep went out to hold the road, Noreth's army would ride through them like grass. Fear coursed through her, filling her stomach with a roiling mass of dread. She shoved herself out of the chair, pacing back and forth before the coals.

There had to be *something* that could be done. Something to stop the army. She wanted to transform into a dragon and attack. She wanted to wipe the army away with a great wind. Tear up a mountain and throw it into their path.

Turning back toward the mantle, her gaze caught on the spiral of darkness of the Black Horn. She strode over to it and snatched it off the mantle. Her fingers wrapped around it and the horn felt rough and cold against her skin.

It didn't matter that it was useless. It didn't matter that the Horn wasn't real. She had dreamed of the powers it held for years, and the hope was too ingrained in her to do anything else.

She raised it to her lips and blew.

A long, rich note rang out of the horn, thrumming against Eliese's hands and filling the room with a wave of sound. Even the stones beneath her feet vibrated.

Eliese yanked the horn away from her mouth and stared at it.

She lifted it again and blew. This time the note was thinner. A third blow made barely any noise at all.

Eliese stared at the horn for a long moment, her mind racing.

It was Keeper Oriana. She'd put some magic, some energy into the horn.

Eliese closed her eyes and focused her mind on the horn. For a long moment it felt thin and still and lifeless in her hands. Until it felt like more. There was a depth to it, a hollowness. She breathed out, drawing from the pool inside her, spilling it out like she did with the tea.

Instead of dipping into it she plunged in, scooping the longing out in a great splash.

Her hand began to burn, then sear and she dropped the horn onto the chair, cradling her hand against her chest. Across her palm, wide red blisters rose. Wincing, she picked the horn back up and brought it to her lips. Taking a deep breath, she blew and a wavering, low note rang out from it. Not as loud as the first had been. But she'd done it! She had added power to the horn!

Eliese looked from her palm to the horn. Inside her the pool of longing swelled and surged. She felt exhilarated and exhausted. And her hand stung with pain.

Oriana. She needed Oriana. Eliese took a step toward the door, hope bursting open in her chest. The Keeper could put power into it. More than before. And then the horn would...

Eliese paused. It would do what? The stones around the room hadn't been transformed into an army. The horn had done nothing but blow like a horn. Granted, if a little magic made it that loud, a lot of magic might make it deafening. But Noreth wasn't going to be scared off by a loud noise.

The idea snagged in her mind. A loud noise. The war cries of two young boys had started a rockslide in the gorge. Maybe a deafening horn could do something more. Maybe she could throw a mountain in Noreth's path. She ran toward the door. How many hours until dawn? She'd need at least two. There had to be at least two.

Eliese ran through the keep. The council room was empty and dark, her father's study the same. She ran outside and found the walls lined with men and torches. The sky above twinkled with more stars than seemed possible, and the eastern sky was still black.

Eliese ran up the stairs to the top of the wall, past the watchmen. Through breaks in the parapet she could see the blackness of the gorge. If there was an army there, it was hidden by the shadows.

Halfway around the wall she found Marcus and grabbed his arm. "Keeper Oriana, where is she?"

Marcus looked at her in surprise. "Gone."

Eliese stared at him, her mind trying to wrap itself around the word.

"She left from the council, hoping she could get the reinforcements to send troops faster. She's been gone for hours."

Eliese sank back against the wall. Oriana couldn't be gone. She needed to fill the horn.

"What's wrong, Eliese?"

Eliese explained how Oriana's power had fixed the horn, the words spilling out of her mouth. When she finished, his brow wrinkled and he shook his head. "I don't know, El. The watch blows horns all the time in the gorge and there's never rockslides."

"They never stand where we did," she said. "It's the narrowest, steepest part of the gorge. It echoes and…"

Marcus's face was troubled. "Eliese, I know you've always had a…fascination for that horn, but…"

"You didn't hear it," she insisted. "It's more than a horn."

He looked at her for a long minute. "I believe you," he said finally. "But Oriana is gone. There's no one to put any…whatever into it."

Eliese shifted her grip on the horn and pain lanced across the blisters on her hand. Her hand tightened on it for a moment. "Maybe there is," she said quietly. She told him about putting her own power in.

Marcus's face grew more astonished the more she talked.

"You did it?" he asked.

"Not as loud as she did, and it really hurt." She held out her palm to him. "I guess you are right about my tea."

Marcus held her hand out toward the torchlight and winced. "If a little bit hurt this much, how are you going to put enough in to make it really loud?"

Eliese's will faltered for a moment. Even what Oriana had put in wouldn't be loud enough. The Keeper's words came back to her mind. *If I were to try to fill it, it would kill me.*

But maybe she wouldn't have to fill it. Just put some power in. It would hurt, of course, but she could stop before it killed her.

She needed to go. Turning to Marcus she grabbed his hand. "When do the men go out to fight?"

"Your father plans to take our position in the pass at dawn." His eyes were troubled watching her.

"I can't bear the thought of you all going out," she said. "I can't bear the idea of not knowing what is happening to you."

"Eliese—" he began.

She shook her head. "If I had tea I'd brew it and wish we could know each other were safe. Once we drank it, we'd know if—if anything happened to either of us."

But Oriana had said the magic was in her, not in the tea. Eliese couldn't walk off this wall and not know.

She pulled Marcus's head down until his forehead leaned against hers. "I want to know that you're safe," she whispered, the longing for it rushing up and spilling out of her, flowing into him. "I want us to know that each other are safe."

Without the tea, the desire flowed more freely. She took a deep breath and in her chest she could feel it—she could feel that right now he was safe. Troubled, but safe.

"Can you feel it?" she asked.

He nodded slowly, watching her with a mixture of awe and uncertainty.

She hesitated just a moment before stretching up and kissing him on the cheek. His skin felt warm and he leaned into her. She wanted to stay here forever.

But her fingers were wrapped around the Black Horn and the troops clanked and rustled nearby, preparing for the dawn. She pushed herself away from him.

He looked down at her, his eyes buoyant and fierce, and grinned. "I like how it works when there's no tea."

"I do too," she whispered.

Then, before she lost all courage, she turned and ran.

THE BLACK HORN

Eliese scrambled up onto the windowsill of the back watch tower. This side of the keep was the farthest from the road and it pressed up against the steep cliff. Down into the gorge was a sharp drop, and the top of the cliffs still towered high over her head, so it was inaccessible from above and below. But here the thin goat trail wound along the rock face, scratched into the escarpment.

All of the guards were up at the top of the tower, so no one stopped Eliese as she scrambled through the window. It was a long drop to the ground, but she dropped quickly, before she had time to be scared. She hit the ground hard and the horn cracked against the stones of the keep. Her breath caught at the thought of it breaking. There was only a thin sliver of a moon hanging low in the eastern sky so she couldn't see the horn well, but she ran her fingers over the spiraled horn and it felt undamaged.

The trail scratched out ahead of her, barely visible, but the bottom of the gorge was in shadows. Carefully she began down the path. In the steepest places she leaned on the cliff, trying not to think about the drop off next to her feet. Last time she'd carried the horn here she'd imagined herself transformed into one of the battle maidens of old. But she was no such thing. She was just herself. No different than she'd ever been. As common as everyone else and terribly small in the face of the wide world.

We might not be enough, Marcus had said. *But we have to try.*

She focused on the feeling in her chest of Marcus. He was safe, she was sure of it. But also frightened.

Maybe this is how every brave person felt. Inadequate, but trying anyway.

It felt like hours before she caught sight of the huge boulder they'd dubbed Lookout Rock as children. Her eyes stung from dust and her palms were raw from the rocks when she clambered onto it. She was so tired that if she laid down, she'd fall asleep.

The eastern sky had lightened from black to blue, washing out the stars. She could just make out the outline of the keep. The biting smell of smoke wafted up, lifted high above the ground by a careless breeze. She stepped to the edge of the boulder and looked down. In the pre-dawn light she could finally see the floor of the gorge.

Hordes of Wildmen filled the base of the canyon. Below her, straight down the sheer face, orders rang out and the clumps of men began to shift, organizing themselves into loose lines.

Eliese shrank back from the edge and slipped the horn out of the sling. The sky had bleached to a pale yellow. It was minutes from dawn. Small figures moved along the top of the keep wall, but her father and his men hadn't emerged yet.

She thought of Marcus, preparing with the others to fight and knew deep in her gut that he was safe. For now.

In the pale light the horn looked thinner, less substantial than ever. It looked as though it couldn't hold a cup of water, never mind a well of magic. She held it in trembling hands. The world was lifeless and empty around her, made of nothing but thin morning light.

Closing her eyes, she reached into herself, searching for the pool.

And felt nothing.

Her heart began to pound and her hands felt slippery on the horn. She took a deep breath and focused on her longing.

"I want the keep to be safe," she whispered. And with those words, the flood gates opened. The pool within her surged up, pouring out in a river. Her hands on the horn began to sting, then burn and she almost stopped. But then she pictured the men of the keep, standing ready to sacrifice their own lives to stop the enemy. She gripped the horn harder and dropped to her knees, willing more and more power into it.

Pain seared through her hands and up her arms. She could feel the pool inside her emptying. But the horn wasn't full yet. And then it wasn't just the pool flowing out of her, it was something more intrinsic. An energy that came from her muscles, her bones, her mind. With a cry she dropped the horn, cutting off the horn before it pulled so much out of her she wouldn't even be able to blow it.

When the rush of power had stopped, blood dripped from her palms. She curled forward, crushed by exhaustion and pain. Her body pressed down heavily against the rock. With a monstrous effort, she cracked her eyes open.

A sliver of the sun crested the horizon, lighting the stones around her with deep, rust-red.

Below, the army began to creep forward, and out of the corner of her eye she caught some movement. The gates of Stone Gap cracked open.

The thought of her father and Rellien and Marcus and the men propelled her to her feet.

With fear rising to choke her, Eliese heaved the horn up to her lips and filled it with her anguish and fury. She willed the gorge to fall, willed the rocks to collapse. The note began hollow and haunted. But then it grew, sharp and clear. It cut through the air and her desire sliced through the morning with it. She blew again, a wild blast fierce and free. It echoed off the stone walls of the gorge, crashing against itself. The echoes slammed into each other, swelling rather than fading away until the very earth shook.

The approaching army paused.

And the rock face shifted.

In a breath Eliese crashed to her knees on a promontory, jutting out into a rushing sea of rock. The rock shook and she peered over the edge. The army below scattered and began to run, crashing into each other, crying out as the rocks surged down, filling the gorge between them and the keep, crushing the front lines.

All around her, boulders and stones crashed through a sea of smaller rocks, tumbling down the slope. Rocks raced down the slope above her, smashing into each other before launching out into the gorge. She clawed her way to the cliff wall, as far as she could get from the edge, fighting against the falling rocks and the crushing exhaustion. She curled into a ball, wrapping her arms over her head.

Rocks pelted her from above and beneath her body the boulder groaned and shook. Her hands and arms were on fire with pain, and everything inside of her felt empty. Hollow.

She was terrified for a moment of the pain she knew was coming. When she dared to peek up above her, it was nothing but a waterfall of falling rocks. More and more came until the entire world was a rush of stone, falling to crush her.

Darkness crept in from the corners of her view and she gave in to the merciful exhaustion as everything went black.

To: The Shield and all the Keepers at the Stronghold
From: Keeper Oriana at Stone Gap

Enclosed is the official record of the events from the last day at Stone Gap. They are momentous for the country and fascinating in their own right. Noreth and the other warlords rode with the advanced guard and all were crushed. The Wildmen are in disarray and leaderless, fleeing back into the wilds. With Noreth dead, perhaps the next leader will be more inclined toward peace.

But in a personal note, I would like to apologize for two misjudgments I made.

The first involves the Black Horn.

I examined it myself before the battle. Eliese had brought it to me in the hopes of finding that it held some great magic that would protect the keep. Although it was ancient and strange, I could sense no power in it. I told her that even if it could be filled, it would be nothing more than a horn.

However, I heard the horn call from a great distance away, and there was... *something* in it, something more than a horn blast.

The legend of the horn claimed it could call forth an army of stone men, and that is essentially what it did. Whether that was coincidental or not, I do not know. If the horn has survived the rockslide, it should be examined more thoroughly.

The other thing I misjudged was Eliese herself. The folks in Stone Gap believed that she had magical skills. If she brewed someone tea, anything she desired while brewing would come to fruition. I think even she had a faltering belief that it was true.

I admit I doubted.

But she made me tea, and wished that I would keep the soldiers of Stone Gap safe. Which is what I intended to do by calling the reinforcements to hurry.

But just after I drank the tea, I also inspected the horn. I put energy into it, just to see if it would hold. It did. The horn seemed almost hungry for it. It was just a little bit of energy and I'd almost forgotten about it. But that power let Eliese know what the horn was capable of. And so it turns out I did help Eliese keep the Gap safe after all.

I do not know what happened to Eliese, but I cannot imagine she survived. Her father sighted her just before she blew the horn, standing on a rock in the center of the widest slide. But both sides of the canyon for two hundred paces has collapsed. The gorge is unrecognizable and utterly blocked.

And beyond the rock slide, the amount of power she must have poured into the horn to create such a sound—it's a wonder she survived long enough to blow it.

They mourn her in Stone Gap, even as they hail her as a hero. The locals have already written songs about Eliese and the Black Horn, of her magic and her sacrifice.

In truth, not everyone mourns. One man, a lieutenant Marcus, claims he knows she lives. He leads search parties incessantly, scouring the gorge for her. His confidence is unshakable and he insists Eliese "wanted him to know if she was safe."

I've been pondering what sort of spell a bond like that would entail and am having a hard time imagining one. He calls it magic. And it very well might be. But it may just be love.

Either way, I keep being tempted to believe him. After all, I misjudged Eliese before.

So I believe I will remain a few more days, just in case Marcus turns out to be right.

Your servant,
Oriana

About the Author

JA Andrews is a writer, wife, mother, and unemployed rocket scientist. She doesn't regret the rocket science degree, but finds it generally inapplicable in daily life. Except for the rare occurrence of her being able to definitively state, "That's not rocket science." She does, however, love the stars. She began writing stories and creating coloring books because these sorts of things need an outlet. And now good markers are a deductible business expense. She spends an inordinate amount of time at home, with her family, who she adores, and lives deep in the Rocky Mountains of Montana, where she can see more stars than she ever imagined. Her website is www.jaandrews.com.

THE ICE OF HEAVEN

A LITTLE MERMAID STORY

CORRIE GARRETT

The roof of my world is untouchable, a frozen skin that protects us, and yet also protects itself. Far before my fingertips can reach the pink ice, the aqua grows bitter cold and my body grows sluggish. I know my suspicion is beyond unlikely, but I believe something is coming through.

Strange shadows play over the surface, casting blue and even black shafts of unlight over my tail. Vibrations shake the aqua below the ice, and it's not the vibrations of meteoroids, whatever my sisters say. Besides, we are not turned towards the belt now, so where would the rocks be coming from?

I let myself sink down until I float in a pocket of warm aqua. A safe place to study the skin of the sky.

If the noise is not cracking ice or meteors, it is something else. The vibrations run and run and run. They grow so faint at times that they are only whispers of energy, but I swear they have never entirely stopped.

What kind of beast never sleeps for days at a time? I quiver. Perhaps ice is its food. Is that possible?

I'm not the only one drawn by the vibrations. A leviathan drifts toward me, but I am not worried. She is higher than I. Her great bulk and hot blood can withstand the cold at the base of the ice.

I've heard that a great leviathan once shattered the ice with its tail. The cracks ran halfway around the world, letting the aqua spill out in great sheets above. And the leviathan, for all its dumb curiosity, realized it had endangered all things. It plugged the great hole with its own body until the aqua froze and the skin of the sky was healed. They say the ice froze around him and you can still make out his shape in the bulbous mound.

This one casts me into complete shadow as she noses the pink ice. I can hear the slow, gentle beat of her great heart, and feel the current from each swash of her double fins. I can hear the gush as she opens her mouth and extends her ridged tongue to scrape along the bottom of the ice.

She can't break through... can she?

Normally I would not even wonder, but with something gnawing away at the top and this mother leviathan rasping like a fractive coral below... could it happen?

I push myself deeper, out of my warm spot. I will watch and listen, but from a little deeper.

The darkness down here is broken by a school of twinkling ripplefish. They are waking and the tiny pebbles glow to life in their skin. I can feel the faint hum of bioelectricity from each one. It perceptibly warms the aqua and I let them crowd around me as they also enjoy the faint warmth I bring.

We have thirty-seven words for warmth in our language, and one hundred and three for types of darkness. More, if you count the words that mean both a temperature and a quality of dark.

The ripplefish cloud and clump around my upper body, and again I hear the long, slow rasp of the mother's tongue.

Does she want what is up there? Does she know what is up there?

How could she? And yet the sea snakes know where the garuda's eggs will pop out of the steaming vents, while never having seen a garuda. We cannot figure it out, but we can follow the sea snakes.

Another scrape.

The heartbeat and breath of the leviathan dominate the aqua now, but I can still discern the faint hum from above. It might even be louder.

Should I alert the pod? Would they believe my suspicions anyway? And will I miss the most amazing confrontation ever documented in this circum if I go?

My tail coils and jerks in indecision and my long ears twitch to catch each detail.

Is it me or does the rasping sound higher-pitched? Is the ice thin enough to reverberate differently—like in the caves of the Tormented Sea?

I must see what comes through. My mother insists I should trust my instincts, so I will.

What she means by that warning, often conveyed as she presses my head to her chest, is that I ought to choose a companion. She fears I stare at the ice to the detriment of my future and my pod. But I am not trying to avoid my instincts. If I ever find someone who will stare at the ice with me, who will study the vents for weeks, who turns the heaviness in my arms to bubbles, I will not ignore it.

In the meantime, I need to know what is up there.

We are most likely the only inhabited planet in the galaxy... but likely does not mean certain. True, our planet is perfect for life in a way that almost defies imagination or accident. But could the Creator not have done the same elsewhere? He is not obligated to tell us, after all.

Of course, their world would need an icy crust, like ours, to block the harmful rays from the sun. It would need the perfect balance of aqua and aether to sustain a full ecosystem. An ecosystem that extends all the way to a dominant predator like the leviathans. Their energy, heat, and waste fuel the cycle that allowed intelligent life to arise here.

A planet can't be too close to the sun, of course, or the aqua would be destroyed, and you can't have life without it. It needs some direct light, though, or the pink ice would turn black and freeze all the way to the core until the plant cracked apart like a rotten egg.

A perfect world like ours, often protected but darting forth regularly into the light, is too precise to be accidental.

There are places where the ice is transparent as filtered aqua and our gazers can see the heavens. I have never been there, but I've met a few who have.

They found that another world has aqua, and they suspect microscopic life. But the planet has no atmospheric crust, and it directly orbits the sun. Most likely that would sterilize all but the hardiest, simplest cells.

And yet... there is something humming up there above the ice right now.

Humming so loud, in fact, that the leviathan pauses its licking to listen.

If there are others, and they discovered how to safely break through the skin of heaven, would they travel through the aether and share their knowledge?

A sudden jolt makes me recoil. It almost felt like a quake. Did the ice crack? There is no need to go for anyone now. My pod will have felt that. Perhaps others as well.

The leviathan is excited. Her heart is going faster, her respiration as well. The ice must have opened!

I want to see it. I want ever so dreadfully to see it... but the cold will kill me. I can't even reach the ice when it's unbroken, let alone if the cold of space is rushing in through a crack.

I can't see beyond the mother's great bulk and masking heat, but I have to assume...

Her heat!

With a snap of my tail, I surge upward. The leviathan is in such a heated hunt now, she will have warmed a significant area around herself. They don't usually pause for so long, or I would have realized before.

I aim for her round, bulbous belly, about a third of the way down, where she can't see me.

There are no more vibrations from above. No tug of escaping tide, as I'd always imagined would happen if the ice broke.

Perhaps I am wrong...

When I get to the underbelly of the leviathan, I find the globe of blood-warmed aqua around her is nearly twice my length. Plenty of room to skirt up and around her without risking a frozen stupor.

I whisk myself past her wrinkled underbelly and past the striated fibers that attach her side fins. The fins are still small and stubby, not done growing back since she came out of hibernation.

Now I am angling up and... yes! The ice is open.

The sky has a hole.

I know I will always count my life forwards and backwards from this moment.

The hole is only a tail length above the leviathan, and it is a strange shape. It is not a long crack or a rough puncture, but instead is square, like a perfectly grown salt crystal. Very few things are that shape.

It is larger than me, but still only a small fraction of the leviathan's size. The mother tilts her head to eye the strange opening, and extends her tongue again to feel the smooth edges.

The narrow channel between her bulk and the ice will be a dangerous swim. If she thrashes or rears up I could be crushed against the ice. Or worse, thrust out of the hole on a wave of aqua and left gasping and dying on the roof of the world.

Only... I have always longed to see the face of heaven. Someday I will swim to the clear ice observatory, but I suspect it will not satisfy my longing. I don't want to see through a glass, darkly, but face to face.

I hover near her side, eyeing the hole, the distance, and listening for all I'm worth. From this angle I cannot see through the hole, but if I get underneath, what will I see?

Who will I see?

It is silent up there now. Whatever has been humming for so many days has fallen silent now that the ice is open. Has the leviathan scared it away?

I do not believe that.

I must know.

With a flick of my tail, I surge into the danger zone. I will only have moments to look, but I will do it. I can't linger long, for even if the leviathan does not slam me into the ice, she may decide to eat me while she ponders.

A few seconds and I am there. I flip onto my back. I am a hairs-breadth from lying on the bulging head of the leviathan. The square opening yawns above me.

I see sky-darkness, as I have heard described. And yes, even the shifting, twinkling lights of stars, filtered only by a few feet of aqua!

The curve of something large and reddish-brown obscures part of the darkness—and I realize it is our Giant. The protective planet that guides our orb through the heavens like a shepherd.

My gills shudder and flap with wonder. I am lightheaded with awe. I barely notice the white and black blobs on the edge of the scene.

A blinding flash of light stabs my exposed eyes.

I recoil instinctively before the pain has even registered, slamming my head and back into the leviathan. Was that a punishment? Did the stars blind me?

I can't see anything. I twist sideways and flap away like an injured eel. The leviathan knows I am here now, I must move.

But still my eyes are useless, and my panic has disoriented me. Worse, the leviathan's muscles are tensing beneath me. A surge of aqua pushes me backwards—is she flapping her tail? Or sucking me in? Either way, I fight the current.

My long tail beats against the surging aqua, and my hands desperately clutch at the lumps on her back. If I stay right on her, she can't eat me. But then she bucks.

I tuck my head, but my back hits the ice above me. The cold burns each knob of my spine. What was I thinking?

When something sharp and hard clutches my tail, just below my dorsal fin, my heart nearly stops.

Oh, Creator, what is that? It cannot be the teeth of the leviathan, not right on top of her back. And that means...

I thrash for all I am worth. The end of my tail is no thicker than my arm. I can slip loose...

I can't.

I am inexorably drawn back towards the unnatural hole.

The leviathan is my anchor now, my safety. I clutch her as if she were my own mother. But my fingers are weak, their strength is nothing compared to the claw clamped on my abused tail.

I suck a deep breath of aqua, and another. If I cannot prevail, I won't be dragged up like a cringing little crab. I release my hold and throw myself at the claw.

I clutch the strange, metallic arm. I am almost upright when it pulls me out of the aqua and onto the roof of heaven.

Jack planted his boots firmly on the shaking ice as he twisted the control levers to extend the grapple arm into the water. His team had been digging through the ice for a hundred and fifty-six hours, over thirty shifts. If he lost the thing he'd seen...

It was their last location, after a year on Europa, and it had taken longer than they hoped. The ice in this area forced them to dig a series of terraces and ramps from which to work. Normally they would be at least forty feet above the water. Instead, on the lowest terrace, they were only five feet above sea level. Their temporary camp was set up on the third terrace, and the support crew was on the second terrace, holding Jack and his teammates' lifelines. Team 2 was ready to jerk them to safety if this ice-shelf cracked. Or if that whaleshark thing roiling the water below proved to be more intelligent than it seemed.

Jack twisted the second joystick to raise the grappling arm out of the water. They'd been documenting the huge whaleshark when something smaller darted into view. He'd thought at first it was some sort of snake or eel—long and skinny. But it had paused long enough for him to get a good look at it. Through the enhanced visor of his EVA suit, he'd seen something very like a face.

Cameras ringed the hole and filmed continuously. His team had also mounted large lights to illuminate the site. The lights used significantly more wattage than the cameras however, so they used them sporadically. Jack had been startled by the face in the water, but not too startled to ask Mi Sun to turn on the lights. He wanted at least one lit image of the thing.

Then one of the lights exploded. Perhaps its casing had been compromised by the thin atmosphere of Europa, or perhaps it had degraded during the trip. It wouldn't have been that big a deal, easily replaced, but it had startled the things in the water. The large animal began to thrash about and the little one slipped away.

At least, Jack thought it did as he blinked the bulb's after-image away. But then he saw the tip of its tail just beyond the lip of the hole. It was no easy thing to use the grapple while a huge monster lunged against the very ice he stood on. But Jack wanted that creature. There was a reason they let him have the controls during their last exploratory session. He could finesse the machinery like nobody else.

"Xen support, ready tank 3," Jack called out. "And give me a little slack on the line." He could feel his vest tightening. His counterpart was ready to jerk him away.

The extension arm rose dripping out of the water. A creature clung to it.

Mi Sun swore softly in Korean, something she was not prone to.

Jack swung the grapple to the tank. He couldn't let the thing die out of the water.

Xen support had activated the pumps, with hoses they'd already run to the hole, and the medium-size tank filled with sea water at the rate of forty gallons a second.

Jack released the claw just above the tank and the creature dove in. Truly, it raised its arms, lowered its head, and dove in.

The tank was only half full, but it was enough for the sea creature to be completely submerged.

The whaleshark was still near the hole. Jack could see its bumpy, purplish-gray back rippling past. Then that groping tongue came back. The whole moment was surreal. Was he really here, on a far-away moon, watching an alien monster swim beneath his feet? Had he really plucked a specimen from the ocean that looked... terrestrial?

A scratchy, metallic voice blasted out of his earpiece. "Point team, prepare to retreat to Terrace 2. Please confirm."

Jack confirmed on autopilot as he retracted the grappling arm to rest position. The support team would attach the safety cables that secured it while not in use. Mi Sun was unscrewing the broken light with the multitool in her suit glove. Leo sheathed the cutting blades that they'd used to break through the ice. A few minutes later, they ascended together to the second terrace, carefully stepping up the ice steps they'd cut to this level.

Jack's vest, attached to the lifeline, remained uncomfortably taut. The support team must be feeling a little jumpy and he couldn't say he blamed them. The whole team had hoped for such a sighting as they'd had today, with more than microbial creatures, but after months of trying, their expectations were low. No one had anticipated such a wild moment a few seconds after they'd cut through.

When his feet were safely on the second terrace and twenty feet of ice separated him from the ocean, Jack allowed himself to look at the sleek creature in the tank.

"It's a mermaid," Mi Sun stated. He was glad she'd said it first. Nobody would dare give her grief for it. It was exactly the word he'd been thinking, but he was embarrassed to say it out loud. They were scientists, for Musk's sake.

"No," one of the xenos said through the microphones, though he didn't sound convinced. "It's an unknown aquatic creature. Hereby to be known as Specimen R-4."

"Let's raise the heat on that tank," said another xeno. "There's already ice forming along the periphery and R-4 seems to be hugging the heater vents."

The xeno specialist used the heads-up display in his suit to increase the output from the radiant heaters in the base of the tank.

The mermaid—er, specimen—was curled around herself on the floor of the tank, with her tail pointed toward them.

The specialist stuttered. "That might be a defense mechanism, see how coiled it is? I—I should be recording this. Of course, I should. Open Log for new specimen." He began a voice recording. "Specimen R-4 seems aware of our presence and is orienting itself ventrally..." He continued making observations, but Jack tuned him out.

He'd caught a mermaid! Jack had always had a strong sense of wonder, of the majesty and infinite possibilities of life. He didn't know any astronaut who didn't start with something like that. It took powerful motivation to reach the upper tier of a scientific field and *then* devote the next two-to-five years to becoming an astronaut.

But all those years of study—when math and engineering and the all-but-divine procedures filled every waking hour—those years had coated his sense of wonder in layer after layer of obscuring grime.

When he saw the mermaid come out of the ocean, his faculty for mystery and fantasy exploded back to glorious life.

She had a face. A face. Two eyes, a pointed nose, a mouth with thin lips. Her round, smooth head seemed a bit small for the length of her long, snaky tail, but the longer he looked, the more perfect she seemed. Her ears were large and moved independently, like a horse's. One tilted toward the heaters, then toward the crowd of astronauts in front of her. The other lay against her head, only popping up when Mi Sun repeated incredulously, "Say what you will. That is a mermaid. And I need a drink."

"We're on the clock now," Jack reminded her. "We have six hours to return her to the ocean or else move her to a permanent tank."

The procedures were very clear. They couldn't keep a specimen in a temporary tank for longer than six hours. Too many risks and they weren't here to kill half the things they found. They had brought specimens back to their ship, none larger than his thumb. Some for dissection and further study, and others to bring back alive.

Anything they were not going to use went back within six hours. They'd hoped for something larger before they had to leave this site. When Leo had a few drinks, he admitted he still hoped for a primitive, diplodocus-like, aquatic predator.

The mermaid was unexpected, to say the least. The previous unmanned expeditions to Europa—Pernicus III and IV—had punched through the ice and sent back evidence of life, even of potentially large species, but this was unreal.

Her eyes darted from one to the other of them, and down the icy steps to the hole. She could probably only see the edge of it from this angle, but she knew where it was. Occasionally she looked up at the dark sky and Jupiter. Her arms relaxed slightly and the specialist started a whole new paragraph on her six digits, claws, and opposable thumb.

"Breathe," Leo said. "You're going to hyperventilate."

Jack took a deep breath, then realized Leo wasn't even talking to him. The specialist gulped a breath and kept on.

"We have to assume she's intelligent," Jack said. "We're all thinking that, right?"

A moment of tense silence fell. As a team, they'd had plenty of time to discuss their various views on the likelihood of intelligent alien life. Their opinions ranged from: "Definitely—somewhere," to, "Unlikely to matter."

None of them expected to find it here, in their own solar system. Out there, in the galaxy that they knew more about than most people—it didn't seem so crazy. But Europa was in their own backyard, so to speak.

One section of the procedures covered this possibility. It was shorter than the section on the possibility one of them turned into a psychopathic killer and sabotaged the ship.

"Can you hear me?" Jack said. He placed his gloved hand on the wall of the tank. He was not qualified to do this, but none of them really were. The xeno specialists were mainly botanists, microbial scientists, and one evolutionary macrobiologist.

The mermaid twitched an ear toward him, but otherwise gave no response. She looked at him and then gazed away at Jupiter again. Had she ever seen it before? Not through the ice.

Did she know what it was? What they were? Did she think at all?

Or was this a galactic practical joke, to put un-intelligent life in something so familiar and... and beautiful?

He qualified that thought as soon as he had it. He knew that he didn't understand this creature in the slightest. Any emotional response was the result of heightened emotions over a successful mission, a dangerous close call, and her remarkably human facial features.

But... the same way that he could look at a nebula or a Roman aqueduct and see nothing but beauty, he could call this creature beautiful.

"If she's intelligent, we have to put her back," Mi Sun said. "Right?"

The specialist laughed a trifle hysterically. "But will we ever see them again? This is the chance of a lifetime. We need to get the interior tank prepped. We need to get the whiteboard and the lights."

Jack's hand was still on the wall. The mermaid uncoiled herself. Her movements were fast and fluid. The dim fading sunlight reflected off the iridescent scales on her tail and back. Jack's childhood fascination with fantasy was flowing back to him. He'd supplanted those dreams with better, truer ones—or so he thought. Now he wondered if the earliest dreams had been the higher ones.

Jack kept his hand where it was as she swam close. Her nose almost touched the plastic as she studied his fingers. Her eyes were covered with a greenish film, but he could see dark pupils contracting beneath. Wonder. Fear.

"Perhaps they're nearsighted." Mi Sun put her own hand on the wall.

"Maybe." Jack's ability to think methodically was rapidly deserting him. The mermaid's gaze travelled to his arm and up to his visor and back again. Jack knew he couldn't read into her expressions, but she gave something very like a shrug and retreated to the warm bottom of the tank again.

Jack reminded himself to breathe. "She can't see us. She can't even see our eyes through our visors. If she saw our faces she might respond." He wanted nothing more than to take off his air-tight helmet and see her face to face. That was the height of stupidity. What was wrong with him? Was there some truth in the fables of sirens luring men into the waves?

The captain had been standing silently to the side of the group. It was his decision ultimately. If he decided to put her back now... Jack's gut clenched at the thought. But then, they would be leaving within seventy-two hours. What would happen if they *didn't* put her back?

The captain collected his thoughts. "Let's get Specimen R-4 to a permanent tank. We will temporarily assume that she—I mean, it—is of high intelligence and proceed with all caution. I will extend the specimen return clock twenty-four hours. At that time, if we can't make a unanimous decision, we will err on the side of caution and return her to the ocean."

Jack kept his hand on the tank as half the team began the trek up the icy stairs to the domicile at the top. Surely in twenty-four hours he would have a handle on the joyful madness that had seized him.

I press my chest against the warmth of the false floor, my face and arms too. It is heavenly warm now, though I was very afraid for a few moments that the harsh cold would send me into a lethargy. This heat is like the heat of a steam vent. After warming my front, I flip over to warm my back and tail. If those black and white manatee things—moving so fat and slowly around me—should choose to dump me out on the ice or grab me with that claw, I need enough body warmth to survive.

I do not think they will try to kill me. The suffocating aether surrounded me for less than three heartbeats before they put me into this strange, tiny ocean of aqua.

Now they are moving again—except for that one who stands with his flipper pressed against the warm ice. The ice is very strange. It is transparent, even clearer than they say the observatory is. It does not smell like any ice I know. I suspect it is something the manatees have cut and formed to build this cage, the way we cage the sea cows at times for their protection and our sustenance.

I focus on the creatures nearby. For their short, rotund bodies and slowness I call them sea cows or manatees, though they stumble upright on the dry roof of the sky. Perhaps they are not adapted to the aether after all. Their bulk would be better suited to the buoyancy of the aqua.

I am wiser than I was before. I realize these things are not the Creator or his helpers. They must indeed be the other people we have imagined. But they are slow, so very slow, and they do not have eyes to see and ears to hear. They make loud clacking noises and bright lights. None of these things make them unworthy, but they are certainly not gods.

I ignore them for now. If they take me out, I shall dive for the hole. If they leave, I shall jump out of this tank and flop my way down to the hole. I think I could make it before I froze from the icy breath of the heavens.

If they do not leave... well, I shall endeavor to face whatever may come with serenity as I wait for a chance to go home. In the meantime, I have the opportunity to study the heavens as no one of my people has ever done.

I study the sphere of our Giant. It ripples with beauty. Hundreds of colors, swirling in bands like the stripes of the shadefish. I have always pictured it solid and still, as the surface of our own dear orb—how my affection for home rises as I rest here above the crust! But the Giant is anything but solid. What makes the bands? Does the ice float free down there, on the uncovered currents of an unimaginable ocean? Or is it... my mind boggles. I am realizing how little we know.

Do they know these mysteries? I cannot reach the creatures through the dead ice cage to ask my questions. Would one of them get in here, so that I could talk to it? Would they dare? Would the aqua hurt them? It pinches my mind to imagine the possibility, but there is no denying that they are crawling around with no aqua in sight except mine.

But I need to touch them to talk. To see if they can talk.

My manatee begins clacking again. It waves a flipper upward, and I realize the claw is descending toward me. This time...it is holding something translucent and shapeless. I barely trace its outline before the claw is in the aqua and something is swooping around me. It is like the tentacle of a squid or the sack of jellyfish.

I am swished about this way and that and then I am lifted. With wonder, I realize I am in a moving bubble of aqua. The claw does not clamp me this time, but lifts my bubble out of the cage.

Then I am lifted higher and higher and my gills shut tight in fear. There is the hole—so tiny below me! Fathoms below me, and nothing between me and it but the aether of death. If I thought I was on the roof of heaven before, now I know better.

There are walls of ice all around me as I soar upward. There are roofs upon roofs.

My ears stretch painfully.

I ascend too rapidly.

Do they not know?

We cannot...

When I awake, I am in another of those flat, ice cages. I flip around looking for the sky or the Giant, anything that anchors me in this new place, but none of that is visible. I am in a large cave with many strange things around me. Five of the manatees stand nearby and clack loudly.

One of them—my manatee, I think—puts its flippers to its head and twists. Perhaps I should be shocked to see its head pop off, but this is all so strange, I have no capacity for horror.

Instead, I stare in fascination. It is not a manatee at all.

It is a person. The eyes are brown and round, the lips thick, the nose very wide—but definitely the face of a person. The head is too square, the ears shockingly flat. Then I look at the eyes again and I forget that it is all wrong.

Because it is all right.

These eyes would look at the ice for many days, I feel sure. They would want to know the secrets of the vents even more than I.

A ripple of laughter squirts out of my mouth. I would have to draw him away for times of rest. And I would. Because I would always long for his attention—for the focused look of wonder I see now.

Except... I jerk out of my dream. This is not a person who could be a companion. His face may fulfill my dreams in a way I never imagined, but his short, stubby body is useless. Even if the rest of his manatee body is a shell, whatever is within is not...normal. He is not a true person.

Perhaps the sadness is visible in my face, because he comes forward and puts his hand on the cage again. He has removed more of his shell. I can see his fingers now. Five short fingers with flat nails. They are different than mine, but strong, I can tell. I press my fingers to the ice and twitch my ears. He is not clacking now, but the other manatees are.

They begin removing their shells as well, and I see all manner of faces. They are strange and wonderful, but none of them are as perfect as my manatee.

What is he thinking? What do his uncovered eyes mean? He does not have the protective eyelid and it makes his eyes look vulnerable and sad.

I want to know what he is thinking, but that is impossible. I cannot touch him, and he cannot touch me.

The other manatees move about the cave, removing more and more of their shells. Without the bulk, I realize they are faster than I thought. And they are at home in the aether. It is incredible. They trundle about like crabs balanced on two legs.

It is warmer in here. They seem to like the warmth even more than I. In fact, now the dead ice of the cage is hotter than the aqua, almost burning hot to my fingertips.

Still my manatee stays beside me, and though it is hot for my hand and cold for his, we keep our hands together.

When I look only at his eyes, the cave fades away. Anything is possible. The garuda might come forth and dance with the leviathan. The shadefish might swim sideways. My young sisters might play in the nest of the shrike unhurt.

I knew the Creator was strange and unbound, but I am now humbled before the complexity of his creation. Who are these people, and why did he bring them here?

Jack kept his mouth shut as much as possible while the teams worked. He was afraid if he spoke he would spout poetry or insanity. The mermaid was looking at him now.

"That's uncanny," Leo said. "It's like she's staring you down."

"Just stay there," the specialist told Jack. "I'm recording everything. Clearly the specimen is copying you—possibly recognizes your features. I'm going to set up the portable x-ray. If she'll stay still like this, we can get some great shots. Then we'll move on."

Jack grunted. Her eyes were tragic. Was it because they'd taken her out of the ocean? He wanted to tell her that they would put her back soon. If that were true.

But she didn't give off a fearful sadness. It was as if she looked at him and her heart broke.

He pressed his lips even more tightly together as the x-ray machine whirred to life. Leo came and draped him in a lead apron. Still she looked in his eyes.

His fingers were numbed with cold but he couldn't think of moving them. He focused on her face and imprinted it in his mind. This was a moment no one on Earth could imagine, and Jack was having trouble imagining his life when it ended. Did all great discoverers feel like this? Did Galileo glue his eye to his newly invented telescope, afraid to go back to his humdrum life after his first look at the wonders of the universe?

If Jack's team knew how unhinged he felt, they would tie him in his bunk.

He answered the occasional comments and questions as normally as possible while they worked around him. But the whole time he felt he was really having a conversation with the mermaid.

She was intelligent. Not like a dolphin or an elephant, but like an angel or a star.

What a fine thought for an astronaut.

It seemed an eternity until everyone left the specimen dome of their temporary shelter. Jack didn't realize what he was waiting for until it happened. Until he was alone with her. It only happened because the next burst of messages from Earth—which had been delayed by a solar storm—finally arrived.

Jack wasted no time. He knew the video records were going. He knew anyone could come back at any moment. He didn't care.

He climbed the rungs attached to the cage and opened the hatch at the top. The water was cold, but not colder than the Polar Bear Plunge he'd done with his three sisters every year of high school.

The mermaid swam to the hatch as well. Jack didn't pause before putting his hand in the water. He wasn't surprised when she grasped it in her long, jointed fingers.

Only when she pressed his palm to her forehead, and he felt the force of her thoughts in his mind, did Jack surface from the wonder. Was he delusional? Was he having a psychotic break?

Then he squared his shoulders and plunged into the fantasy.

His hand is rough and hot against my forehead and my eyelids. Does my skin feel slick and strange to him? Do my thoughts? He doesn't jerk away.

He presses his fingers gently to my head, barely brushing my eyelids. I ought to clarify my thoughts to something very simple for him to understand—if that is even possible—but I cannot. My thoughts are a mixture of my past: my mother, my sisters, my pod; and this moment: his eyes, his face, and his unknown and mysterious past.

My people talk this way, through touch and thought. Those closest to me can understand any ill-expressed thought or half-toned emotion. Can he understand anything?

Many pictures crowd his thoughts. I've always considered my thoughts as a form of song, of sound, of tones, and clicks of joy. His thoughts are largely silent. Faces, explosions, colors I've never seen. And hands. Hands working, hands holding, hands learning tiny intricate motions and building huge machines. He understands the world through his hands. Perhaps that is why he put his hand in the aqua rather than any other part.

My eyes are in his thoughts—I see them. I picture his eyes and he seems to pause. Brown eyes and green.

But then the chaos is back. Between my noise and his visual churn there is a vast difference. It is not all incomprehensible, but it is not a conversation either. It's almost unbearable. I yearn to communicate, and each tiny glimmer of understanding builds my excitement. His frantic desire to understand stains all his thoughts. It's like salt on my tongue.

What language can I use to express what I feel? That I found something worthwhile, something I never thought I'd find. That I am sad to know it will never be mine.

Ah, that is a pattern he understands. He pictures ice, the thick ice that protects us and protects itself. Perhaps it would have been better if the ice could have protected me from him. Even if I get home again, how will I move past this moment? How will I be satisfied without the unbearable mystery of understanding?

Now he is picturing the ice turning green, a blue sky, more upright manatees—is it his world? There is no aqua—wait, yes, there is. He shows me an ocean. But there is no ice! It must be ever so hot.

He laughs and shivers, his fingers briefly flexing against my head. This is cold, his laugh says. The laugh is both a picture and a sound. I hear it distantly above the aqua. I laugh as well. Not in amusement, but in purest joy. This is discovery. This is... everything I want. The mystery of the ice. The mystery of the heavens. The mystery of thought—which I didn't know until now was a mystery. All wrapped up in one person.

But I want to know, too. He pictures the hole. A monstrous beast—the leviathan! Each thought that connects sends a thrill from the base of my head to the tip of my tail.

I sing a song of leviathans traveling. Of gentle hearts and flashing teeth. Of mothers, calves, and solitary fathers. Of warm blood, warm waste, warm meat—everything a leviathan is to us. I don't know if he understands my song.

His pictures flash alongside as he listens. A blue aqua ocean—so blue. Fat, floating leviathans... or something similar. I stroke the thought in my mind—longer, faster, bigger teeth, double fin.

Another noise comes from above the aqua, from his mouth. Does he think I can hear him?

I tentatively bring my face to the edge of the aqua. Only an inch separates me from the open aether.

Don't. His hand is large compared to his short body. He pushes on my head now. His fingertips reach from ear to ear as he tries to shove me further under.

But he has little leverage—this I can understand—and I have a strong tail. I push myself up until the tips of my ears extend from the water. It is hot, oh so hot, but I don't think it is hurting me. In fact, there is a little aqua in the aether, I can feel it. I raise the top of my bare head into the emptiness. The heat squeezes my ears and makes my eyes tingle.

I clamp my gills shut and raise my face out of the aqua.

He widens his brown eyes and his mouth opens. That is shock if I have ever seen it. Now he does look rather like the stupid sea cow. Oh, my manatee. How I love him already.

I grasp his hand, which has slipped away. It doesn't seem as hot, compared to the incredible heat around me. I want better communication than a hand, however.

It works best head to head, or head to heart. He is already leaning only inches from the aqua. It does not take much effort to put my hands on either side of his face, next to his strange little ears.

The skin is rougher on his face, like sandscales, and easy to grip. I pull him down and press my forehead to his own.

Be careful. Don't get hurt. The concern coming from him is as clear as my mother could have conveyed it. It doesn't matter that I don't know where he comes from or what he is—I know he is good.

Good. I see faces in his thoughts with glowing light. Faces with wings—wings! —called angels. I see my face.

I want to teach him the words he needs to know to say it properly. I want him to teach me the words I need to know. I duck back down to get a breath and come back up to him.

My head presses to his again. Now I can hear his voice clearly. I don't know what the sounds mean, but I could probably reproduce them if I had enough time to practice.

I don't have time. His silent pictures flash faster in desperation. Pictures of time too short and round shapes with ticking black hands and thunderous voices counting down to blast-off.

Why? I want to know. Stay.

Come, he says.

Come?

Jack's head pulsed with the sound of her thoughts. It was a beautiful maelstrom, like an outdoor concert under the stars, and the band was playing every song at once.

Her cold hands cooled his burning, chafed cheeks, and her nose nearly touched his own. He was leaning precariously off the top rung of the ladder, nearly headfirst in the tank. If he'd thought of it, he might have been afraid at how easy it would be for her to pull him under.

He didn't think of it.

This was a revelation people gave their lives for. This was why translators spent their lives among lost Amazonian tribes. This was why those marine biologists risked destroying their brains with neurotransmitters to communicate with dolphins. This kind of raw connection with a completely other being was the thing.

What did anyone really want out of owning a pet, making a friend, or even marrying except knowledge of the *other*?

Come.

She rocked her head against his. She didn't understand in full, but enough.

200

Jack heard the uncertain melody of her consideration and was shaken.

She would give up her whole world, possibly her life. Because he asked it.

No, no, no. He tried to take it back. Already, her presence had changed things. Word was going back to NASA. Decisions about future trips would be made. Submarines, linguists, scientists. And if she came with them...

"Jack! What the hell? I'm coming!" Leo's voice broke the concert to pieces.

She dropped her hands and fell back into the water with a ripple.

Unsteady, Jack teetered over the open hatch until his groping hand found a rivet.

His eyes were unfocused. It took precious seconds to fix on Leo's face, and by then more crew were flooding into the dome.

Jack looked back into the water, feeling empty and feverish.

Hands grasped the thick waistband of his EVA pants—did he still have those on? —and guided him down the ladder.

When his feet got to the ground, he closed his eyes.

Leo smacked his shoulder. "Why did you open the tank? Did it try to pull you in? What happened?"

"No. She didn't pull me in. She... talked to me."

He heard the specialists playing back the video. He saw the concern in Mi Sun and Leo's eyes. "I know I ought to explain—" Jack continued.

"Bloody right," the captain said. "You better start."

"I can't."

The questions fired at him like BBs and ricocheted off. His mind was not there. Was it like a drug, that kind of communication? Would he grow addicted?

Grow addicted? Heck, he was consumed by it and he'd only touched her for a few seconds.

They couldn't dump her back in the ocean. He would lose his mind if this was it.

They couldn't take her. She was a sentient person with a family(?) and a future.

A sharp prick in his arm startled Jack. Their first-line medic was doping him with something.

"Hey. I'm fine. I need to... " Need to what? Rethink my life?

"Jack. You've been standing stock still for thirty minutes. We need you to snap out of it. I've given you some oxycodone for stress."

Stress? Jack laughed. He felt distant from everything happening around him. Numbers and screens and procedures. He was in an adjacent world now. A world where an exquisite thing pressed her head to his and made songs. She swirled in the tank, her face always toward him.

"Jack!" A hand slapped him across the face now. Then it came back to feel his head. "Good grief. This is serious. He's freezing cold."

Their hands felt hot and rough on his face and neck. They pulled him, but he would not walk away. He could hear their whispers, but he didn't care. He had to stay. He would protect her. Translate. Mediate.

He could hear the shift of their heavy clothes and the canvas of the stretcher creaking as they unfolded it.

Another prick on his arm and he was pushed backward onto it, his muscles barely responding.

His feet and boots felt unbearably heavy.

His eyes couldn't focus on anything. Leo and somebody else carried him out of the specimen dome and into the domicile living space.

He kept hearing her songs.

I flick nervously from one end of the cage to another. They took him away. I wonder if another manatee will come to the hatch to talk.

I am torn. I want them to understand, but I don't want to touch any of them. The bright connection to my manatee was wonderful but painful. I feel weak and I don't want to plunge into any of their chaos-minds. Perhaps it weakened my manatee, too. Perhaps that is why they carried him away. What an odd, unnatural thing—to clutch someone and shuffle them away. Without aqua, everything is strange.

I am so tired.

I wait. The cave empties again. No, that is not quite right. One of the manatees has stretched itself on the floor of the cave like a rock. Does it think it's hiding?

I smile when my manatee finally returns.

His eyes are better than I remember. His nose less bulbous. His ears tiny but not so ill-shaped as I remember. The more I look at him, the more perfect he appears.

He steps over the manatee who is being a rock and comes back to the round opening in the cage. When it unseals, I am there.

He does not clack at me this time. He puts both hands in the aqua and I grip them tightly. They are not so hot and rough as I remember either.

Only a single layer of aqua separates our faces. I feel a moment of uncertainty as he moves his hands to feel my ears and cup my cheeks. My instinct is to talk again, to finish our conversation—if it could be described as that. Because it certainly needs to be finished. A precipitous sense of incompletion has hung over me since we broke apart.

But how can I trust my instincts now? What possible instincts could I even have for this impossible moment?

Like the great leviathan of legend, I sense I have broken a layer of protection I didn't even know was there. I touched him and cracked through it. No, it was before that. The danger was there from the first moment I swam to the hole and the manatees saw me and I saw them. I don't know exactly what the danger is, but that it exists—I know.

How dangerous a thing have I done? How do I plug the crack if I can't see it?

Is there a sacrifice I need to make? How? What?

In the end, I can only heed my mother's advice. I follow my instincts and rise to press my head against his.

And when I lay my fingers on either side of his jaw, I can feel where his gills will be. I can feel a fluttering beneath his skin.

Ah. Not my sacrifice at all then, but his.

We think together of songs. Of undersea ships. Of mysteries.

Of unthinkable gifts.

About the Author

Corrie Garrett lives in the Los Angeles area with her husband and four kids. She has been writing for six years, featured numerous times on Wattpad.com, and with short fiction published on

EveryDayFiction and other ezines. Corrie loves classic science fiction, from Isaac Asimov to Andre Norton, and enjoys writing science fiction and fantasy with an old-school vibe and a bit of romance. Her second love is retellings - be it myths, Bible stories, or Jane Austen. Her website is www.corriegarrett.wordpress.com.

GIVE ME THE SEA

VILLE MERILÄINEN

—Shiver, a dark place—

Rem?

    Rem?

       Are

          you

             still

                there?

Rem lay on his back, eyes shut against the dark. His hair was damp, his clothes too, and the shivers cold sent through him wrote the name of this city in his bones. Nemi's voice echoed around him, a tether to the outside, but he couldn't answer yet. His body still bled outside the dream, and an answer before his soul was properly severed would've moved his lips somewhere afar. *Better let the old carcass rest,* he thought, though the distress in the girl's tone made him ache.

When Nemi's calls faded completely, Rem got up and listened to the darkness breathing. There were others here with him. He felt their exhales hot on his skin when he walked through the cellar, could hear them shifting in sleep and the rustling of their sick lungs. Rem reached out a hand to touch one, found soft fur, curled a finger around the smoothness of a fang. The creature allowed the intrusion.

These were the beasts who hunted his people, and whom Rem hunted in turn. They were a symptom of the approaching end of his home, but for now they were impotent, content to sleep in Shiver's deepest pits and wait. Rem walked among them without fear.

He found the stairs leading up, placed a foot on the first, and slid it sideways on the icy surface. It was too slick to climb with any kind of haste, and so, with great care, Rem found a foothold and leaned onto the wall for support. Frost creeping through the cracks in the stone stung his palm, and the faint vibration of rushing water within the wall told him his location in the city.

The wall was broken in places, letting moonlight stream in. He climbed out of the cellar to a riverside street, leading towards the cathedral overlooking the city. Across the water stretched a stone bridge, thin like his arm, up to the broken stained glass on the cathedral's side.

When he'd last been in the cathedral of Bastion, of which this was a copy, he had watched the ceremonies from the shadows of the rafters. A low sun had painted glittering dresses in warm gold as he listened to rapturous chanting for the glory of Death Herself and her dethroning of the God Bled Dry.

The soft patter of his footsteps sounded profane now, breaking the deep, deep silence, inside which the pews and altars were smashed and all colour was the blue of the moon.

Rem made his way through the desolation to the entrance, pushed apart the wooden doors great enough for gods to walk through, and found snow falling outside. It had covered the streets and turned the glow of gaslights into pale haloes. He walked down the cathedral steps to a labyrinth of bridges and stairs, descending into a city surrounded by a forest to the south, east and west, and a fall into emptiness to the north.

He stopped under an archway when Nemi's voice reached him again. Carved into the stone was a basin where water sat still and unfrozen. Rem peered through for a glimpse of the outside. Nemi had brought his body back home, laid it on the bed, and now sat by his dry, lifeless remains with her fists wrapped together and pressed against her mouth. Poor, nervous thing. This was the risk he took, wading out at night, and she never got used to it no matter how many times he bled out in her arms. He pressed his fingers against the water, but despite the gentleness of his touch, they broke through. Any clear surface was enough to see outside, but with his body so hurt, he needed a hard reflection to leave.

A wail broke Rem's concentration, and the image in the basin faded as he wheeled towards the sound. Nemi must've botched the exsanguination. The creature had chased Rem here as drops of shadow in his blood, eager to finish the hunt it had begun outside.

Rem rushed to the end of the terrace and leaned against the balustrade for a look below. The streets there were cracked, buildings collapsed, and the flames of the gaslights floated freely around as fireflies over shattered lamps. They made the snowflakes glow like embers, and lit up the many eyes of the beast infecting him.

From his perch, Rem regarded his quarry with sudden terror. The beast reared itself when it saw Rem watching it, screamed at him with such force the drifts around it whirled into flurries. It was lupine in form, but its oversized head was full of eyes; Rem counted them all as he approached and felt his stomach lurch when he found the last one. Seventeen yellow, slitted eyes, as were said to watch all the world on the crown of the God Bled Dry, before he fell from his throne.

"Forgive me," Rem said, when the beast ran out of breath and its wail turned into a rasp. "The only absolution I can offer is a long wait."

Rem descended the winding steps, and the beast came closer. Not as a challenger would, but with hesitation, even timidity. Rem grunted when the creature spoke, or tried to—it made a sound like a deep inhale, and in it, Rem thought he heard a plea for help.

He shook his head, and the creature lunged, screaming again as its jaws opened to swallow him.

Rem dodged with the swiftness of thought, as only a lord assailed in his realm could. The beast crashed against the steps and recovered to find Rem circling it on the street with a hand lifted. The flames swarmed into a globe over him. The beast wheeled around, but before it attacked again, Rem lobbed the gathered fire at it.

The third scream, the last, was not for wrath. Rem watched the beast's fur burn away and reveal wristlets bent out of shape by the growth of its limbs. As it burned to cinders, he saw human eyes looking up at him, and the ghost of a man full of childlike fear.

Then it vanished, the infection cleansed. The soul of this one was Rem's burden now, one of many inside his towers, pits and cellars.

Once Rem closed the door after him, the only sound in the house the beast had guarded was his own breathing. This was a replica of his home. The blueness that governed the city had crept even in here, dyeing the stacks of books and ledgers on the table, the shelves full of many more tomes, and the dusty piles of journals stacked next to the armchair and used as stands for coffee cups. The hearth was a blotch of ink in the back of the room, darkest in a dark space, and permeated an uncanny coldness when Rem passed it on his way to the bedroom.

Nemi's crooning was clearest here, and he could even locate where she sat in the real room. The bed was empty, and so was the low stool beside it, but a ray of moonlight through the window laid her shadow on the floor. A part of her still belonged here, and always would.

Rem went to the mirror on the wall, above the drawer opposite to the bed. The reflection showed the room lit softly with candles, but not himself. Nemi's shadow moved on the other side, and when Rem gave it a glance over his shoulder, he saw it getting up here as well. She paused in front of the mirror and looked straight at him, cocked her head as though she guessed he was there. Her hair was straight and black, like his, but reached her hips instead of being shorn short—looked like a burial cowl, Rem thought.

Rem pressed his hands against the mirror, felt the glass bending at his touch, and pushed himself through.

⟶∘⟨⟩∘⟵

—Bastion: A home—

Despite his sudden lack of skin, the warmth of his house sent a pleasant quiver through Rem's spirit.

Nemi had left the room. From the kitchen drifted the scent of boiling vegetables, but instead of humming as she often did, Nemi only stared vacantly into the pot as she stirred the steaming soup. At least she was eating again. She stood a head's height over Rem, though he wasn't short himself, and was too thin for someone so tall. Maybe she'd once been a willow who had dreamed of being a girl, and seized the chance to become one after she was cut down and fed to fire.

Nemi gave him a sideways glance and, though his form was little more than a visiting breath from a cold room, did a double-take. "Rem? Are you back?"

He could not answer, but went to his body and brought his unseen arm to its wounds. A tingle raced up the suggestion of a limb, and he pushed it deeper into the torn flesh. Nemi peered into the room, and her grey eyes shot wide from the sight of his flesh mending. Her legs turned into a billowing cloud of black smoke as she swooped to the bedside and closed his hand in her fists.

"You were gone for so long," she said, when Rem's lids cracked open. Her voice trembled with the nearness of tears. "I thought I didn't dry you fast enough and the sickness got you. I was so scared you'd—"

"You did well," Rem said. No need to trouble her further with an admonishment, not when he hadn't been in any real danger. "But I fear I've no time to rest. I saw something in Shiver, something that's worried me awhile. I need to get back out there."

He sat up despite Nemi's protests. "What's so worrisome it can't wait until the morrow?"

Rem lifted his shirt for a gander at the white stripes on his belly, the marks where claws had raked him the night before. Alongside them were many more, some faded, others nearly as fresh. "The beast who did this was once a man."

Nemi looked at him with fright and dismay. "A man?"

"A pious man, I think." He climbed to his feet, faltered, and leaned on Nemi for support. Her legs reappeared from the cloud of smoke. "Which means they need a blasphemer all the more out there."

"You're not—"

"To them I am," Rem said. She didn't like being talked over, and he'd already done so twice within the minute. She might've grumbled about it to someone else, but she was Rem's child, in a way; he had found her inside Shiver, lost and confused in the snowfields outside the city. She looked about fifteen, older than Rem, though he'd brought her through the mirror only a year ago. Not that appearances mattered much—Rem had looked the same for a lifetime, as had everyone in Bastion but for one of its inhabitants. Only Pontiff Sola Astrondos aged, aged terribly at that, as though he suffered time's grinding wheel on his shoulders to spare his flock from it, in the manner of the martyrs of Death Herself of whom he and his followers preached.

Nemi helped him to his staff leaning against the hearth, a gnarled branch set with a bell. The bell chimed softly every time the staff thudded against the floor as Rem made his way to the wardrobe by the door. Nemi followed gingerly, watching how white his knuckles clutching the wood were.

Bastion was never dark, not like Shiver, but blazed with gaslights and lanterns hung over doors, with candles by the windows and torches on the ramparts. Rem tugged his scarf tighter around his throat as he waded out onto the snowy streets, where mounds rose high from the long winter. From the houses stacked atop one another came sounds of prayer, pleas for Death Herself to deliver the faithful into the warmth of her sleep. Nemi peeped inside here and there, watching the nightly rituals, but Rem only listened with smouldering thoughts.

Bastion was the nexus realm of countless dreamers, each of whom had built a world of their own within themselves. It was, Rem suspected, a part of the reason why the city had become stuck in time. The worship of a death god was only a symptom of the collective wish to fall into solitary dreams and never wake up.

"Bastion is dying because of them," he said, when they came to the end of the residential street and took a turn for a boulevard, towards the cathedral. "I wonder if the beasts are an answer to their prayers."

He cast an eye towards the mouth of an alley, where a man and a woman slept in a pocket of shadow, huddled against each other under a blanket. Dead, but not with their precious deity—their bodies had frozen long, long since, but the chiming of Rem's bell still made them twitch. He could have delved into their worlds and pulled them out, but they'd come alive in their own time—and slip away again as soon as their apathy climaxed.

Only the beasts seemed to bring a permanent end. Rem returned from every fight, but so far, none of the victims had.

"You keep putting yourself in danger for them," Nemi said, when she noticed him observing the couple. "And what for? Being sneered and spat at, when there'd be a bowl of warm broth and a warmer fire waiting for you at home."

"You're starting to sound like the preachers, Nemi, and I don't like it in the least." They came to the rise of the cathedral, simpler than Rem's archway labyrinth. He paused when the steps made him run out of breath. "Someone must care. If no one did, we'd all sleep until the beasts found their way into our homes." He pressed his staff hard against the stone stair to push himself ahead.

Nemi watched his climbing with a frown, and stared at her shoes as she followed. "Do you think you'll be allowed inside? At this hour, no less."

"I must. I've long contemplated the possibility of the worlds within changing the person, instead of vice versa, but only in Shiver saw it clearly. If I'm right and the monsters are people who've changed, I'll need help finding out how to stop it."

They reached the top, and Nemi gave him a slanted smile. "You're more optimistic than I am if you hope the church would offer any."

Rem rapped the gilded door, rapped again, but no one came to greet them. Only after he hammered it for a full minute did an irate and bleary-eyed woman in silver-lined cleric's robes appear behind the smaller side-door near the grand main ones.

"Death's grace, what is this racket?" she demanded, wiping her eye with a knuckle and hoisting a lantern with her free arm. Her expression of irritation turned into one of weariness when Rem stepped closer to her light. "Ah, the blasphemer himself. I should've known."

"I must speak with the pontiff, Yulia." He made to brush past her, but the woman grabbed him by the wrist. Rem stopped, not from the force of her hold, but to inspect her arm. The skin of it was loose and wrinkled, and her face was sallow, with dark patches around the eyes. She hadn't slept for so long her body had begun coming apart.

"Run on home, Rem. You can see the pontiff tomorrow— once the mass begins, the same as everyone."

Rem yanked himself free. "Step aside or I'll set you aside. This is not a courtesy call."

"Are you truly so foolish as to threaten—"

"I have more important matters tonight than to argue with you," Rem snapped. "I don't care to be here any more than you care for me. I won't trouble him longer than I have to, but I *will*—"

Nemi's cloud of smoke swooped under his legs, slipped past Yulia, and vanished into the gloomy foyer. Yulia spun in place, shrieking at the intruder, then slapped a hand to her mouth. For a moment, she wheeled between Rem and the interior, then grumbled, "No longer than you have to. And wipe your shoes."

—*Bastion: The grand cathedral*—

Rem and Yulia caught up to Nemi in the cloister connecting the main body of the cathedral with the monastic dormitories. The clergy's dwelling sat on a cliffside overlooking the ocean, far above the walls of the city. It was one of the oldest buildings in the city, not as majestic as the halls they'd just left, but imposing in its own right with its sharp spires and angles.

Nemi ignored Yulia's scorn and gaped openly at the sea every time they passed a window on their way through the vast corridors towards the pontiff's chamber. The interior was lavishly decorated, with rugs soft and fine, gold-rimmed paintings of past lords, and vases full of exotic flowers filling the halls with their redolence. None of it entranced her as profoundly as the sight of moonlit waves, resting calm and still to mirror the sky.

"It's beautiful," she said, and Rem caught a hint of melancholy in her tones. "The walls are too tall to see it from the city. So close, and yet I've never seen it."

Yulia replied with only a scoff Nemi barely noticed. "Has anyone ever crossed it?" Nemi went on. "Do we know what lies on the far shore?"

"There are stories," Yulia said, "but to the best of my knowledge, people have never made it across."

"Amazing," Nemi breathed. "Rem, do you reckon you could imagine something so vast in Shiver?"

"Maybe, but it'd take a while," Rem said. "But what would the point be? What good is something that leads to the unknown?"

"Not knowing what awaits beyond leaves everything possible."

"What a strange child," Yulia muttered. "Of course he'd know—he's the one who makes it. Do you have no control over your own design, girl?"

"She has nothing *to* design," Rem said.

Yulia swung around to face him with a mystified look. "I'm not sure I understand."

"I don't have a world inside me," Nemi said, dropping her gaze to her feet when Yulia's puzzlement sought her instead.

"Nonsense," Yulia said. "All people do. Death Herself shattered the world of the old god and placed its shards inside us. This is Her truth."

"Spare us from your sermons," Rem drawled. "Nemi is a child of Shiver, different from you and I. Do look livelier, dear," he added upon noticing Nemi's abashment. "It's nothing to be ashamed of."

Yulia stopped and glared at him with lividity. "I will not stand for heresy in this house, Rem. I do not know how you've wormed your way into the pontiff's favour, but say such things again and I will throw you out and ensure you lose it. You have not dreamt a human being into existence."

Rem smiled calmly, at her, then at Nemi. "Human beings do not turn into smoke with a thought, Yulia."

"You dare suggest—"

"That there are things more frightening than her locked away in Shiver. It is far from unfathomable I'd come up with something sweet after a while."

Nemi blushed a little at that, but the next Yulia glanced at her, her embarrassment had turned into a hint of smugness and her feet into clouds.

Yulia looked as though she might've argued, but a screech from the floor below made the three of them freeze. Rem was the first to dart into motion, staff chiming as he raced down the corridor. Yulia cried an objection after him, but she was already alone—Nemi was a cloud with the boy, circling his staff as though he carried an open flame.

The sound had come from the women's wing, but there were no guards present to stop Rem from entering. He dashed towards the commotion, and turned a corner to find six guards—one of them a man—wrestling down one of the lupine monsters. The guards had captured it in a net, and left a streak of blood on the floor as they dragged it out of the room. At first, Rem thought it was wounded—but then saw the remains of the residents past the struggle. Four beds, three bodies.

Rem raised his staff and struck it down hard, making the bell swing from side to side and clang. It only earned a snap of,

"Hey! You're not supposed to be here!" from one of the guards, but the corpses lay still, beyond his help.

The beast, however, went mad at the sound of the bell. It screeched and thrashed, poked its claws through the netting, as though reaching an arm out towards Rem in a pleading gesture. "It's the blasphemer! Get him out! Don't let him near her!" said another guard, as they began to drag their quarry towards the exit to the courtyard. Yulia grabbed Rem's arm when he took a defiant step towards them and spun him around.

"That's enough of you," she said. Her breath wheezed despite the short run. "As though it wasn't bad enough to demand an audience in the middle of night, next you go running amok—"

"You knew," Rem hissed. His glower was enough to startle Yulia into letting go. "You've known they're people all this time. I've had my spirit torn out twice the past week trying to find out where the beasts come from, and you've had the audacity to mock my efforts." He cast a glance to his side when Nemi rematerialised, gave a low grumble at the nervous way she looked at him, then swept a gaze down the doors along the hall. "Do your people sleep easy, Yulia, knowing this could happen to them? Do they *pray* for it to happen? I refuse to believe even the faithful could slumber so deeply they wouldn't come to see what this awful howling was, unless they already knew."

Yulia stared him down, coldly said, "I will see you out now."

Rem averted his eyes from hers, gripped his staff with both hands—and swung at her. Nemi shrieked as Yulia struck the wall and slumped against it. Rem readied himself for the guards, but found the bloodstains on the carpet reaching the exit. The hallway was silent, and no one shuffled inside the rooms.

He knelt by the cleric to make sure she was out cold, then gestured for Nemi to follow. She lingered by the unconscious Yulia, hands over her mouth, before going after him. "Is she... Is she okay?"

"She'll have a headache tomorrow, and that's better than she deserves." He slammed a fist to his thigh. "This quite changes the intent of our visit."

Returning upstairs, Rem stormed into the chamber of Pontiff Sola Astrondos. Nemi had become a half-cloud to keep up with him, and when they entered the chamber, reverted into physical form so suddenly from shock her legs reappeared in mid-air and she stumbled.

On the walls and along the floor, covering the ceiling and the roof, were thick, limb-like vines that crawled further with a squelching sound. Their tips squirmed like fingers.

"Close the door," Rem said. Nemi did as told while he went to the pontiff and examined him. The ancient, withered man was dead—not as profoundly as he wished to be, but retreated from the coils of the living into his own world.

Nemi stepped beside the boy and tilted her head, suppressing a shiver as she watched the elder. "Can you draw him out?"

She turned to Rem when he didn't reply, and found his face set with a grim expression. Disgust, perhaps. He then lifted his staff and struck it down in a rhythm, making the bell tinkle. "Find me a mirror once you've lain me down."

Nemi caught him when his heart stopped beating and he toppled.

—Amaranth, in the sea—

Rem entered a room like the one he'd left, but without the growths to tarnish its splendour. Through the windows, whose curtains fluttered with a salty breeze, wafted the scents of hundreds of blooms, not arguing with but complementing each other. Sunlight danced on the floor with the thin shadows of the curtains.

He looked around for a way out. Nemi had set a mirror on the table behind him and peered into it on the other side.

I'll
    wait
        here.
            Please...
                Don't be long.

"I won't," Rem said. Nemi gave no indication she'd heard.

He went to the window, past the empty bed. The sea glistened under a brilliant sun, and by the shore he saw the lonely figure of Sola Astrondos. Amaranth was a simple world, fit for someone who already had everything outside but his youth. It was an island with the one tower Rem was in, and a vast garden of rainbow hues. For all its beauty, it was a mockery of its master's wishes: Ever abloom, never fading.

Rem's staff lay beside his corporeal self, but his footsteps on the stone path to the shore were enough to alert the resident of his approach. In Amaranth the pontiff appeared as a boy of Rem's age, and the two of them, like he and Nemi, looked much the same. Nemi had stolen in her a part of Shiver's darkness, and moulded it into a talent unique to her. Rem had done the same when he crawled out of a giant orchid's embrace in Amaranth, with the skill to cross into other worlds, and so the pontiff's surprise at seeing another soul left quickly when he found a likeness of his own dark features coming down the path.

Astrondos swept a melancholy look over Rem before he returned to observing the sea. "I feared you'd come. Don't you have better ways to spend your nights, blasphemer, and others to save?"

"I know the nature of the beasts," Rem said. "And now I've seen yours too, Father." The young pontiff flinched at the title. "Amaranth bleeds through to the outside. Are you and the beasts connected?"

After a moment of silence, Astrondos asked, "Tell me, Rem. What do you see in waves?"

Rem lifted a brow, gazed out to the sea. "Your room, where our bodies lie and your vines squirm."

"Then what of the shores of Bastion? What do you see in the still sea?"

"Nothing but calm plains, endlessly."

Astrondos gave a small laugh at that, and faced the boy. "I've never crossed them. Nor has anyone. They've tried, but though the winds are calm near the city, out in the open blow terrible storms, and every time a ship has sailed off we have found its wreckage washed back in the days after. No one tries anymore, and the ships of cowards who lost their wits remain as monuments to the futility of such efforts." He glimpsed to his side, then returned to observing Rem. "I'm surprised you never tried, given how eager you were to sail away from Amaranth."

"Don't change the subject, Father."

A scowl visited Astrondos' features. "You asked what connects my sleep and the beasts. The ocean is a part of it.

"You should not exist, Rem. I never wanted something like you to walk out of my garden, but I do see the steps leading to your creation. I wished for a way to let others into Amaranth, so I might offer them the paradise I spoke of. I have long run out of faith in Death Herself and the notion that we would be her chosen people, when we do not even have the power to end ourselves." Astrondos glanced Rem up and down, with jealousy in his gaze. "And now that creatures with that power have appeared, you use the gift I yearned for to take them away from us."

"I would gladly not abuse this 'gift,' and be spared from having a legion of monsters asleep in me," Rem grumbled. "But when good men and women become reflections of the God Bled Dry and rampage through the city, how could I refuse to step in their path and protect my home?"

A grunt fled Astrondos. "You've seen them for what they are?"

"I told you I knew the truth."

"You did, but I didn't expect *this* truth."

Rem froze. When he found his voice anew, he demanded, "What else are you hiding?"

Astrondos let his gaze fall from the sea to the waves lapping to the shore at his feet, until Rem snapped, "Father!"

"I wish you'd stop calling me that," Astrondos said coolly. "Your creation taught me two things about these worlds of ours: That they *can* be entered by others, and that they have the potential to be infinitely deep. That girl—Remi?"

"Nemi."

"Nemi," Astrondos repeated, in a musing tone. "No less conceited of you. You've told me she has no world of her own, but I don't think that's true—she simply does not know how to find it. If you have one, and one vast enough to give a part of it to another person, then I am firm in my belief they can be layered endlessly." He smacked his mouth. "But, perhaps each world can only have one person born of it, a centrepiece. I have not succeeded in creating another image of myself, and unless you've kept something from me in turn, neither have you."

"If this were true," Rem said, folding his arms in a tight bunch, "as you've given life to me, would this not make you the centrepiece of Bastion? And you have the nerve to call me conceited."

"It does, and I have proof of it. Not yet solid, but so far undisputed." He took a few paces closer to the waves, so that they wet his ankles. "I suspect all the others, every other soul, are trapped in Bastion, the way you send your prey into Shiver."

Rem stammered, "Why? How?"

"I don't know, but perhaps it has to do with our mythos. Those beasts... Have you been to mass for some time?"

"Please, Father. You know me better."

"Yes, for an incorrigible bastard," Astrondos muttered. Rem's brow lifted with indication he'd heard. "Then you wouldn't know I've told them of how you were born." He gave a cruel smirk at Rem's surprise. "Not *you*, personally, but of someone like you embedded into a prophecy, who would bring Death Herself back to us. Now all of Bastion believes they could birth our saviour.

"When you told me of the girl, I took note of how similar her making was to yours. So simple, to reach inside our worlds and shape them surrounding one wish, yet neither of us has replicated it." Astrondos curled his lip and sucked on it. "And yet, when others reach the deep, deep, deeper sleep vital for such a pure wish, they instead find something from which they cannot return, and become beasts." Rem choked, and Astrondos smiled. "But, they aren't people who change—they *revert*. The fanged horrors are their true form, shrouded over by the might of Bastion's lord to make them look like you and I. For what purpose, I cannot tell. Perhaps to pacify them, perhaps to disgrace by making them worship an old enemy and their jailer." His smile weakened, and he looked away from Rem. "I have long wondered about my appointed position, yet cannot recall when I rose to power, or whether I received it through trust or violence. I believe Death Herself is not a goddess to be worshipped, but merely another dreamer, accursed with the gaoler's mantle. Bastion is the world within her. From Bastion sprung Amaranth, amongst countless others, but only from Amaranth came something new: you, and your Shiver. Thus, I am the reflection of the purest wish of Death Herself, just as you are mine and Nemi yours."

Rem was quiet as his mind worked to process this. Finally he asked, "The vines in your bedroom... What were they?"

Astrondos folded his arms behind his back and faced the sea. "My last effort to deliver on what I've promised. You came to be when I tried shaping Amaranth to find a way to let me cross into other worlds. In all my efforts to renew that miracle, I stumbled upon a way to let mine shape Bastion." He gave Rem a look over his shoulder. "My garden will dig deep into the soil, break the earth, crush the city and the walls. The ocean will swallow everything, the way the beasts were meant to before your interference. The people will drift into cold sleep under the waves, where sunlight won't reach them, and never awaken."

Rem approached the young pontiff with his fist raised, but Nemi's voice around him startled him into stopping.

Rem!
  Rem!
    Please...
      You
        must
          come
            out!

Astrondos looked around, as though trying to follow the voice. "Well, you have some time, but not much longer. I will awaken at dawn, and cannot complete what I've begun tonight. What will tomorrow bring? The day after? Who knows. I certainly do not."

"I won't let you—" Rem shouted, but the next instant seawater filled his lungs and washed him back to the garden. He struck the wall of the tower, coughing and sick from the salt. Another wave sent him scrambling up the tower and for the mirror.

—*Bastion: The grand cathedral*—

Rem revived amidst verdant chaos.

Nemi clawed at a stem tangled around his leg, and cut him loose when Rem's body and soul reunited. A cocoon of thorny vines had formed around the pontiff. Blood seeped through, painting the stalks red.

A growth of branch-like thickness fell on Nemi. She escaped in a puff of smoke, and the vine began to thrash as though it were an arm. It drove the two away for fear of being crushed, and as they raced out of the room, the stems crept after them and out the windows to encircle the building.

Even with the ongoing calamity, the halls were empty, though no longer silent. From every room came joyous prayer, voices calling for the arrival of Death Herself.

Pillars fell, floors crumbled, steps cracked with Amaranth's invasion. Only Rem and Nemi fled from it, and when they reached the safety of the city proper, they turned and stopped to watch how the vines wrapped around the cathedral, smashed its windows and spires, and stilled. The stalks glowed in the lights of the city, but not even here did anyone come out to the cold to see why sculpted marble rained that night.

Nemi gasped and wheeled away from the destruction when a howl reached them along the alleys. She forced her eyes shut when a woman's scream replaced it and was cut short.

"Will you hunt?" she asked Rem, who still watched the painted glass gleaming where it stuck to the stalks.

Inhale, exhale, two, three, four.

"Not tonight, Nemi."

Nemi woke up to an empty bed beside hers.

Sunlight cast a pale ray onto the dust on the floor. Without church bells to disturb her, she'd slept late into the morning. She called for Rem, but received no response.

A row on the street caught her attention, and she got up for a look out the window. People had gathered outside and now spoke in urgent tones, watching the ruined cathedral.

Rem's coat and shoes were gone, and so Nemi donned hers and went outside. Rem's footsteps started towards the city gates, but were disturbed by dozens of others where he'd stepped off the porch.

"You! You, girl!" cried someone. Nemi turned to face a woman pointing a finger at her. "Has the blasphemer done this?"

"The pontiff has," Nemi said.

"Liar!" the woman said. "Why would the pontiff keep us from getting into the cathedral?"

"It *must* be the blasphemer's doing!" came a man's voice from the crowd. Nemi couldn't see the speaker. "I saw him leaving the city! He has cursed us and fled!"

Left the city? thought Nemi, and dashed off when someone suggested they'd fetch axes and try to chop up the vines.

She found his footprints in the new snow at the outskirts, easy to recognise from the prints of his staff beside his left foot. Rem had followed the wall, veered away from the woods outside Bastion. *A good thing at that,* Nemi thought with relief. *If the people had found him while looking for axes, they might've split* him *while they were at it.*

The winds blew cold that morning, and Nemi wrapped her arms around herself while she followed the trail between the wall and the firs down to the shore. Rem stood on the beach, gazing out to the open sea. Even with her worry, Nemi couldn't help but to feel a pang of wonder at seeing the ocean from up close.

"You should have woken me," she said, making Rem turn with a start. "I would've loved to join you."

Rem cast his eyes down. "I couldn't sleep."

"Small wonder, with all you've learned." She stepped beside him. For a while, they watched the slow waves in silence. "You have nothing to fear," she then said, and wove their fingers together. "Even if you slept, you wouldn't turn. I know you wouldn't."

Rem gave a mirthless chuckle. "It's not fear keeping me awake. Only thoughts."

Nemi nodded, and looked up at the cathedral up on the cliffside. "What're we going to do?"

"Nothing."

She let go and faced him. "Nothing? We cannot just—"

"Did I ever tell you how you came to be?"

She faced him with a frown, but tilted her head with a puzzled expression at his sombreness. "You found me out on the snowfields. I remember."

Rem shook his head. "No, before that. I fell into slumber so deep my body stopped breathing for years. All that time I spent shaping one wish inside Shiver." He gave her a look from the corner of his eye. "And that wish became you."

Nemi said nothing, only looked at him with her mouth slightly open.

"I'm sick of Bastion, Nemi, have been for a long time. Sick of how everyone here is resigned to waiting for the end to come. You came alive from the desire to be free of them, and to wander far from here." He looked to the sky, at the few clouds drifting towards the horizon. "Father envies my talent of being able to walk in other worlds, and I envy yours. I never wanted you to see the ocean because I was afraid you'd turn into smoke and let the wind carry you away, like I've always wanted."

"Rem…"

"If death is what they want, I'm ready to let them have it. Father thinks Bastion is just another world of a faraway sleeper.

That means *we* can escape it, together, and I think the way out is found across the sea."

"If that were true," Nemi said, with a finger on her lip, "why do you see your reflection and not what awaits beyond when you look into a mirror here?"

"I don't know what to look for. When I first awakened, I saw nothing beyond Amaranth either. It was only after I made myself a raft and set off, lonely in Father's absence, that I found my way to Bastion." He shook his head. "It was an awful time, drifting alone on open seas. I never dared to face the waves here, fearing there'd be nothing beyond and I'd lose my way again." He set a hand on her shoulder. "I'm ready now. If we are to be lost, I'll gladly be lost with you."

Nemi's gaze swept the wall of the city, the forest around them, until she let it rest on the waves. "We'd need a boat."

Rem smirked, cocked his head towards a path down the shore. "I know where to find one."

Rem led her far down the beach, where the sand hiding under snow turned into rocks and grew into cliffs. There they found a hidden cove, where ships lay moored and gnawed at by time. The ground beneath them was blackened, and Nemi recalled some of the things he'd told her the night before. Maybe this was where they'd burned the wreckage of failed voyagers.

Tucked between the time-lost sailing ships was a single-mast sailboat, small enough to be manned by the two of them, and in seemingly fine condition. Come the evening, they rowed the boat out of the cove and out into the open, where the sails picked up wind and sent them gliding towards the unknown.

—Open seas, and desolation —

Rem struggled to pull down the sail before the wind rent it to ribbons, but even with Nemi's help, couldn't lower it fast enough. The canvas ripped free from its bindings and their hands, fluttering away into the dark.

The storm had risen without warning, as though it had lain in ambush for them. Wave after wave gushed over the railing and soaked the vessel with icy seawater. Nemi had turned into an apparition, with only her arms at cold's mercy. Rem had no tricks for braving it but the act of gritting his teeth.

The nails and planks creaked with the battering, and Rem knew they fought a losing battle. With the sail lost, he went back to bailing out the boat, but for every bucketful he emptied, another wave crashed against him.

"We're going to sink!" Nemi screamed. Rem barely heard; though she floated only paces away, helping him bail in a frenzy, the storm silenced her.

When Rem turned to yell encouragement, she dropped her bucket. He tried to catch it when it rolled towards him, but the boat rocked and tossed the bucket out of his reach.

Nemi floated in place, staring out, arms limp on her formless body's sides. She didn't respond to Rem's calls, and he wiped spray out of his eyes to see what had startled her. He saw nothing, but the night was strangely darker on her side than his, the rumble of thunder deeper.

Rem's bucket fell from numb fingers and chased after Nemi's when he realised the size of the wave about to hit them.

Rem woke up coughing and spluttering. Even before his eyes opened, he rolled to his side in a shallow pool and vomited salty water. Bile spread around him as his lids cracked and he pushed himself up.

The water reached halfway up his forearm, and on the bottom of the pool was a mirror showing his dishevelled reflection. Rem shivered with cold as he climbed out, clothes dripping onto dry earth.

He was in a garden—or what once had been, worlds apart from the lushness of Amaranth—and looked around in wonder. The trees were white husks, the flowerbeds rotted, and the stone paths amidst the ruins crusted with dirt. There were channels for artificial rivers leading towards the dome where he'd awakened, but they, too, were dry.

The further he went, the more his wonder at the new place turned to sorrow. Ahead Rem saw a building, one that had once been as enormous as Bastion's cathedral, but now had fallen to dilapidation and collapsed in places. When he crossed the gates separating the garden from the building, he found skeletons in rusted armour. Rem realised the stains on the path weren't dirt, but old blood. There was more of it inside, and more bodies; some were three times Rem's height, others roughly his size. None of the giants wore armour, and when

Rem stopped to inspect a mummified one, the amount of holes perforating its skull told him he might've found the remains of creatures like the ones in Bastion. It occurred to him he'd never seen a skeleton before, only read about them, and now wondered if one of Bastion's citizens had been dissected, would their skull have looked like the lesser skeletons' or the giants'.

Past mountains of bones he found a throne room, and on the throne sat the sole corpse who still wore flesh. Seventeen yellow, slitted eyes, as were said to watch all the world on the crown of the God Bled Dry, stared down at him from atop a face curtained with straight black hair, so much like his own, like Nemi's.

So much like his father's.

Across the corpse's throat ran a glistening cut. Rem went to him, lifted his head—heavy with the weight of the crown—but found no life in his eyes. He touched the wound and wetted his fingertips with blood, as though it had been made moments ago. None of it flowed.

Rem spun in place to take in the piles of skeletons around him, noting how many of them were giants. Whether Death Herself was one of them, had left long since or had never existed, he couldn't guess. He stayed for a while, trapped in thoughts, as he considered the meaning of the corpse before him. Whenever the God Bled Dry was mentioned in the myths, so was his immortal throne. Death Herself was supposed to have cast him down from it, but she was never said to have taken his crown, nor that she sat on it in his stead.

With a last sombre look at the fallen king, Rem left the throne and the palace.

The front wall was broken down, and Rem crossed the rubble for a view of the world outside. The sight awaiting broke his heart: The slopes past the gates were dyed a dead shade of grey, as though they had drunk so much blood it had salted the soil and left it barren. The greyness stretched to everything in Rem's sight, from the fields far below to the ruins of what may've once been cities, and farther still to the distant mountains and the iron veil of the sky.

Rem watched the barren lands for a time, but with nowhere else to go, returned to the pool.

Nemi was there now, visible through the mirror on the bottom. He saw her from a downward angle, as though from the sea. She had lain his body on a beach, and now held his head on her lap and sang softly. Worry creased her brow, but she contained it well, even though Rem had never drowned before.

The sight made Rem gag. So lost in awe at everything around him, he had forgotten to focus on himself. He was *there* in the once-garden, in body and spirit, but also in Nemi's arms.

"Nemi!" he called. He fully expected her not to respond, but the girl flinched and looked around.

"Rem?" she replied. Her voice was muffled, like she spoke through a wall, but he *could* hear her.

"Come to the water," Rem said. Her gaze darted a different way at every word. "Maybe you can see me."

Nemi looked at his closed eyes on her lap, then gently laid his head down on the sand and came to the water's edge. She seemed to be so near, but her expression was doubtful, and at last she said, "I see nothing."

"I've crossed to a new world," Rem said. Again, she looked around for him. "Whole."

Nemi jumped to her feet. "What? But, you're here with me!"

"I saw." He chewed his lip as Nemi returned to the body and inspected it.

"You're—" she said, cut herself off, looked around with horror. "Rem, you're... I think you're dead. I don't know how I didn't notice it. It's so different from before."

He gave her a solemn smile she couldn't see. "I think we stumbled upon a way to escape."

Nemi came to the water, shaking her head, and sank her hand. "But... you need a hard reflection."

"The same thing happened when I left Amaranth. I fell into the waves, and when I recovered, I was in my bed in Bastion, where everyone acted as if they'd known us all their lives."

"Us?" She gasped, and her puzzled expression turned to sadness. "The time you spent dead—"

"Yes. A wish to be free isn't all you are." He took a deep breath, paused for a time. Nemi looked straight at him all the while. "I couldn't bear the loneliness of the sea, Nemi. I drowned myself."

Nemi averted her eyes, faced the body. "Then, should I... should I try drowning myself as well?"

Rem considered a moment. "You can't cross on your own. You don't have the gift."

"Then what?" He saw more than heard her growing panic. "I don't want to be alone either. I searched the beach, and there's nothing here. Just a strip of sand rising from the sea."

"Come to Shiver."

Her expression turned as dark as the storm clouds earlier. "Don't mock me, Rem."

"You can do it. Close your eyes and think of home."

"Like so many times before, when it never worked?"

Between them was silence, until Rem heard her calling for him. The sound came from the edge of his consciousness, and when her voice rose to a cry, he was slipping away.

—Shiver, a dark place—

Rem waited a whole day before Nemi found her way to Shiver.

He had lain on the roof of the copy of their home and watched the sky. It was always dark, but the stars moved and rearranged, creating for him a cosmic kaleidoscope to help pass the time. He sat up with a start when the door beneath him creaked open.

Rem jumped down to greet Nemi as she stepped out. On her face flashed profound relief, but as soon as the flash was over, she crossed the distance between them and slapped him so hard he fell over.

"Don't you ever leave me alone like that," she grumbled while Rem clambered to his feet.

"It worked, didn't it?" Rem said, rubbing his cheek.

"I cheated." She looked away from Rem's surprise, and answered his unasked question. "I didn't return here like you meant me to, but the way the beasts chased you. I scraped your skin with my nails until you bled. Not dry—my nails aren't sharp enough for that—but enough for some of my smoke to infect you. Then I waited, slept, until I stole my way here." She pressed her arms together, hands on elbows. "It took longer than I thought. There was only dark for a while."

"Ah," Rem said, with a touch of disappointment. "More dark for a while longer, I fear."

"What do you mean?"

"I want you to stay here. Bastion is dead to us. Dead to all, I think, whether Father succeeds or not."

Nemi's puzzlement only grew. With a frown, she said, "I thought our plan was to escape. Are you now leaving me here? Abandoning me to the same loneliness that once conquered you?"

"There is nothing outside. I found only an empty opening ahead of me, with no place for us to go. I could draw you out with me—but why would I? Better I crown you the queen of Shiver and bequeath it to you, while I dream its growth." He took Nemi's hands. "But I won't abandon you. I think I've pieced together the reasons for Bastion's obsession with death. Father thought that we, you and he and I, are reflections of Death Herself... but I fear we may be dreams of the God Bled Dry instead."

Nemi gasped. "You found him?"

"And found him true to his name, trapped in a strange dreamstate where he bleeds but does not live. Is it any wonder the world within such a star-crossed creature should seek an end so fervently?" Rem shook his head and let go of Nemi. "I doubt Death Herself was ever a real creature, but something borne out of his desperate wish for a release. I can give him that, by casting him from his throne."

"And if he perishes from the fall, play the part of Death Himself," Nemi said with a half-smile.

Rem nodded. "The stories speak of his throne so often that it makes me wonder its importance. If I pushed him aside and sat on it, perhaps I could dream forever. But, my world is one of life. Shiver may be cold, but it yearns for warmth and sunlight and springtime. You aren't alone, either—the dungeons are filled with the creatures I captured from Bastion. They sleep now, but if my will is strong enough, may one day wake up in our shape."

"What makes you think they won't eat me instead, hunt like they hunted before?"

"Father thought they were captives in Bastion, and after what I've seen, I suspect the same. I saw the aftermath of a terrible war. The people of Bastion, I think, were enemies of the God Bled Dry he ensnared in a failed effort to save his people." Rem paused, searching the towers growing around Shiver. "Everything is changing, whether because the God has begun slipping away or because of Father's efforts. I won't let the same happen here. If I can remake them in our image, I will ensure they share our yearning for peace."

"You're determined to do this?" Nemi asked, with the kind of sorrow creeping into her voice as every time she wished him a good hunt. "You say the world is empty, but I'd gladly walk it with you until we find something. Anything. I love you, Rem, my dear friend. I don't want you to dream out there alone."

Rem gripped her hand. "You haven't seen what I have, and because I love you as well, I don't want you to. Whatever caused Bastion's creation is long past, and it has scarred the land in ways that will never heal. Maybe that world is just another layer in a never-ending chain of dreariness, or maybe it's the end of all the worlds, a place where death alone can thrive. It doesn't matter; from there, I will spark something new."

Nemi sighed, caressed his knuckle with her thumb. "Will you visit me?"

"Some day, if I can. It will be so long away you might forget about me."

Nemi glowered at him. "This isn't the time for jokes, Rem."

"It's not a joke. I have a grand design for Shiver, and seeing it through will be taxing. Loneliness *will* be your companion for the times ahead, but if there is anything I can do to ease it, please, tell me. I will make it my one wish to give you whatever you ask before I turn my focus on my own vision."

Nemi bowed her head, stayed silent in thought for a full minute. Finally, she looked out towards the darkness past Shiver's cathedral, the same place where Bastion's walls had hidden the ocean, but where in Shiver was bleak nothingness.

"Give me the sea," she said, "and fair winds on which to ride over the waves. Give me lands far beyond and fill them with wonders, so I'll forget I've forgotten you." She lowered her gaze to the snow at their feet, traced a slow look up Rem's body as though etching his shape into her mind. "Give me an adventure that leads me through your dreams and brings me safely home, so that I might one day see what's become of the heart of Shiver and this grand design of yours, and so that I might remember you when I find you waiting for me."

A smile eased onto Rem's face, and he laughed when it infected her dourness. "I'll try."

Nemi embraced him, hugged him so tightly she felt him melting against her. In a moment too short, he was gone; with his body in good health, he needed no mirror to exit Shiver. The thought of leaving was enough.

STILL WATERS

—An old garden—

The wind swept dry leaves across the garden as Rem rose from the pool.

There was a curious warmth near his heart now, one that had been absent for some time. It gave him comfort knowing Nemi was back home, despite the isolation she would have to endure.

Instead of heading straight for the throne, Rem climbed to the top of the palace. As he trod through the carcass-strewn halls, he wondered whether it was safe to try to force the beasts into human form. From the havoc he saw from the balconies up high, and what he'd seen in Bastion, it seemed they only knew how to destroy. Could he change their very nature by simply wishing it away? Maybe not, but what else was there but to try? Nothing in this world, certainly. Bastion had been blessed with snow to hide its desertion, but there was nothing to drape the dead earth here. It occurred to Rem he'd never seen grass outside Amaranth, and decided he'd grow fields of it somewhere in Shiver for Nemi to find. Flowers, too, hills full of them.

Rem leaned against the balcony's weathered railing for hours, waiting for night to come, but it never did. The sun didn't move from its position near the mountaintops, nor did the clouds veiling it. Eventually, he decided this world was what Bastion sought to become—dead and still.

The static view led his thoughts back to Nemi and her emptiness. Maybe she had no world of her own because she didn't need one. She was born of the yearning to be free, and now she was, without ever needing to worry about the siren song of deathlike sleep. Rem couldn't have wished for a better centrepiece for Shiver.

Rem returned to the throne, took a firm hold under the old king's arms, and lifted him from his seat. For a moment, holding the corpse aloft, Rem thought of giving him a proper burial, but then only turned and cast him into the nearest pile. The crown shattered on the floor, its gemstone eyes rolling every which way, and the king's glistening wound splashed its last drops against the desiccated flesh of his old underlings and enemies.

The act of irreverence stung Rem less than he thought it would. Perhaps it was a fitting end for the blasphemer, before he became something else. A strange lethargy overcame him as he took the seat and reflected upon his transformation. Death Himself didn't sound right. There was too much life inside him. Too much hope.

Dreams filled his waking vision, sweeter than they ever had before, and Rem let them steal him away. He envisioned a world lusher than Amaranth, and the fair winds Nemi desired, carrying seeds of green across the earth. He pictured the tides burgeoning from melting snows, first as puddles, then vast as lakes, and finally as the sea that seemed to flow through all the worlds, hiding limitless mysteries from those who stood at its shore.

His lips curved into a drowsy smile as he pictured Nemi travelling across the land, searching for all the wonders he left for her. One day, he would grow a grand tree in Shiver's most distant corner, and around it a field of flowers with petals as bright and red as the blood in the old king's wounds. She'd first be dazzled by the shadow of the tree, then the field when she'd reach the lip of the valley.

And finally, she'd find him there, waiting.

Sleep became irresistible, and Rem drifted away. Through the haze of his dream he caught occasional glimpses of Nemi wandering his earth, most often alone, but now and again with companions who shared her journey after people began to crawl out of the cellars. Eventually she left them all, when the winds were strong and carried her away across the ocean that belonged only to her. She was quick to care, but quicker to forget, and at times Rem was certain she was so swept up in her adventure he was a distant memory as well.

But, whenever those thoughts threatened to mar his dream, a voice stirred him. It was small and distant, but as clear as though it came from just below his ear.

Rem?

Are

you

still

there?

About the Author

Ville Meriläinen is a Finnish university student by day, author of little tragedies by night. His short fiction has won the Writers of the

Future award, and has appeared in various journals and anthologies, including Pseudopod, The Death of All Things, *and* Disturbed Digest.

The Uses of Disenchantment

Joanna Hoyt

One

J orinda! When she was born she didn't cry, just stretched her hands into the light and laughed. She learned early to crawl, to walk, to run, fast and light and fearless. She fell in the river and was fished out still laughing. She only cried by night when she woke from frightening dreams, and by day whenever anyone tried to hold her back or shut her in. Finally her mother Aleit let her go wherever she wished, except for the old castle in the woods.

Aleit didn't forbid Jorinda to go to the castle. If she'd done that, Jorinda would have run to it. Aleit said that if Jorinda went there the witch would catch her and lock her up so she'd never be free to roam again. The next time Jorinda woke weeping she said she'd dreamed of the castle. She never went that way.

Aleit was a weaver, quick at plain work and skilled at tapestry panels, and she taught Jorinda her trade. Jorinda's hands were quick and deft. By the time she was ten she was faster than her mother at plain weaving, though she didn't care for it; she begged until her mother taught her tapestry work. She learned tapestry quickly, and it took her fancy. She'd weave and smile until her mother shook her by the shoulder and sent her out to play. Then she'd blink, rise, and skim down the street like a swallow, the other children pelting after her.

Jorinda wouldn't copy designs. She'd agree to, but when her mother came back to look at her work there'd always be a difference: a laughing snake in the rose border, flowers blooming in the desert, a fountain rising from what had been a still pool. Fortunately, buyers liked her changes more often than not. They liked Jorinda, too: her long dark hair, her eyes like windows open on the summer night, her courage, and her laughter. They didn't see her night terrors and fits of weeping.

As Jorinda entered womanhood, she had suitors aplenty. She'd dance and sing with them, talk and laugh with them by the hour, but if their talk turned toward marriage she turned it away. If they persisted she ran from them, lightly, gracefully, too fast for them to catch. Finally Melcho the smith's son backed her into an alcove before asking. She stared at him, her face pale and set.

"Just answer me, Jo," he said. "You know I love you. But if you won't have me, tell me, and tell me why, and I won't trouble you again." She shook her head. He tried again. "All right, so you don't want me. But why? What's wrong with me?"

"With you? Nothing! But all the nights, and all the mornings... always... and no way out... I couldn't. " She put her hands on Melcho's wrist, swung him round and ran past him into the woods under the stars. Nobody asked Jorinda after that. Not until Joringel came.

TWO

Joringel's father, Othmar the cloth-merchant, had boated downriver to the village once before and left again with some of Aleit's best work. He'd sold it for a good price, but he'd had to pay dearly for it too, so when he came back down the river he brought his son.

Joringel's winning ways brought goods into his father's store cheaply and sent them out again with a fine mark-up. He was handsome, but that wasn't all. With the farmers who brought fleeces to sell Joringel was grave and quiet. With the young women who spun and dyed the wool he was quick-tongued and full of laughter. With the priests who came to commission altar-cloths Joringel was devout, or full of subtle questions, depending on the temper of the priest. His delight in the girls, his interest in the priests' lives, his respect for the farmers was unfeigned. His pleasure in pleasing them all was the most real thing he knew, and he went through his days with a brightness around him.

His father sometimes saw him shadowed. Joringel didn't always keep his mind on the work at hand; sometimes there were errors in the figures, or in the orders, and Othmar reproached his son. He didn't swear at Joringel, or beat him, but Joringel's eyes dulled and his face went salt-white. Afterward he stayed away for hours.

Plenty of girls were charmed by Joringel. Sometimes he'd take one of them to fairs and dances for a few weeks until the night when the girl went back early to her mother's house, angry as any girl might be with a suitor, while Joringel came home in the small hours with shadows behind his eyes. He never went back to those girls. It was no good asking him why. Othmar didn't worry; a single young man was bound to please female workers and sellers and customers as a married man couldn't. If Joringel worried he didn't let on, just moved smiling through the days. Until he met Jorinda.

THREE

Joringel stood in Aleit's weaving room, admiring the panels she and her daughter had made. He smiled at each piece that Aleit praised until he came to the tapestry in progress on Jorinda's loom. Then he froze like a rabbit under a hawk's shadow.

The woodland scene was detailed enough to show the song-swelled throat of the nightingale perched on a low bough. Around the nightingale rays of golden light stretched like the strings of a harp, like warp threads on which the bird's song was woven, like the bars of a cage. From the position of those bars, and from the light on bough and bole, the sun seemed to shine from the right, but on the left something glowed low and golden as a setting sun. It was so hidden by the trees that Joringel couldn't tell its shape. His blood beat hard, and he kept his mouth shut, knowing that if he opened it he would cry out—in fear? in longing?

"She's made a mistake with the light," Aleit said. "Never mind that one. But see, this here..."

"No, she didn't make a mistake," Joringel said. "It's real."

A shadow fell across the weaving. Jorinda was back from running. She smiled at him.

"You've seen that place?" she said. "Who are you?"

"I'm Joringel," he croaked. "Othmar the merchant's son. I came down the river."

Jorinda's smile deepened. She'd never been more than three days' journey from the town. She asked about the places Joringel had seen. They talked all afternoon, but not about the picture.

FOUR

After that Jorinda and Joringel were always together, rowing on the river, running in the forest. Three weeks later they were betrothed. Othmar went on down the river. The wedding was set for the day after his return.

"You can help me set up a new shop." Joringel smiled at Jorinda. "With your fine work and your fair face, we'll have all the custom we could wish for."

"A shop?' Jorinda echoed, frowning. "Why? Let your father mind his shop while you and I travel on the river together."

"How will you weave on the boat?"

"I can weave in winter. But you wouldn't tie me to a loom in summer, when there are stars in the water and dances in the cities!"

Jorinda's eyes were frantic, and when Joringel looked into them he saw his own reflection, worried and alone. So he promised that she'd travel with him and see all the places he'd told her about. She laughed. His reflection in her eyes was surrounded by light. Slowly it grew handsome again.

One evening as they walked in the woods Jorinda asked Joringel to tell her again about the midsummer fair at the northernmost point of the trade route, when the sun set for only an hour before it rose again, and all the long day drums played and dancers leaped. She laughed and said, "So many places, and I'll see them all!"

"Come now," he said, trying to laugh, "you might say something about loving me, not just the places I might take you."

Her eyes narrowed. "When it's you I'm thinking of, I'll tell you," she said, and she turned to go. Joringel took hold of her arm. Jorinda's face crumpled. Aleit would have understood that look. Joringel had never tried to hold her back before. He only knew that she looked as though she hated and feared him.

"Don't do that!' he cried. "You're mine, and..."

"I am not!" Jorinda pulled away from him. "I thought with you I'd be free. I don't want a cage! If I wanted that I could have married Melcho. I could have married any of them. I thought you were different."

"People aren't so different. Places aren't so different. You learn to please people, to get by, wherever..."

"Nowhere in the world is different," Jorinda said, stricken. "Nowhere is free."

They stood a pace apart, each staring at an ugly and hostile stranger. Into the silence fell the song of the nightingale.

Jorinda turned, listening. "One place is different," she said. She turned and ran. Joringel ran after her, crashing heavily through the brambles.

He found Jorinda at the edge of a green glade. The golden light of the setting sun at his right pierced through the gaps between tree trunks in long rays like the strings of a harp, like the bars of a cage. On the bough above Jorinda's head a nightingale sat, its throat swelling with song. Across the glade to Joringel's left something flashed golden in the sun. Joringel couldn't see its shape through the trees. He shut his mouth to keep himself from crying out.

Jorinda saw the castle walls leaping into the sky, saw the windows blazing with reflected light. In the heart of the blaze, pictures formed. Wide meadows, swift rivers, high mountains glowed and vanished. Her figure passed among them, walking, then running. As Jorinda's heart clenched with longing her image in the glass lifted its arms, which softened and spread into wings, which bore her up and up into the light.

The real Jorinda stared at the image in the window. That was what she had desired all her life: freedom from work and expectation, from the wishes of lovers and family and neighbors. She didn't forget Aleit's warning, but the golden light threw a long shadow over her memory of the town, and it seemed to her that Aleit had tried to keep her caged—Aleit, and Joringel.

She heard Joringel's voice behind her crying "Jorinda! It's the enchanted castle! Jorinda, come away!" She heard the sound of a cage door closing. She would not let it close on her. She stepped into the glade, singing, and raised her arms like wings.

Joringel, knee-deep in tangled undergrowth, afraid to move, heard her voice fading into the song of the nightingale, saw her hair spreading to cover her back and arms, saw her body shrinking and the light hardening around it into a cage of gold. The caged bird gazed at the light that quivered in the bars and sang for joy.

Something moved between Joringel and the caged bird. First it was a screech-owl that cried out as though with Joringel's own pain. Then it was a woman. A smiling young woman lovelier than Jorinda, if that was possible. A sallow old woman with bleak lines carved in her face, with bleared red eyes, like any witch in a tale. He had to push past her, reach into the cage...

He couldn't move. *Coward!* he told himself. *Take a step toward her. Now. Quick. Before she does... whatever witches do...* He couldn't. Or wouldn't? *It's a spell*, he thought, half desperate, half relieved. *She's bewitched me. It's not my fault, I can't...*

The witch laughed. Joringel still couldn't move, but the laugh tore words from him.

"Let her go! Give her back! You... you..."

"Let her?" the witch wheezed. "*Let* her? She came to me willingly enough, didn't she? Didn't want her lover, her hero, her pass to freedom. Found something better. I can make her happy, fool boy, and you can't." She lifted the cage, walked toward the castle. *Move!* Joringel told himself. *Stop her!* But he didn't.

At the castle door the witch looked back. "Run away, lover-boy," she said. Her voice was Jorinda's voice, sweet as it had always been, but with contempt underneath... had that always been there too? Joringel turned and ran, stumbling, blind, until a stone rolled under his foot. He went crashing down into darkness.

FIVE

Joringel woke in the gray dawn, cold, bruised and dew-drenched. He sat up stiffly and thought what he could do.

He couldn't go back to the village. He couldn't bear to be blamed for not protecting Jorinda, or to admit that she'd left him. There were jealous young men in town who'd be glad to see him miserable and shamed. Worse, there was Aleit.

He couldn't go back to his father, either.

He'd go back to the castle. He'd be a hero now, if he hadn't been before. Surely he could find it again...

He spent the morning looking, finding neither the castle nor anything else he knew. Eventually he gave up trying to find anything and followed where his feet took him.

At sunset they took him to the edge of a green glade. The sinking sun fell below the cloud-margin. Red light spread like fog through the glade, slid like blood down the castle walls. The screech-owl cried. Joringel fled.

For three days he wandered in the woods, his steps always bending back toward the castle, his legs and his will quivering as he tried and failed to force himself to cross the glade and pass into the shadow of the door. On the last evening he was too tired to run and too weary to try to convince himself that he'd be any braver if he returned again. He turned his back on the castle and walked steadily away.

At the next sunset, hungry and tired, he stumbled from the woods into a wide space of gnawed turf. He smelled wet wool, and as he watched the flock of sheep plodded up over the hill. A dog followed them, but there was no shepherd.

The dog raced round the flock, setting itself between Joringel and the sheep. Joringel backed up, looking for a stick, a rock—anything to use if the dog came at him. And it came, but whining rather than growling. It stopped, started away, looked back at Joringel, returned, went again. Joringel followed it.

The shepherd lay on his face in the tussock-grass of the hollow, his right arm bent awkwardly under him.

"What happened, father? Can I help?"

The old man didn't answer. Joringel knelt by him. The old man's skin was warm, his pulse uneven.

The touch seemed to reach the sufferer, who made a sound like the dog's whine, wordless. Joringel felt over him, finding neither wound nor broken bones, and then gently turned him over.

The right side of the old man's face drooped. His right arm and leg hung limp. His eyes scanned Joringel's face while his mouth made formless sounds.

"Be easy, father. Lean on me. Don't try to talk yet. Can you point which way I should take you?'

The old man pointed with his left hand and let Joringel hold him up from the right side. He swung his left leg along willingly; his right leg dragged, a dead weight. Joringel was nearly exhausted before they came in sight of a light—a horn lantern swinging from an old woman's hand.

"Geert?' the woman called. "Geert, man, what's keeping you?"

"He's here, mother," Joringel called. "He's hurt." She hurried toward them, lantern raised.

"Ai, it's the apoplexy again! Well done, boy, we're almost home."

Home was a one-room cottage with rough stone walls and a thatched roof, a fire, and a smell of food that almost made Joringel forget everything else. He'd seen such homes before, and pitied those that dwelled in them, but he was past that.

After seven days the sounds from Geert's mouth began to shape themselves like speech. By then the woman, Imma, had shown Joringel how to tend the sheep. He knew the commands to give the dog. He'd seen the plants that could sicken the sheep. He knew how to move so as not to frighten them. Imma was busy carding wool and minding the garden and the old milk cow and the old man. They needed Joringel's help. They enjoyed him, too; in the evenings, with the sheep penned safely and the fire burning low, Joringel told them tales of the places he'd seen. He didn't tell them much of himself. When Imma asked what he was he said, "A pilgrim. A penitent." He hadn't planned to say that, but it seemed to match the name he'd claimed, Gotthilf. She looked at him and asked nothing more.

The days were hard and good. The nights were bad. Joringel lay in sweet-smelling dry fern under a wool blanket and dreamed that he stood sick and shaking at the edge of the glade.

SIX

Jorinda didn't see the bright bars of her cage. She saw only the pictures that shimmered between them.

There was a forest whose silver-leaved trees shot like fountains into the sky. In their shade the unicorns danced, melting into shadow when other humans passed by, never hiding from Jorinda, who danced with them, swifter than wind, softer-footed than sunbeams.

There was a path up a towering cliff where only Jorinda dared to climb, tracing the veins of quartz with her fingers, touching the bright spots of tourmaline. When the path failed and the cliff bent back above her she leaned back and let the wind take her. Once again she was a bird not a woman, beating her strong wings, rising beyond the last sharp crest into a gulf of light. On the cliff's far side a cataract flung itself into a deep pool and flowed out into a river like...

Like what? Jorinda could remember nothing before the forest and the cliff. A shadow stirred at the edge of her mind, at the edge of her sight; a shadow-beast, winged, larger than any bird. Fast as Jorinda was, the shadow was faster. It was gaining on her. In a moment it would catch her, it would make her remember... She flew frantically, straining her wings, straining her heart.

In the eastern sky she saw a cloud that looked different from its neighbors. Shapes moved behind it. It wasn't a cloud; it was a window into another place. It was closing. She flew toward it frantically, folded her wings, fell through. The shadow-beast was too large; it was checked, and vanished as the window closed. She flew on over rolling grasslands toward distant music.

A fire burned on a hill. Around it a circle of people danced, leaping like flames. She wheeled in the air above them, dancing too. See, here it was, here was the thing she had dreamed of, that she was going to see with....

The shadow was there again. It rose like smoke from the fire, flew at her with eyes like sparks. She had a moment in

240

which to flee toward the not-cloud in the northern sky. She hovered instead, trying to remember: whom had she been going to see this with?

The smoke, the shadow, closed around her. It was the dark, the walls closing in, the thing she had always feared, the thing she had fled until the last time when she ran from Joringel.

His name brought the true pictures back to her: the dances and the promises, the quarrel in the woods, the sun-slants in the glade, and then...

The slanting light was still around her. She couldn't have been dreaming long. Where was Joringel? She turned to find him, to step toward him.

Her body, turning, was not the body of a girl but the body of a bird. She spread her wings to fly to him and felt the coldness of the bars. Who had done this to her?

"You did it yourself, dearie," a cracked voice whispered next to her. "Same as they all do. Took what you wanted. The man, then the dreams. Kept you happy for a while. Finding out there's other dreams, eh? Dark dreams? Don't fret, dearie. Fold your wings and forget him. Look at the bars. Look at the light. You'll have your sweet dreams again. Just keep moving through them, and don't ever look back."

SEVEN

The leaves fell, and then the snow, and Imma grew accustomed to Gotthilf. No one could have asked for better company by day. Sure he wasn't used to farming, you could see it by his fine soft hands, and by how quickly he tired of the heavy work, young and strong as he was. Still, he learned, and she'd have been hard put to do without him through the fall, with Geert stricken, and the late hay still to bring in, and the firewood to gather. There was less work in winter, of course, but still it was a mercy to have a sturdy young man to clear the snow away from the door, break the ice on the sheep-trough, and carry loads of hay from shed to byre. Not only that, but he spoke to her and Geert politely as if they had been a lady and a lord, and the stories he told! He was better than a minstrel at a fair. Her own son Huppert had bidden fair to have that way with words, but he'd seen less to tell about, and then he'd died of summer sickness.

Geert saw the likeness too. Imma understood that, seeing how Geert's eyes followed Gotthilf, seeing how he gave Gotthilf Huppert's boots that they'd never had the heart to throw away. So she was hardly surprised when Geert looked over at her, one cold morning when Gotthilf was out fetching more wood from the shed, and said, "He's done a son's work for us, and should have a son's part."

"Aye, if he wants it, but I doubt that."

"Then why should he stay the winter?"

"Why indeed?" That was all she said. Geert slept long and deep. It was Imma who woke in the night to hear Gotthilf moaning to himself like a sick dog, Imma who stood over him in the dark, saying prayers and bits from the holy book: *He maketh me to lie down in green pastures; he leadeth me beside still waters; he restoreth my soul.* He was a kindly boy, Gotthilf, but she thought his soul needed restoring. She didn't ask about his secrets. She didn't tell Geert what she'd heard. When the mud began to show through the snow and the first soft wind came over the southern hills, Geert spoke of sons again, and Imma didn't argue.

Joringel was almost frightened by the spring. Winter had shut him into a small world where he was a help and a strength and a gift. The thaw melted the walls. Soon it was time to take the sheep abroad to forage. Geert walked the fields with Joringel, pointing out plants that could poison a sheep.

"Imma showed me already," Joringel protested.

"They look different now," Geert said. Sure enough, Joringel didn't recognize the delicate new leaves of spotted hemlock in the water-meadow. "The poison's worse in them now," Geert told him. "Keep the sheep to the hill here—it's sparser, but it's safe." Joringel listened gravely. When Geert spoke thanks and offered him a son's share Joringel tried to hold that same courteous attention on his face while his mind stuttered and surged like the melt-swelled brook. He saw himself reflected in Geert's eyes, heard himself reflected in Geert's words, and he should have been glad, but he was thinking of Othmar, wondering if he was now telling another young man "You've been as good as a son to me—as good as my Joringel who disappeared."

"So mind the flock well," Geert said, "for it'll be yours, and the cow and the calf and the holding too. And when the snow's off the ridges Imma'll take you to meet the neighbors."

"You're too kind," Joringel said thickly.

Geert stayed near home the next day with the ewes too pregnant to walk far. Joringel took the rest of the flock to the hill above the water-meadow. He tried to imagine himself staying forever at the croft, being introduced to 'neighbors' a day's walk away as Geert and Imma's foundling son Gotthilf, spending his days within three days' walk of the stone hut, never again seeing the summer dances of the north or the great fairs of the south... *Grus Gott*, no wonder Jorinda had been mad to get away!

He had guarded his mind against thoughts of Jorinda by daylight, until then. Now the pain cut across his heart, and the blame of himself. It was the blame he minded most. Well, was it fair? What could he have done? Could he have fought an enchantress? What had he ever done to make Jorinda take away her love and admiration and leave him cringing in the cold? Hadn't he given her everything, just as he had given his all to this poor couple who knew nothing of the life he had been meant to live?

He was like one of the generous and ill-treated heroes of the old tales. That solaced him a little. He lifted his face to the wind and imagined himself as the unjustly banished prince, gazing back toward his father's kingdom that lay beyond the empty hills...

The empty hills. How long had he stood dreaming? Where was the flock? He knew the answer by the lurching of his stomach even before he heard bleating from the water-meadow. He ran down the slope, shouted to the dog, drove the sheep back, cursing them and himself, hoping that they hadn't been astray long enough to eat the hemlock... or at least to eat much...

That hope didn't last long. Before they'd gotten a mile back toward home, two pregnant ewes and one young one were gasping and another was passing blood. Joringel would have hurried the beasts back to Geert, but the dog stood in front of the herd, stopping them. Joringel remembered Imma's words from the last autumn: *If they do take sick, let the beasts rest... if you're near the house give them charcoal...*

He told the dog to stay and hold the sheep. He ran for Geert. Halfway back it occurred to him that he could equally well run in the other direction, find himself another refuge, be someone else's beloved almost-son; better so than to face the disappointment in Geert's eyes. Yes, that would be the wiser thing, he told himself. He didn't turn around.

Imma was angry, and Geert disappointed, and both bewildered by his carelessness. He'd had all the way back to think of an excuse, and he hadn't thought of one. When he and Imma reached the flock the three sheep were dead, and two more were gasping. Imma gave them charcoal and prayed over them. One died. One lived. That night neither Geert nor Imma asked for stories, and Joringel didn't offer one. He thought silently of the dead ewes and of Jorinda.

That night he dreamed. Jorinda called his name inside the castle. He stood in the middle of the glade. The lovely young witch stood in the doorway.

"Come, hero, come, lover, come, prince," she said. "Come please her again, the way you please everyone. Come let her down again, the way you let your old peasants down, the way you let your father down. The first time you failed her she ran to me. Next time where will she go? The river, maybe, without a boat, with a stone bound in her clothes?"

Joringel wouldn't run away. He couldn't go on. He woke groaning. Imma stood over him, praying in the dark. *He leadeth me beside still waters*, Imma whispered. *I will drown in them*, Joringel thought, feeling the nightmare closing over his head and filling his lungs again.

EIGHT

Jorinda felt her heart withering under the witch's voice. She looked toward a shining bar, sang softly as though entranced, until the witch fell silent and—surely? —went away. Once she thought she was alone Jorinda tested the gap between the bars. It looked almost wide enough to pass through. She shut her eyes and pushed her head through. The bars gave a little; she could get out...

The bars tightened around her neck, cold, hard, choking. Somewhere a harsh bell clanged. Terror clutched Jorinda's throat, tighter than the bars. It was almost a relief when the witch came back, laughing, and bent the bars enough to thrust Jorinda back inside.

Dreams, then. Dreams were all she had. But surely the dream-world must contain some path outside the witch's hold. Jorinda stared into the lights of her cage again, willing herself to see what she needed to see.

There! A tiny golden key hung by a thread from the top of her cage. In the bar near her left eye there was a flaw, a shadow. She saw herself taking the key in her beak, tapping at the shadow. The shadow became a hole, the key slid in and turned, the door swung wide, and Jorinda was free. The cage behind her fell into tinkling shards. Before her the castle walls dissolved, leaving the witch weeping helplessly. Jorinda circled above her. How beaten the witch looked...

The witch looked up and smiled. "Sweet dreams, dearie," she said.

Jorinda trembled and came back to herself. There was no key, no open door, no vanished castle, only the shut cage of dreams.

She tried again, too many times to count. The shadow-spaces between the bars were filled with the witch's face and voice mocking her every time the dream broke. She began to realize that she was dreaming as soon as she thought she had found a way out.

Jorinda began to think that it would be better to forget true escape, to lose herself in the sweet dreams gleaming from the golden bars. What else could she do? She'd been enspelled. She'd tried to break free, and she couldn't. She was like the queen's daughter in the old tale, the fair and fearless one, carried away to the dark places below the earth, beyond help...

But she'd come of her own will, the stubborn part of her mind said. She was held by the magic of the castle, but hadn't she run there on her own two feet, leaving Joringel shouting behind her?

Joringel... Thinking of him, she almost felt him near. Joringel, coming back to rescue her, his face bright and strong, understanding in his eyes. Coming to set her free and never try to hold her back again...

No, that was no good; she knew better. The light behind Joringel was golden as the bars of her cage. She was dreaming again. She was seeing what the witch's magic gave her to see. It was sweet, but she was no more content with it than she'd been with the pretty tapestry designs Aliet bade her copy.

She had sat over those designs, looking and not looking, thinking and not thinking, until she saw the change in them, the thing the first weaver should have put in to give the picture life. Perhaps she could do that again.

She shut her eyes. Joringel's face still glowed behind them, bright against the golden light, and she held her mind on that image—not wanting, not blaming; seeing. What she saw changed.

The golden light behind Joringel's head faded to the grey of a cloudy morning. He stood on a greening hill, a flock of sheep about him. His face was bearded, weathered. The stubborn set of his jaw and the bitterness in his eyes were new to her.

As she watched his face took on something of his old look, and he smiled a little. What was he thinking?

Wondering it, she felt her mind slipping away into the dream-world, but this time she knew she was dreaming, and she knew the dream was his. He dreamed he was the hero-prince in exile, slandered by his enemies, falsely suspected by his father, abandoned by his love. But over the hills the messenger rode to tell him of the kingdom's need, to take him back to struggle and victory, to his father's contrition and admiration, to the love of a better woman...

He stood there, dream-bound, while the sheep wandered away. Somewhere a dog whined. Something was wrong. Jorinda wanted to warn him but she had no voice in his world.

He felt the warning. He pulled loose from the dream. For a moment she felt his dismay, and then he was gone.

He was dreaming again the next time she was able to reach him. She stood behind him, powerless, invisible, as the witch mocked him, as a voice like hers called desperately for him inside the castle. She heard what the witch said to him.

"The first time you failed her she ran to me. Next time where will she go? The river, maybe, without a boat, and a stone bound in her clothes?"

"Don't listen!" Jorinda cried. "It wasn't you, mostly—it was me, wanting what wasn't real. I've learned. I want to live!" But she couldn't find her voice, and she and he were both dreaming; they couldn't reach each other, they couldn't help.

Again she felt Joringel's mind pulling away from her, back into the waking world. For a moment she felt a presence near him in the dark, heard an old woman's voice murmuring "...hopes all things, endures all things..."

She'd tried hoping all things, and where had it gotten her? To the castle and the cage. She didn't see much virtue in enduring. That was what you did when everything else had failed.

Well, so it had. What was left, then, but to sit in the darkness and wait and endure, as Joringel also must?

NINE

Joringel couldn't think why he should get up the next morning, or what he could say to the old people who surely no longer wished to think of him as a son. But Imma was tending the fire, and Geert was rising effortfully, and Joringel couldn't just lie there and leave the work to them, so he went out to unbar the gate for the sheep. When Imma set food before him he couldn't refuse it. When Geert said those of the flock who weren't too great with lamb for walking needed to range further so they didn't exhaust the near pasture Joringel took them. He spent the day watching and came home, not comforted, but quieted. He answered courteously when Geert or Imma spoke to him; otherwise he held his peace.

Seven more days passed so, and seven nights which Joringel spent dreaming of the castle, and of Othmar, and of sheep. Then the lambing began.

They'd done all they could to be ready, fencing off a clean dry corner of the pen, scattering straw, crutching the wool around the ewes' tails and udders. Even so, there was little sleep once lambing began. In the first three days nineteen ewes gave birth. It was a loud business, and messy, and twice Geert had to reach in and help the birthing, but when Joringel cleaned the blood and mucus from a lamb's mouth and heard it cry for the first time he thought the labor worthwhile. That was the first day. The second day one of the lambs was born dead. The third day two sets of twins came weak and misshapen.

"From what their mothers ate?' Joringel asked.

"Aye," Geert grunted. "They'll never thrive. Best not try to save them." Joringel spent that afternoon digging a hole to bury them.

When he came back he heard a ewe screaming. It was almost as bad as Jorinda's voice in his dream. Joringel might have bolted if Imma hadn't come up beside him.

"Is it one of the mothers whose lambs died?"

"Nay. It's a lamb set awry in the womb, and the mother straining to push it out. Geert's done what he can, but it won't turn right, and he won't leave her."

Joringel didn't dare to ask whether that also was from the hemlock-sickness. He went back to the lambing pen. Geert sat on his heels by the ewe, breathing almost as raggedly as she did.

"Can I help?" Joringel asked.

"Best let be," Geert answered. "I've tried, but I can't turn it further without tearing her."

"But you're still here."

"Aye, waiting with her. What else?'

Joringel sat down by Geert. He rose to pen the rest of the flock, and again to fetch clean straw for another ewe, but he kept coming back to the old man and the sheep. He slept by them, started awake when Geert took his arm.

"Look, lad, she's done it!'

The screaming had stopped. The ewe stood heaving. Behind her a lamb lay tangled in the bloody mess of afterbirth, its head out, showing white amid the red. The old man dried the lamb and set it close to its mother's side as its younger brother slipped easily into the world.

"Healthy?"

"Aye."

Joringel slept and dreamed that he stood on the hill above the water-meadow under a clouded sky. There were no sheep around him. Had he lost them again?

No, they were penned. He'd come out alone because he heard the nightingale singing like all the sorrow of the world made sweet. If only it didn't remind him so of Jorinda. Jorinda, who he'd wanted at his side and in his shop and in his bed without ever troubling to know her. Jorinda, who he'd driven away. Jorinda, whom he couldn't help now any more than he could help the ewe. Jorinda, with whom he couldn't even sit to watch and wait...

The nightingale sang again, and while the notes were the same they wrought on him differently. They might almost have been a voice saying *Come*. He came, stepping slowly across the twilit grass.

248

Something lay in the grass ahead of him, dark red as dried blood. Was Jorinda dead, then, or hurt? He flinched, but the nightingale called *Come,* and he remembered the lamb's head rising white and clean from the puddle of afterbirth, and he stepped forward.

The sun slipped out between the clouds, and the blood-color freshened and showed a gleam of white in the center. A scarlet poppy lay there in the grass, its petals filled with light as a glass is filled with wine. In its center a dewdrop shone like a pearl. *Come,* called the nightingale. Joringel plucked the flower and carried it with him under the trees, moving carefully so as not to shake the dew-pearl free.

He didn't come back to the treeline by Geert's house. He was in the witch's glade again, where he'd come and failed over and over. But this time he had the poppy in his hand, and the memory of his waiting, and the nightingale calling.

The witch was calling too. "Come, hero, with your magic flower and your precious water-drop. Come turn your sweetheart back to a woman again, and let her look at you as she looked last time." He winced, but he came on. Geert and Imma's eyes had reproached him almost as Jorinda's had, and he hadn't run from them. He would not run now.

He woke to sunlight spilling through the open door, to Imma singing.

TEN

Gothel walked among her nightingales, singing in her cracked old voice. They sang too, preening themselves. The new one, Jorinda, wasn't singing, and she had her eyes shut. Gothel closed her own eyes, let her mind slip into Jorinda's dream.

Well now, it wasn't her own dream, it was that boy's dream, and Jorinda had gotten into it somehow. Clever girl. She'd gotten into his dream and she'd called him, and now she thought he was coming back.

She thought she wanted him back. That was strange. Or maybe it wasn't. Hadn't the foolish girl Gothel had once been wanted Heinrich when he ran his fingers through her hair, when he promised to take her away from her cold house and the sound of her father coughing his lungs out and weeping? Hadn't she been glad to marry him?

She'd learned, oh yes, she'd learned. They'd not been married a year the first time he questioned her sharply about how she'd looked at another man. They'd not been married two years the first time he hit her. Still her pride had sustained her until she noticed women following her with their eyes, laughing at her behind their hands; and then men watching her too, speculating on whether she really was the whore her husband took her for. Then she fled with a satchel of dream-giving herbs and a dusty volume from her husband's highest shelf, fled to the abandoned castle that was rumored to be haunted even then.

She was fool enough to be happy again when she first arrived, to think herself safe in the golden light, until the darkness broke into her dreams, and her own dreams opened into the dark dreams of the women she'd left behind. She learned a different kind of pleasure then, as the women who'd laughed at her fled singly and secretly to her castle to hide from nightmares, sleeping or waking, and to drown themselves in sweet dreams. None of them had ever reached into another's dream, though, not until this Jorinda with her foolish handsome boy.

Jorinda! Her eyes were open now, and one was fixed on Gothel. She'd seen Gothel's memories just as Gothel did.

Gothel was too wise to show fear. She grinned at Jorinda.

"So you can do it too, dear? I thought I was the only one who'd learned to go half-free, to call the others in."

Why not go wholly free? Jorinda asked.

"You still think you can disenchant yourself? Once you've laid the spell on yourself?"

"Not alone, maybe," said a voice behind Gothel. Gothel wheeled away from Jorinda's cage.

Joringel stood in the doorway with a wilted poppy in his palm. Light from the high window glanced off a dewdrop in the flower's center.

ELEVEN

The young witch's eyes burned into Joringel's. "Left your old peasants to fend for themselves, have you, hero?"

He drew a deep breath, forced himself to answer.

"I told them who I was, and why I had to go. I left when the lambing was through. The shearers will come soon, and they'll take word to the next steading that Geert and Imma need a helper."

"So you've nothing to blame yourself for. You never have." The witch advanced on him. He looked for Jorinda behind her.

He saw a table, stone benches, shelves, all covered with caged nightingales. More cages hung from the ceiling.

He strode toward the witch, his left hand advanced under its coat of scarlet petals. The witch stepped aside to let him pass. He touched the flower and the dew-pearl to the first cage within reach.

The bars were cold as ice against his hand. They melted faster than ice. The flailing bird within seemed to melt too, growing larger and fainter at once. Then it solidified into a woman in her middle years, soft-faced and fair-haired.

"Georg!" she cried, throwing her arms around Joringel. He stiffened. She pulled away. "Georg? What have you been doing? You stink of sheep."

"No... no, I'm not your Georg, my name's Joringel..."

"How dare you lie to your mother! I was the only one who kept watch for you all this time. I knew that you weren't really dead, that it wasn't really you in that coffin..." She slapped Joringel hard across the face.

The witch looked at Joringel almost gently. "Best leave her to me, hero," she said. She turned to the woman. "Hush, dear, you've made a mistake, this isn't your son. Your Georg's over here." She took the woman by the shoulders, turned her toward the cage that stood empty on the table. The woman gazed into the bright bars, smiled, shrank back into a nightingale as she stepped through the golden door. Joringel looked from the cage to the flower in his hand.

"Oh, you can call her back again, boy," the witch said. "For what?"

"Where is Jorinda?"

The witch smiled.

Joringel swept the poppy petals along the row of cages on the highest shelf. Gold light fell like rain. A flight of nightingales circled the room, drifted to the ground, rose again as women, young and old, staring at him with hungry eyes.

"Helmut, you came back to me, you loved me! I knew you would..."

"Where's my daughter gone? Where's my Hanne? She was right here with her baby boy... have you stolen her away, you brute?"

The birds in the remaining cages chattered and screamed, beating their wings wildly. Joringel cowered under the weight of their fear. He turned, half-blind, and stumbled away again, beaten and ashamed...

From the shadow behind the open door a nightingale cried *Come*. He turned to look. The witch stood in the shadow with her hands behind her back.

"Come out," he said.

She sidled out, keeping her right arm low against the wall. He stepped to meet her. She clutched a cage in her right hand. The nightingale in that cage watched him steadily from one bright eye. He reached out, the flower in his hand.

The cage broke and the bird dissolved. The witch's face dissolved too, faded, resolved itself into something quite different from the young woman's lovely mask or the old woman's frightful one: a fine-boned face with deep-set eyes, no longer young.

"That's how I saw you in your dream," Jorinda said to the woman. "That's your real face, then. I like it better than the others."

Joringel stood staring between them. Was this another trick?

Jorinda flashed him a bird-bright glance. "Don't you understand? This is Gothel, how she really looks. You've disenchanted her too."

"Not on his own!" Gothel said. "I made him."

"So you did want to go free."

"I did, once it was too late, once I'd put it out of my own power. But now there are all these others. How can I leave them all with the pain they ran here from? But how can I not? If you've taken the power from me..."

"But not from them," Jorinda said, looking back into the shadowed room. The top shelf was filled with cages again, and all the birds were singing.

Almost all. An old woman with fierce eyes stood by the shelf.

"I'll stay waking now," she said. "My dreams weren't what I wanted, only what I thought I wanted. And I needn't hurry home. I've learned what I had to, but I doubt I can say as much for the ones I left. Let this be my haven for a little while, while I learn if there's any way to be free."

"And your Heinrich?" Jorinda asked Gothel.

"He's dead too. I've no one left to fear."

"Go on, then," the old woman said to Gothel. "And you, boy, give me that flower. I'll give the rest their chance, though most won't want to take it. How could you help them? You'd look to too many of them like a piece of their dreams, and you haven't been fool enough to enchant yourself."

"I have," Joringel said. "Jorinda freed me." He gave the old woman the poppy, turned back toward Jorinda.

"Yes, I'll come back with you," she said. "In case you or I need freeing again." She slipped her left hand into Joringel's hand where the poppy had been, gave her right hand to Gothel. They stepped out of the castle's shadow together, setting their faces toward the village and the long slow work of waking.

About the Author

Joanna Hoyt's fiction has appeared in publications including The Centropic Oracle, Crossed Genres, *and the* Mysterion *anthology of Christian speculative fiction.*

FAITH

SHERWOOD SMITH

"My dog can talk."

Fay said it like it didn't matter, as she fell into step beside us, her round shoulders hunched into her old purple coat.

"What?" I yelled.

"What?" Melissa yelled.

Fay shoved her lank blond hair behind her neck and nodded, still no sign of a smile on her face. "Yup. Probably won't last long, but it's fun."

"How did that happen?" I asked.

"Saw a triple shooting star, so I did this ritual I read about."

Melissa was silent.

I hurried into speech. "What's he said?"

Fay shrugged, the worn seams of her coat straining, as she sidled a glance at Missy. "Dog stuff."

Melissa still said nothing.

We'd just crossed to the school parking lot when the principal's voice ripped out at us. "Reed!"

Melissa flinched, and I jumped, but Fay just hunched tighter, looking kind of like a rock on legs.

"Faith Reed, come here!" Mr. Conley was standing on the steps just outside the gym building, watching the students come to school.

Mr. Conley glared at us until we were right in front of him. "Reed, has your mother seen that memo?"

"Yes, Mr. Conley," Fay said in the thin, flat voice she always used with adults.

"Well, where is she?" he roared.

"She's in the hospital, Mr. Conley," Fay said.

"What?"

"Foot problem, Mr. Conley. Waitresses get it. She'll be out soon."

The principal stabbed a finger toward her face. "Your brother," he said, loudly enough for everyone in the parking lot to hear, "is going to flunk out unless we get some cooperation. One graduate to four flunk-outs is not a good record, even for you Reeds. You just pass that on!"

"Yes, Mr. Conley."

The principal glared at Melissa, then me; even the furrows in his face looked mean. The kids streamed around us, some with sideways looks.

"Go to class," he ordered.

We hurried away.

"Is your mom going to be okay?" I whispered.

Fay gave her head a shake. "Nothing wrong with her. Matt's problem, not mine."

We ran up the steps, into the relative safety of the corridors. Kids yelled and screamed, lockers slammed, and bodies rushed by.

Melissa said, "I think it's humiliating that he should single us out like that, for something that isn't even our fault."

I knew why the principal had done it—to make Melissa and me feel embarrassed, so we'd stop hanging out with Fay. Teachers had tried it, too, but there were usually sneakily nice and reasonable about it. Mr. Conley didn't have to be subtle. No one stood up to him, ever. Our parents were still afraid of him, just as they'd been when they were in school.

Our lockers were right in a row. "Library after school?" Fay asked, looking at both of us. "You don't have ballet, Missy, and I know you don't have band practice." This last was to me.

"But I might," I said. "Mrs. Lopez threatened us with extra practice if we can't get that jazz thing right. Of course, maybe a miracle will happen and we will," I said.

"I can't," Melissa said quickly. "Madame has invited me to observe the senior technique class. I can learn a lot that way."

"Oh." Fay hunched a little further into her coat. "Okay."

We walked in silence toward homeroom, Melissa and I to Mr. Kent, A-L, and Fay on down the hall to Mrs. Nashimura, R-Z.

As soon as Fay was gone, I said to Melissa, "You can watch the seniors do ballet any day, can't you?"

Melissa rounded on me. "She lied to us." Her blue eyes were fierce, her pretty mouth tight. The only reason the three of us hadn't been made fun of long ago was that Melissa was the prettiest girl in the school, and probably the most talented. She gave a quick look around to make sure we weren't overheard, then dropped her voice to a whisper. "I don't care if she lies to Conley, or even to teachers. But not to us."

"You mean about the dog?" I'd almost forgotten it, after that scene with Mr. Conley. When Missy gave a short nod, I said, "She's just doing some kind of story-game. Like being an alien, or the Middle-earth Radio thing."

Two years before, Fay had had this idea that an alien had traded bodies with her. She'd said it to everyone, and we'd gone along with it. Missy seemed to enjoy it as much as I did, same as when Fay had announced the summer before that she had found a radio station that tuned in to Middle-earth. For a while she brought us news, every day, about the doings of the Fourth Age Gondorians and Hobbits and Riders of Rohan.

"She knows it's not real," I said. "It's just acting—like she did just now with Conley."

I knew as soon as I said it that this had been a mistake, because Melissa's mouth got tighter. Before I could start on the difference between games and realities, Melissa opened the door. "Then maybe it's time to stop," she said over her shoulder, and she went into the classroom, her head queen-high, her skirt swirling around her long ballet-trained legs.

A group of boys watched her, and one of them said something I couldn't hear, but she ignored them as she slammed her books onto her desk.

I was still blocking the doorway, so I went in. Of course no one noticed me—something I was glad of, because I needed to think. It was the first time Melissa had ever said anything outright that meant the friendship might break up. Lately she'd been getting busier and busier with her ballet, while last year we met at the library practically every day. Before that, we'd met at the park and played out our versions of stories we read or saw. But now it was changing, and it was more than going from fifteen to sixteen; the two most important people in my life were pulling away, and I didn't know how to fix it. I felt sick inside, much worse than Conley had tried to make me feel—and then I'd only felt bad for Fay.

At lunch we sat together, as always. But instead of story talk, Melissa went on brightly about tests, and teachers, and even the weather. I did my best to keep that stupid conversation going. Instead of talking, Fay was quiet. In fact it was hard to look at her, sitting there so short and square in the ugly neon-purple coat all of her sisters had worn—after they, too, got it as a hand-me-down.

I ate as fast as I could and tried to get things back to normal as I held out my lunch bag to Melissa. "I'm full," I said. It was my turn to have leftovers. "Anyone want that extra ham sandwich?"

But then Melissa put her bag down on the bench and got up. "I promised Miss Dobson I'd come and watch the tryouts for the musical. I better go talk to her. See you guys later."

She walked away. I leaned over and picked up her lunch bag because I knew Fay wouldn't. In all our years together, Missy and I had never seen Fay bring a lunch, but she never asked to share, and she wouldn't scrounge. Plenty of people scrounged, football players especially. But not Fay. Though she would take leftovers rather than let them go to waste.

So I pretended to see if Melissa had left anything in the bag that I'd like, and I said, "This *Brigadoon* thing is really important to her. Dance scholarships and things."

Fay stared stonily at the ham sandwich in my hand, so I shoved it into my coat pocket. When she did speak, it took me by surprise. "She doesn't believe in magic anymore."

"It's not that—" I started, but then I stopped. I just couldn't say anything about lies. *If you play around with little girls who lie, you might become a liar too*, Mrs. Kemble had said to me in fourth grade, her crow voice plenty loud enough for Fay to overhear. *You're a nice girl from a nice home, and your parents have good standards....*

That line we'd heard a lot, but it had always been meaningless. My house was too small, and we all hated it, but we couldn't afford to move. And people said it to Melissa, whose parents were divorced.

I handed Melissa's bag to Fay, hoping at least she'd take the apple, but she set it gently down. Her face was blank, her neck invisible. She looked at me the way she looked back at adults like Mrs. Kemble and Conley the Creep.

I searched for a way to sidestep the subject of lies, to heal the breach, and then I saw it.

"She's making her dream into reality," I said, remembering something Melissa had told me recently. It had sounded something like one of those stupid things teachers tell you, like, "achieving your goals," but it fit now. "Even when we were middle-schoolers and played those games in the park, you know what her part always was: she had to be the princess, or the shepherd girl, or the witch's kid who saved the prince, or hypnotized a dragon, or saved the world—by dancing."

I smiled at the memory of Melissa's scrawny form dancing among the trees. When she'd danced she wasn't scrawny, she was light and graceful. That day her long brown hair was crowned with a garland of leaves that the three of us had put together, making her look like something out of Greek mythology and not a real human being. Grownups used to stop dead on the path, watching her.

"Dance is magic for her," I finished. "And all her energy is going into making it real."

"Magic," Fay said in her flattest voice, "already is real. Gandalf said as much in *Lord of the Rings*. But not everyone can see it."

Could I talk about lies without having to say the word?

"But Gandalf isn't real," I said.

"Of course he is. Tolkien believed in Middle Earth," Fay stated. "You can see it in that poem, 'Mythopoesis.'" She pronounced it carefully, and probably wrong. None of us knew how to say it—the teachers had never heard of the poem. The only poems they seemed to know were ones like "Daffodils."

The bell rang, startling us both. I was angry with myself for getting sidetracked into arguing about whether Middle-earth was real or not, when what I wanted was for the three of us to go back to being best friends.

But Fay stood there stolidly, looking at me with that round, blank face, Melissa's lunch bag sitting forgotten on the bench between us. She said, "Missy doesn't believe me, and you don't either."

So that was that. I walked away, and she didn't call me back.

My next class could have disappeared into a time warp for all I noticed. I sat there staring at my notebook, getting madder by the minute.

I couldn't believe it. Fay wanted me to prove our friendship by believing in lies. Who was that supposed to impress?

In band that afternoon, we sounded terrible.

"Well," Mrs. Lopez said, "since some of you can't seem to find the time to practice at home, we'll use our scheduled hours after school. Report back at three-oh-five."

Everyone else groaned, but as I put my flute away, I was relieved. Now I wouldn't have to see Fay at three. I wouldn't have to do anything about that promise to go to the library.

But after practice, I got a nasty shock.

Mr. Conley was standing there on the steps, as if he hadn't moved since eight that morning. Seeing him, the band members kind of froze up in the doorway, like a clump of zombies.

"Come here." He crooked his finger at me.

The other students swarmed around me like fish in a stream, glad to escape the hook.

"Yes, sir?" My voice quavered. I hated it.

"The United States mail never seems to reach the Reed residence, and they do not possess a telephone. On the chance," he said with heavy sarcasm, "that Mrs. Reed has miraculously recovered from her foot injury, you may deliver this to her while you are consorting with your friend."

And he thrust a sealed envelope into my sweaty hands.

He turned away. I gulped some air in past my pounding heart.

I didn't tell him that I'd never been to Fay's house—didn't even know, except kind of generally, where it was. Nor did I ask why I should do his job for him, especially one (I realized as I looked at the address penciled on the envelope) that would take the rest of the afternoon. One didn't refuse Mr. Conley.

Instead, I went back into the gym and borrowed someone's cell to call my mom. "I have to do something for the principal," I said. "I guess I'll be home later."

There was a tiny silence; then of course Mom said, "Well, try to get home before dark."

I thought about everything on the long bus ride across town. If I had any kind of dream, it was to get a long way away from this town and Conley the Creep. But I had to learn how to deal with the Mr. Conleys of the world.

College was the way, I thought as I leaned my head against the dirty bus window and watched the streets lurch by. I thought about how money was a constant worry in my family; Mom's hours at the flower shop were always getting cut back, and though Dad had recently been promoted to manager at the gas station where he'd always worked, his raise had gone straight into the family fund to take care of my great-aunt Sarah, who had Alzheimer's.

Reality for my parents was the town where they'd always lived, the jobs they'd always had, and the people they'd always known. I wanted more choices, and the ability to make the right ones.

The bus reached the highway outside of town, and I got off. So far I'd managed not to think about what I'd say to Fay if I saw her.

I'd never been asked to Fay's home. Though she, Melissa, and I had been best friends for years, we'd always met at the park, and then at the library. Every year Missy and I invited her to our birthday parties, and Fay always thanked us, but she always had something to do those two days. The only two days of the year she was busy.

We hadn't questioned her about it; it was just the way things were. And considering how much the adults of our town were always complaining about the Reeds—whether Matt, Mark, or Luke, or Charity or Hope or Prudence—it was easier that way than to explain that we were friends with one of the Reeds you didn't hear much about.

Their place was easy to find. One side of the highway was nothing but scrubland, the other a group of rotting buildings, long abandoned. Near a clump of dusty trees squatted a rusting old trailer, with a kind of shed made of battered pieces of sheet metal hammered to the back. Several junker cars rusted around the trash- and weed-choked yard.

I trudged up the rutted dirt road toward the trailer. My heart started hammering when I saw a group of older boys, all tough-looking, standing around the engine of an ancient pickup. Nearby, four or five younger kids were playing some kind of game. They were all thick-built, like Fay, but some were blond and some redheaded.

They stopped playing when they saw me. "Get lost, butt-nugget," a boy yelled at me.

The others laughed, then the big guys looked around.

"Well, hel-lo, baby," one said, with a nasty sneer. "Come on over, let's check you out!"

The others greeted this with yells of brainless laughter and disgusting suggestions. Fear choked me. I was ready to drop that envelope and run.

Then a pair of legs appeared from under the car, followed by a muscular torso and a square face with blond hair.

"Shut up," the young man said, and they shut up.

I stared. It was Joseph Reed, the oldest, the only Reed to be graduated from high school, though several of them were over eighteen. He was also the only one with a job; he worked, as it happened, for my dad.

He'd never talked to me before, but it was obvious he knew who I was. "Fay's inside, doing homework," he said, pointing an oil-blackened thumb over his shoulder.

I didn't tell him I wasn't there to see Fay. Glad the envelope was in my notebook pressed tight against my chest, I just nodded and went by. The guys were all silent, but I could feel their stares like radiation burns on my back.

Sagging steps led into the open door of the trailer. The first thing that met me was noise from a loud television set. The front door stood wide open, but it did nothing for the thick air inside, which smelled of cigarettes, beer, cooking oil, and hair spray. I stood uncertainly in the doorway, peering into the gloom.

In a corner the TV blared, completely ignored by two huge women, one with bright yellow hair, the other with even brighter red hair. They sat by the kitchen counter, the redhead fixing the blonde's hair. Heaped-up ashtrays, dirty dishes, and empty beer cans lay everywhere.

The blond woman raised a beer to her lips, then saw me. Squinting, she said, "You lookin' for someone, sugar?"

"Are you Mrs. Reed?" I asked.

"Depends on what you want," she shot back, and both women let loose with loud shrieks of laughter.

"Mr. Conley sent me with this," I said, trying to keep my voice even, as I pulled out the paper. My forehead panged with the beginnings of a headache, and I wondered if Mr. Conley had meant for me to go through this nightmare in order to end a friendship that was likely already finished anyway.

Mrs. Reed held out her hand for the letter. Her nails were an inch long. Ripping open the envelope with one of those crimson nails, she said, "Who are you?"

I didn't want to tell her my name, so I blurted out the next thing that came to me: "I'm in Fay's class."

As soon as it was out, I regretted it.

She put her head back, expelling a huge cloud of smoke. "Faith!" she screeched. Then she squinted at the letter and dropped it onto an ashtray on the floor. "Matt again," she said, and laughed.

Then Fay appeared from a back hallway. When she saw me she hunched up, like someone had smacked her.

"I'll be going," I said quickly. "You're busy—"

"Stay awhile." The red-haired woman poked my shoulder, propelling me toward Fay. "Get the kid to talk a little. Ain't natural, sittin' all the time with a book like that."

Fay looked from them to me, then said, "Come on."

The trailer's hallway reminded me of an old train: narrow, airless, dark. Trying to find some kind of easy way out, I said, "Are all those your brothers and sisters out there?"

I didn't even know how many of them there were. Too late I realized the question might seem an insult.

"Sure. Rest are cousins," she said, using her flat voice. "That's my aunt Leah out front."

"Does everybody have Bible names?" I thought that question, at least, would be safe to ask. But she didn't answer right away, just pushed aside a hanging beach towel in a doorway and gestured me inside.

It was a tiny room with four futons on the floor. Most of the room was an even worse mess than the living room, except for one corner. There, three plastic boxes stuffed with neatly folded clothes stood next to a tidily made-up futon. On the top of the crates sat an old, cracked radio, propping up a row of library books.

Fay's radio, I realized. Her bed, her clothes. Her books.

She turned around and faced me, her arms crossed. "Grandma named us," she said, still flat as poured cement. "Ma not being married, Gran paid for the hospital, so long's she could name us. Had us all baptized, too. Anything else you want to know?"

Her anger made mine come rushing back. If her magic was so real, then why was she living in this disgusting dump? The tiniest spell could at least empty an ashtray. "Is that the radio where you listened to Middle-earth?" I asked, pointing.

Fay's cheeks showed dull red, but just as her mouth opened, a set of clicking claws ticked right up behind me, and I got thumped in the back by a stout dog with a shaggy tan coat.

He slobbered onto my hand, which I snatched away and wiped on my coat. I asked, "And is this the dog that talks?"

The dog bounded past me to Fay, jumping up with his paws on her chest. She grabbed his paws and held him, though the dog must have weighed at least as much as she did. Looking him right in the muzzle, she said: "C'mon, Aslan, tell her hello."

I felt as if someone had doused me with ice water.

The dog dropped down, panting, his tongue lolling out, and thumped his tail. Fay glanced up at me once, then bent close to him. "Please. Say something."

She's crazy, I thought, backing up a step. *She's a crazy girl living with a lot of horrible crazy people, and I never knew it.*

A sudden gulping sob stopped me in my retreat. Fay buried her face in the dog's dirty ruff. "Talk," she cried into his fur. "Talk. Please, Aslan. Please." And she cried, not noisily like a baby, but the terrible soundless sobs of a person who has lost everything, her whole body shaking.

I stood there, my anger gone. *Now what do I do?*

I looked at Fay, who crouched on her futon, still holding the dog. He sat patiently under her tight grip, his tail stirring as he looked up at me.

I looked at the dog, then around at the room again. *This is Fay's reality,* I thought. *No wonder she believes in magic. What else could rescue her?* A great wave of pity swept through me, piling up behind my teeth and tongue, but I didn't say anything, because I knew, as surely as I knew she had never come to our birthday parties, had never asked to share our lunches, that Fay would hate pity.

I dropped onto my knees at the other end of the futon and held out a hand to the dog. Maybe I couldn't say anything, but could I show her how sorry I was?

Her head was still buried in the dog's fur. I looked past her, wondering what I could do or say next. My eyes lit on that radio, and I remembered all those Middle-earth reports. How much Missy and I had loved to hear those stories! Heck, how believable they had been—true to the characters, as if J.R.R. Tolkien himself had made them up.

This isn't *her reality,* I thought. *She's made a reality all for herself, filled with magical happenings and interesting people and faraway places. And in its own way, it's just as real as Missy's dream to dance with the New York Ballet.*

My pity was gone. In its place were admiration and envy. The radio, the dog, even the trailer—I remembered once in the fourth grade, she told us her house could fly. Trailers moved, and with a little imagination, maybe they could fly. She'd taken bits of her horrible life and made it fun.

"It doesn't matter," I said. "I believe you, Fay. I believe you."

She lifted her head, just a bit. Her red eyes were more suspicious than anything else.

I threw my arms wide. "You're right," I said. "I've been thinking, and you're totally, absolutely right—magic can be found if a person looks hard enough. I'm sorry I was so blind."

She gave a long sniff and sat up, knuckling her eyes. "Wh-what made you change your mind?" Her breathing was still ragged.

"There's magic here," I said. "I can feel it."

She gave another sob, but it was the relief kind, the storm-is-over kind. The dog thrust his muzzle under my hand, then sniffed at my coat pocket, where the ham sandwich from lunch had sat all afternoon, forgotten. I pulled it out, unwrapped it, and gave it to him. Fay and I watched him gulp the sandwich in two bites, then look from one of us to the other, hoping for more.

I patted the dog's head absently, smiling at Fay. At last, she smiled back.

"Food!" the dog barked. "More food! Food!"

About the Author

Sherwood Smith studied in Austria, finally earning a master's in history—she's been a governess, a bartender, and wore various hats in the film industry before turning to teaching for 20 years. She began her publishing career in 1986. To date she's published over forty books, nominated for several awards, including the Nebula, the Mythopoeic Fantasy Award, and an Anne Lindbergh Honor Book. Her website is www.sherwoodsmith.net.

WASHING OF THE WATER

JIM JOHNSON

The distant glittering waves of the Couran Ocean gently pushed the sun up out of their embrace and into an unusually clear blue sky. Gray gulls cried out shrill welcomes, and local fishermen greeted each other with what, from their tone, sounded like friendly insults as they shook out their nets and sails. And yet all Camille really heard were wordless whispers driving her southwest toward the ancient city of Bridges.

She squinted at the sun, shading her eyes with a free hand. Under most circumstances, she'd have considered the lack of rain, fog, or threatening clouds a portent of a good day ahead, but not today.

The silent voices rattling in her mind suggested today would be a grim day.

She shrugged in her heavy cloak and chainmail and adjusted the weather-beaten packs slung on her shoulders, as well as the sword hanging from her waist. Once settled, she limped onto the northernmost span leading toward the city of Bridges, the whispers dogging her all the while. They, along with her mount, had been her only companions these past months, and even with them, she felt more alone than she had in years.

As Camille trudged along the crumbled northern edge of the bridge, she glanced down toward the shoreline and the rotting wooden piers poking into the water like gnarled fingers. The fishermen were moving out in their little single-mast skiffs, no doubt planning for their first catches of the day.

Her command of the northern dialects was poor, and the fishermen far enough away, that she could only just barely hear their calls to each other. She could not discern their meaning. Their comments, laced with laughter, roused her confused curiosity. That anyone could still find levity in these dark days was nothing short of amazing. The Empire had seen precious little joy of late, from the southernmost steppes to the Northern Shore and every province in between.

And the dread in her heart at having to approach the massive wooden doors closing off Bridges from the rest of the world did nothing to set her mind at ease. She had intended to bypass the city completely in her desire to get back to the capital quickly, but no. Her ineffectual meditations had been chaotic since leaving the ancient Valanth Priory, and that had been weeks ago. Murky signs and strange portents and the constant whispers had pushed her toward Bridges. And, like a broken branch helplessly following the current, she'd let herself get swept off the homeward path toward the uncertainty that waited for her here.

She glanced up at the unnatural clear sky again and mustered up some gratitude that rain seemed unlikely for the day. Her beloved jaunter, Visala, was no doubt still securely fastened to his picket pin, enjoying the water and grass near their makeshift campsite. She didn't plan on being in Bridges more than a couple hours, no matter what the whispers might suggest, so she had thought it better to leave him off the span and out of the city.

If Bridges was suffering as much as the rest of the Imperial cities, horsemeat on the hoof would be a temptation few could ignore, even if an ordained Sentinel of the Crown were seated on his back.

She moved closer to the city's gates, barely registering the heaps of refuse and rubble strewn along either side of the span. Bridges had clearly been hit as hard as the rest of the northern Empire she'd seen of late. That fact pressed another layer of despair upon her senses, like the weight of water on her lungs when she dove deep on a too-rare swimming indulgence.

She stopped before the city's massive wooden doors, closed fast against the rising sun. Bridges was the northernmost city of the Empire. If it had suffered as much as the smaller settlements farther north, what hope was there that any Imperial cities had escaped the plagues? Had the wave of plagues, famine, and warfare spread so far? Was there any community, any blade of grass, any clear pool of water, left untouched?

There had to be. If she was sure of anything, it was that there had to be some glimmer of hope, some spot of radiance left in the Empire. Otherwise, what was she fighting for; what purpose did the Sentinels serve? Why should they defend the citizens and scour the known world for ancient knowledge and storied relics if there was no light left shining?

No. She shook her head and stretched out her cramped legs. No despair. She'd been riding hard and had been conserving her strength for whatever awaited her beyond those massive wood and metal gates. She had been drawn here, to Bridges, for a reason; it was time to find out why and by whom. The whispers in her mind were maddeningly vague on all fronts, but the answer awaited her within. She was certain of it.

She lifted her gaze along the tall doors, stretching some thirty feet overhead. They were carefully set into the stone walls, with no seam visible as near as she could tell. Bridges had been one of the very first Imperial cities, built in an age when the ancestors knew how to build things to endure. Their techniques had been lost over the ages, and the city and its strangely solid constructions still stood—for the most part, anyway.

Looking over the side of the elevated span, she saw several other bridges connected to various other roads that all converged on the city. Two had collapsed at some point in the past, which suggested either wartime damage or, perhaps, that even the ancients hadn't had all the answers.

Camille refocused her attention on the doors in front of her. No point musing on what might have happened in the past. Her present and possible future faced her behind those city doors. She studied the dated yet intricate designs carved into the doors, appreciating the detail and precision of the craftwork. Her eyes fell upon an arrow slit set halfway up the doorframe. She caught the distinct glint of an eye looking down on her through the slit, an eye that then disappeared from view.

She didn't need to call out. If the door warden had seen her for who she was, had seen the distinctive badge on her cloak shoulder or her surcoat bearing the double-looped cross, they'd know who and what she was. Even if she could no longer perform her office thanks to the inchoate voices rattling in her mind and the battering of her hope over the long months.

The clanking and grinding of the door's mechanisms sounded, setting her nerves even more on edge. She flinched back in a mix of surprise and not a little fear, though she tamped down the latter and allowed the feeling to flow through her like water in a channel, down into the stone beneath her booted feet. She took one long, calming breath as the doors swung open with a long groan.

The door warden, a graying branch of a man dressed in dingy green linens and wools, slipped out from the depths of the long tunnel behind him and approached. The threadbare, faded Imperial sergeant's badge embroidered on his cloak shoulder and the double-bladed halberd in his hands marked him as a career soldier from the old guard. No doubt stationed here as a door warden in the northernmost city as a form of retirement. Or punishment, though that seemed unlikely. A darker thought tried to manifest itself, but she pushed it aside.

Camille offered him a smile. "Good morrow to you, Sergeant. I see you served with the Seventh Legion. The Sentinels are eternally grateful for your service."

She didn't need to elaborate. Every Sentinel and Seventh Legionnaire knew of the Day. It was embedded in all their memories and would be passed down to new members of both organizations for as long as there was ink to put to paper or voices to recite songs.

"You do this old soldier a kindness, Sister-Sentinel. A compliment from your kind is more than I could have hoped for, being stationed this far from the comforts of home."

That dark thought her subconscious had been nurturing against her better judgment flared up, and it took a strong dose of willpower to push it aside again. She'd been right to think it—the man wasn't here for retirement. He'd been posted here to help defend the empire's northern border.

She couldn't hold off any more. She had to know. She limped over to him and raised an open hand in greeting. "I am Sentinel Camille. May the Empress smile upon you."

He raised a gloved hand in response. "And may she nod favorably in your direction. I am Sergeant Andrus."

She met his eyes and offered the briefest of smiles before touching her right palm to his and then letting her hand fall to her side. Out of habit, she hooked her thumbs into her sword belt. "I've been north on Sentinel business. What times have befallen the Empire such that they send youngling recruits to patrol the outlying villages and... experienced soldiers such as yourself to the cities to act as wardens?"

He used his free hand to pull thoughtfully at the inch-long growth of stubble on his chin as he stared at her. His bright green eyes were clearer than she might have expected from a man of his apparent age. "You've seen a campaign or two yourself, Sister-Sentinel. You may have spent months far to the north, but you know why I'm here."

The truth in his voice speared her deepest soul, and yet she had to ask because it was so hard to believe. "Is it really so bad for the Empire, then? That we arm our sons and our elders and press them into the field?"

The door warden nodded, the corners of his eyes glimmering with tears. "As well as our daughters and ladies, gray and fair. And all else who fall in between. Every able body or near-able body has been pressed into service. The plagues require it."

Camille swore quietly under her breath, confident her secret god would forgive her the moment of blasphemy. "I've been gone far too long then, friend. I followed signs that have brought me to your post. May I pass and enter the fair city of Bridges?"

He sized her up, smiling all the while, and then moved his halberd to a resting position. He took a precise step back and to the left. "The city is open to you and to yours, Sentinel Camille. I will not bar the way."

She bowed low, a sign of respect for him and his veteran status. "Thank you, Sergeant Andrus. May you soon be returned to your home and your loved ones." She moved past him and into the dark tunnel leading into the city proper. The piles of refuse were less present here, whether because of Andrus's diligence or some other reason, she didn't know.

He called out to her as she walked away. "May you find what you're looking for during your time with us, Sentinel."

She paused and offered a nod, then focused on her footsteps and followed them into the city. If she could somehow stop the voices in her head, and nothing more, she'd consider this journey to Bridges worthwhile.

Once out of the largely empty tunnel, she entered one of the major thoroughfares. The street stretched out ahead of her in a perfectly straight line, leading off into the far distance where the southern gates stood closed beyond a tunnel similar to the one she'd just left.

As she started along the wide stone street, curious locals dressed in drab workday linens and cottons paused their morning gossip and trading to glance at her. She steeled herself for the inevitable, and tried to reach deep within herself for her reservoir of power. It took far longer than she wanted to admit to muster enough energy to prepare a weak calming spell in case she needed it to stave off the inevitable requests. Hardly enough, but it would have to do. She could do no more.

Their whispers started not long after she started walking along the avenue. "A Sentinel... here?" "Relief coming for sure." "Help is on the way?" "Tell mama—someone's come."

Camille focused straight ahead, but both her peripheral vision and her Art told her that she had attracted a small crowd that grew every few steps. She cast her prepared spell, and felt a little of the tension in her back and legs ease, though not by much. The spell was barely a tickle, nowhere near the power she used to be able to muster. The tightness of her lips and the weariness on her heart remained unabated. The whispers in her mind shifted in tone, modulating to a dull roar that hung in the background, mocking her and her failed talents.

One brave lad pushed through the crowd and boldly stepped in front of her. "Good Sister-Sentinel, hear my plea?" Fortunately, his language was one of the more common northern dialects, and she was able to discern it well enough, even through the buzzing in her ears.

A gentle request made of her could not be ignored, as much as she might have wanted to. She forced herself to stop, reluctant to push the boy aside in her efforts to get to the old Sentinel barracks. She focused on the tow-headed boy, his arms held tightly across his chest, shifting from one thin boot to the other.

She offered a weary smile. "My good cousin, how best may I serve you?"

He nodded toward her cloak shoulder. "Double-looped cross on a blood-red badge. You're a curate, or that's a stolen cloak."

She bristled on the inside, but she clamped down and forced herself to remain calm. "No one accuses another of stealing a Sentinel's cloak."

The boy, who couldn't have been older than ten or twelve, puffed up his chest. "What does that make you, then? That badge says you're a curate."

Camille shot a hooded glance around her. There was no easy path out of here—the press of the crowd had grown too much in the few moments she had stopped to talk to the boy.

She took a deep breath and nodded. "I am a Healer and a Sentinel. But I have not been sent here to…"

She had no chance to get out the rest. She was immediately pelted with pleas for help—'Mama is sick,' 'I've broken a finger,' 'The plague runs through the central district…' One after another, the requests hit her. She was forced to lock off her heart and mind to them. They couldn't see her shame or know her secret guilt. Not here, not now.

She mumbled a hasty excuse and then pushed through the crowd of desperate citizens. When the locals started moving after her, continuing to call out their pleas, she broke into a run and made for the solace of the Sentinel barracks. Her heart broke at leaving needy people behind, but she had to get away, to secure the relative peace of the Sentinel barracks. Without her abilities, there was nothing she could do for them.

After several twists and turns through the city streets, with the whispers chasing her all the while, she managed to lose the pursuing citizens. Eyes full of tears and a sob threatening to rend her throat, she pushed on toward the squat stone and brick structure that encompassed the sole Sentinel presence here in Bridges. She made straight for the front door.

She crashed through the unlocked door and slammed it shut behind her. She leaned hard against it and finally let out the sob she'd been holding back. She wrapped her arms around herself and gave herself the luxury of a short cry. What good was a Healer who couldn't heal? She could barely manage a small spell for herself, but even that simple charm had left her ragged and shaking worse than a snot-nosed initiate. The whispers hadn't just pushed her toward Bridges, they had somehow stripped her of her gods-given talents.

Camille took a few deep, shuddering breaths and pulled herself back into some semblance of order, dredging up memories of the smooth, clear lake near her family's home to settle her mind. She'd lost herself countless times in its still waters, and it was a regular mental retreat for those times she needed to refocus. Even the endless whispers struggled to shake that vision.

Once collected, she stood up away from the doors and took stock of the entrance to the barracks. Much as she expected, the barracks was deserted. Even at the height of the Empire, the barracks would have been lightly occupied, with less than a dozen Sentinels assigned to the city and the surrounding territories. Army regulars and local militia and guards would have managed the safety and security of the city's denizens, and the Sentinels would have been tasked with pursuing the Empress's will out on the frontier or elsewhere within the northern reaches of her domain.

Camille locked the doors of the barracks, which would keep the citizens out physically, though their distant cries for her assistance penetrated the wood and stone and beat upon her like a campaign drum—a constant cry for help. How could she stand to ignore them for long? What could she even do without access to her healing Art?

She found an empty seat in the barracks and sank down onto it—no. She was just one Sentinel, one Healer, and there was no way she was going to attempt to take on the needs of an entire city. The last census she'd seen, years ago, had put the city's population at around nine thousand souls, though that had to be before any recent disasters, plagues, or battles. Regardless, she suspected that if she managed to regain her talents and then stayed to help everyone in need, she'd probably never be able to leave.

She held her face in her hands for a few more desperate, centering breaths, and then forced herself to stand up, and to search both floors of the barracks. She worked her way methodically through the various rooms, efficiently rifling through each chest and box and bag she found along the way. She found a few items of interest, and carried them back to the barracks' simple kitchen. She settled onto a low bench next to a long table.

She pulled together a quick, cold supper from the supplies in her pack. She gnawed on the remnants of a hunk of cheese as she reviewed the shaky, spidery journal entries of the last Sentinel posted to Bridges, Brother-Sentinel Alois. She'd found the slim volume on a small table next to an unmade bed.

The journal was much as she expected, a daily accounting of people the Sentinel had healed or treated, the mundanities of his life, and general reflections particular to him, all of which carried a thread of worry throughout that he might soon be reassigned. It seemed the Empress had few Sentinels left to do her dirty work.

When she finished skimming the journal entries, she sighed in frustration. She'd already figured out that the man had disappeared—the empty barracks was sign enough of that. Either he must still be in the city or he had left Bridges on some Imperial business. The latter seemed unlikely, since it was standard practice for Sentinels to log their arrivals and departures. And besides, if he had left, he would certainly have taken his journal. The leather-corded book was only a third filled with ink, and Alois had been diligent in recording some sort of comment every day for the last several months. She suspected a more thorough search of his quarters would reveal more journals, older than this one.

No, he had to still be in the city somewhere, either working his healing craft or, perhaps, injured or dead. She recalled one of the comments from the crowd—plague in the central district—and wondered if he'd be found there.

The barracks doors suddenly rattled. After a moment, a quiet rapping startled her out of her musing. She sighed and then moved over to the door. "Yes?" The whispers in her mind started to rumble, growing in volume.

"My name's Mora. May I come in? I help Sentinel Alois from time to time."

Camille frowned, but pulled open the door. She squinted into the sunlight streaming over the city walls. "As long as you're not here to ask for healing or poultices, come in."

A young girl dressed in a dingy brown sack dress hurried in, her sandaled feet slapping on the flagstone floor. She had a simple rope belt wrapped around her waist and a rough-hewn wooden double-loop cross pendant hanging from her neck on a frayed leather cord. Her long brown hair was tied back in a simple but serviceable braid.

Camille closed the door and shot home the bolt. "My name's Camille. I'd welcome you into the Sentinels' barracks, but it seems you know your way around."

Mora had moved over to the large hearth set against one wall and had already lit the kindling that had been set in it. The girl was quick. "Oh, yes, I come here every day to speak with Brother Alois and to look at his books."

Camille quirked up an eyebrow. "You can read?" The girl

didn't appear to be much older than ten. Her dress and demeanor didn't exactly scream out a connection to the wealthier class that could have afforded lessons for their children.

Mora glanced at her as she built up the fire. "Yes, Sister. Brother Alois taught me. Or at least he *was* teaching me."

Camille stared at her as the voices banged around in her mind. Alois had made no mention of training a commoner in his journal. "Indeed? Would you happen to know where he is?"

Mora's face fell into a frown. "He told me a few days ago that he couldn't wait any longer, and was going to go into the central district to try and help those he could." She rummaged around in a basket set near the hearth and started pulling out onions and root vegetables. She placed them onto a low wooden table set near the hearth. "That's the last I saw of him."

Camille crossed her arms in front of her chest. "A few days, you say. What's happened in the central district?"

Mora shrugged as she gathered a few more vegetables and then replaced the basket cover. "The plague has returned, or so the people of the central district claim."

"Why would they lie?"

Mora shrugged again and then produced a small chopping knife out of her satchel. She sat down at the table and started to chop the vegetables arrayed in front of her. "To get out of there. The city council set a new edict that the doors to the central city were to be barred until further notice."

"To protect the rest of the city?"

Mora paused in her chopping to stare at her with strangely hooded eyes. "I don't know."

And yet Camille suspected Mora knew exactly what she was afraid of. She stared at the girl in silence for several heartbeats, then nodded and took a seat at the table across from her.

Mora shot her a wary look and then resumed chopping the vegetables. "You arrived today. How long will you be in Bridges?"

Camille focused on Mora as she spoke, wishing she could push a gentle probe with her Art to pick up any of Mora's surface thoughts. But she could sense nothing—the girl was a blank slate. Any control she had over her Art had all but vanished. The whispers mocked her again.

No. Brother Alois must have taught Mora something more than just how to read—the girl must have something of the Art about her.

Something in her eyes must have given her away, because Mora stopped chopping again and shifted the knife in her hands to a defensive grip. "Are you going to try to hurt me?"

Camille's voice escaped her. That wasn't the question she had expected. She raised both hands palms out, and shook her head. She swallowed hard and forced her voice to reconnect. "I wouldn't dream of such a thing," she lied. "That's not what Healers do."

Which was generally true, except in extraordinary circumstances, which Mora was starting to feel like. "Did Brother Alois teach you anything aside from how to read?"

Mora didn't change her stance or shift her grip on the knife. "And what if he did?"

Camille slowly rested her hands on the table, but readied herself if Mora decided to strike out with the blade. "It's just a question, no more. We're a long way from the capital, and I have no interest in reporting him or you to the Stone Guard."

God, that's the last thing she'd do to a girl so young and with apparent ability in the Art.

Mora gave her another hooded look and then slowly lowered the knife to the table. "Can you swear a solemn vow on that?"

Camille met her eyes and focused, unblinking. "I just did. I'm sure Alois told you that a Sentinel's word is their law. If we break it, we don't deserve to wear the white surcoat or the double-looped cross." She injected as much confidence and surety she could muster into her words.

Mora's features seemed to soften. With one more lingering stare at her, Mora shifted her focus anew on the pile of vegetables and resumed chopping. "All right, then. I believe you, Sister-Sentinel."

Camille sighed and tapped both hands on the table. "Please, just call me Camille. This isn't a day for ranks or protocol."

Mora quirked up an eyebrow as she chopped. "What is this a day for?"

Camille snorted. "Surprises for one. Answers, hopefully." She reached out for a slice of potato and popped it into her mouth. She chewed the dense, moist wedge thoughtfully, then swallowed. "What are you making, anyway?"

Mora shrugged as she neared the end of the pile of vegetables. "A simple stew. I also brought some flour and meaty bones to make stock. Brother Alois usually brings fresh baked bread from the market, and…"

She stopped and stared at the closed barracks door. "I… I guess he won't be bringing bread today." She sniffed and Camille caught the glimmer of a tear before she lowered her head and started transferring the chopped vegetables into a pot.

Camille took a steadying breath. "In answer to your question, I didn't intend to stay here long. I even left my horse picketed outside of the city, near the shoreline. I had thought to check in with the Sentinels here and then be on my way."

Mora finished moving the vegetables into the pot and glanced at her as she hung the pot over the fire. "Where would you go?"

"Back home, south to the capital to report in to the Grand-Master, and then farther south, to home."

Mora rummaged in her satchel and tossed a couple of bloodied bones and a handful of herbs into the pot. "Where's home?"

Camille sighed as the room started to fill with the smell of simmering vegetables. "Caulber-on-Routh. It's a small fishing village a few days' ride out of the capital."

"Nice place?"

Camille shrugged. "I haven't been home in almost a decade, but yes. I remember it being a nice enough place. Lots of hills and trees, quiet brooks, quiet people. A large lake to swim in."

Mora shook her head and then stirred in some water and flour to her stew. "I can't imagine a quiet place to live. Bridges always has something going on, even at night."

"I can imagine. Does the city not have an imposed curfew?" Some of the beleaguered Imperial cities and larger villages had resorted to mandatory curfews to try and give the overworked local guards a chance to rest and regroup, to varying middling success.

Mora shrugged. "We do have one, but there's hardly anyone here to enforce it. Just old men and women with slow hands on pikes, and a few soldiers not much older than me."

Camille sighed, saddened all over again. "And if the plague has returned to the central district, they'll be even more overworked containing anyone trying to escape."

Mora met her eyes and nodded silently. The look on her face made Camille's heart yearn to reach out, to offer some comfort. Mora wasn't much older than her sister, assuming she was still alive. Camille hadn't seen Yvaine for more than five years.

But... Camille shook her head, pushing the past into the back of her mind, past the rustling voices. There were more immediate matters at hand. She brushed her hands off on her surcoat and stood. "Mora, I need to find Brother Alois. Would you be willing to help me?"

Mora stirred the pot of stew and avoided her stare. "Why me?"

Camille started gathering up her gear. "You're a local, for one thing, and you've worked with Alois recently. And, if I had been him, I'd have taught you something about the Art and how to scan for a person by using it."

The look Mora shot her told her all she needed to know. Camille offered the girl a brief smile, then held out her hand toward her. "Come. Help me find Brother Alois."

Mora stared into her eyes for a long moment, the nodded. She wrapped a towel around the pot handle and removed the pot from the fire, and set it down on the hearthstones. "I don't know how long we'll be, but I don't want this to burn."

"Well-reasoned. The fire should be fine left alone, yes?"

Mora nodded. "We leave it burning from time to time." She gathered up a few odds and ends and stuck them in her satchel, and then cleaned off her small chopping knife and placed that in her satchel as well. "We should head for the central district's main gate, though you'll have a hard time getting in."

Camille opened the door and led the way out of the barracks. "Oh, I don't know. I think we'll be let in easily enough."

"Why do you think that?"

"Because if the plague has returned, the people the city guards are most likely to let pass is a Healer-Sentinel and her assistant." Even if said healer couldn't heal. Camille offered a grin she didn't really feel, which Mora made no effort to return.

Just as Camille had suspected, the guards posted to the central district's barred gates took very little convincing to let them pass through. Camille caught the subtle warding gestures the guards made as she passed them.

Camille glanced at Mora as the guards locked the gates. "Getting in was easy enough, but getting out might be a bit more challenging."

Mora glanced at the gates and then refocused on her. The confidence Camille had seen earlier had faded. "I suppose."

Camille took a deep breath then focused on the area around her. This section of the central district was mostly shuttered shops and closed residences. It was near midday, but there were hardly any people about. The flagstone paths were in need of sweeping, and there was a decided silence in the air that echoed of death and despair. Wood smoke lingered on the air as if from some distance farther away, deeper into the district.

"So, assuming Brother Alois taught you something of tracking with your Art, would you be willing to focus and attempt to pick up his trail?"

Mora took a deep breath and then nodded. "I'll try. Brother Alois was a good teacher."

"Then close your eyes, focus on what Brother Alois looked like when you last saw him. Reach out with your senses, and tell me what you see."

Camille tamped down a surge of bitterness that she didn't have the ability to do what she was guiding Mora to do, but nothing for that now. Her talents were locked away somewhere within her mind, and she didn't have the means to break them out.

Mora closed her eyes and seemed to focus. She shifted on her feet, and then, with her eyes still tightly shut, started to slowly walk along the main thoroughfare. Camille raised an eyebrow, but remained silent. Either Alois had taught her well, or the girl had more potential that she had first guessed at. She followed along behind Mora.

"You're doing quite well, Mora. How long did Brother Alois train with you?"

Mora closed her eyes. "Nearly every day for a few months."

"Did your parents not worry that you were spending so much time with Brother Alois?"

Mora flinched, but to her credit, did not retreat. "My father is dead and my mother is a drunk. No one cares about the time I spent with Brother Alois other than him and me."

Mora opened her eyes and gestured toward a nearby alleyway. "The path continues through there."

Camille glanced that way, and nodded. "Very good, Mora. Your control is remarkable for someone with no formal training. If you ever decide to get out of Bridges, you might be able to find work as a seer or tracker."

"Or a Sentinel?"

Camille considered that, then finally nodded. "Certainly, or even a Sentinel, if you felt so called. I'd want to talk to you at length about that choice if that's the road you choose to walk."

"Would you not recommend joining the Sentinels?"

"I would, of course, recommend joining, but you have to know why you'd want to join. Serving the Empress and serving the Empire's people are very different things. You'll want to evaluate both before doing so."

"I thought all Sentinels served the people."

Camille couldn't help but snort. "Many do. Some join for less noble reasons."

Mora frowned at that, but Camille couldn't bring herself to add any more for fear of completely disillusioning the girl.

"But we can discuss that in further detail later. For now, focus on Brother Alois. Let's see if we can find him or his trail."

Mora stared at her as if she wanted to ask a question, but then shook her head and focused. "Give me a moment... there." She gestured toward the alley again. "That's the direction he took."

Camille gave Mora a gentle nudge. "Lead the way, Mora. I'll follow the trail."

Without comment, Mora stepped toward and into the alleyway. Camille followed along in silence. The whispers were back in force, even louder than before. Camille frowned, and focused less on the path and more on Mora's back as she walked ahead.

How was Mora so effectively managing her abilities to follow Alois' trail? No Sentinel initiate that she could ever remember had exhibited such control at such an early age. She had read most of the training registers in the formal library. There had been some standout recruits and high-functioning Sentinels in the past, but if Mora were to pursue Sentinel training, she'd almost certainly be the most powerful practitioner ever trained.

Not that a prodigy wasn't possible—Mora certainly could be that. But there were no prophecies any more, no legends of heroes to come. There had been some dusty tomes of the ancient religions that she had taken a special liking to, even had read up on the ancient goddess of the moon, Del'shaya, and taken her on as her private inspiration, but nothing that she could remember reading suggested that someone in a generation could display the Art that Mora was displaying now.

Lost in her thoughts, she nearly crashed into Mora, who had stopped in front of a stone archway set into a narrow alley. Inside the arch was a straight stairway leading down into darkness.

Camille caught herself before crashing into Mora. "My apologies."

Mora nodded toward the archway. "The trail leads in here. I'm sure of it."

Camille studied the archway. "This is old, older than most of the other parts of the city I've seen so far."

Mora stepped into the archway and ran a hand along the stones. "We're deep in the central district. This was the core of the city from which the remainder was built around. We're in the heart of Bridges."

Camille flinched at the certainty in Mora's tone, the comfortable means by which she described the area. "You've been here before." It was a statement, not a question. The hackles on her neck itched.

Mora focused on the stairway ahead. "I stumbled into this and then sought out Brother Alois." She shrugged and then glanced back at Camille. "I showed it to him."

"Why?" Camille had blurted out the question before really thinking about it.

Mora shrugged and her voice took on a strange, ethereal tone. "There are things down here, things that were meant to be found, but had been lost."

The voices in Camille's head reached a crescendo, making her wince back from the archway. She tried to gather up her Art to try and block out the noise, but it was simply too strong, or she was too weak. She cried out and staggered back, and tried to swat away Mora's hands as the girl reached out to her, but found she couldn't resist.

Mora took hold of her hands, and in that moment, the voices were silenced, as if they had never been there before. The subtle ache on her mind eased, and she found she could think and breathe more clearly. A glimmer of her own abilities flared for a moment in her mind, but then was gone again.

Camille stared into Mora's eyes. "What did you just do?" She was afraid to pull her hands away. She didn't want the voices to come back, and she desperately wanted to feel her Art blaze within her soul again.

Mora's dark brown eyes bored into hers. Camille fancied she saw a glimmer of golden light behind those dark orbs, but surely that was a trick of the sun.

In that same odd tone, Mora said, "The dead have been trying to distract you, to fill your mind with lies and noise and chaos. I've blocked them, for now."

Camille couldn't pull her gaze away. "But... how?"

Mora shrugged toward the archway. "I don't know, but I want to find out. The answer is in there." Her voice continued to hold an unearthly quality, almost as if a second voice was speaking simultaneously, adding a deeper echo to her words.

Camille shot a fearful look at the archway. "What's down there?"

Mora broke off the eye contact and gently pulled her toward the stairway. "A long passage down to the original city cistern, and more. Come and see."

Camille dragged her feet, but didn't lose contact with Mora. "Is Alois down there too?"

Mora nodded, but stayed focused on the stairs. "I believe he is here as well."

She led Camille into the archway and then onto the first wide flagstone step leading down. Camille took a good look at the darkness ahead and pulled back on her arm.

Mora stopped and glanced back. "What?"

"It's too dark down there. We can't see where we're going."

Mora inclined her head as if in thought, then nodded. "Alois didn't teach me how to make light."

Camille stared at her. "And I can't use my abilities." She offered Mora a sad smile and then produced supplies from her satchel and sparked off a couple of candles with flint and tinder.

Now armed with some light, Mora resumed leading her down the stairs. Camille focused on the steps, but then got comfortable with the pace and motion, and studied the walls around them as they descended the long staircase.

"The workmanship on these stones is remarkable. There's no mortar that I can see, and hardly any gap between the stones."

Mora remained silent, steadily leading them onward.

Camille reached out and let one hand skim along the surface of one of the walls, marveling at the smooth stone finish. After what seemed like a hundred or more steps, they reached a landing that then turned on itself and led to another archway. This archway had a pair of ornate metal gates bolted into it with some sort of black-finished metal she wasn't familiar with.

Both metal gates were open, and it took a moment or two for her eyes and mind to bring clarity to the pattern of the swirls of metal comprising the gates.

She stared in surprise. "That's... not possible." Both gates were made of thin metal that had been shaped into dozens of connected double-loop crosses, each one a near-perfect representation of the same double-looped cross she bore on her surcoat and shoulder badge.

Mora kept hold of her hand and glanced at her. "This is why Alois came back. And why we must come here."

Camille nodded mutely, her mind whirling at what this could possibly mean. "I want to say this is impossible, but..." She reached out a tentative hand, then more boldly reached out and wrapped a hand around one of the gates. The metal was cold to the touch and had a slightly greasy texture to it that she could not place.

"The double-looped cross has been a symbol of the Sentinels since they were formed some two hundred years ago. But this gate... this part of the city is far older than that."

"How much older?" Mora asked.

"Gods, I don't know. Ten times that, perhaps? More? The ancients faded from the world more than a dozen centuries ago. They built the core of Bridges, this center of the city. If they built this gate..." She trailed off, at a loss as to what that might even mean.

Mora cleared her throat. "If the ancients built this gate, then the Sentinels, or some form of them, have been active for far longer than you have ever imagined."

Something in her tone sparked off a memory in her mind. Camille forced herself to let go of the gate and focus on Mora again.

Either it was a trick of the candlelight, or Mora had taken on a glow of her own, almost as if her skin was radiating light. Her facial features had changed somewhat as well, though that might have just been caused by the random dancing shadows in the room.

Mora gestured toward the stairway leading down. "Shall we continue?"

Camille's heart quailed, but she rallied. If Mora turned out to be an agent of evil, she'd fight as hard as she could. She wondered if it would be enough, given what Mora seemed to be capable of. Finally, she nodded. "Lead on. I'll follow."

Mora let go of her hand. The voices in her head returned, though at a lower sound level than they had been at before. Mora led the way down the stairs. The stairway continued down for another hundred steps or so, and as they descended, the temperature in the air dropped steadily.

By the time they reached the bottom of the staircase, which opened onto another stone archway, Camille had pulled her cloak around her to help stave off the sudden bout of shivers.

Mora, who seemed unaffected by the cold though still clad in her simple shift and sandals, glanced at her and gestured toward the long hallway leading away from the stairs. "We're nearly there."

Camille shifted her hands under her cloak, tucking her thumbs into her sword belt again, making sure her right hand wasn't all that far from the pommel of her sword. "What are we going to find?"

"Answers, and truth." Mora turned to focus squarely on her. "And hope."

The word was spoken so plainly and yet with such gentle force. Unbidden tears sprang to her eyes.

Hope. Something she hadn't felt for a long time. Not since before leaving the capital a year or more ago to begin her mission into the northlands. Her mission had been one of desperation, sparked by the loss of faith in the ability of the Sentinels' leadership to stem the outbreaks of plague.

Mora nodded, perhaps sensing the chaotic thoughts in her mind. "Go, Sister. Go seek what you need."

Camille wrapped her cloak more tightly around herself and nodded in silence, and backed away from Mora and turned to walk down the hallway. The stonework in the corridor was every bit as polished and clean as the stairwells had been, but this hallway had an additional feature in that there were panels of text inscribed into the walls on both sides, as well as on the ceiling overhead. The language was foreign to her, the pictographs vaguely familiar in some places but utterly alien in others. An ancient tongue, certainly, lost to time. Even though she had not yet reached thirty years of age, she was one of the more learned of her order; the language laid out on the stones all around here looked like nothing she had ever seen before, except perhaps in a vision or a dream. And even then, her dreams had never been reliable.

As she moved down the hallway, marveling at the text all around her, the voices slowly faded away, replaced by the staccato of dripping water. It had been a subtle shift, but it slowly grew in volume as she neared the end of the corridor, which opened up into a large chamber, so large that it swallowed up her feeble candlelight.

The stone hallway opened out onto a sort of stone platform that ended in a tall stone wall. Beyond the wall stretched a glasslike surface of water, smooth for as far as she could see. Steady dripping from somewhere in the darkness beyond her vision suggested that the cistern had to be fed from somewhere above, though they had to be far enough below the surface of the city that perhaps the cistern tied into the sewer system somehow and then to the streams and ocean beyond.

On the left side of the platform was a stone statue of a woman, easily ten feet tall, holding an ornate double-looped cross in one hand and a thin stone sword in the other. The sword resembled the quick court swords favored by the western countries, unlike the heavier, broader blades used by most in the Empire, including the Sentinels. The woman's features were sublimely wrought into the stone, the face so finely carved that she thought the woman might turn her head and talk to her.

A crumpled form was curled up against the statue's base, wearing a white Sentinel's surcoat. Camille rushed over to the statue and knelt down next to the body, carefully reaching out and turning it onto its back.

The body was that of an older man, with rugged features, a couple days' scruff of beard, and wide, sightless eyes. His sword belt and healer's kit were stacked to one side of the statue. The body had to be Alois.

She rested a palm against his forehead, which was cold to the touch. She thought to reach down with her senses, but of course she had no talent to flex, and so no way to determine if there was any vestige left of him, some memory, some spark of life.

But no, he was gone. She didn't need her Art to identify the faded lesions on his arms and face.

"He's dead?" Mora stepped into her peripheral vision.

Camille stared at the dead man and nodded. "Looks like he made it this far, but then got overtaken by the symptoms." She glanced at Mora. "Do you know when he started to exhibit signs of the plague?"

Mora shifted her eyes to Alois's prone form. "No. I was never that close to him and wouldn't have thought to look anyway."

Camille shifted her stance to sit on the stone floor. The steady dripping of the water soothed her mind and her soul, despite the dead brother laid out before her. She was reminded of that smooth lake near home, and tamped down a sudden strong burst of homesickness.

She let the leading edge of it wash over her, then forced the rest of it away. Mora stepped over to her and knelt down.

"Why do you resist? Why not let the grief wash over you, consume you, and let it take away your pain and anguish?"

Camille held back the tears, but knew it was a losing battle. "No, there's too much. I need to hold it back. It's all I have left." She gestured toward Alois. "You said I'd find hope here, but there is only more death in a room of mysteries."

Mora stretched out a hand and rested it on her shoulder. "There is life here, and hope. You have to open yourself to it."

Camille shook her head, losing control of the arcane dam she had built to hold in her feelings, her emotions. "No, no! I can't. There's nothing here, there's…"

Mora moved closer and wrapped her in an embrace. Camille took hold, held tight, and didn't let go. It had been years since she had let anyone embrace her, and the pent-up emotions and feelings welled up and spilled over her dam, and then broke loose.

She held Mora tight and let it all out, sobbing into her shoulder, crying for all the people she had tried to heal over the years but had failed. The soldiers on the battlefields too far gone for her to save, the confused citizens pushed from their homes, the unborn babies lost to their plague-stricken mothers—all of them.

All those voices she'd lost over the years, the ones she'd been unable to restore. Camille heard them all now, their mute accusations deafening to her ears. Their cries washed over her, consumed her, but then...their cries started to modulate. A bright light pushed against her closed eyes, and after a sobbing breath, a strong burst of honeysuckle and lavender exploded in the air around her.

Confused, she shot open her eyes. Mora sat next to her, haloed in radiant light that had no other source than the girl herself. Camille blinked a few times at the sight. Then, she managed to shield her eyes and focus. There was a fine streamer of golden light connecting Mora to the statue, and a spray of like-colored light connecting the statue to the pool of water beyond the retaining wall.

Camille stared in wonderment. "What is this?"

Mora's features altered slightly and a fresh gust of honeysuckle assaulted Camille's senses. Camille focused on the girl's altered face, which now largely matched the one carved into the stone statue. The halo of light surrounding Mora, or what used to be Mora, spectrum-shifted to something closer to white, rather like... like moonlight.

Camille's hands shot up to clasp together. She whispered, "Del'shaya?" Impossible, and yet...

The slight smile, serene and immortal, shone on what was once Mora's face. "You recognize me, daughter."

Camille didn't know whether she should bow, or offer some other form of obeisance, so simply stared. "I have never seen you before. There are no paintings, no engravings of you anywhere that I have traveled. I know you only through a few ancient ballads and some scraps of rough translations, and... through my heart and my prayers."

Del'shaya's image flickered briefly and then she moved to wrap her hands around Camille's. "In the darkest places of my arcane prison, I heard your prayers, daughter Camille. Across time and space and concepts you can only dream of, I heard you. And I came."

Overwhelmed, Camille could only shake her head in wonder. "Imprisoned? I don't understand."

Del'shaya simply smiled and gently squeezed her hands. "Far too much to explain, and I with far too little time. I cannot linger. I must rest and gather my strength. But know this—your prayers and your faith woke me from a deep slumber I thought to never return from. And that allowed me to reach out one tiny tendril of hope, to this place, this statue. The one shrine to me left standing in all the Empire. Maybe all the world."

Camille nodded mutely, turning to focus on the statue that was still connected to both the pool of water and Mora's slight frame.

"I found my way through the water and into my shrine, and managed to issue the briefest of messages to the girl who owns this body." Her image flickered again, and the light emanating from her faded to a degree.

"Mora? Mora heard your call?"

"Yes. And used her cleverness and small size to find her way down here. I communed with her briefly, weak as I was, and she agreed to find the Sentinel you see fallen at your feet."

Camille nodded, eager to hear more. "Alois. And he helped Mora?"

"To an extent." Her form shimmered in the light again. "I grow weak, daughter, and I must rest. I return Mora's body to her, and my essence to the water, to rest and recuperate. There is so much to tell you, but it will take time."

Camille tamped down a burst of frustration, and shifted to rest on her knees. "What must I do?"

"Teach Mora the healing arts. She has the ability within her. Latent, and potent, but unfocused and untrained."

Camille flushed despite the chill in the air and she hung her head in shame. "I... I've lost my ability to heal. I have no Art left to use, much less teach." Admitting it out loud formed a thick lump in her throat.

Del'shaya offered another serene smile. "Silly daughter. You cannot lose that which is yours by heritage. You've merely misplaced your hope, not your gifts." She nudged Camille's chin up so that she had to meet her eyes. "Do not despair, my daughter. There is a new light dawning. Will you embrace it?"

Camille stared at her goddess's fading form, at her features that were slowly morphing back to Mora's own image. "It's been so long since we've had any hope. The plagues and the wars have burned most of it away."

Fading faster now, as if losing her grip on the world around her, Del'shaya nodded. "The Empress. She is to blame. Her soul is darker than the night." Nearly gone completely, she squeezed Camille's hands, hard. "Train Mora. Train others. Find my history here in Bridges. Spread my name and my word. Defend your people and the world from the plagues and the Empress and her cruelty. Keep the faith, daughter. I charge you to be my first servant of this new age."

The last sentence was nearly inaudible. After she had spoken it, Del'shaya's light faded completely, and the tethers that had connected Mora to the statue and the pool of water faded into nothingness. All that remained was the flickering candlelight.

And the voices… the voices were gone. That realization brought another one with it in its wake, a far stronger one: her Art! The wellspring of her soul, the center of all her power, had reopened. The bright pool of her talent was open for her use.

She reached down deep for a thread of power, and harnessed it to imbue her cloak with light. Once her cloak was ablaze in silver light, she gently blew out her candle.

Camille's eyes adjusted to the new lighting, and then she focused on Mora, surprised to see the girl staring back at her with equally wide eyes. "Do you have any idea what just happened?"

"I heard it all… in my mind."

Camille pulled Mora to her and hugged her tightly, sensing through her resurgent Art that the girl had the ability to be a strong healer and Sentinel. Unfocused, raw power. She could be one of the strongest healers in this generation, if she wanted it. For the first time in a very long time, Camille's heart lifted up in a flare of hope. She had come to Bridges with nothing, but had rediscovered everything.

She squeezed Mora gently, and then stood and helped the girl stand as well. "My dear Mora, I think we have a lot of work to do. In Del'shaya's name, let us begin."

About the Author

Jim Johnson was born about the same time Apollo XII landed on the moon and shares a birthday with the Kindle. He is the author of the Pistols and Pyramids weird western series and the Potomac Shadows urban fantasy series. He's also written a bunch of other stuff in and around the SFF genres and pen and paper RPGs.

In rare moments when he's not writing or publishing, Jim plays board games and card games, eats more pizza than he really should, and makes a brilliant bowl of popcorn. He also likes to live dangerously by running last click. You can learn more about him and his writing at www.scribeineti.com.

OF GRIEF AND GRIFFINS

M.C. DWYER

I n her long years of walking the tide-littered beach, she'd found a number of strange and incomprehensible things. There was the blown glass vial that glowed with inner light when she filled it with fresh water, casting strange shapes on the walls of her cottage. There was the enormous sea creature that had taken five minutes to walk the breadth of. There was the stoppered bottle with a rolled up parchment inside that stubbornly resisted all her efforts to open. There was also the occasional body, washed up from some shipwreck out at sea. These she dragged up to the tree line and buried properly.

She never wondered about their histories; she wasn't curious about the strange paths that had led them to her doorstep. She was too tired to be properly inquisitive. Once, long ago, she would have speculated, conjuring up fantastic stories that would have kept her niece in fits of the giggles for hours on end as they acted out the stories on her bedspread with her assortment of ragdolls.

But that was a very long time ago. Her niece was gone, along with her brother. She'd left it all behind and escaped here, to this lonesome, sandy stretch of beach where no one bothered her. Where she could try to forget. Here, she was not Renata the powerful; she could just manage to be Wren the ordinary.

And so Wren the ordinary woman spent her days tending her garden, fixing the thatch on her roof, and walking the beach after the tide went out, sifting through the flotsam for anything useful.

On that morning, she spotted what looked at first glance to be a large, dead bird. Its head was resting on the sand, and one battered wing was cocked up into the air. Its feathers were reddish brown under the dusting of sand. It was also, she realized as she approached, enormous. The bird's head was at least as big as hers, and the hawk-like beak could have snapped her in two. Wren sidled up cautiously, staying out of reach in case it wasn't as dead as it looked. As she rounded the creature, she saw its legs; one drawn up tight to its body and the other cocked at an unnatural angle. She then saw what she at first took to be a second body underneath; the back end of a large cat, reddish brown in color, lay on the sand. A large, bloody gash glistened in the morning sun, and as Wren watched, its chest gave a short, shallow heave.

Wren scrambled backward, landing in an undignified heap in the sand. Fortunately the beach was as empty as ever. As she stared at the creature, her perspective shifted and she realized there was only one body. The feathered body of the bird shifted nearly seamlessly into that of the cat, with a line of feathers running down the spine all the way to the tail, which was long, like a cat's, but had a feathered tip. This flexed briefly, as did the cocked wing, and Wren saw the chest lift again in another labored breath.

The wound on his body was not glistening with seawater, but rather still sluggishly bleeding. The creature was alive, but would not be for long.

Wren sat for a moment in silent thought, weighing out several possible courses of action. The easiest would be to let the creature die. She owed it nothing, and it would likely protest any treatment she tried to give, possibly injuring or killing her in the process. She could, by the same token, end its suffering immediately. Or, she supposed, she could try to stop the bleeding and stitch up the wound.

The creature opened one enormous eye that focused on her briefly, then slid closed again.

Almost without realizing it, Wren found herself on her feet and heading for her cottage. She smiled wryly at herself as she gathered linen, needle, and thread. She was going to try to save the creature, come what may. She sensed the quiet simplicity of her life slipping away, and couldn't decide whether she was glad or not.

Once more on the beach, she approached the creature. She found herself, not for the first time, lamenting the loss of her library. It would be helpful to have some idea of what she was treating, and whether she could expect intelligence, or even magical assistance from the creature. Her own magic rose up inside her at the thought, curling seductively in the corners of her mind, but she sternly banished it. She'd sworn never to touch it again.

The creature was where she'd left him, though she had to wait a long minute before she saw his chest rise and fall. Deciding the gash was the first order of business, she started talking quietly, telling the creature what she was doing. If he were intelligent enough to understand her good intentions, maybe she'd survive this.

Wren's voice was rusty from disuse, but warmed up quickly. She placed a hand on the creature's flank, and the skin shuddered at her touch. Still murmuring, she pulled the edges of the wound together and began stitching. The gash was long, and by the time she reached the other end, she was practically straddling the creature's back. She tied off the thread and slid down with a sigh. The wound should be wrapped, but that would only be possible once the creature stood up. It'd have to wait.

A short walk down the beach produced driftwood suitable for a splint, and Wren approached the creature's front end with less trepidation than before. He hadn't hurt her yet; he was either too worn out or intelligent enough to understand what she was doing. She reached for the creature's broken leg, talking all the while. She felt the break as gently as she could, but the creature did not respond. He'd either passed out or— no, his chest was still moving, though just barely.

It was a bad break, and would have to be set before it was splinted. Wren looked at the leg somewhat ruefully. It was as long as her arm, and twice as thick. With a shrug and a murmured apology, she grasped the leg above the foot and pulled.

The creature awoke with a piercing cry, and kicked spasmodically with his uninjured leg. Wren found herself flung backward through the air. She landed in the sand with a thump and the world went dim for a moment. She came to almost immediately, then wished she hadn't, since she couldn't breathe. She tried to tamp down the rising panic, assuring herself she'd just had the wind knocked out of her. She hoped it was true.

After what felt like an eternity, she was able to suck in a lungful of air, and sat up, coughing, to take stock. She was sore, and a painful spot on her side suggested a bruised or cracked rib. Her magic woke again, whispering promises of help, but she pushed it down with a violent exhalation of air that ended in a hiss of pain.

Putting her hand to her injured side, she crawled back over to the creature, who was awake, and eyeing her balefully.

"What?" Wren asked, wheezing slightly. "Did you want the leg to heal crooked?"

The creature opened its beak and hissed, not angrily, but thoughtfully, then craned his head to peer at his stitched up flank. He snapped his beak once, then carefully held out his injured leg in her direction.

Wren picked up the strips of linen and wrapped the leg, then tied the splints in place as well as she could.

Wounds dealt with as well as she was able, Wren hiked back up to her cottage and dragged out her copper washtub. The creature would need water, and she didn't have anything else large enough for him to drink from. It took several painful trips to fill the tub, but the creature lowered his head and drank thirstily, nearly emptying it again. She dragged the tub back up above the tide line, then hiked to her house once more for a supply of fish. What she had was mostly smoked, but it was either that or potatoes and greens, and she suspected the creature would prefer meat.

Wren set the food in front of the creature, who sniffed it delicately, nudged it with his beak, then swallowed it in one bite. One thing was clear: if he was going to stay long, Wren would need to spend more time fishing.

The food and water seemed to revive the creature, who furled his wings and settled himself more comfortably on the sand.

"If you can walk, you need to move about fifteen paces that way," Wren said, pointing inland. "Otherwise you're going to get wet in the next few hours when the tide comes back in."

The creature looked at the sea, then up at the high tide mark, then let out a very human sigh. Gathering his three whole legs under him, he managed a painful crabwalk, and after a couple short rests, got himself into the shadow of the trees above the tide mark. He collapsed with a hiss of pain.

Wren's ribs were sending definite messages of distress by this point, and she carefully sat down a few yards from the creature and leaned against a convenient tree, one hand clenched against her side. Experimentally, she tried to draw a deep breath, but had to stop when the pain caused her to cough, which in turn hurt even worse. Not just bruised, then. When the coughing subsided, she sat back with a groan.

The creature gave her an inquiring look, head tilted to one side in a very bird-like fashion.

"Broken rib," Wren sighed. "Nothing I can do about it." After a pause, she added, "Thanks for that, by the way."

They sat in silence for a short time, until Wren felt well enough to once more make the hike back to her cottage. Without a backward look, she heaved herself to her feet, and made her painful way home.

The creature was still alive in the morning, but Wren was beginning to regret that she was. Her chest ached from the broken rib and her exertions of the previous day. Taking some long strips of cloth, she wrapped the ribs snugly then brewed some willowbark tea for herself. Once the willowbark took hold, she wandered down to the beach to check on the creature. He was sitting in the shade of a tree, legs tucked underneath his body and staring out at sea. If Wren had been sure he was intelligent, she would have called his pose pensive.

"Morning," Wren said. It was an observation, not a greeting.

The creature snapped his beak at her but otherwise ignored her.

Griffin.

The word appeared fully formed in her mind, taking Wren by surprise. Had she known what a griffin was? The thought had a slightly foreign feeling to it, and she looked at the creature in sudden suspicion. He eyeballed her as only a creature with monocular vision could manage, and the thought appeared again, with emphasis.

Griffin. Not "creature."

Gritting her teeth, Wren threw her mental defenses into place, walls slamming down around the edges of her mind.

"Stay out of my head," she managed through clenched teeth.

Presenting themselves on the doorstep of her mind, as it were, were the words, *Don't leave your mind open to every passing traveler if you don't want your thoughts read.*

She glared at the creature. Griffin. Yes, she did remember reading about such a creature in one of her books, long ago. They were thought to be mythical. The creature staring down its beak at her was unfortunately all too real.

Realizing that her tea had gone cold, she quickly drank it down and then turned and stalked back to her cottage. She slammed around, making herself a simple breakfast of toast and dried fish and then dumping it into the fire when she realized she'd charred it black. Still muttering imprecations against mind-reading mythicals, she got on with her daily tasks, trying to ignore the creature on the beach. Who hadn't had any food or water since yesterday. Wren sighed.

Retrieving the water bucket, she began the long task of filling the washbasin, making sure her mental barriers were in place before she returned to the beach. The griffin ignored her, staring out to sea with an unreadable expression on his hawkish face.

It's rude to stare, he said, not turning his head.

Wren's cheeks colored, but she held her ground. "I brought you some fresh water. I can bring fish, too, but it'll take awhile. You ate most of my store last night."

At this, one of the griffin's eyes darted in her direction. *I can eat raw fish,* he said. *I may be able to fish for myself by tomorrow.*

"Not with that leg, you won't. And if you think I'm going to resplint it for you, think again." Wren turned to leave, then tossed over her shoulder, "I'll bring you what's in my traps when I check them this afternoon."

She was halfway down the beach before she heard the faint, *Thank you.*

Walking her tide traps hurt. Spearing the fish hurt, too. But then, so did breathing. By taking it slow and stopping often to breathe, Wren managed to collect a sizable collection of fish. It would have been too heavy to drag at one time, so she made several painful trips across the beach. By the time she returned with the next load, the griffin had already finished the previous bucketful. She dragged in the last bucketful and dumped it in front of him with a rueful sigh.

"You're welcome," she said, watching him snatch each fish and toss it back with a flick of his beak. Within moments, this last batch was gone, as well. Ignoring her, the griffin limped over to the water and finished that off, too.

"Is there anything else you'd like?" Wren asked, irritated at being disregarded.

The griffin's head snapped up, and his eyes darted from side to side, scanning the ocean.

Duck, was all the warning she got before something slammed her to the ground.

From her prone position, she watched in incredulous shock as another creature straight from mythology launched itself at the griffin with a shriek. It was scaly, with the lizard-like head and wings of a dragon but only two legs: a wyvern. As she watched, the wyvern locked its clawed wings with the griffin's front legs, clawing at the broken one. The hind legs kicked, trying to tear open the griffin's stomach, but the griffin put his catlike rear legs to good use, blocking them at every turn. Their relative positions left the griffin with the advantage of two extra limbs, which he used to beat the wyvern around the head.

Wren watched the battle unfold with increasing detachment, as she realized something was wrong in her chest. Her ribs were on fire, and she felt a tingling sensation from the arm that was pinned underneath her body. She tried to roll to her back, but only succeeded in wracking her body with coughs that sprayed the sand with red and left a metallic taste in her mouth. She knew she should be panicking, but couldn't seem to summon up the energy.

"Help?" she managed to say, or at least think, before things went grey and fuzzy. The sound of the fight had vanished, and there was a sudden wash of magic, warm and inviting and teasing all at once, that washed over her and was gone. And then she must have been hallucinating, because warm hands were turning her, checking her injuries, and then placing themselves at her temples and delving into her mind to unlock her magic.

"No," she tried to protest, but it was too late, for the sweet sweep of magic—her magic—had washed over her, soothing the pain and easing the fear of death.

"Foolish child," a voice muttered, and then the hands lifted her, carried her, and as her magic carried her to oblivion, she found just enough of a spark of energy to feel resentment.

Not a child, she thought, and was met with vague amusement. And then she knew no more.

Wren awoke some time later; how much later, she never knew. She was in her cottage, wrapped in a blanket but still in her bloody tunic. She felt—fine. Better than fine, actually. Ruefully, she took stock, and found her magic batting at the edges of her mind like a playful kitten, asking to be played with. She sternly pushed it away, but found it strangely recalcitrant. Rather than do battle with her own mind, she decided to ignore it.

Her cottage was as she left it, though one or two things had moved slightly as though they'd been used and then replaced. She fingered the teakettle thoughtfully before shrugging and setting it aside. Stripping off her bloody tunic, she held it up to the light and sighed. It had been looking old and worn before the wyvern attack; now she may as well tear it up and replenish her bandage supply. Moving to the small chest at the foot of her bed, she opened the lid and carefully lifted out a cloth-wrapped bundle. She gently removed the outer layer and held up the revealed tunic. Memories washed over her, piercing her heart with grief. She'd last worn this when—no, better not to awaken the memories any further. Her fingers smoothed the embroidered flowers around the neckline, and she dropped it over her head with a sigh. Some faint scent of cinnamon lingered, and without willing it, the memory slammed into her.

Cinnamon rolls, oozing sugary goo as they dissolved under the weight of their own sweetness. Renata had made them for her niece. Never one with a robust appetite, Elory had been uninterested in food the past few days, and her wasted frame was looking even thinner than usual. She could, however, occasionally be tempted with something sweet. Thus, Renata had spent the morning in the kitchen, bumping elbows good-naturedly with the cook who tolerated her sporadic inroads into his sacred territory for Elory's sake. All the servants loved little Elory, and wasn't it a shame she'd never walk again, but the little mite was so cheerful that it just melted one's heart.

As she carried them up to her niece's room, Renata smiled. She'd found a new book of fairy tales in the market, and was going to attempt a little bribery if the cinnamon rolls weren't tempting enough on their own.

Renata bumped the door to Elory's room open with her hip, and felt her smile widen further at the sight of Elory's rumpled curls.

"Aunt Wen!" she said softly. At eight years old, her r's no longer troubled her, but she'd called her Aunt Wen from the beginning, and Renata didn't mind.

"I brought you a snack," she said, placing the tray by Elory's bed.

"I'm not hungry," Elory whispered, clutching one of her ragdolls closer.

Renata sat on the edge of the bed. "That's too bad. I was going to read you a new story while you ate..." she trailed off, pulling the book from a pocket in her overdress and caressing the cover. "There are some fabulous illustrations in here." Opening the book randomly, she held it up out of Elory's sight and exclaimed, "Wow! A dragon!"

Elory tossed an arm back with an overly dramatic sigh. "Fine! I'll eat something. But the story better be worth it."

Renata grinned. "I'll read you two, and you can judge."

Sometime later, she carried the barely touched tray out the door and nearly ran down her brother.

"She's still not eating, is she?" he said, running a hand through his hair. Elory had gotten her curls from him, and they were now standing on end, lending a half-crazed appearance to his already slightly wild-eyed look.

Renata pulled the door shut softly. "No, I'm afraid not."

He grabbed her arm and squeezed painfully. "Should we try calling the healer again? Maybe a different one?"

With a sigh, Renata placed her free hand on top of his. "If magic could cure her, Elan, she'd be healed already. Don't you think I've been trying?"

Releasing her, he leaned against the wall and slowly slid down. "I know. I just feel so—helpless."

She put a hand on his shoulder. "I know. I do, too. I—"

The sudden rush of magic stopped whatever she was going to say, and she cried out at the strength of the power washing over her. Her brother looked at her in dawning horror, and pulled away with a gasp.

"Elory! I need to get to Elory!"

Pushing past her, he flung open the door.

"Papa!" Elory cried, pain sharp in her voice.

Renata tried to stand, but another wave of magic slammed her to her knees. She tried to crawl towards the two figures who'd gone blurry in the maelstrom, but barely had the strength to hold her mind together. Working slowly, with mental fingers that shook from the effort, she wove protections around herself, whimpering slightly when she wasn't quite quick enough.

With a final gasp, she finished, and collapsed to the floor. She could see her brother holding Elory, could see the lines of magic he was trying to weave around them both, but could do nothing to help. She was unable to do so much as close her eyes, which she hoped and prayed for as the storm continued, sucking every bit of life and magic from the two people she loved most—the only people she loved—in the world.

They found her hours later, barely breathing, curled absurdly around a tray of cinnamon rolls and a book of fairy tales. The house was a shambles, as though a tornado had swept through. And Elory, Elan, and every man and woman who served in their house were dead.

Wren dashed the tears away fiercely, and snarled at the questioning tendrils of magic. Magic had destroyed her family and her life. She'd given it up in her exile, and sworn never to touch it again. Whoever—whatever—had released it to heal her, it made no difference. She would not use it again.

With a sigh, she stood up, smoothing the tunic down. The overdress had been lost long ago, but the tunic could be worn with trousers just as easily. She drew a pair on, and admitted to herself that the lack of broken ribs was quite pleasant, if one ignored the invasive healing method forced on her.

She made her way outside, where she saw the griffin virtually unmoved from his spot under the trees. He had to have moved, though, because the wyvern's body was gone, and its skin draped over a bush a ways down the beach.

As she approached, she realized he'd discarded his splint, and the gash on his side looked almost completely healed.

You're looking less like death, yourself, the griffin returned, cocking an eye at her.

Frowning, she tried to reestablish her mental barriers, but it was like trying to catch dandelion fluff. Every swipe wafted it further out of reach. She stumbled dizzily, and sat down quickly.

Useless child. The growl reverberated in her mind, and then he was there, again, in her head, building up fine, strong walls around her thoughts before locking himself out.

You shouldn't have been able to do that, Wren murmured, poking at the walls from the inside.

The griffin gave a mental shrug. *You should eat something before you pass out.*

"Thank you for your concern," she said drily. "Unfortunately I've had house guests lately and they've eaten me out of house and home."

With an enormous sigh, the griffin snapped his wings open and half bounded, half flew over a distant rise, then returned a short time later with a heavily-laden branch which he dropped in her lap.

"Did you just destroy one of my plum trees?" she asked suspiciously, looking over the fruit. At the same time, she was filled with a certain amount of dismay. The fruit had not been ripe the last time she checked it. How long had she been asleep?

You have another one, the griffin said, staring once more out to sea.

Wren sighed, but pulled a fruit off and started to rub it clean on her trousers. "You need two plum trees to get plums," she said around a juicy bite of fruit. As long as he'd left the rest of the tree undamaged, it would probably be fine. It looked like he'd simply nipped off one of the upper branches.

The griffin eyeballed her briefly, then returned to staring out over the water.

Wren finished off her plum, then another. By the time she'd eaten six or seven of them, she was starting to feel better. She tossed the pits down into the sand where the tide would take care of them, then stood up and dusted off her seat.

"I'm going to go wash up in the stream," she told the uninterested griffin. "Do let me know if any more wyverns show up? There's a dear."

Bathed and clothed once more, Wren decided the next order of business was to check her fish traps, and then see if weeds had completely overrun her garden, as she feared. Her traps were emptier than she would have expected, and she wondered if the griffin had been checking them. It would have been difficult for him to do so, built as they were for human hands, but he seemed to have managed. Wren gave a mental shrug. At least he wasn't going hungry. And if he was as healed as he appeared to be, she wouldn't have to haul fresh water for him, either.

When she checked the tide pool, she grimaced. An octopus had gotten stuck. She had no interest in attempting to capture or kill it; it was one of the few food sources she refused to take advantage of on her island. If it ever came down to starving to death or eating octopus, well, she'd dig her own grave while she still had the strength.

There was a sudden rush of air, then a thud as the griffin landed beside her. The wind of his landing threatened to unbalance her, and his sudden appearance had done her heart no favors.

"Yes?" she asked. "Did a dragon show up?"

The griffin ignored her, peering intently into the tide pool. With a leap that knocked her to her backside in the sand, he plunged his front legs into the pool. There was a moment of wild splashing in which the water turned black with ink, but after he plunged his beak in, it went still. With a toss of his head, the octopus went into the air, flinging black water everywhere. Wren scrambled back to avoid the splash, not wanting ink stains on her last viable tunic.

The griffin dropped the octopus on the sand, and started tearing into it with great gusto. Wren gagged and quickly turned her back.

"Let me know when you're done," she said, sticking her

fingers in her ears and starting to hum.

Octopus is not only tasty, but good for you, too.

"I'll take your word on that."

You should try some.

Before she had time to react, Wren had a long, slimy octopus arm dropped in her lap. She pushed it off with an oath, even as her stomach heaved. By a monumental effort, she managed to keep her breakfast of plums down, but she had to scrub her hands clean in the pool to rid herself of the feeling of the octopus' skin. Finished, she stalked away, followed by the griffin's silent laughter.

"Jerk," she muttered, and went to vent her feelings on the weeds in her garden.

Life continued in this fashion for another week or so, at the end of which she'd replenished her stock of dried fish, started harvesting potatoes, and begun to dry plums. By the end of this time, she'd learned very little about the griffin, beyond the fact that he was adept at magic, and was concerned about an attack from sea. This last fact she'd garnered mainly by observation; the griffin steadily ignored most of her conversational overtures.

To be fair, she hadn't offered much information, either. She'd never told him her name, or why she was here, alone. Though she wouldn't have told him that even if he'd begged sweetly.

What they'd achieved was a somewhat wary truce, living side by side with minimal interaction. Wren got on with the business of survival, storing up food and firewood against the coming winter, and the griffin watched, waited, and healed. She had yet to see him actually fly; some of his flight feathers had been damaged in his initial arrival, and hadn't yet grown back in. When they had, Wren supposed he would leave. The thought left her feeling strangely unsettled. Though why she thought she'd miss that arrogant jerk was a mystery to her. Nevertheless, that evening found her making her way down the beach to the griffin's nest.

He'd managed to assemble a sort of roof woven from living branches; it was enough to keep the rain off when it fell, as well as provide some shelter from the sun. He sat there now, gazing at the darkening sea, though what he hoped to see in the darkness was anyone's guess.

Wren held up a speared octopus, a sort of peace offering. She'd killed the octopus the same way she killed spiders—quickly, and looking away as much as possible. It still turned her stomach to see its loose arms flopping.

The griffin's gaze darted from the octopus to Wren, then glinted with amusement that was clearly communicated mentally.

Thank you, was all he said, however, so Wren let it pass.

"Do you have a name, griffin?" she asked, when he'd finished destroying the carcass and tossed back the last bit of meat.

Yes, he replied.

After a moment, Wren sighed. "Do you intend to tell me what it is?"

Yes, he said again, and though the light was now completely gone, Wren could tell he was laughing at her.

She tried again. "What is your name?"

After a pause, the griffin said, almost reluctantly, *Faldor*.

"Faldor," she said, rolling it around on her tongue. "My name is Wren."

No, it isn't, the griffin said bluntly.

Wren's sudden flush was hidden by the dark, but she couldn't keep the anger from her voice. "I thought I told you to stay out of my head."

The griffin was silent so long she'd given up on getting a response.

Your name wasn't in your mind, he finally said.

Despite staring at him for a considerable length of time, Wren got nothing further. She threw her hands up in annoyance and went to bed.

When Wren went out the next morning to start her chores, she found Faldor running back and forth on the sandy beach, beating his wings and taking great, bounding strides. A couple of times he managed to stay aloft briefly. Coming to a stop, he mantled his wings and inspected the damaged feathers.

Wren wondered why he didn't just regrow the damaged feathers with magic, the way he'd healed his other wounds.

I didn't heal the others, the griffin said, head still tucked under a wing.

Wren sighed and reestablished her mental barriers. She'd lost the habit of guarding her thoughts since coming to live on her island; obviously she needed to get back in practice.

"What do you mean you didn't heal the others? Do griffins naturally heal quickly?"

There's nothing natural about griffins, he snorted. *And no, it was your magic that healed me. Apparently it didn't recognize the feathers as a wound.*

After pondering that for a moment, Wren said, "I was unconscious. How could I have healed you?"

I didn't say you did.

Talking to the griffin was an exercise in patience. Wren took a deep breath and replayed the griffin's words. "Alright, how could my magic heal you if I was unconscious? Don't I control my magic?"

The griffin threw back his head and opened his beak in a hiss. After a moment, Wren realized he was laughing. *Wouldn't that be nice.*

Wren spun on her heel and started to walk away, only to be brought up short by the griffin, who leapt in front of her.

Are you planning to use your magic?

She shot an angry look at him under her brows. "You've been in my head. You should know better than anyone that I have no intention of using any magic—mine or otherwise."

The griffin managed a very human-looking shrug. *It's polite to ask, but since you don't mind—*

And then somehow he was past her walls, and the magic was pouring out of her like water through a sieve. As she watched, unable or unwilling to stop it, the damaged feathers straightened and lengthened to their proper shape.

Collapsing to her knees, Wren found tears were running down her face, and realized that she did mind, very much. A foolish reaction, she scolded herself. She wasn't going to use her magic; why should she care if someone else took it? And a neat trick, that—one of the first things she learned at the Wizard Hall was that you could draw from your own pool of magic, but no one else could. What the griffin had just done should have been impossible.

Dashing away her tears, she stood up, and faced the griffin.

"You're welcome," she said, and walked away.

From that point on, the griffin was as likely to be seen as a diminishing speck in the distance as he was under his tree. He started with short flights, just circling the island, but as he gained endurance he would vanish for hours at a time, until Wren began to wonder if he would come back.

Did it matter to her if he didn't? Wren wasn't sure, and hadn't had to decide, because he always returned eventually.

Early one evening, he returned in a bigger hurry than usual, crashing rather than landing in the space before her cottage, and calling for her in a tone of voice she'd never yet heard from him. It sounded almost frightened, with just a touch of rue.

She came to the doorway, a bowl full of bread dough in her hands, and looked inquiringly at the griffin.

Where's the wyvern skin? he demanded.

Wren reached a hand inside the cottage and pulled it off the peg where it hung. She'd been fashioning it, at his offhand suggestion, into a cloak. It was finished, or close enough. She held it out to him.

In a rush of wind and leaves, the griffin shook himself and dissolved. Wren watched in open-mouthed stupefaction as in his place, a russet-haired man took shape. He stumbled slightly, then regained his balance to step forward and lift the cloak from her nerveless fingers.

Tossing it around her shoulders, he bumped her chin up, forcing her mouth closed, and fastened the cloak.

"I need your magic," he said, his voice unexpectedly deep.

Looking up into his golden brown eyes, Wren only managed one word.

"No."

The man—Faldor—sighed, then spoke quickly. "I've been rather careless, and I'm sorry for putting you in danger, but unless you know how to fight a chimera, I'm going to need your magic."

Wren felt the blood drain from her face. A chimera? Here? Still, the thought of him using her magic again made her feel squidgy inside. His hands were heavy on her shoulders, and his gaze solemn, even as a savage roar echoed down the beach.

Wren wrestled briefly with herself. He'd take it either way—let him have it. Could *she* defeat a chimera?

Closing her eyes, she whispered, "Take it."

Pulling the hood up over her head, he said, "Stay under the cloak. It's fireproof." And then her magic left her in a rush that left her dizzy and sick on the ground.

After a moment, she managed to open her eyes and saw Faldor, once more in griffin form, leaping up to meet the strangest creature she'd ever seen. It had the basic shape of a lion, but too many heads. One was cat-like, and had a scant mane, much like a lion's. The other was a horned goat, if goats had the sharp teeth of a carnivore. It flew with the help of leathery wings, and its heavy, scaled tail had two barbs on it that glistened wetly in the light of the descending sun.

The battle was fierce, and impossible to gauge. The two wrestled in the air, rolled on the beach, then separated only to clash again. The air was thick with Wren's magic, as well as the heavier feel of the chimera's. On the surface, the chimera seemed to have the advantage. It had an extra set of teeth as well as that poisonous tail. It also, Wren realized as she was forced to duck, could breathe fire. The wyvern skin protected her beautifully, but the thatch of her cottage was ablaze.

Yanking out the burning thatch, she stamped out the fire, then returned her attention to the battle. While she'd been distracted, the tide seemed to have turned slightly in Faldor's favor. He was using her magic to weave a web of some sort around the chimera, and with each fiber he wove into it, the chimera seemed to slow.

Even as she watched, the chimera's tail slipped free of the net of magic, and swung around to pierce the griffin's unprotected flank.

"Look out!" she cried, and without thinking reached for her magic. She had it gathered, ready to launch, when she realized what she was doing and froze. Fortunately, Faldor saw the attack and bound the tail off with one more twist of magic. The chimera, completely encased in magic webbing, dropped to the beach and dissipated into a fine mist, which in turn vanished.

The griffin landed heavily, then winced. While he inspected himself for injuries, Wren continued to stare. She'd nearly broken her vow. In the heat of the moment, she'd almost forgotten what she'd promised Elory and Elan at their grave.

She remained frozen even as Faldor resumed human form and approached, limping slightly. It wasn't until he grasped her arms and shook her slightly that she focused on his face.

"I killed them," she said, matter-of-factly. Her mental walls were down, but she didn't even feel a hint of Faldor's presence.

"No, you didn't," he said. "It wasn't your magic that summoned that storm, and the fact that you survived is a miracle of no small order."

"I should have saved them," she protested, as tears started streaming down her cheeks. "I should have been able to save them."

"Listen to me," Faldor said, giving her another shake. "You did not kill them. You could not have saved them. You should not have been able to save yourself. That storm had one purpose—your death. The person who sent it is responsible, not you."

With a faint thread of hope blossoming inside her, Wren rubbed her eyes and sniffed. "Truly?"

Faldor turned his eyes heavenward in supplication. "Listen, my idiot child. There is a wizard out there who has been systematically targeting magic wielders of any power. He killed your family. He killed my wife. He's tried to kill me. So far he has failed." He shifted slightly and winced. "So far. As far as I know, we two are the only ones who have survived his attempt on our lives. And unless you want to spend the rest of your life on this godforsaken island, you will abandon this idiotic vow and help me find the murdering bastard."

Wren stared at him wide-eyed, his fingers squeezing her arms tight enough to bruise. "Alright," she whispered, before she even knew she was going to.

"Truly?" he asked, staring into her eyes.

"Yes," she answered, and felt a great peace settle on her heart.

Faldor winced again, and said, "We need to leave soon. He'll have tracked the chimera, so we're no longer safe here."

Wren nodded.

It took only a few moments to bundle up the few things she wanted to save and stow them in a pack. Looking around her cottage, she felt a wave of sadness wash over her. This island had been peaceful, a refuge in a stormy passage of her life. When the ship had dumped her here so many years before, she'd fully intended to end her days here. Instead, she'd found peace, and a measure of healing.

Moving to stand in the doorway, she looked out over the darkening sea. The griffin was waiting for her, favoring one leg, and with a thought, Wren sent a breath of healing magic over it. He darted a glance her direction, then looked away. Her magic curled up like a cat in her mind, purring at her.

Wren took a deep breath and strapped her pack on. Whatever came next, she would not forget her time here.

She climbed onto Faldor's back and buried her fingers in the feathers of his neck. "I'm ready," she said quietly.

Her stomach gave a lurch as he leapt into the air, but settled as they gained altitude. Faldor's gaze flicked around to look at the emerging stars, and taking his bearings, headed off into the night.

The stars above reflected into the ocean below, which appeared calm and flat from this height. Snuggling deeper in the griffin's feathers, Wren drifted off to sleep in a placid sea of stars.

About the Author

M.C. Dwyer has been a student, a librarian, a store clerk, a teacher, a student again, and an occasional world traveler. Some day she'll figure out what she wants to be when she grows up, but in the meantime she enjoys binge-watching kdrama and creating new fantasy worlds to escape into.

CPSIA information can be obtained
at www.ICGtesting.com
Printed in the USA
LVHW081548290920
667401LV00002B/293

9 780989 191562